# WHE
## YOUR NAME

## Gemma M. Lawrence

●

© Copyright Gemma M. Lawrence 2020
All rights reserved

# CHAPTER 1

*Move, Elena. Now!*

Listening to that inner voice, the primal thing that is instinct, Elena turned and bolted up the steps to her front door.

Only minutes before life had been normal, safe, her mind planning the best route for a run that would help cleanse her body of the wine she'd polished off with Charlotte last night.

But that was before she caught sight of the man striding towards her as she stretched out her body, using the wrought iron railings that separated the pavement from her home for support. Someone she recognised, but had never met. Someone she'd passed in her road a couple of times or glanced at as he lingered opposite her building, his phone pressed to his ear. Uneventful moments with a stranger and seemingly nothing to do with her. But deep down, she had the unfathomable feeling it was *everything* to do with her. She'd ignored it though, not wanting to make the same mistake as before. Stupid, given her family's circumstances.

He was tall, lanky, and with hard eyes and a face taut with purpose, he kept his pace. She hesitated as the first pang of unease fluttered in her stomach. But when a car crept into her peripheral vision, pulling up in the road like a dark threatening cloud, its door opening, ready to swallow her whole, the feeling quickly morphed into a tight knot of dread. Then, instinct kicked in and sparked her body into action.

Muscles tight, she hurled herself up the steps and reached for her keys as his footsteps sounded close behind.

'Easy now,' he murmured as he wrapped one arm tightly around her waist and ripped the keys from her grasp with the other, disarming her of her only possible weapon. 'Best you don't struggle.'

'What are you doing?' she cried as she struggled to be free, fear and confusion crowding her mind. 'Stop it! Get your hands off me!'

There was no time to process what was happening. No time for anything at all except to deliver a sharp stab of her elbow to his stomach, freeing herself from his grasp. She jumped from the top step and rushed out into the street. She didn't know where she would go, but to run was her only option.

Now, she sprinted and only two things sounded in the quiet London street: the air she forced into her lungs and footsteps pounding the pavement – a mingle of hers and his.

The surge of adrenaline was doing its job but the footsteps behind were getting louder, getting closer. He was gaining on her. She worked harder, feeling her legs tire, knowing they would soon cramp, having worked hard with little warm-up. Would she be lucky enough to bump into another early morning runner, or someone out walking their dog? Anyone who could help her? She remembered her mother's words in times of confrontation. 'Keep well out of it,' she heard her say. 'Never get involved. Call the police if you can, but never get involved. If you don't want to get hurt, that is.' Sound advice, but now it was her in trouble and that made it a whole lot of different.

But she was out of luck. They were alone, the chill of the spring morning keeping people locked within their homes, shrouded in warmth. But despite the quiet, she didn't scream. There was no time for that. She had to conserve her energy for the sprint.

*Keep moving.* Sweat trickled down her back as her body worked to counteract the exertion and fear.

She felt him close now and risked a glance over her shoulder to see him sprinting hard behind. Now she screamed, as his fingers grabbed at her top and pulled her back against the bony contours of his body. He hurriedly patted against her clothing, searching for her phone. In one swift action he grabbed it and tucked it into the back pocket of his jeans.

'Nowhere to run now,' he said breathlessly, as the mix of chewing gum and stale cigarette smoke hung in the air. It turned her stomach, but so did the fear.

She fought hard to be free of his hold, but in the struggle he still managed to grasp her arm and yank it hard behind her back. Pain ripped through her shoulder and she shrieked as joints cracked and tendons pulled.

'Now, we're going to take a little trip, you and me,' he said, his body pushed against hers as he continued out into the road and towards the car that had found them again. 'And you're going to be a good girl and make this easy.'

'*No,*' she cried. '*Stop. Help me. Help me!*'

He wrapped one arm around her waist and lifted her feet from the ground, walking her forwards as he clamped his other hand over her mouth, stifling her cries.

Desperate, she screamed into his hand as she battled against being bundled into the car. If that happened, she was as good as dead. She scratched and kicked, her legs flaying, wild and uncoordinated, until her foot hit the door with a sickening crack. White-hot pain seared through her leg, knocking the air from her lungs as it stalled her fight. Now he had a better opportunity to get a tighter hold and as he squeezed hard, it was clear that as well as hold her, he wanted to hurt her.

*Oh God, this is happening. This is actually happening.*

'Drive,' he ordered as he rammed her into the car and pushed her across the leather seat with a force that made her head hit the window.

'*No, no!*' she screamed as she lunged for the door release, tugging at it frantically. But it was useless, the door locked tight.

The car picked up speed and she clocked two more men. One driving, one passenger.

'Oh God, oh God, what's happening?'

'Listen to me,' the man beside her ordered as he grabbed her arms and dragged her round to face him as a shrill cry burst from her mouth. 'You ain't going anywhere, so do as you're told and shut the fuck up.'

Unable to stop herself, she sobbed loudly as he forced her wrists together and pulled them down onto the seat between them.

'Are you going to do it? Are you going to shut up?' he barked, his face inches from hers. 'Or will I have to shut you up myself, because you really wouldn't like that.'

His words hung in the air. She didn't doubt his threat, so she suppressed the hysteria, swallowed it down, desperate to reduce the sounds that escaped from her mouth, terrified of what would happen if she continued to make too much noise. He chuckled, happy he'd made himself clear, and the sound was thin and ugly as it reverberated through the car.

He loosened his grip enough to pull a cable tie from his pocket. With this he bound her wrists, his fingers thin but strong as he wrapped it tightly. Next, he pulled out a ragged piece of material and covered her eyes, the knot catching in her hair. He shoved her along the seat as instinct screamed. She should do more, fight her captors, but how? There would be no fighting this man and surviving it, of that she was sure. So she sat in darkness as the sound of rustling, the click of a lighter and the acrid aroma of cigarette smoke filled the car. The sound of his drag on the cigarette and the long exhale filled her mind. Swirling smoke mingled with her incoherent thoughts.

The car slowed as smooth road changed to gravel that crunched under wheels. They pulled to a stop and the engine died. Doors clicked open and the car shifted as the men got out, slamming the doors behind them.

She sat in silence, sensing nothing but the thumping of her heart. She waited for the activation of the central locking system, but it didn't come. With trembling fingers, she wriggled the band of cloth up and squinted. Blinking, she willed her blurry vision to clear and peered through the windscreen. They were in a clearing, surrounded by woodland, with nothing but a dilapidated wooden shack ahead of her, and that's where the men had grouped together – talking, planning – and taking no care that their captive was alone, sitting in an unlocked car. Unsure if this was a trap, she used the time too, needing a plan of her own.

She watched for a moment longer and

when they didn't bother to look her way, she moved into action. This was her chance. Placing her hand over the door handle, she carefully pulled it back, listening for the click of release. Holding it there for a second, she waited to see if any of the men had noticed. Still nothing, no reaction from any of them as they continued on with their discussion. With great care, she pushed open the door and slipped out, crouching down low, keeping herself small.

One of the men shouted out as she stumbled into a run, the hurried strides of escape, and she heard the sound of boots on gravel as they kicked into action. They noticed her now; they were all watching her now.

*'Jesus, get her!'* the man who had taken her off the street roared, the fury in his voice igniting panic deep within her. But she kept going, her desire to survive so much stronger.

She saw the edge of a long gravel lane between the trees and stumbled through low scrub and brambles to join it. Thorns as sharp as barbed wire caught her legs and ankles, ripping and tearing skin, but she didn't care, didn't even feel it, as she hurried on. Whatever the cost, she *must* get away, and the gravel lane was her quickest route. But her thoughts clouded as the ominous sound of footsteps pounded behind her again, crashing through the undergrowth, snapping branches as they went. She screamed as terror clawed at her throat.

She had made it to the lane when his hand brushed against her back once more. It would be him; she was sure of that. He wouldn't let her escape. He'd be the one to take on the challenge to get her back, so with every ounce of energy, she tried to quicken her pace. But it was no good, fear had exhausted her body. Another swipe, and this time, his hand grabbed hold of her clothing. Unbalanced and without a sure footing, she began to fall and threw out her hands to lessen the impact as they slid against small stones that grazed her skin. With no time to react, she was hoisted up and, with little care, thrown over the man's shoulder.

'*No!*' she shrieked, banging her bound hands against his back. '*Let me go!*'

He gripped harder. 'Shut up, bitch,' he snarled as he strode back to the others. 'I'm not letting you out of my sight.'

Her vision of brambles gave way to the wheels of the car she had just fled. But rather than make his way to it, he kept walking. She began to sob, unable to fight anymore, and slumped against him, rocking in time with the motion of his stride.

'Who the fuck didn't lock the car?' he bellowed to the waiting men. 'Do I have to think of everything?' He strode into the shack, tipping her onto an old ripped sofa. Rusty metal springs poked through blackened fabric, likely torched at some point in its history. It was the only item within the shack's rotting walls, and it plumed out thick dust that filled her lungs and burned her throat as she landed hard onto it. She was 5'4" and of slim build, but still it groaned under her weight. Her eyes darted around the shack with only muddy earth for a floor. One of the men stood by the entrance, blocking any further attempt at escape.

*Oh God, please don't let me die in here.*

The man talked on the phone and paced, a cigarette clasped between his fingers, anger clipping his words as he relayed her little escapade to an unknown recipient. He terminated the call and with a nod to the man who had been the passenger in the car, he walked behind her and grabbed her shoulders, pushing her down into the seat.

'Do it.'

The man before her hesitated, seemed unsure.

'*I said, do it!*' the man behind bellowed as he dug his fingers harder into her skin.

So this was it. She laboured for air as she sobbed, watching the man walk towards her, pulling up the flap of the leather messenger bag slung over his shoulder. Horror surged new energy through her as he produced a vial of liquid and a syringe in sterile packaging, making her wrestle to stand.

'Please... don't...' she gasped, as she fixed her stare at the man in desperation, hoping to touch his conscience. But he ignored her as he pulled out a tourniquet strap, tore open the packet, and drained the vial of liquid into the syringe.

She bucked and fought against the hold on her as the man grasped her left arm. He twisted it within its restraints and wrapped the strap tightly above her elbow until the pump of her blood pulsed and made her veins rise to the surface in long blue lines. Removing the cap from the syringe, exposing a small but effective needle, he pierced the largest vein.

A sound erupted from her throat. A guttural scream. '*No, no, no! Don't do it! Don't do it!*' she cried as she stared in horror, watching the man squeeze on the syringe, letting its sinister liquid seep into her body.

The drug took hold with dangerous efficiency, claiming her, and her head fell back. Only the sound of her scream fading into a long, woozy groan rattled through her mind, and as she drifted away, she stared into the man's eyes, noticing how they had become wide with concern.

# CHAPTER 2

Two days earlier...

'He's there again,' Elena murmured as she stared out of her living room window, the phone pressed against her ear.

'Who?'

'Oh, just some guy,' she said, realising her thinking out loud had become part of the conversation. 'I've seen him around a couple of times, that's all.'

'Well, this is London,' Charlotte said. 'Fourteen million people means we are not alone in this great metropolis.'

'Funny.'

So, what does he look like?' Charlotte continued. 'I mean, how does one recognise a mad axe maniac?'

Charlotte stifled a laugh and Elena immediately felt stupid, as if she was overreacting. But she was sure she wasn't, and as hard as she tried, she was unable to shift the uneasy feeling in the pit of her stomach.

'Sorry, Lena, I'm not laughing at you,' Charlotte said. 'But I think you need to relax. He might have recently moved into the area or could just be meeting someone here?'

'Maybe.'

'And not to open old wounds, but you don't want to make the same mistake as before.'

Elena sighed but knew Charlotte's concern was sincere. They'd been friends long enough for Elena to know that she had her best interests at heart. Since school, it had always been the four of them – Elena, Charlotte, Abigail and Louise. The four musketeers. Unbreakable and prepared to do anything for one another. But now, life had moved on. Abigail was busy travelling the world and Louise had settled down in the country with Tom – 'the one'. So, it was Elena and Charlotte who were the last two standing, still in London and still firmly ingrained in each other's lives. And it had been that way since Charlotte had moved into the house next door to Elena's when they were both nine years old.

'I know, I'm sure it's nothing to do with me,' Elena said, reassuring her friend. 'And you know who says I am over-thinking it?'

'Who? Oh, wait. Adam? Really?' Charlotte said as it dawned on her. 'He didn't want to discuss it?'

'No, not at all. You know what he's like: "*There is always a reasonable explanation for everything, darling. This isn't the movies. Stop worrying about nothing. Blah, blah, blah*",' Elena said in a deep, mocking voice.

They both spilled into laughter, but it didn't relieve her tension.

'Two years you've been together and still he doesn't get you,' Charlotte said with a huff. 'Well, *we'll* chat it out, decide what to do. We're getting together tomorrow night, yes?'

'Yes.'

'So let's talk about it then. Over a bottle of wine.'

'Definitely,' Elena said with a half-smile as she moved away from the window. 'Maybe two.'

'That's my girl. Is Adam back from New York later?'

'Yeah, he should be calling soon, then we're over to my parents for supper.'

'Nice,' Charlotte said, her tone heavy with sarcasm.

'Hmm, exactly. They want to celebrate.'

'Oh dear,' Charlotte said. 'Is your dad in full-on schmoose mode?'

'Yep.'

'Oh no.'

'I know, but unavoidable, I'm afraid. Adam's pulled off some major deal, so they want to hear all about it. Completely boring, but I'll discuss this with them at some point – if I can get a word in. It's the least they can do. Especially as they're the reason I'm 'Mrs Paranoid'.'

'Hmm, I guess peace of mind is the one thing money can't buy,' Charlotte mused.

'No, but it pays for the security, I suppose.'

'Ever the optimist, Elena.'

'Always.'

Elena checked the window again after finishing her call. The man had gone. *Is that a good thing? At least when I can see him, I know he isn't lurking in the shadows. Or worse still, in this building, climbing the stairs.*

Her ringing phone punctured the silence, and she jumped, letting out a startled cry.

Checking her phone, and with a soft laugh at the absurdity of her reaction, she accepted the call. 'Hey, Adam,' she said as her heart calmed. She sank into her favourite button-backed armchair, a vintage piece, and the first item she'd purchased from a quaint little shop in the East End of London after securing the apartment. Looking out at the dusk skyline, she watched wispy orange clouds glide across the navy sky, the dying embers of the early spring day.

'Lena, hi, how're you doing?' Adam replied. 'All the better for speaking to the love of your life?'

'Well, obviously,' she said playfully. 'Glad you're back safely. Good journey?'

'Great, apart from the delays and the people.'

She chuckled.

'I'm serious, Leens,' he continued. 'I think there must be some unwritten rule that allows people to become complete morons the minute they step into an airport terminal.'

'Adam,' she chided. 'They can't all travel

business class like you. Be kind.'

'I'm killing them with kindness,' he said. 'Best thing for them.'

'You're a nightmare. What time are you going to get here?'

'Thank you, and my driver is negotiating us through the traffic as we speak,' he said. 'London is even more chaotic tonight.'

She heard the *tap, tap, tap* of a keyboard. He was working as he talked, but it didn't surprise her. He rarely gave her one hundred per cent of his attention and she was used to discussing whatever she needed over a laptop or in between phone calls.

He continued. 'I guess I'll be thirty minutes, maybe forty, max, so unlatch the door and I'll run in and freshen up before we go.'

She hadn't wanted to mention the man across the street because she knew the reaction she'd get, but it was unavoidable now. 'No, use your key please. I'd rather keep the door locked.'

'Really, Lena,' he sighed. 'Tell me you're not worrying about that man again,' he said, the humour gone from his voice.

'Well, if you must know, yes I am,' she replied. 'He was out there just now, actually. He's only just gone.'

'For God's sake, we've spoken about this. Not everyone is out to do you harm, remember?'

'That was five years ago, Adam,' she retorted. 'And he was a total weirdo.' She tutted. 'I wish I'd never told you about it now.'

He sighed. 'Okay, okay, I'm sorry. I've been travelling and I'm tired, that's all. I'll use my key. We can talk about it when I get there.' His voice sounded kinder now, more patient, but she wasn't sure how genuine it was.

She wound up their call and decided that a quick shower would help to clear her mind and get her ready for the night ahead.

It had been a long day, but she loved her work. After finishing university, she had floundered, but it had been three years since she had secured a job as a conservator at the British Museum. It was history that she loved, not her father's beloved law, and building a picture of how civilisations lived from the fragments that were left behind. It was rewarding and paid well enough to mollify her parents, even though they did little to hide their disappointment when she told them she wouldn't be pursuing a career in law too.

She didn't let it concern her though. She was happy where she was in her life, living in her top-floor apartment in a row of converted Georgian townhouses with heavy black front doors and iron railings that spoke of grander times gone by. Burton Street was close to the Museum and a stone's throw from Tavistock Square Gardens, a haven of outside space. It had everything she needed. It was home.

Once showered, she dressed in a smart

black dress – the expectation to dress for dinner was always a given at her parents' house – and attempted to tame her hair. This was a constant struggle, mainly because she had no patience for it, and because it was happiest trailing down her back, in long, dark waves. But for tonight, she styled it into a bun at the nape of her neck and teased out sections to frame her face.

She was ready and covering her lips in gloss when the key turned in the lock. Adam pushed open the door, dropped his case and came to her, wrapping his arms around her waist. He smothered her 'hello' with a kiss.

'Well, I do believe you missed me this time,' she said when he pulled back.

'Yes, actually, I did,' he said with a smile.

He kissed her again, just as his phone rang, breaking the moment.

'Sorry, darling, I have to take this,' he said with a sheepish smile. Elena nodded, used to these interruptions and she rectified her smudged lips while he dealt with business. When he was finished, he disappeared to shower and change and returned with a small gift bag.

'What's this?' she asked.

'I wasn't going to come back from New York empty-handed, now, was I? Go on then, open it,' he said, watching with interest.

His reaction could have meant that he wanted to see her joy, but she understood him well enough to know that if it was like any other gift he'd given before, it was because he didn't know what was in the bag either. She knew he lived by the notion that there was nothing wrong in getting his PA to organise little things like gifts, because he was always too busy earning the money to buy them.

She reached into the bag and pulled out the recognisable blue Tiffany box. Inside was a double chain bracelet, held together with the iconic 'Return to Tiffany' heart tag. It was delicate and pretty – and absolutely not what Adam would have chosen.

Her suspicion was confirmed when he murmured, 'Hmm, not bad,' as she held it up.

'Adam it's lovely. Thank you,' she said, ignoring the sinking feeling within her. She planted a kiss on his cheek and reminded herself that a gift was a gift, by whatever means.

'You're welcome darling,' he said as he gathered up his things ready to leave for her parents'. 'Now let's not be late.'

\*\*\*

The next morning, she woke to a silent room and a note from Adam saying that he had headed straight to the office, to get his report in.

She relaxed for a while and enjoyed the peace, not wanting to drag herself from her bed and start the day.

The visit to her parents had been like any other and, as predicted, her father was in top-level schmoose mode, with him and Adam sharing enough affectionate back slaps to emphasise just how highly regarded he was by her parents. And that meant that, in their eyes, it was only a matter of time before 'boyfriend' became 'husband'. The only problem with that idea was that she wasn't sure how she felt about it. Her mother had been her usual graceful self, not a hair out of place, and had given them both two-cheeked kisses with an extra hug for Elena. Never too close though – Elena knew the drill. Big displays of affection were for gameshow contestants, as her mother put it, and not the family.

Words like 'bonds' and 'hedge-fund' had littered the conversation with Adam in his element and very soon Elena was bored and on the outside once more, looking in. She hadn't managed to discuss her concerns with her parents either, because every time she tried, the conversation had been steered back to Adam and his rousing anecdotes. Although it left her more than a little frustrated, she allowed him his moment, knowing that discussing her concerns on 'his night' was likely to lead to arguments on their journey home and she had no appetite for that. The chat with her parents could wait.

She sighed and hauled herself out of bed. Today was a day for coffee. Lots of it, and for starters she'd go for the best. She'd stop off at the coffee shop at the top of her road – her local and her favourite.

She checked the window again. No sign of the man.

*It's nothing to do with me. Why would it be? So just stop worrying.* She showered, dressed and applied a little make-up, all the while letting the thought of fresh coffee hurry her along.

As she opened the door of Marco's, delicious, warm, coffee-infused air wafted into her face and filled her with a sense of cosy familiarity. She loosened the pashmina wrapped around her neck and shuffled her way through the empty tables that would soon be busy with a throng of people. But now, still early, there was only a queue of workers requiring their daily hit of caffeine before they braved their commute.

Marco was a stout Italian man in his fifties. He was kind and funny and loved to share wild, heavily embellished stories with his customers, especially the regulars. His eyes lit up when he saw that she was next in the queue.

'Elena, my beautiful princess. How are you today?'

'I'm good Marco, thanks. You?'

'Better for seeing you, my darling,' he said with a wink. 'Is your man back from America?' he asked, with particular emphasis on the A in America, a play on his embellished accent.

'Yup,' she said, wriggling the bracelet on her wrist. 'More presents.'

'Ah, yes,' Marco nodded, thoughtful for a

moment. 'More trinkets. But I wonder if he realises his greatest gift is you, Elena.'

She laughed. 'I doubt it.'

Marco didn't laugh, but smiled kindly. 'I would make sure any man who came near such a beautiful flower as you, would be made aware of what a precious gift you are.'

It was a paternal role Marco played with Elena, and his words touched her. Within five minutes of arriving, he'd spoken with more affection than her father had managed in an entire evening.

'Marco, you're so sweet, thank you.'

'Here's my little piece of advice for today: make sure you have people in your life who appreciate you, my darling.'

She nodded. 'Well, I'll try,' she said, reaching for her purse.

He held up his hand. 'No, no. Consider this one 'on the house', and you have a good day.'

'Thanks, Marco. You're the best,' she said as she turned, too close to the person standing behind. As she bumped against the unknown commuter, a trickle of hot coffee spilled through the plastic cover of her cup, burning her fingers. She flicked it away as she looked up to apologise.

The man, dressed in an open-collared shirt under a thick navy cashmere coat was miraculously free of spilt coffee. He was calm, assured, and had the looks to back it up. Standing so close, she caught the warmth from him and the sweet, musky notes of his aftershave, which only served to fluster her more.

'I'm sorry, are you okay?' he asked as he reached out and placed a steadying hand on her elbow. He smiled, in complete control and clearly poles apart from how she was feeling. He studied her for a moment, waiting for her response, his head slightly tilted to one side as he watched the embarrassment flush over her face. It was clear he was enjoying the moment.

'Oh, no, I'm fine. I'm sorry. It was my mistake,' she stammered, trying to feign calm.

'Well, as long as you're sure,' he said, holding her gaze before pointing to the messy cup in her hand. 'Can I get you another?'

She had lost her thirst for the coffee in her hand as even breathing became an effort. 'No, but thank you, it's fine,' she said, nervously tucking her hair behind her ear, feeling the weight of his scrutiny of her.

He held her there for a little while longer before nodding, deciding the moment was over. He moved his hand from her elbow and stepped aside, gesturing for her to walk by, still smiling but with eyes fixed on her.

*One foot in front of the other, Elena.*

As she left the coffee shop, she glanced back, fully expecting those eyes to be watching her leave, but she was disappointed to find he wasn't doing that at all. He was at the counter, completely at ease, giving his order, their encounter nothing but a blip in his day. She chuckled to herself that she'd dared a sneak peek at him, like the silly schoolgirl she'd reverted to. She shook her head and made her way to work. It would serve to provide some light relief with Charlotte later if nothing else.

# CHAPTER 3

Her mind drifted in and out of consciousness like the ebb and flow of the tide. She couldn't open her eyes. They were too heavy and it would take too much effort, so she avoided the task. She could be hovering on the edge of life or death. She didn't know or care. She was only *here*, lost in a surreal dream.

Blackness.

She woke in a haze to voices, which spoke in low muffled tones. Male voices. Someone used her name. 'They' seemed to know exactly who she was but she was in the dark still, in every sense.

She was unsteady, her head spinning as if she was drunk. But whatever coursed through her system had blocked the fear and panic for a moment, had saved her from its vice-like grip, and she lingered in a strange calm.

Blackness.

Waking again, as if floating to the surface of an ocean, she became aware of her surroundings once more. Now there was more clarity, as the drug loosened its hold on her. She tensed and held her breath, ready for attack. Opening her eyes, she squinted, letting them adjust. She was alone and relief washed over her. Her body was heavy, a lead weight, and she lay on a thin blanket. She was fully clothed with nothing torn or exposed and was in no pain. *Small mercies.* Carefully, she ran her fingers over the rough floorboards, the edges catching on her skin, and she remained there, unable to move.

She was no longer in the shack. Now she was in the middle of a room with faded, discoloured floral wallpaper on the walls. It had begun to peel away and exposed crumbling plasterwork beneath, blackened with damp. The room was empty of furniture, except for a small wooden chair in the far corner, eerie in its uselessness. Wherever she was, the long-since-abandoned building was rank with dereliction and decay.

To her left was a door and to her right was a window with long wooden boards laid across it, and this was where her attention focused. These lengths of timber were not to protect from intruders, they were a barrier; to keep someone contained. The first fluttering of panic began to take root within her as a fog of claustrophobia inched into her consciousness. *Don't think about it. Focus on something else, anything else.* She kept her eyes on the window behind the wood, staring at the fragments of glass that gave a glimpse of the outside world, where life was continuing as normal. The glass was covered in thick dust and grime and was cracked in places, but even so, she could just make out some blurry sky. The pink clouds against the dark blue could have signified dawn or dusk, she couldn't be sure, the sands of time lost in her black oblivion.

It was very cold.

She lay there for a moment, letting her body adjust, to come to. In time, she became more alert, but if the drug that ran through her system had anaesthetised her sense of fear, it had not dulled her sense of pain. The nagging jab of discomfort soon escalated into a deep, aching pain. Every muscle in her body hurt, but the main centre of her pain was in her legs. Lactic acid trapped inside strained muscle, which if she had the will, would have had her squirming to find comfort and ease.

Her ankle smarted too, throbbing and sickly warm. Tentatively, she wiggled it but knew the only way to assess the damage properly was to get her weight onto it – if she ever got the energy to stand.

Her hands were still bound with the plastic cable tie. Two pink circles ran over her wrists, so she moved them as best she could to aid circulation and ease the stiffness that had crept in. The grazes on her palms were sore but superficial, but these became insignificant compared to the bright, zinging pain in her right leg – rips in her skin made by thorns and brambles when she'd tried to escape. Long slithers of dark, blood-red lines ran up the lower half of her leg and nestled in between them was a long, deep wound, the length of her hand at least. Blood glistened in the torn skin and there were smears of dried blood and dirt around it. It was a mess, but in her panic, she hadn't even felt it snag. Nausea moved through her in waves, so she turned her head away, as pathetic tears threatened. But nothing came, her eyes as dry as her parched mouth.

Awake now and senses snapped on like a switch, she needed to move. She was too vulnerable on the floor.

'Come on, get up,' she whispered into the silent room. She rolled over and hoisted herself up onto her right elbow. The room seemed to sway and black dots danced about in front of her eyes. She had moved too fast and needed to grip the floor beneath her to steady her senses. With no improvement, she admitted defeat and lay down again, staring at the peeling ceiling. 'Take it easy,' she said, breathing away the urge to vomit.

Once the nausea had passed, she tried again, the knowledge that they would soon return keeping her motivated. This time she was successful and rose to her feet, careful to keep her weight on her left foot. She stood for a while, letting herself adjust, and although the room swam again, she was in control of it, holding her hands out for balance.

*Well done. Good work. Now walk.*

She placed her right foot on the floor,

putting a little weight onto it, testing it out. It ached and was sore, but she didn't have the shooting pain that she imagined she'd feel if it was broken.

*It's just a sprain. That's all.*

Putting harder pressure on it now, she shuffled around the empty room careful not to make too much noise, scared to bring attention to the fact that she was awake. A small sob caught in her throat. She needed to take small steps, both physically and mentally, because, in terms of the latter, she was holding on to her sanity by a single thread that might just snap if overloaded with the knowledge of the horrors that lay ahead.

Sweat trickled down her back as she tried to calm her panicked mind. Was she being held by these men to be raped, killed, or both? Was this a kidnap and ransom demand? Or was this all of the above? She knew the risks of kidnap. Of course she did; her family's wealth was no secret. Her parents had to face the fact that this scenario might become a reality many years ago and had taken all of the necessary precautions. They had fitted panic alarms, trackers, CCTV equipment, all installed at their home to secure their safety as much as possible. They had all been educated about what might happen if one of them was abducted, and the list was long and not exhaustive; the removal of extremities – fingers or ears, or both – to send to the family, a ploy to keep them focused and away from the police. The knowledge sent a fresh wave of nausea through her.

She paused, focused her mind and concentrated on the next steps. If this was a ransom demand, she was reasonably safe if no call had yet been made. She just had to figure out how she'd stay that way.

She blocked that thought from her mind and managed a circuit of the room, shuffling on shaky legs, holding her bound hands against the crumbling wall as best she could. It was pointless, but as she reached the door, she grasped the handle and turned it, careful to be quiet. As predicted, it remained rigid and unmoving, but the desperation still hit her and she began to sob as she rested her head against the flaking paint. She held her hands against her mouth to stifle the noise, hoping that the emotion would soon subside. Thin tears ran down her cheeks as she moved across the room to the blanket, her only source of comfort. She sat with her back to the wall, facing the door, keeping watch. Sleep would make her vulnerable, but with no apparent control of it, her head would drop until she snapped awake again, her eyes focused on the door.

The sound of a key clunking in the lock jolted Elena out of her restless sleep and back to her grim reality. Instinctively, she sat upright and pushed herself against the wall for support, dizziness and nausea her friends once more.

The smoker, who could only be known as Cigarettes now – a caricature, she knew, but still terrifying nonetheless – stood in the open door.

'Well, well,' he said with a sneer as he used the weight of his body to shut the door behind him. 'Our sleeping beauty is awake.'

Heart hammering, she pushed herself harder against the wall, wanting to dissolve into it, to become invisible. His heavy boots thumped against the dry floorboards as he strode towards her. He crouched down, taking a long drag from his half-smoked cigarette and made a strange whistling sound as he sucked the fumes through his teeth and down into his lungs. When he had held it there long enough, he blew it out into her face in one hazy, toxic cloud. It burned her throat, making her cough and gasp for air, which seemed to amuse him. Laughing, he did it again.

He rested his elbows on his legs and in the dim light, she stared at the thick black tattoos that snaked out from beneath his t-shirt and down his arms, rather than look him in the eye. He stared too, watching as if she was a prized animal, his face only inches from hers.

'Now, my little princess. What are we going to do with you?' he said with a smile that made her want to scream.

He took hold of her bound hands, gripping hard, and turned them within his own. He looked with fascination, his fingers digging into her clammy skin.

'Such delicate hands,' he said as he brought them closer to his face. 'It would be such a shame if you were to lose one of those pretty fingers. Or even two. It would make them ugly. Deformed.' His gaze roamed from her hands to her eyes. 'You wouldn't like that, would you?'

'No,' she said as she struggled to free herself from his grasp.

'No, you wouldn't,' he replied with a sigh. 'It would be very painful too. Here in this room, with no way of numbing the flesh before I made the cut. There would be a lot of blood. Your blood. You'd scream, beg me to stop.'

'I just… I just want you to leave me alone,' she stammered, her voice faltering as the mental image of what he proposed burned into her mind.

'Oh, is that right,' he goaded with an amused expression. 'I see. The lady wants me to leave her alone.'

He dropped her hands as if they disgusted him and wiped his own on his trouser leg.

'Well, I can't do that,' he said as he reached into his pocket, his eyes on hers as he pulled out something thin and metallic which glinted in the low light.

The sight of the blade made her dart sideways away from him, but he was quicker and reached out for her, pulling her back.

*'Oh God, no!'* she shrieked as she hugged her hands tightly against her body.

He snatched them in his and slipped the blade between her palms as she let out a piercing scream.

He held her firm and wiggled the knife which cut through the tie, snapping it apart, freeing her hands as the plastic fell to the floor. Laughing, he tucked the knife back into his pocket with a glint in his eye that gave away how much he enjoyed this little game.

Hands free and through anguished sobs, she lunged away from her tormentor, desperate for some distance. But as she shuffled along the floor, she caught the humour in his face flash to anger. He reached out again. Now, he wrapped his hand around her neck, covering her throat. She froze, her attempt at freedom thwarted. Eye to eye, she stared straight into his cold soul.

'Did I say you could move?' he hissed.

With ragged breaths, she brought her hands to his, grasping them, trying to ease the pressure.

He laughed and released his hold, happy he'd made his point. With one last act of violence, he struck her forehead with the heel of his hand, cracking her head into the wall behind.

She cried out as fresh pain reverberated through her skull and down the core of her body, connecting with the throb in her leg.

'Later, bitch,' he muttered as he walked to

the door, slamming it shut and locking it.

She let out shallow gasps as his footsteps faded away. She was alone again and had never been so grateful.

Fresh glinting pain glowed in her head as she reached up and gently touched the egg-shaped lump that had formed. She didn't stop the sobs that escaped, not that she could have if she tried. She wanted to get out of this. She wanted to go home. She wanted to survive.

After a brief respite, the sound of the door opening again made Elena jump to her feet. Cigarettes strode in again, a large bottle of water in his hand.

'What's going on?' she stammered, keeping herself steady as her mouth salivated at the sight of the water.

He didn't speak but walked towards her, unscrewing the lid from the bottle.

She reached for it without thinking, wanting to get the cool liquid into her body, but he swiped her hand away and instead held the bottle to her lips. She let him do it. However she was going to get it, she needed that water and drank greedily, using her mouth to tip the bottle lower for a better flow. He resisted and only allowed a few gulps before he removed the bottle and replaced the cap. 'That's all you're getting.'

It wasn't enough. Not even close, but she said nothing and just watched as he tucked the bottle under his arm.

'Move,' he ordered as he pulled at her arm.

'Where are we going?'

'We need you to stay alive at this point and even though I don't give a fuck if you sit in your own crap, you need to come with me.'

Walking her across the room and through the door, he pushed her to the right, alongside the staircase, its balustrades kicked out, by vandals perhaps. Dirty, peeling paintwork covered the walls and uneven floorboards creaked beneath their feet. They stopped directly outside the door at the end of the corridor, its top hinge missing, making it hang precariously on its side.

He released his grasp on her. 'Go on. Off you go. Do what you need to do,' he said as he lit a cigarette.

She did as she was told, happy to be free, and pushed the door carefully. Inside, and with the door pushed shut as much as the broken hinge would allow, she discovered the remnants of a bathroom. It was a shell, with large gaps where the bath and sink should be; exposed pipework the only indication of their presence, long ago. She looked up at the rafters that let small shards of light beam down through cracks in the roof. What was left of the ceiling littered the rotten floor from years of water damage and she couldn't be sure that it would take her weight. Huge black graffiti was scrawled across the walls, the only evidence of past visitors to this desolate place.

In the far corner of the room was an avocado-coloured toilet pan, with no seat and a large crack running through the centre of it. More wood covered the window above it. Tentatively, she moved towards it and pulled hard at the slats, but it was no use, they were fixed firm. No escape from here either. She glanced around. She was expected to use this room but found that, mercifully, she was far too dehydrated to pee. So she stood for a while longer, wanting to delay, but once she had prolonged the moment for as long as possible, she opened the door.

The man shoved her – a harsh, unspoken instruction to move forwards. He walked close behind and as she neared her room and the top of the stairs, he grabbed her neck, a helpful reminder not to make any attempt at freedom.

In her room, he released his hold and pushed her away, making her stumble for balance. The movement pulled on her wound and she felt it throb. She hoped this would be the moment he would leave her, but he stalked towards her, swiping the back of his hand across his mouth as if the sight of her whetted an appetite in him.

She backed away, sensing that this visit was, in fact, far from over. 'Leave me alone,' she snapped as she glanced at the open door.

'Maybe you want to be nice to me,' he said as he moved closer. 'I can get you more water, if you pay me a little attention.' Close enough to touch now, he slowly backed her up against the wall.

'I want you to go away.'

'Fine, I'll go,' he assured. 'Once you're nice to me.'

She stared at him as he leant in close, too close. This was another subject in the lesson of abduction only she and her mother had been educated on: that sex was maybe an option to consider, if necessary. A bargaining tool, to help placate the abductor, to get him on side and maybe prolong or save your life. Still, the idea of it abhorred her, here, in this dank room, with this disgusting man.

She edged away enough to slap him hard across his face. 'You get away from me.'

He raised his hand to his cheek and glared at her. 'Now, that is not nice,' he growled as he took a step back as if to turn away from her.

He moved so quickly that she only registered the impact of the back of his hand against her cheek by the pain that seared into her skin and bone rather than from sight alone. She cried out as she lurched sideways.

Steadying herself, she turned and faced him, her hand to her cheek. 'My father will kill you when he finds you,' she spat as she tasted the coppery twang of blood in her mouth.

He moved closer, fury blazing in his eyes. 'He's got to fucking find me first, little bitch. And you.'

'Oh, he will!' she snapped. 'And he won't stop until he's crushed you. Like the insignificant weasel you are.'

She watched him raise his hand again and bring it down hard against her face, collapsing her body to the floor as a dark void of unconsciousness enveloped her.

# CHAPTER 4

Endless days passed. Each one the same routine of torment. Cigarettes would come to her room, offer her the tiniest drop of water and sometimes a little bread, and then he would taunt her, telling her she'd get more if she was prepared to be nice to him. She would take the water and snippet of food and refuse anything else, but there was no more violence.

He would never force himself on her, never disregard her refusal and brutally take what he wanted anyway. He could, of course. They both knew she would be unable to stop him from doing whatever he wanted, in whatever way that pleased him, but something seemed to stop him. Although she could see the desire to do her harm in his expression – she only had to look at the way his eyes scanned her body – there was always restraint. It made her suspicious as to what lay ahead for her, what orders he was being given. But whatever might befall her, she held on to the fact that she was unharmed for now, and she was grateful for it.

Her face was still tender from his backhanded slap, but it was healing. She massaged it gently, hoping to get some fresh blood flowing to it, focusing on anything other than her constant state of hunger and the dull ache in her leg. She fantasised about favourite drinks or food just so she could salivate and lubricate her dry mouth, but, in time, even that failed. But there was a glimmer of hope. She remembered that the last time she'd worn her hoodie she'd tucked a packet of gum in the pocket, so she reached in, hoping it hadn't tumbled out when her phone was snatched from her. She felt the foil paper crinkle in her fingers and breathed out with relief. She pulled it out. The packet was full, only one tab missing. Heaven. She rubbed the cuff of her sleeve over her teeth and carefully bit a tab in half, rationing them, and tucked the packet away. She chewed, and was so hungry that she knew its final destination, but she didn't care.

She scratched a line into the dusty plasterwork to mark a new day. She was keeping track, making a timeline of misery. Fourteen lines were stacked in a row already, and these were her conscious days. She had no way of knowing how many days she had spent in an abyss of darkness. But she wouldn't let herself dwell on that. She had to focus, stay strong.

The sun was bright and high in the sky. Iridescent specks of dust sparkled and danced within the shafts of light and she found it soothing to watch. She thought of her family, her friends, Adam. Her old life. She'd been missing long enough now. Surely they must know that this was a ransom demand? Surely now they must realise that someone had been watching, had been waiting, ready to place her in this hell. And now all she could do was to keep the faith that someone out there in the normal world would be close to finding her.

Watching the sunlight – and with a mixture of fear, boredom and hunger – she stood and went to the window. Unable to fight the desire to be free, she tugged and pulled at the wood, hoping to dislodge it in some way. She jabbed her fingernails under the screws and twisted, but it achieved nothing, only to snap and tear her nails. The screws were held firm, tight and unmoveable. It should have broken her, but it didn't. She glared at them and inhaled deeply, feeling the fire ignite within her. That's when she knew she would continue to fight. She may be hidden, captured, but she still had strength. She wouldn't let them win. She also wouldn't discount another escape. Cigarettes just needed to be careless. One open door would be all it would take. She just had to bide her time, and she had plenty of that. She had an endless amount of time.

***

The quiet in her room was broken by the approach of a car, followed by the sounds of activity downstairs. More voices. Her heart pumped wildly and she felt her pulse throb in the wound on her leg. She braced herself as she listened to footsteps climb the stairs and sat up straight, ready, as the key turned.

'Hello, Elena.'

Noticing his eyes first and then his mouth, she instantly recognised the man she'd seen in the coffee shop.

'You!' she cried as she jumped to her feet, an action that left her unsteady.

The reason for their encounter became startlingly clear, and the knowledge was devastating. It was no coincidence. He had orchestrated their little meet-and-greet that day, a little escapade for his pleasure, no doubt, before the hell he would inflict. Humiliation radiated through her. He'd been so calm, so self-assured, and she had allowed thoughts of him to slip into her mind for the rest of that day. He'd been a funny story shared with Charlotte that evening too, and all for what? Being here now, his captive.

He used her name. What else did he know about her? Everything, probably. He'd need this information. Things to use as he saw fit.

Standing in the centre of the room, an air of power surrounded him – something she had noticed in the coffee shop that day and now here. His eyes bore into her, demanding her complete attention, and in the circumstances, she gave it.

He moved closer. 'You made an attempt to escape, I hear,' he said as he stood opposite her with folded arms. He was taller than her and it required her to look up if she was to maintain the eye contact he was demanding. 'Please don't try that again. I don't want to sedate you.'

She didn't believe him but nodded anyway, letting him know that she understood.

Cigarettes strode into the room, his smile as cold as the frigid air.

She stepped back as panic pooled in her empty stomach. Cigarettes walked to the chair, picked it up and slammed it down next to her. The stench of stale nicotine lingered in the air as he stood behind her and grabbed her by the shoulders, allowing the memory of her sedation to come flooding back.

'Sit down,' he demanded as he shoved her down onto the seat.

Frightened little gasps whooshed out of her as she stared at the man opposite.

But he didn't look at her. Instead, he pulled out a mobile phone from his pocket and punched in some numbers. It was a small, cheap phone. One that had been purchased for this job alone and would likely be disposed of immediately after its use. He held it to her ear and she listened to the ringing tone until there was a click and then her father's voice.

'Hello. Hello. I'm here. Where's my daughter. Let me speak to my daughter.'

'Dad,' she whispered, unable to stop the tears.

'Elena. Oh God, Elena,' he said. 'Have they hurt you?'

'I'm fine…' she lied as the phone was dragged away from her ear, her time up.

'You will be contacted again with instructions,' her captor said. It was a quick transaction with no emotion and his eyes were on her as he hit the button terminating the call.

She glared at him. *Go on, look if you must. Come a little closer and see my hatred for you. See how it fills my soul.*

She may not be able to say it or even properly show it, but she could feel it. No one would take that away from her.

While hatred briefly fired her up, the sound of her father's voice only heightened her sense of isolation, and the danger she was in. She was all alone in this room with two men – one of whom wanted to do her harm. The other, she was yet to find out.

Cigarettes huffed with disgust and scratched a fingernail along her neck as he walked away, making her wince as it left a long thin welt on her skin.

'Leave it,' her captor warned. 'Get the hell out of here and go downstairs.' He watched Cigarettes move to the door and leave the room before turning to face her.

'I hear you've been testing his patience,' he said as his eyes scanned her cheek.

Even in her perilous state, she gave a

small, cynical laugh and despite her best attempts to control it, a seething feeling grew within her.

'Are you deliberately trying to make this harder for yourself?' he asked as he meandered across the room and leaned against the wall opposite her. It wasn't necessary for him to be near for her to feel his power. It filled the room.

'Like my welfare really matters to you,' she muttered quietly.

She wasn't stupid. This was a dangerous game, but she couldn't stop herself.

'Elena, be careful,' he warned, his voice low but powerful, meaning every word. 'I only know because the man downstairs has been bringing me up to date. Your swollen cheek confirms it.'

'Ah, I see. Is that why you're here? Do you want me to be nice to you too?'

He raised his eyebrows. 'No, that's not why I'm here.'

'Well, that's what got me this,' she said pointing to her face. 'I bet your little henchman didn't share that, did he? I wouldn't give him what he wanted for a measly bottle of water, so he decided to get busy with his fists. And just so you know, I'll fight you too, just as I refused your friend. Even if it means more punishment, I don't care.'

'You need to take it easy with that attitude.'

She didn't reply and tried to hide the fact that her body had begun to tremble.

He was quiet too, perhaps allowing her little outburst, or about to react, she wasn't sure. She braced a little.

'But you're right,' he said, finally breaking the silence. 'I wasn't aware of what had happened. He failed to share that information with me.' He paused. 'I thought I could leave things to him in the early stages, but it seems I was mistaken.'

'Early stages? How long do you expect this hell to continue?'

'Until your father does as he's told,' he replied. 'But the fact that I'm here now is probably in your best interest.'

His words deflated her. 'Really? I can't see how,' she said as she shifted in the chair. 'And anyway, I'd go as far as guessing that it's more the case that it's in *your* best interests that you're here? For the money, the end goal we're all focused on, for different reasons.'

He strode towards her, not stopping until his hand met with the back of the chair, bringing his face close to hers. 'That's enough!' he thundered. 'Do you think this is a fucking game?'

The full force of his body near hers and the intensity that radiated from him made her cower from his glare. She shook her head, the ability to speak having deserted her.

His eyes bore into her and she braced for

an impact that would launch her from the chair.

She glanced at him, and although there was anger in his eyes, there was also control. Not like Cigarettes.

He released his hold and moved away from her. 'Relax, I'm not going to hurt you.'

She straightened in the chair and kept her eyes to the floor.

'But you're lucky it's me you're testing,' he said. 'I'll let it pass, for now, but you might want to keep those kinds of comments in check with the others from now on.' He turned and looked at her, ready to open the door. 'Do you understand?'

She nodded silently, not trusting herself to say something that would get her into more trouble.

'And that's exactly the right decision,' he said, as if reading her mind.

After effectively putting her in her place, he left the room, locking the door behind him.

She wanted to hurl the chair towards the door, show some act of defiance, but thought better of it. Testing his patience was not conducive to her survival, she knew that. She'd pushed boundaries with him in ways she'd never have done with Cigarettes, but she'd be wrong to trust him when he said he would let it pass.

She'd done well. She was still alive and unhurt. Now, all she had to do was stay that way.

***

Elena snapped awake, her senses on high alert. The wind howled outside her window, blowing icy gusts of air through cracks in the glass. Although it was spring, a frost still descended on cloudless nights and a cold chill penetrated her bones. She was agitated and jittery, feelings she couldn't shake since meeting her captor. Things were taking too long; she should have been released by now. She shivered. A running vest, a light hooded top, and calf-length leggings offered no protection in the frozen room.

She sat up and readied herself as footsteps climbing the stairs punctured the silence. The key turned and her captor walked into the room. He locked the door and she stood, not wanting to feel vulnerable on the floor.

'Hello, Elena,' he said as he approached her.

If there was one thing Elena was familiar with, it was quality, and everything about this man smacked of expense. It was clear he had money, lots of it. She just had to look at him to see it. His clothes, although casual, were well made, and the exclusive, chunky wristwatch at the end of his arm removed any sense of doubt. But it made perfect sense to Elena that someone in the game of demanding huge ransoms from London's elite would have a lot of cash to spend.

'What's happening?' she asked. 'Are you here to release me?'

'No, not today,' he said as he pulled out his

phone.

'Then what's going on?'

'It would seem that your father needs a little nudge in the right direction.' He held out the phone and snapped a picture of her, blinding her with the flash. 'This should be enough to focus his mind.'

She blinked until her vision returned and hoped that in her current state, with her unkempt appearance and decaying surroundings, her father would be given ample evidence that this was as real as it gets. It didn't surprise her. Nothing did as far as her father was concerned. Of course he'd want more proof before he'd even consider giving away a slice of his wealth. But she couldn't bring herself to think of what trinket Cigarettes would painfully cut away from her body if her father still refused to believe this reality.

He tucked his phone into his back pocket and although he didn't seem to be deliberately staying with her, he didn't seem in a rush to leave either.

'If you're here to take me to the bathroom, I don't need to go,' she said as she folded her arms tightly, nerves creeping in. 'Just so you know.'

'Well, thank you for sharing.'

Embarrassed, she continued. 'I mean, I just need water. Please. I'm so thirsty.'

'Water will be brought up to you shortly.'

'Shortly?'

He nodded and the air was filled with silence. After a moment, realisation hit her. She held her arm across her body, in a pathetic attempt at protection.

He cocked his brow as he figured it out. 'It's okay. I'm no thug. Forcing myself on a woman is not my thing.'

Relief made her legs falter, but she managed to stand firm.

'It's a shame your little 'kidnap buddy' doesn't feel the same way,' she murmured.

Suddenly, a thought occurred to her. An interesting and potentially life-saving one. Maybe he wasn't a thug. Maybe there was a part of him, a good part, that she could appeal to and she considered the option of negotiating a way out of here. She could test him out, try her hand. It was worth a shot. She moved a little closer and looked up at him, leaning in ever so slightly, an action designed to make him look down at her, bringing them closer together.

'Look, I understand what you need to do here. You want to show me who's boss, especially with the others around. But we could make this easy. I could make it easy,' she said as her mind raced. She wasn't even sure where this was going.

He listened without speaking and, unable to read his expression now, she continued on.

'If you let me go, I would persuade my father to pay you. But this has to be just between us. Don't you see, you'd still get your money and I would get my freedom – unhurt.'

He folded his arms. 'I understand your desire to leave, I really do...'

'So let me go. You don't have to discuss it with the others. We could work together, perhaps you could sneak me out.'

He raised his eyebrows at her suggestion, but the hint of a smile never left his lips. 'It is a mess,' he said, seeming to entertain her request. 'I hadn't expected it to take this long.' He sighed, running his hand through his hair.

A tiny glint of optimism flashed inside of her. 'Well, you can change it. There's still time. You can do the right thing if you want to.'

'I don't know.' He studied her again. 'You'd still be able to convince your father to pay me, even if released? You think he'd do that?'

His tone was strange, but she ignored it, blind to what it meant and hurried on. 'Yes, yes, absolutely. I would get the money somehow,' she said, knowing she was making promises she couldn't ever keep.

He began to laugh, a deep, resonating laugh that gave away what was really going on here. 'Nice try, Elena.'

Humiliation radiated through her and she took a few steps back to separate herself from him and this moment.

'You... you... pig!' she snapped.

'That's better,' he said with a dry smile.

'I much prefer your true colours. They shine so much brighter when you're angry,' he said as he moved closer, not allowing her the distance. 'You can try to play me again if you want. I'm not going to deny that I enjoyed it, but it won't get you anywhere. Do you understand? Because I see right through you.'

'Leave me alone!' she spat, angry with him, but furious with herself.

'Have it your own way,' he said as he strode to the door, locking it behind him.

She was alone again and worked hard to calm herself and her pounding heart. With clenched fists, she screeched with frustration and sunk to the floor, pulling the blanket close to bury her face within it in an attempt to block everything out.

# CHAPTER 5

Elena had scratched ten new lines into the wall since her pathetic attempt at negotiating a deal with her captor. Time dragged so slowly she was sure it had stopped completely – herself and her captors suspended in their strange little existence together – while the outside world continued on without them. She'd had little or no contact with any of the men apart from receiving her daily dose of water and a little bread. She spent her time pacing the room, trying to combat the negative energy that seemed to surround her since she'd made that embarrassing error.

It was dark, the day done, but no stars peeped through the gaps of the wood at the window. The key turned and the man who had sedated her, the doctor, appeared. He approached, carrying his messenger bag and, as he did, all other thoughts of why he was here faded into insignificance as she fixed her eye on the open door behind him.

*Careless.*

She watched him, slowly taking a few side steps to keep the doorway in her view.

'What do you want,' she asked as she paused, her body still but ready for flight.

'I'm here to check you over.'

'But I'm fine. I don't need checking over,' she said as she balled her fists. 'And you don't need to come any closer.'

Another step.

'Well, I have my orders,' he said, eyeing her cautiously as if she was a dangerous animal, observing, waiting, trying to predict her movements.

'I don't care. I don't want you anywhere near me.'

She glanced at the door as his eyes did the same. The mix of realisation and panic washed over his face as she shoved him hard and lurched forwards, straight out of the door.

His shout echoed in the empty room as she willed her fatigued body into action and used the finial of the top bannister to turn and launch herself down the stairs. Thudding against cracking wood, she jumped the last four stairs and tore across the hallway. Ignoring the dim light that shone from the room to her right, she only focused on the old front door and the freedom it would provide.

Cigarettes appeared and she shrieked and backed up, turning towards the corridor adjacent to the stairs. They rushed behind as she hurried on, hoping to find another room, a window, anything to break free. Finding another door, she pushed it open and slammed it behind her.

Darkness surrounded her. 'Come on, come on,' she whispered through panicked breaths as she shuffled around the room, running her hands along the walls, willing herself to find the cold smoothness of glass. A window that wasn't boarded, that she could smash and climb through. But there was no time to do a full circuit before she heard them, just outside the door. So, using the thin light that shone through the frame of the door to guide her, she darted back to crouch into the corner of the room. She waited, listening to their quiet voices and the pounding of her heart as the door swung open and Cigarettes' shadow loomed in the doorway.

'There's nowhere to go,' he murmured. 'I'm gonna find you and then we're gonna have a nice little chat, and we both know how it's gonna end, don't we. How itchy my hands get when I'm angry.' He stalked the room, taking his time; predatory. 'And right now, I am so fucking angry.'

His statement caused fear to prickle her skin. She understood exactly what was coming her way, but once he was farthest from the door, she leapt to her feet and snuck out behind him, back into the hallway. The doctor appeared and lunged at her, but, somehow, she managed to avoid his grasp and pounded on towards the front door.

She grabbed the old, battered brass handle with both hands and yanked it hard. But the door wouldn't budge. The door was locked, and frustratingly solid for such a derelict place. She sobbed, rattling the handle in her hands, and banged against the old wood as she glanced behind to see the doctor striding towards her.

'*No, no, no!*' she cried as he grabbed her and wrenched her away from the door.

The sight of Cigarettes forced a scream from her throat as he wrapped his hands around her waist and lifted her from the doctor's hold with such savage force her feet didn't touch the floor.

'*No!*' she shrieked as she clamped her hands over his in an effort to release his hold. '*Somebody help me! Help me!*'

'Keep screaming, bitch,' he said through heavy breaths as he carried her thrashing body back up the stairs to her waiting prison. 'No one can hear you – except the druggies and whores outside. Do you think they give a shit about what's going on in here when they don't even know what day of the week it is?'

'*No, please! Don't put me in there!*' she cried out as she struggled hard against him, unable to combat his furious strength. '*Please! I can't go back! I can't go back!*'

'You *are* going back,' he thundered as he dragged her to the room and dropped her to the floor, not giving her any time to react before wrapping his hand around her throat, squeezing hard. 'And if you try and escape again, I'll kill you myself. Do you hear me!' he roared.

Hot pain gripped at her throat. Unable to

breathe, and eyes wide with terror, she could only whimper as she readied herself for the violence she knew was coming.

He released his hold to grab her hoodie and gave two sharp backhands to her cheek with a force that knocked her to the floor. She cried out and sobbed uncontrollably, unable to take any more.

'*Shut up!*' he bellowed as he stood over her, panting with anger and exertion, appearing to consider doing more but holding back. After what seemed like forever, he moved away, slamming the door behind him.

A strange throaty cry escaped her mouth as she dragged air into her lungs.

*He hasn't locked the door. He's coming back. Oh God, he's coming back.*

The sound of multiple footfall confirmed her fears and with anguished sobs racking her sore body and echoing around the empty room, she scooted back away from the door as it swung open.

'No more. Please, no more,' she cried, her voice hoarse.

Cigarettes shoved the doctor into the room and threw his bag at him. 'Sedate her,' he barked as he strode to Elena and grabbed her wrist.

'Wait... No...'

'I've had enough of your games!' Cigarettes snapped as he watched the doctor pull out another syringe from his bag. 'You will learn not to fuck with me.'

She struggled against his vice-like grip that kept her hand immobile as breathless pleas escaped her lips. But, watching the doctor hurry, and unable to stop what was about to happen, a strange acceptance descended on her.

Now, she turned to Cigarettes and fixed him with a cold glare. 'I hate you,' she spat as the doctor hurriedly pricked a vein in the back of her hand. 'I hope you rot in hell.'

He laughed as the drug took hold and it echoed in her mind as she succumbed to the sedative.

\*\*\*

Lying awkwardly against the hard floor beneath her, Elena awoke, just as she had been left the fateful night before. Exhausted and stiff, and with the musty scent of the floorboards beneath her, she stretched out carefully and stared at the soft dawn light that had begun to creep into the room. She imagined herself a bird, soaring through the morning air, free and unrestrained.

She sat and held her cheek, her skin smarting and eyes sore from crying. She was even more dehydrated from it. Slowly, and with much effort, she pulled herself up and made her way to the pathetic blanket.

The lock turned and she froze, preparing herself for more torment. Her captor walked into the room. Not Cigarettes or the doctor, but the man in charge. He made his way to her.

She groaned. 'What now?' she asked as her eyes began to fill with tears. 'Are you here to punish me too?'

'Jesus,' he said as he caught sight of her.

'Oh yes, that,' she said as she turned to face him, watching him wince. 'Does it make you uncomfortable, to see the violence inflicted on me? That I discovered the hard way that old blue eyes down there does not take kindly to me leaving this room.'

'I think running for the door is a little more than that,' he remarked.

'Whatever,' she muttered as she shuffled to her blanket. 'Anyway, what do you care?'

She eased herself down carefully, placing her hands to her side to steady herself, still dizzy from the effects of the drug. 'You're a monster, just like him.'

'I'm no monster,' he said as he walked towards her. 'And I get no pleasure from seeing you in this state.'

'So, why didn't you stop it? Stop him? You're the boss, aren't you?'

'I was not here last night.'

'Of course you weren't. How convenient.' She raised her head to him. 'Well, you need to keep your guard dog on a lead. He bites when he's angry.'

He ignored the backchat and crouched

down beside her. Reaching out, he took her hand and checked over the small mark on the back of it. Her hand felt warm in his, but she snatched it from his hold and stared at him.

Would things have been different if he had been here? Maybe. But right now, she didn't care for the finer details and let anger fuel her on. 'You can keep your false concern. You are no different to the others, despite what you may think.'

'Maybe, Elena, but you do need to understand that nothing is going to change,' he said calmly. 'The rules are simple. You will remain here until the ransom is paid and until that is done, it's only you who will suffer from these little attempts at escape. You must see that.'

She did see that. Her bruises and aches demanded it, including the inflamed wound on her leg – still wet and refusing to heal. Resigned, she nodded and shuffled uneasily under his gaze.

'Are you suffering any effects of the sedative?' he asked as he looked her over.

She shook her head. The effects were, mercifully, nothing like the first time.

'Here, have this,' he said as he produced a bottle of water from his pocket.

She snatched it from him, a reflex action to get the liquid into her dehydrated body. She unscrewed the cap and drank down half the bottle in a few large gulps, feeling the cool liquid lubricate her mouth and pool into her empty stomach.

'I'll get you a couple of painkillers too,' he said as he watched her drink and scanned over her body. 'And I'll see to it that you get more to eat and drink than you have.'

She nodded and replaced the cap, saving what was left of the water for later. Maybe he had noticed how her clothes had begun to hang on her frame, just as she had. 'Do you expect me to thank you?'

'No, I don't expect anything from you, but you're right, I am the boss and I will see to it that you get what you need.'

'I'm not interested in you or some twisted code of honour you may have,' she whispered as emotion tightened in her throat. 'I just want to go home.'

'I know, Elena. I know.'

\*\*\*

The chaos of Elena's new existence calmed considerably following the last visit from her captor. Since that time, it was only the doctor who would come to check her over, escort her to the poor excuse for a toilet and give her a sandwich and a fresh bottle of water. Every day she hoped that would be all she'd have to deal with.

She understood the significance of this gesture. Her captor had been true to his word in providing better living conditions for her. That fact alone kick-started another emotion within her: one of gratitude, and that worried her a great deal. It would have been easier if he had been like the stinking cigarette man, but he wasn't. He was much more complex than that and she found herself both fascinated and terrified of him.

As well as drinking the water she was given, she would use a little to cleanse her body too, as best she could. It was all she could do. She may be held like an animal, but she wouldn't be reduced to one. They wouldn't take her dignity. It took time, her body aching and fatigued, slowing each movement, but she had the luxury of that, for now, as she awaited her fate. With weary fingers, she pulled her hair into a long braid, an effort that would require her to pause and catch her breath.

Feeling cold, she wrapped the blanket around herself and pulled her knees up to her chest. Her skin was hot to the touch, probably the start of a fever. Her leg also throbbed in a way that told her it was infected now. She pressed the palm of her hand to her forehead in a bid to soothe the headache that had taken up residence there, and watched the sunrise shining through the gaps in the wood.

The lock turning startled her. She hadn't heard the warning sound of approaching footsteps and stumbled to her feet. Her captor walked in, a small paper bag in his hand.

'Are you here to release me?' she asked.

'No,' he said as he handed her the bag. 'Not today.'

She opened the bag and took in the thrilling sight of a large doughnut and bottle of water. Divine. Her mouth watered and stomach growled in anticipation. She looked at him.

'I suppose this means you don't plan on dispatching me anytime soon.'

'This is a business transaction,' he replied. 'And I, for one, don't want to hurt you.'

Her stomach turned. She nodded.

He moved to the door, having done nothing to her and expecting nothing in return.

'Thank you,' she murmured. 'For the food.'

He turned to her as he opened the door, his head tilted, intrigued. 'You're welcome.'

She waited for the lock to turn and ripped open the bag, grabbing the sugary doughnut. She couldn't think of anything, her ever-present fear, her infected leg, or the fact that this locked room was becoming her cocoon. Nothing, except the divine sugar-coated glory as she stuffed it into her mouth, its jam oozing and mingling with the sweet, spongy dough. With meticulous care, she sucked the sugar from her fingers and licked her lips until they were clean. Next, she opened the bottle of water and swiftly gulped it down, not caring in the slightest how she may have looked. So much sugar would take her on a strange high, but if that was all that would happen in this awful reality, it wasn't so bad.

She leant against the wall and waited for her body to process everything she'd just given it, and for her heart to stop pounding in her chest. It made her feel alive though, still part of this world, and while she could still enjoy the vibrancy of it, she'd fight to remain so.

\*\*\*

The night was long and endless. Whichever position she lay, she couldn't shake the shooting pains in her leg. Heat radiated from it, and her, and little beads of sweat formed on her forehead. But even burning like a furnace, her body shivered uncontrollably. The fever was setting in hard.

She pressed her leg against the cold floor in an attempt to cool it, but nothing helped, and after a night of no sleep and watching the dawn break, she feared the next visit. The thought of being so unwell, so vulnerable with these men, frightened her.

'Calm down,' she murmured to herself, providing her own comfort in the gloom. 'Just keep breathing. It's going to be okay.' She repeated the last part over and over again, creating some sort of mantra in her mind.

Grabbing the half-empty bottle of water at her side, she downed a few gulps and trickled the remaining water over her wound, watching the blood and pus mingle together and ooze down her leg. She tried hard to think back to that day in the woods but couldn't remember seeing anything in her path that could do such harm.

*Well, that's what you get for misbehaving, girl. You clearly didn't learn, did you.*

'Shut up,' she said to the irritating voice in her head and concentrated on what she was doing, only stopping when footsteps climbed the stairs.

Her captor appeared as she struggled to her feet. His gaze went to her leg and the little trickle of blood making its way to her foot. 'What's going on?'

'It's nothing. A cut on my leg, that's all.' She tried to straighten up, but the effort was too much for her fatigued body and, empty of food and dizzy with fever, her vision blurred. A darkness hovered on the edge of her consciousness, a black fog that threatened to claim her.

He moved closer. 'Elena.'

His voice was distant, dreamlike, as the room spun and her eyes fluttered closed. Her knees buckled as the sounds of movement echoed in the room, of shoes against floorboards. She was spinning, falling into the dark, until firm hands were upon her, scooping her legs from beneath her.

It jolted her awake. 'Don't,' she murmured and tensed, holding her body stiff, afraid of what he would do.

He held her close enough to feel it. 'It's

okay, there's no need to panic. I'm just getting you comfortable,' he assured as he carried her to the blanket in the far corner of the room. 'We need to check you out.'

With the cold floor as her only comparison, his warmth against her shivering body was comforting. She let her head rest against his chest and breathed him in. It was impossible to be so close and not do so.

*The fever is making you delirious. You're in this hell all because of the man placing you down on the blanket. Remember that.*

Her senses returned and she lifted her head, her conscience pricked with a strange guilt.

He looked her over, and she noticed the glimmer of concern in his eyes as he did.

He turned and left the room, leaving the door open, and she found herself staring at it, looking through it, knowing that it led to both danger and freedom. More footsteps and he appeared again with the man who had previously sedated her following close behind, his bag in hand. Elena tried to move, frightened at the sight, but the attempt was weak.

The doctor took a good look at her injury while her captor held her ankle. His hold was warm, gentle. She glanced at him, and noticed something in his eyes. A hint of something deeper, something that belied the stern mask. The sight of it made the first building block of judgement begin to crumble. She had wanted to hate him, and part of her still did, but she was knocked off balance by his reaction. They'd be motivated to keep her alive and well in order to get their money, that was a given, but she didn't expect to see this, and didn't like where she was heading with it. She needed him to be the monster. Not the man. Certainly not this man, showing something that looked remarkably like compassion.

'It's nasty but not too deep,' the doctor said. 'It'll heal, but only if we stop the infection.'

'Get it done,' her captor ordered.

The doctor nodded and took out a bottle of antiseptic and a large piece of gauze from his bag and began the task of cleaning the long wound. He was efficient, but he wasn't gentle, and the antiseptic burned in her wound like liquid fire. She gasped with each swipe, sucking in air through clenched teeth, breathing away the stabbing pain as he worked.

Finally, after an age of tortuous cleaning that left her exhausted, the doctor spoke. 'The wound has been left unattended for too long to successfully stitch it now, so these are the best chance of pulling it together as it heals,' he said as he placed some butterfly stitches across the tear. Once done, he placed a rectangular dressing over the length of the wound. He reached into his bag again, pulling out another syringe and two vials of liquid.

'No, don't,' she cried, trying to pull away.

The doctor looked at her as he spoke. 'This is a shot of antibiotic, that's all. It's all I've got, but your leg is infected and will get much worse if we don't do this. The other is a simple painkiller.'

Her captor reached out and pulled up the sleeve of her hoodie. She watched as he did it, as if she was his property for him to make the decision for her.

*But that's exactly what I am, and there's nothing I can do to change it.*

She held her breath as the doctor administered the injection, but he was gentle, and it was a stark contrast to the way he had sedated her before. When no black oblivion descended, she breathed a little easier knowing he hadn't lied.

When he was finished, they discussed her injury. Nothing to be done, they said. She'd been lucky, they said. She could have laughed at that because she didn't feel lucky at all.

'The painkiller will soon kick in,' the doctor said as he pulled out another bottle of water from his bag and handed it to her.

As she sat with her back against the wall watching the doctor leave, she resisted the urge to thank him. He was elusive. He didn't fit in here at all. Cigarettes, absolutely, but the doctor seemed out of his depth. And she was unable to make up her mind about the other man who was now standing above her, making no move to leave.

The door clicked shut, and he looked down at her. 'You need to get some rest,' he said, a soft command.

But she didn't want to rest. 'You need to let me go.'

'I can't do that.'

*Of course you can't do that. I'm your prize – and an expensive one at that.*

He stood and walked to the door.

She laid herself down on the blanket, desperate to fight the sense that she would never leave this place, that she would never again see the outside world. It was a futile attempt because however hard she tried to overcome the sense of dread, it would always return, stronger than before.

# CHAPTER 6

Staring at the ceiling, Elena kept her mind busy trying to remember exactly how long it had been since her infection had cleared, or how many days she had been here, locked in this room. Her idea of marking the days on the wall had become an unreliable source too, because some days she would forget to do it, and other times she couldn't be bothered by the pointlessness of it all.

Childhood memories drifted into her mind. Happy times. Iced drinks on hot summer days, creamy hot chocolate after playing in the snow. Hot apple pie after a Sunday roast. Only the good times, her mind cutting out the bad. Self-preservation at its best. She thought of time spent with friends, her tribe, and the adventures they shared. The messy, deep roots of friendship. The fun, the dramas, and the laughter. Not normal laughter though, but the silent kind. The belly-aching kind, the kind that would leave them spent, and eyes wet with tears.

She was lonely, homesick, and just wanted someone to talk to. Someone to touch. A connection with another human. She wanted to use her voice, discuss things, and feel part of life again. Essential human necessities, but things she was currently deprived of. A suspended animation of sorts. Waiting, hoping for her life to continue.

The sound of the key fired energy in her belly, ready for attack. The doctor walked in carrying a stainless-steel bowl filled with water in one hand and a plastic bag in the other, both of which he laid down in front of her.

She looked at the washbowl and bag, and then at him. 'I assume this means I'm not going to be released today?'

'I'm not here to make conversation,' he said. 'You know that. Especially after your previous attempt at escape.'

They both glanced at the locked door.

'No, I suppose not.' She smiled. 'It's all right, I've learnt my lesson. I'm not going to whack you over the head with that chair, rummage through your pockets while you're out cold, find the key, and make my way down the stairs.'

He looked at her, eyebrows raised. 'But you've clearly given it some thought.'

'I have a lot of time to think in here, and it would be a lie to say I haven't brutally killed you all, many, many times. Up here, in my mind,' she said, tapping a finger at her temple. She shrugged. 'But another escape won't happen, I know that, especially if that other man is downstairs. He'll get angry again, and the pain he inflicts is very much real. And I don't feel like living in that reality. Not today.'

She saw the twitch under his eye that betrayed his discomfort.

'Let's talk about your leg,' he said. 'How are you feeling now? Any fever, or pain in the wound?'

'No, none. There's no pain in my face either, so I assume my bruises are fading.'

He nodded, confirming it.

'My body heals itself well it seems. It's just my mind I'm concerned for.'

He didn't respond to her comment, but waved a finger towards the bowl. 'You can wash with this water. It's cold but fresh,' he said. 'There's a cloth, some soap and a toothbrush in the bag. I'll come and collect it later.'

Surprised to be given such luxuries, she leaned forward and caught his eye. 'You're so different from the other man. The nasty, cigarette smoking one. How did you find yourself here?'

The corners of his mouth curled into what would have been a smile, if he had let it continue, but he concealed it well. 'My history and reason for being here is no concern of yours.'

She continued. 'No, I suppose it's not, but you're medically trained. You should be somewhere other than here. Somewhere safe and good and appropriate for someone whose job it is to keep people alive.'

'I'm keeping you alive. Is that not safe and

good and appropriate?'

'Yes, it is. Unless that's all about to change?' she said, frustratingly unable to read his expression.

'I take the orders, I don't make them.'

'And if that order came, could you do it?'

He glanced away.

'Could you?'

'I'm not prepared to answer that.'

She held her head up. 'My name is Elena Dumont. I'm 27 years old and I have a mother, father, and brother. I like coffee first thing, my favourite of which I get from a little café at the top of my road. I have the reputation between my friends for being overly sentimental when I've had too much to drink. My favourite colour is yellow, and when I'm nervous I talk too much.'

Confusion replaced his discomfort. 'What are you doing?'

'I'm sharing information about my life, so that you know me. So that I'm not a stranger to you anymore. Making you realise that I am a human being. I live, I breathe, and what is happening here is wrong. I want you to see that.'

'It won't change anything.'

'No, maybe not, but you can't blame me for trying.'

He nodded but said no more and closed and locked the door behind him, leaving her alone again.

Despondent, she dragged open the bag and

found all that he had promised, and more. A bottle of water and a sandwich sat on the top of everything else. A proper little care package. She was being allowed to clean herself up, and she didn't know what to make of it. She certainly needed it – her skin was sticky, and her deodorant had given up the ghost a long while ago – and it didn't take her long to realise who was responsible for this treat. She grappled with the gratitude she couldn't help but feel.

She ate, consuming every last morsel of food and water and then dragged the bowl a little closer. Tracing her finger over the logo of a popular high-street chemist on the cardboard wrap around the washcloth, she found that she couldn't let it go. It should have been of little consequence, but for some reason, it mattered. It was from a shop, and a shop meant the outside world, and the outside world meant people. So she folded it and tucked it into her pocket, wanting to keep it near.

She plunged her hands into the water and soaped the washcloth, and began the task of cleaning herself up. The water was cold but refreshing and she washed herself quickly and as thoroughly as she could, slipping the cloth inside her clothing, rather than undressing. That would leave her too vulnerable if someone decided to barge in on her – namely Cigarettes. Feeling so much fresher and to finish off, she dunked the toothbrush into the soapy water and scrubbed her teeth. She also decided that today was a day for a whole tab of gum.

Expecting no further visits, she jumped with surprise when the lock on the door turned and her captor strode in. Despite a sense of anxiousness as to why he was here, she couldn't dismiss the tiny buzz inside that it was he who had come to her. She also couldn't help notice how he looked, a crisp cotton shirt over his broad shoulders, his dark hair shiny and loose, falling a little over his forehead, and a face that was freshly shaven.

'Good morning,' he said as he stood a few feet away from her. She watched as he moved, as he came closer, and prepared. She may be fascinated by him, but she also knew it was best to be on guard when he was around. But as the scent of him lingered in the air, she became distracted and couldn't resist inhaling the mix of aftershave and fresh, clean clothes. A pleasant scent, and one that she became lost in for a moment. She kidded herself that the only reason for it was because he was clean. Catching him watching, she snapped her eyes away, but not before seeing his apparent amusement at her reaction. Her face flushed with embarrassment. She'd been careless. He'd use that to his advantage, she was sure, so she moved away from him, hopeful that a little distance would help.

'How are you today?' he asked.

She looked down as she considered how to

best answer the question in her current frame of mind. She wanted to tell him how she felt. She wanted to tell him to stop this right now and let her go. She wanted to ask why he was being so kind to her in this place of danger, or how she wanted to stand next to him and breathe him in instead of this musty old room.

She said none of these things.

'I'm fine. In the circumstances,' she said and looked straight at him. 'Are you here to release me?'

He smiled, as if he recognised her internal conflict. 'No, not today.'

He held her gaze so that she was immobile, unable to move. 'I see you've cleaned up.'

Strangely nervous, butterflies took flight in her stomach. 'Yes, I did. I assume I have you to thank for that.'

'Perhaps,' he said.

*Stop it. Just stop it. Pull yourself together, Elena.*

She moved out of his orbit. 'I know what you're doing.'

Another smile. 'Oh, and what is that?'

'Manipulating me. You allow me more food and water. You allow me to clean myself up. You visit.'

'These are just basic human necessities,' he countered. 'There's nothing more to it than that.'

'You're being nice to me. Kind, even.'

'Would you prefer it if I didn't do those things?' he asked, a dark glint in his eyes.

'Yes. No. I don't know,' she sighed. 'You're playing the good guy, trying to confuse me—'

'Maybe I am the good guy, Elena. Ever thought of that?'

'But it won't work.'

'Really.'

'You think I'm going to fall for your charm like some doe-eyed schoolgirl, but I'm not.'

He crossed his arms. 'But I do have charm.'

She saw the humour in his eyes and tried to ignore the energy between them. 'You're arrogant, and no better than the others downstairs.'

'Is that what you think?'

'Well, you're the boss. You're allowing this living hell to happen. Maybe you're the biggest monster of them all, hiding behind that smile.'

'That's the last time you call me that.'

'So what are you if you won't let me go?'

'I'd say with the others downstairs, I'm someone you need.'

She shook her head. 'I don't need you. I despise you. And I can't wait to leave this place.'

Something changed. His smile faded, and whatever game they were playing had come to an abrupt end.

'Okay, have it your way,' he said coolly. 'The door is unlocked. You could walk out right now if you want to.'

'What?' she whispered, unsure and

strangely unhappy that she'd angered him.

He gestured to the door. 'Go on, try it.'

Her tired mind raced with doubt, but even so, she was still ready to do as he said. She hesitated, unease rising in her as she moved but when he did nothing but watch, she allowed herself to hope that she was indeed leaving.

*No. You're not. Don't you go thinking it's that easy.*

She made a steady pace and wished the voice in her head would give her a break and shut the hell up.

'Just remember,' he said from behind. 'You'll get your freedom if you can get past the men downstairs.'

His words halted her immediately, within an arm's reach of the door. Now it was clear. Now she understood. His short lesson about who was in control was painfully complete.

He didn't need to, but continued anyway. 'Those "monsters". That's what you called them, wasn't it? If you can walk past them unharmed this can all be over.'

He'd made his point. He strode to her and stopped close behind, wrapping his arm around her waist in a possessive action, pulling her closer to him.

She gasped, the feel of his body against hers causing a craving to bloom inside. A hunger she knew she shouldn't feel. 'I hate you.'

He watched over her shoulder, amused,

and moved closer still, bringing his lips to her ear. 'No, I disagree. I'd say hatred is the last thing you're feeling right now,' he murmured, his breath warm in the cold room. 'But you need to understand how important I am to you, because I will keep you safe here, but I get to choose how long it takes, and when I let you go.' His lips tickled her skin, almost a kiss but not quite. 'Do you understand?' He moved her braid from her shoulder, letting his fingers brush against her neck. She jumped a little as skin touched skin, sending a shudder down her spine.

She couldn't speak, couldn't think. He wrapped his arm tighter still as her world came crashing down. Everything faded into nothingness until his voice was the only thing she could hear.

'Elena, answer me,' he ordered.

'Yes,' she said finally, on a breath. 'I understand.'

'Good, then we are clear.'

She struggled for air, needing to compose herself as he watched and waited for any quip she might like to make. He released his hold, and cold air trickled against her back, into the place where his body had been. It was true, she understood everything now, the rules of this game painfully clear. She'd been foolish enough to think she could influence him, but he was the master of that, and she'd learned it the hard way. He played her well. He'd tested her, and she had responded in a way that confirmed what they both already knew. That he was in control and would remain so until he decided what to do with her.

But she also knew him a little better now too, having managed to read a few signs of her own. She'd registered the quickness of his breath as he stood close and the gentle touch of his fingers as they lingered on her skin. She was important to him somehow, and not just because of the money.

She wasn't sure if the thought terrified her or filled her with a strange sense of calm.

# CHAPTER 7

Elena had just managed to find sleep when she was interrupted by another visitor entering the room. When it was Cigarettes who sauntered in, she tensed and clutched the blanket to her body, wanting to hide from his glare.

'Get up,' he ordered.

She jumped to her feet, not waiting to be told twice, fearful that a second order would be followed by a fist to back it up.

He reached for her and shoved her forwards. 'Go on, out there.'

She moved and walked out into the hallway and towards the bathroom, her skin crawling as she felt him close behind. Quickening her pace, she pushed open the door, letting it fall behind her, giving her much needed privacy from him.

She did what she needed to do and delayed for as long as possible before she opened the door.

He was waiting. Smiling.

Her stomach lurched. He was even more predatory today. Something was wrong. She caught the low sounds of music playing on a radio downstairs and prayed she wasn't alone with him. Slowly, she walked back to her room, glancing through the balustrades, searching for any signs of life.

As she walked through the door, he took hold of her arm, pulling her back.

'You know I'm just biding my time, don't you?'

She turned and jerked her arm free, taking a step back from him. 'I don't know what you mean.'

He moved closer. 'What I mean is that when the moment comes, I'm going to come up here and get you all to myself.' He took hold of her hair and gripped it tight. 'And we're going to have a little fun together.'

Despite her struggle, he leaned in, his eyes travelling down. 'I'm going to taste you. All of you,' he said with a low chuckle. 'There's no escaping it, princess. And I'll make it last and last until you can't take anymore.'

She grabbed her braid and snapped it out of his grasp. Stepping back, and nudging the chair behind, she lost her balance and tumbled over it, a cry escaping her lips.

Footsteps thumped up the stairs and her panicked mind registered the appearance of her captor.

'What the fuck is going on?' he demanded. 'You just had to take her to use the bathroom and then leave her. That's all you had to do.'

'And that's just what I'm doing,' Cigarettes replied.

'So you're done,' her captor said, his voice thin and tight.

'Am I?'

'Yes, you are. Now get the hell out of here.'

Her captor moved closer to Elena and helped her to stand. She found herself grabbing his arm for protection as she cowered close to his side.

He clocked the gesture but ignored it and kept his focus on Cigarettes. 'Go downstairs. I won't warn you again.'

Cigarettes paused, staring at the man beside Elena, sizing him up. Eventually, he moved, a strange curl of his lip giving away what he'd just seen.

He left the room, slamming the door, and only then did her captor turn his attention to her hand clasping his arm. She snapped it away, suddenly aware of what she'd done.

'Everything okay now?'

'Yes, I'm fine,' she said through quickened breaths, embarrassed that she'd briefly forgotten herself for a moment.

'That man is all bravado,' he said as he picked up the chair. 'He's frustrated. He's under strict orders, so he makes threats.'

'Someone like him doesn't care about orders,' she said as she hugged her hands across her body. 'Probably goes for all of you.'

'Elena, you don't need to fight me,' he said. 'I'm very different to that man.'

'Doesn't mean I trust you,' she replied.

'Really? I think the way you just grabbed my arm gives away more than you realise.'

'No, I'm just surviving, that's all. That doesn't make you any better than them. You're just the safest option amongst a half-wit doctor and a terrifying psycho. Simple as that.'

A smile crept over his lips. 'Well, that's good to know,' he said. 'And thank you for speaking your mind so eloquently.'

She smiled too and managed to relax her tense shoulders a little. 'Well, you haven't raised your fist to me, so I suppose I should thank you for letting me. And I suppose I should thank you for coming up here when you did. You didn't have to do that.'

He moved a few stray hairs from her face, making her skin tingle as his fingers brushed against hers.

She smoothed a hand over her braid, suddenly self-conscious. 'I'm a mess.'

'You're not a mess,' he said softly as his eyes lingered on hers.

She felt her body sing, as if needing to be closer to his, without her having any control of it.

They remained this way until she wasn't entirely sure what he was going to do next.

Finally, he spoke. 'I'll make sure food and water are sent up later.'

He walked away from her and opened the

door. As he pulled it back, she saw Cigarettes standing on the other side, his hands shoved in his pockets, and a nasty knowing sneer on his lips. One that comes from having heard all of their conversation.

Fear made her flinch as the door was shut and locked.

\*\*\*

Elena hugged her knees tightly to herself as she listened to the loud music that played downstairs. It felt endless, and must have been playing for a couple of hours, at least. What were they doing down there? The chaotic guitar riffs and aggressive lyrics only managed to heighten her state of panic. The raised voices too. An argument. Whatever was happening was escalating quickly. Something crashed on impact, loud and heavy. Furniture perhaps, she didn't know. After that, silence – from the voices and the music. And that's when she knew she was in trouble.

Footsteps slowly climbed the stairs, purposefully, ominously, and Elena knew immediately who it would be. She jumped to her feet as Cigarettes pushed open the door, his breathing heavy as he leant against the frame. He was clutching a large bottle of whisky and eyed her as he drank. He sauntered into the room, unsteady as she froze to the spot, her heart pumping and her body preparing itself for attack.

*Fuck.*

'Thought I'd come and keep you company,' he said as he walked towards her. 'Must be lonely up here all on your own, sweetheart.' He chuckled and took another swig from the bottle.

She watched him move and worked hard to quell the fear that threatened to take over. Immediately, she doubted her captor when he said he'd keep her safe, feeling naïve for trusting him as she had. Was this part of a warped plan to subject her to an ordeal that would break her spirit a little more?

'So, I've been thinking, sweet cheeks,' he murmured. 'You're up here all alone, and I'm downstairs, bored out of my fucking brains. What do you say to our own little party up here?'

'Where are the others?' she asked unsteadily.

'The doc is just taking a little nap, and pretty boy is not here,' he replied as he held the bottle but took no care, letting whisky spill out and splash on the floor.

*Fuck, fuck, fuck.*

They stared at one another before he moved swiftly towards her. She moved too and rushed to the door, panic moving her forwards, but he reached out and grabbed her arm, dragging her back, hard against the wall. He used his body to keep her still and leant his arms either side of her face, steadying himself. She moved her head to one side, away from his and the stench of his breath. Her blood ran cold. He was here, as promised, unrestricted and looking for a little sport. To take his time. She didn't know how she was going to do it, but she was going to fight him, she was sure of that. She needed to work her sober mind into outwitting his drunken one.

His breathing quickened, his arousal evident as he pushed against her. His face was close to hers, invading her space, and her stomach turned.

'Pretty little thing, aren't you?' He lifted one arm off the wall and ran a nicotine-stained finger down her cheek.

'Leave me alone,' she said, trying to mask the panic.

'And why would I do that?' he sneered as his eyes wandered over her. 'Strange what some girls like,' he said, before taking another swig of the bottle. 'I've seen you flutter your pretty eyes at the boss. Turn you on, does he?'

'Of course not!' Elena exclaimed. 'Get off me,' she said as she tried to shove him away, but he repaid that by leaning harder against her, pinning her to the wall. She struggled, but it made him laugh.

He grabbed her braid, wrapping it around his hand and jerked her head back. 'Oh, I think he does, and as he's not here, I'm going to have some fun of my own.'

His words shot through her, her vulnerability triggering a surge of energy. 'Get off me!' she shrieked, and this time she shoved him hard, making him stagger backwards, dropping the bottle as he did. It looked as if he would fall, and Elena raced for the door, hoping it would be enough.

But it wasn't enough. He regained his balance and lunged for her, grabbing her arm again, twisting it up behind her back. 'Where do you think you're going?' he snarled, spinning her around and grasping her face in his hand.

Elena screamed.

His maddened eyes shone in the low light, and he raised his hand, bringing it down hard across her face. A strange crack sounded through the room as she was knocked sideways and off her feet. She crashed into the small chair as heat rushed into her face and shoulder, but there was no pain yet as her brain blocked certain senses, protecting her, allowing her to fight on. She used it and reached for the chair.

He darted to her and kicked it away and out of her reach, laughing as he did. 'I don't think so,' he said as he towered above her.

'No... no...' she mumbled through her jarred mouth as she shuffled backwards, frantic to get away from him, to get as much distance as she could.

He rolled his eyes with amusement and reached down to grab her leg. She thrashed about as he pulled her close, and when she was within reach, he released her leg with a thump and dropped down to straddle her, knocking the wind from her lungs.

She opened her mouth to scream, but he clamped his hand over it, muffling the sound and holding her head still. 'You bitches are all the same, aren't you?' he growled, his body covering hers. 'You need a firm hand and a good, hard fuck and then you soon comply, don't you, bitch?' he said, his face distorted with hatred. 'Then you're quiet little mice, aren't you?'

She screamed into his hand, kicking and bucking beneath him as her survival instinct took over. Her muscles flooded with blood for the fight, and she could only focus on the struggle to free herself from his hold, as each hand fought his own on her body.

Wrenching her mouth free, she began to scream. Her body was empty, devoid of energy, but she didn't care. She fought, refusing to let him win.

He struggled; the synthetic fabric of her sports clothes impossible to rip. She used it and kept fighting. Twisting beneath him, she created enough distance to ram her knee between his legs and freed herself from his grasp as he reeled backwards clutching his groin.

Exhaustion slowing her, she shuffled on all fours, crawling towards the door as she heard a car approach. Inhaling deeply to fill her lungs, she screamed again.

*'I'M GONNA KILL YOU, BITCH!'* Cigarettes roared from behind.

Glancing over her shoulder she watched him lurch towards her. She struggled to stand but he took care of that by grabbing her by the shoulders, hauling her to her feet. He raised his arm, and she braced herself for the blow as it came down hard against the same cheek. No numbness this time, just white-hot shards of pain that shot through her face and head, like broken glass shattering her soul. She crashed to the floor, a strange yelp escaping her mouth as another voice bellowed in the chaos.

Raising her hand to protect herself from more blows, she caught sight of her captor striding towards Cigarettes. Holding him firm, he landed a hard fist to Cigarettes' stomach followed by another to his face that sent him hurtling to the floor.

*Well, now he knows how that feels.*

'What do you think you're doing!' her captor bellowed as Cigarettes slumped to the floor, clutching his stomach.

Cigarettes sneered as blood trickled from his lip. 'What do you care, man? Thought I'd have some fun,' he said breathlessly.

'You disgusting little fuck,' her captor growled as he grabbed Cigarettes by his t-shirt and hauled him to his feet. 'I told you no one is to touch her. What part of that didn't you understand?' He walked Cigarettes backwards and slammed him against the wall, wrapping his hand around his neck. 'And if I find you've even been up here again, I'm going to do you a serious injury, do you understand?'

He slammed another punch into Cigarettes' stomach, backing up his threat, and she watched Cigarettes double over from the force of it. A strange wheezing sound shot from his mouth as the air was knocked from his lungs.

Wanting an answer, her captor continued, vehemence lacing his voice. 'I said. Do. You. Understand?'

'Yeah,' Cigarettes wheezed, still trying to regain his breath, a look of thunder on his face. 'I hear you.'

Her captor threw Cigarettes towards the door, sending him crashing into the frame. He grunted and staggered out of sight. To highlight his point, her captor kicked the door shut, the sound resonating through the empty room as Elena's trembling body jumped.

He stood facing the door, appearing to take a moment to calm himself. She watched as he gained control, shaking out the hand he had used to punch. He turned and walked to her, his eyes bright with anger.

'Jesus,' he murmured as he crouched down beside her and helped her to her feet. 'The bastard really got to you this time,' he said, taking her face gently in his hands, being careful not to hurt her. He winced when his eyes fell over what felt to Elena like a tender bruise forming on her cheek.

She felt the restraint in him and watched him struggle to contain his anger, but she didn't care about any of it. The throbbing cheek, the metallic taste of blood in her mouth, or the ache beginning to bloom in her head. All nothing, except the absolute relief that this man had come in when he had and stopped an unimaginable ordeal.

'Thank you… thank you. It was awful. I thought he… I thought he was…' she stammered as the shock set in.

'Elena, breathe. Take it easy,' he said as he pulled her close and held her to him.

'And I thought you'd let him… I thought you'd allowed it, but you didn't… you came back.'

'I would never allow anything like that to happen, and I won't leave you again. You have my word.'

She focused on her breathing, calmed her racing heart, realising she was lost. Her captor had not sanctioned the violence she had just experienced, and he had saved her from more harm. She felt the shock ease and let herself be soothed by him, wanting to focus only on him and the protection he gave. His body heat warmed her, and soon the trembling stopped.

He was calm now too and somehow different. It wasn't about power. It was about providing a sense of safety. And it was working.

'Your face,' he sighed as he tipped it up to his.

'I'm fine,' she said with an unsteady voice, placing her hands over the top of his. It was an intimate gesture that was inappropriate here, in this room, but she couldn't help it. It was instinctive, and she'd been living on that since her capture and trusted it with her life.

It was simple. He was here again, taking care of her, making her matter, and something shifted in her mind. She was not only seeing the man behind the kidnapper, but was empathising with him too; seeing the person, and not the monster. And that was Number One on the list of Things-Not-To-Do in a situation like this. But to deny it or push these feelings away was pointless. She couldn't even bring herself to ask for her release. She was tired of fighting.

He smiled, but didn't try to hide his concern. 'We need to get you checked over.'

# CHAPTER 8

'Elena.'

The voice saying her name seemed far away. Drowsy, she struggled to open her eyes.

'Elena.'

She didn't recognise the voice at first, but when she did finally manage to open her eyes, she saw the doctor standing at the door. She sat up as dizziness overwhelmed her until little black dots formed in front of her eyes.

'Oh God,' she murmured as she breathed hard to stop the desire to wretch. She sat with her back against the wall and pressed her hand against her pounding forehead to try and ease the pain and stabilise the swimming sensation.

'I'm not here to hurt you,' he said, holding out his hand, sensing her unease. 'I'm here to take a look at you, that's all.'

'No need. I'm absolutely fine,' she said without conviction.

He moved towards her and as he approached, she noticed his split lip and bruised left eye. Cigarettes had really excelled this time.

'I have painkillers here, and I'd like to check the rest of you,' he said. 'I understand you took a bit of a beating.'

She managed a bitter laugh. 'Yeah, just a

bit,' she said, shuddering as she remembered. 'I see you did too.'

'Caught me off guard,' he said as he moved closer and crouched beside her, placing his bag at his side on the floor. 'Won't happen again.'

He was gentle as he moved her face in his hands to check the bruise that was forming there before reaching into his bag. She decided she was glad he was here, keen to know if she was okay, on the outside at least. She knew she was having problems with her sanity, but no one could help her with that.

He pulled out a small thin torch and shone the light into her eyes, making her wince as her head pounded harder.

'Any dizziness?' he asked.

'Yes, just when I move quickly or try to stand.'

'Do you feel sick, or have you been sick?'

She shook her head and immediately regretted it. 'No.'

'Okay,' he said as he put the torch away and pulled out a small bag, handing it to her.

Looking in, she saw a sandwich, a small box of tablets, and a bottle of water.

'Those are strong painkillers. Two tablets. I have kept them in the box so that you can see I'm not trying to fool you into taking something more sinister. They'll help the headache and ease the pain in your cheek.'

'Thanks,' she said as she pulled out the

sandwich. She may be aching, sore and a little freaked out, but she was also hungry, and the sight of the food made her stomach growl.

'I'll check on you again later. Make sure you've kept that food down,' he said as he packed up his bag and rose to leave.

'I'm sure I'll be fine, especially with these,' she said as she checked the painkillers and saw that he was indeed telling the truth from the branded packaging. She may not feel threatened by this man, but she certainly didn't trust him.

'I've got my orders,' he said simply as he walked to the door. As he opened it, the other man, her captor, walked into the room.

She rested her head against the wall, watching as the doctor updated him on how she was doing, before leaving them alone.

'How are you feeling now?' he asked as he shut and locked the door.

'I'm fine,' she said. She meant it. Her face was swollen and sore, but she wasn't dead and had been given enough medication to dull the pain and allow her to cope.

He pulled up the chair and sat opposite her, composed once more.

'Where is that man now?' she asked tentatively.

'Sleeping it off downstairs,' he said. 'He's taken care of. You're quite safe.'

'He really hates women doesn't he,' she said, looking up at him.

'He hates everyone.'

'Perhaps, but women are at the very top of his list. We should be quiet little mice, apparently.'

He smiled. 'A quiet little mouse is something you'll never be.'

She smiled too and quickly winced from the pain. 'Ouch,' she murmured, raising her hand to her cheek. 'But his fist was stronger.'

'You should take the painkillers.'

She nodded. 'I will. I guess I should thank you. If it wasn't for you–'

'You don't owe me anything,' he countered. 'I'm just sorry you got caught up in this mess.'

Somewhere within the confusion of her mind, she found the courage to let go of her emotions. She'd deal with the scars later – if she ever got her old life back. For now, her main source of comfort was his presence. And she didn't care what that meant. She had lost a psychological battle – with him and herself.

'Is this what you like to do?' she asked.

He frowned. 'What do you mean?'

'Sitting with your captives, talking with them?'

'No, this isn't what I do,' he said with authority. 'I've never sat with another captive because I've never been involved in a kidnap before. You're my first. And my last.'

His honesty took her by surprise. She

hadn't expected it, but it didn't stop her from venturing on while he was in a mood to share. 'So how did you end up here? You don't seem to belong. You or the doctor. But you, especially …' She stopped herself, feeling her face flush. *Too much, Elena.*

He smiled, amused at her reaction. 'I'm here because I have to be.'

'Oh,' she said, relieved that he wouldn't inflict this situation on her by choice.

'I've messed with bad people. Owed them a favour, let's say. I will protect you, but that doesn't make me your knight in shining armour.'

She glanced at him. 'You seem to be doing all right so far.'

He leant forward and rested his arms on his thighs, his eyes glinting in the low light. 'That's because some people are worth protecting.'

Her face flushed again, and she moved her gaze to the floor. She could try and combat his statement with one of how she didn't need protecting, but here, in these surroundings, they would both see it for the lie it was.

'Eat and then get some rest,' he said as he rose to leave her. 'I'll come and check on you later.'

She watched him go and listened for the reassuring sound of the door locking. She pondered her plight as she toyed with the food. There was no escaping it. They were connected now, inexplicably linked – captor and captive – bound together by this experience, forging an unbreakable connection only they would share.

She finished the food and took two tablets as instructed. She wanted to stay awake, alert, ready for any more visits, but her body needed sleep, and the mix of trauma and painkillers sent her off before she was aware she'd closed her eyes.

\*\*\*

Elena was woken by a shard of light seeping through a small crack in the window. She shuffled herself carefully onto her side. It had been several days since her attack and although she was healing, her body still ached a little.

She was depleted, empty, and shrouded in loneliness within these four walls. Since her ordeal, she had only seen the doctor who had checked her over and given a little food and water – to drink, and in a bowl to freshen up.

She moved herself to a sitting position, using the wall for support, and rested her head against the flaking plaster. An unwelcome pang of regret visited when she remembered how she had behaved with her captor in the moments after the attack, and it only reinforced her opinion that she was crazy and clearly intent on inviting more danger into her world. But that didn't stop her from missing him or wanting his company.

'You *are* crazy,' she murmured to herself as she shuffled into the sun's bright light, needing to feel the warm rays on her skin. It was healing, and she closed her eyes, letting herself be lost to it for a moment as it warmed her aching bones.

She wanted more of it, so she stood and moved closer to the window and gazed at the wooden barrier, as she had done so many times before. She recognised every knot and swirl of grain. Glancing down at the zip of her hoody her mind whirred as she stared at the little metal gripper. How could she have not noticed it before? It could be a tool. An implement to twist the screws holding the wood in place. She'd certainly give it a try.

Slipping off the hoody, she placed the corner of the gripper into the screw head and carefully turned it anti-clockwise. She felt the bite of the thread begin to slacken and it spurred her on. She just needed more of the sunshine in her room. When the screw began to stand proud of the wood, a new energy filled her, so she kept going, working it slowly to be sure not to break the handle, but also to preserve this new-found vigour. Finally, the screw came free and clattered to the floor. She froze, hoping that they hadn't heard it downstairs.

She waited for the sounds of movement, but when there was nothing, she moved the plank of wood down, in a pendulum motion, and looked out of the window. She could continue of course. She could remove all the screws and kick out the broken glass, enough to jump out. But she knew that wouldn't happen, because what would be the point?

The rays of the sun covered her entirely. No more cracks, no thin shards of light. She hadn't seen this much sun in a long time. She hadn't seen much of anything, in fact, but now, the bright orb filled the room with sunshine. Spring was just starting when she was taken, but now summer seemed to be on its way. She stood in its warm light as it surrounded her like an old friend, something from the outside world, and it made her homesick again.

Wanting to let in more of the light, she wiped the window with her sleeve, and even managed a smile. She thought hard but couldn't remember when she last allowed herself the time to enjoy such a simple pleasure. Religion wasn't important to her normally, but right now, she could understand how moments like these could make a person believe in omnipotent gods in their heavens, giving earthly signs of their existence. She also understood that some things remained constant – the world turned, the sun shone, season followed season, and, for now, she was still a part of it. She hoped to get out alive, but if that wasn't the plan, she resolved to keep this moment as her last memory. And if that time came, she knew that she wouldn't have long to wait before discovering whether there actually was a god in heaven above.

'Good morning.'

'Oh,' she gasped, startled by the voice behind her. He was here. She had been so deep in thought she hadn't heard the lock turn.

'How long have you been there?' she asked, turning to face him.

She watched as his gaze turned to the window and her handy work with the screw.

'Elena, what have you been up to?' he said as he walked towards her.

'It's nothing,' she stammered, her heart thumping at being discovered. 'I just wanted to see the sun, that's all. It's so long since I've been outside.'

'You know I should rectify that. Make it secure again,' he said, pointing to the loose board.

'No, please don't,' she begged, placing her hand on his arm and swiftly removing it. 'I won't do anything else. No more escapes, I promise. I just want this little piece of the outside world.'

He smiled. 'That sounds like a dangerous game.'

She waited in silence as he considered it, watching her.

'Okay, I'll leave it as it is,' he said as he moved closer to her. 'Because you won't let me down, will you?'

'No, of course I won't,' she murmured as

her shoulders slumped. 'And thank you.'

'I've brought you more food,' he said, moving on, and handed her the bag. 'You've been busy. You must be hungry.'

'I'm always hungry,' she said as she reached for it. Her hand brushed against his, causing her to flinch at the sensory overload. 'But thank you.'

'You're welcome, Elena.'

His words were so quiet and intimate, and her name rolled out of his mouth easily.

The mood in the room was calm and she considered if she should be more cautious today, no grand gestures of gratitude. It didn't stop her from smoothing her braided hair in an attempt to tidy herself.

She glanced at him, his hair pushed back a little, as if he'd just run his hand through it and she wondered how it would feel to let her own fingers roam there.

He smiled knowingly. 'Are you not going to ask for your release today?'

'Would there be any point?'

'No, perhaps not.'

'But you do intend for this to be over soon, or am I going to spend the rest of my days in here?'

'Your father knows what is expected of him.'

'So why is it taking so long?'

'We have had a little… resistance, shall we

say. We needed to give him time. Allow him to focus, to understand that this isn't up for negotiation.'

'But he will pay?'

'We certainly expect him to, and soon.'

She nodded and pondered over her next question. 'What's your name?'

'It's probably best you don't know that,' he said.

'For me or you,' she said.

'For both of us.'

'So you may get all this money, but you'll have to live a life of secrets when this is all over. Will it be worth it?'

'Do you care?' he said, intrigued, his lips curving into a smile.

She shrugged. 'I'm not sure.'

'And you're making all kinds of assumptions. How can you be so sure the money will be mine?'

The foundations of all she had assumed shifted beneath her. 'What? But... I don't understand.'

'How do you know I'm not just an intermediary,' he said. 'Someone to arrange this situation.'

'Why would you do that?'

'Like I said, I owe people a favour.'

'Who?'

He laughed softly. 'Again, it's best you don't know.'

'So you do need me alive then,' she said. 'To absolve you of your crime. It'll all go wrong if I die before the money changes hands.'

'Yes, but I always wanted you to survive.'

'Ah, there you go again,' she remarked. 'Showing off your good side.'

Something dark hovered in his eyes. 'I wouldn't be so sure about that.'

'You care that I get out of this alive, I'd say that's pretty honourable.'

'Maybe, but what if I said that there's something else I want now?' He moved closer, so that they were almost touching. 'Something much more interesting.'

'And what is this elusive thing?' she asked cautiously, feeling the intensity of his stare.

'You, Elena.'

It was a simple statement, but it set off a whirlwind of chaos within her. She wasn't sure which of her many reactions she should centre on first – the little flip her stomach made at his response, his intense gaze, or the fact that his statement, which should have worried her, didn't.

His eyes scanned her face, a satisfied glint in his eyes. For a moment she thought he might kiss her and she wondered if she'd let him, but before she could decide, he turned to leave.

'Wait,' she cried, reaching for his arm. 'You can't say something like that and then go.'

He turned, a questioning expression

across his handsome face. 'No?'

She shook her head.

'It might be better that I do,' he said softly. 'Because your reaction has confirmed what I thought all along.' He placed a finger under her chin. 'But whatever is going on between us isn't something for now, and certainly not for this room.'

'But you'll come back, yes?' she asked, caring little about what his words meant, only that he would return to her. 'You'll bring me my food again? Talk?'

'Yes. I'll come back.'

'When? Today, tomorrow? I need to know,' she said.

'I'll come tonight.'

She smiled and breathed in relief. 'Yes. Good. Thank you.'

He turned the lock and she sat down, waiting for him to return.

## CHAPTER 9

The slowness of time was almost unbearable. She had been pacing for what felt like hours, waiting to hear his footfall on the stairs. She'd made an extra effort to clean up and had scrubbed her teeth, allowing herself the luxury of an entire tab of chewing gum. She wanted to please, she wanted to spend time in another person's company. His company. And she was getting restless.

When she did finally hear the thud on the stairs she jumped to her feet, butterflies dancing within, quickening her breath.

'You came,' she said as he walked into the room.

He shut the door and wandered to her, unhurried. 'I have your food.'

'Oh, yes, of course,' she murmured as she took the bag that he handed to her. 'Thank you.'

'And I wanted to check that you hadn't broken out,' he said, his brow raised with amusement.

'And are they the only reasons?' she asked.

'No, but you already know that.'

She nodded, she did know that and had thought of nothing else while he was away. Wanting to fill the silence, she glanced towards the exposed windowpane and tried to order her jumbled thoughts. 'It was a beautiful day today. Where are we now? April? May?'

'Beginning of May,' he said, his eyes fixed on her.

'May. Already?' she said, her eyes wide. 'So much time.'

'You dream of the day you're free,' he said softly, so close now. 'To leave this place, get back to your life.'

She glanced up at him, her body temperature rising, desperate for contact. 'Yes, every day.'

He raised his hand to gently cup her cheek and the warmth of it seeped into her skin, branding itself onto her. An involuntary gasp escaped her lips as the sensation travelled to her core, and she found herself leaning in to his hold, wanting more. The contact was necessary, reviving, and she became rooted to the spot.

'Isn't this breaking the rules?' she asked, wanting to say something, anything, that would hint at resistance.

'I don't give a damn about the rules,' he replied, his mouth now tantalisingly close to hers. 'And neither do you.'

She should pull away, she should resist, but she knew she wouldn't. She needed this, needed him, and gazed at his mouth, anticipating the feel of his lips on hers.

The stillness in the room was broken by

loud voices downstairs. Cigarettes and the doctor were arguing, their voices shouting over one another in a bid to be heard. She blinked, as if jolted awake and stepped back, the moment over.

He exhaled, glancing at the door. 'I need to go and sort that out.'

She hugged her arms around herself, confused, but with warm desire flowing through her veins. 'Yes, of course.'

He reached the door and hesitated, his hand against the frame. Without warning he turned, strode back to her and wrapped his arm around her waist, dragging her hard against him. He pressed his lips to hers with the same urgency and it gave her no time to think, no time to react before her mouth was responding, inviting him in, tasting him. Her body moulded to his, the line crossed and a moral code betrayed, as all she was aware of was the feel of him; his warm, heavenly scent, and strong body against hers.

All noise faded away, from downstairs and in her head, as her hands slipped around his neck and buried themselves into his hair, so soft and smooth, just as she had imagined. Small moans escaped from her mouth as his hands held her firm, unmoveable. Caught in his web.

He pulled back and she gazed into his eyes.

'What have I done to you,' he murmured as he ran a thumb temptingly over her lips, still wet from their kiss.

Something crashed to the floor downstairs. More shouting.

'Jesus Christ,' he growled. 'I really should go and sort that out before they kill each other.'

'Yes,' she whispered.

He reluctantly released his hold and this time, he did leave. She watched, remaining where he'd left her, for how long, she wasn't sure. Minutes and hours held no value here. She ignored the noise. All she could focus on was the memory of his lips on hers, how they tingled her skin. And the thought spun around in her mind, free to roam there. She sensed she was slipping off a precipice, but into what, she didn't know.

\*\*\*

The men had been arguing on and off for the past two days. Tension filled the air and her anxiety tightened, ready to snap. She lay down on the floor and placed her ear against the boards to try and get a sense of what was happening. But it was useless, she couldn't catch any of the conversation.

She backed up as footsteps climbed the stairs.

Her captor stormed in, a thunderous look on his face and a sense of urgency that told her all she needed to know. One way or another, her ordeal was ending today.

She remained still, waited for his next move.

'It's time to go,' he said as he reached into his pocket and pulled out the same piece of cloth that was used to blindfold her before.

'What?' she stammered. 'To go? My father? He paid the ransom, yes?' she asked, questions rushing into her head all at once. 'Did you see him?'

Relief washed over her, and she felt the joy that this horrible existence was soon going to be over.

He said nothing. She stared, trying to read his mood as he frowned and ran his hand through his hair. His mask of control appeared to slip as it had the other night. The sight of it made her feel a strange wrench that after today, she would never see him again.

'No,' he said simply.

She searched his eyes for the answers he wasn't giving. 'What?'

'No, I haven't seen him.' He sighed but continued. 'Your father has refused to pay the money.'

She floundered as his words shot through her like a physical blow, knocking the wind straight out of her. She slumped to her knees and stared at the old bare floorboards. 'He didn't pay?' It was a whisper.

The cloth hung in his hand. 'No, he didn't pay.' He crouched in front of her as he had done so many times before.

'But why wouldn't he?' she asked, unable

to process the absolute danger her father's refusal had put her in. Pain burst in her chest, a large black cloud spilling out its acid rain, burning her insides as hurt and disbelief crushed her. She placed her hand over her heart.

'My father is not paying my ransom to set me free.' She spoke it again, hoping that it would help her to comprehend it. It was too much to hear that her parents had refused her freedom and potentially her life. For the sake of money. They chose wealth over their own flesh and blood. Something seemed to break inside – the part that connected her to her parents by blood – shattering into tiny little pieces, never to be repaired.

Shock stunned her, but slowly, as her mind began to process this new information, this new knowledge, any questions of why he hadn't paid slipped away as a new, infinitely more horrifying one trampled into her mind.

*What happens when ransoms aren't paid, Elena? Come on now. You need to get this question right for the big money prize. You've got ten seconds on the clock. Tick-tock, Elena, tick-tock.*

She let out a strangled cry of terror as it hit her. A juggernaut of thought that decimated and crushed all others in its path. Terrified, she scooted back away from the man who had been so kind to her but was here to finish this ordeal. Once and for all.

'No, no, *no!*' she screamed, all sense leaving

her as the panic burst free.

He lunged at her and grabbed her shoulders as he caught up. 'Elena, calm down. I'm not going to do anything,' he said, locking eyes with her. 'Nothing's going to happen because I'm not going to let it. Do you understand?'

As his words seeped into her mind, she slumped forwards and let her head rest on his shoulder. She let out stifled sobs as his arms enveloped her, and allowed him to soothe her in this moment of need.

She didn't know if he was telling the truth, but she'd let whatever he had planned happen. Even death no longer held its terrifying grip on her. She was without fight.

'I'm getting you out of here,' he said. 'This was never part of the deal and has gone on long enough,' he muttered under his breath. 'It's time to go.'

He wrapped his arm around her waist and walked her to the door as Cigarettes sauntered in, a phone in one hand, the other behind his back. 'My, my. What have I walked into here?'

The sight of him sent a new shockwave of terror through her, and she was unable to calm her trembling body.

'I told you to get the hell out,' her captor ordered as he held her close. 'You've been paid your money, now disappear.'

'Yeah, I know, but I wanna do things my way now. Boss.'

Cigarettes wore a chilling smile as he pulled a gun from behind his back and aimed it straight at them.

Elena cried out and her captor stepped ahead of her, shielding her from Cigarettes. She gripped his arm, crumpling the fabric of his shirt in her palms. But his desire to protect her caused more fear than the gun itself, because the possibility of losing this man to a fatal gunshot wound was more unbearable than being victim to it herself.

'You ...' her captor snarled, his body tense with rage.

'What? What am I now, big man?' Cigarettes said with a cold smile.

No one spoke as they waited for his next move, the seconds more like hours.

Cigarettes kept the gun aimed at them and turned his attention to his phone, punching numbers with his thumb. The man in front of her didn't flinch.

'Mr Dumont, I have your daughter here,' Cigarettes said, his stare fixed on them both. 'See, you're supposed to pay the ransom for your child. That's what you're *supposed* to do,' He paused, listening. 'So why didn't you do it?'

He shifted a little, but the aim was sure. 'No, no, no, Mr Dumont, it's too late for that. Far too late.' He listened some more, happy to entertain whatever was being said. 'Do you know what I'm doing right now?' he asked. 'I'm aiming a gun at your daughter's head.'

He gasped out a laugh, finding humour in her father's reaction.

'Oh, come on now, Mr Dumont, you've made your decision, now it's time to make mine. To kill or not to kill. I haven't decided yet.'

He took one more step forward, and Elena held her breath as movement by the door caught her attention. The doctor stalked in, moving silently into the room. Her captor reacted too, his body tensing in recognition, and suddenly it felt that the balance of power might be tipping in their favour. Cigarettes was too busy tormenting her father to hear the floorboard creak.

'Right, time's up,' he said as he moved, getting a better aim at Elena. 'Time to say goodbye.'

# CHAPTER 10

Elena watched as the doctor lunged at Cigarettes from behind. With both hands, he pulled Cigarettes' arms up to the ceiling as the gun fired, and the phone clattered to the floor.

The bullet rammed into the decayed plasterwork, dusting them all in residue, like fragments of confetti at a wedding.

Her captor rushed forwards to help the doctor overpower Cigarettes who bucked and fought to be free. A foot collided with the phone on the floor, smashing plastic and glass, the first victim of this violence. The doctor snatched the gun from Cigarettes' grasp and tossed it across the floor as she moved her focus to the small burnt hole in the ceiling and the little black lines trailing away from it. It looked like a strange black star. Her own little death star.

'Elena!' her captor shouted. 'Grab the gun!'

She snapped into action, ran to where the gun had landed, and grabbed it. It was heavy and cold in her fingers, and she wanted to drop it, hating the feel of it. A tool to maim and kill.

Cigarettes roared out.

The doctor and her captor worked hard to restrain him, but Cigarettes' rage made him a powerful force. In one swift move, he landed a punch to the doctor that had him out cold before he lunged at her captor. They fought, landing and receiving punches as they moved through the door and towards the broken staircase, stopping dangerously close to the top of the stairs.

Watching the commotion, she aimed the gun, holding it steady with both hands as her jaw clenched. She didn't know how to use it, but she'd figure it out. She wouldn't stand by and watch her captor die if something went wrong.

With his back to the stairwell, Cigarettes drew back his arm to throw another punch, but it unbalanced him, making him step back for a surer footing. There was nowhere to go, only the hollow space of the first stair tread, and the motion sent him spiralling backwards. With rasping breath and bulging eyes, he windmilled his arms in a frantic attempt to stop the momentum that would drag him down. It would have been comical if she hadn't seen his face, ashen with fear as he tried to grab hold of something, anything, in a bid to save himself.

Her captor reached out, but he was not close enough and could only grasp at the tips of Cigarettes' fingers, which slipped away. With nothing to stop him, he tumbled out of sight, his fall and anguished cry silenced by the sickening crack of bone snapping as he hit the floor below.

It was quiet, deathly, except for the quick breathing of her captor who stood and stared at the sight below. The doctor groaned as he regained consciousness but shook his head, quickly alert and staggered out on to the landing. Her captor and the doctor exchanged a telling glance, and they ventured down the stairs. Still silence. She remained, listening to their low, inaudible voices and it told Elena all she needed to know.

Nausea rose within her with an immediacy that wouldn't be ignored. She placed the gun down and hurried to the corner of the room in time to vomit.

She listened to the sounds of activity downstairs as she waited, having no desire to leave the room. Doing that would mean potential freedom and she was at a sudden loss at how to deal with that. She cared little about seeing the remains of a man she hated more than anything. She felt nothing on that score – no regret or compassion, only relief that he couldn't hurt her anymore.

After some time, her captor returned to her. He had a small cut on his mouth where he had taken a blow, and his hair was messed up a little, but other than that, he had no other obvious injuries.

She managed a faint smile as he strode towards her, but her expression crumpled, and she couldn't stop the tears from rolling down her cheeks. He pulled her close, whispering words to soothe and she grabbed him, burying her face in his chest.

He hugged her close, and there was an inevitability to the contact, that it was the beginning of the end for them.

'We don't have much time,' he said with a sigh. 'I've called the police and have given them this address. They're coming for you.'

'What?' she cried, looking up at him. 'What about you? You can't be here; they'll arrest you.'

'Is that not what you want?' he asked.

'No, that's not what I want,' she said. 'Not at all. You must leave. And what about this place? What if they find something that connects you to here? I mean, there's a dead body right downstairs. You've been here. You were fighting. What about forensic evidence? DNA? You'd be arrested for a murder you didn't commit.' Panic swamped her again.

'Hey, take it easy,' he soothed. 'We've already thought of that. The man downstairs is a doctor. He knows what he's doing, and he's taking care of it. It'll be hard for the police to get a match on any forensic evidence. The place is falling apart, it's too contaminated. We've cleared the rooms of anything that could implicate us, just enough to show another person was here. And, more importantly, they'll know it wasn't you. You're safe from blame. Not that they would in the circumstances, but you won't be associated with his death.'

He ran his hands up and down the length of her back as he spoke. She remained still against him as her mind began to work, making a silent vow to protect him from the police and prison, at all costs. She may never see him again, but she would make sure no one would ever know about him or what he did for her. And that would be her thanks to him, for saving her life.

'But you must remember what I'm about to tell you. You will need to give this information to the police.'

She listened carefully, repeating it back when asked. She wouldn't let him down.

When he was finished, he leant forward and skimmed his lips against her unbruised cheek. A small kiss, to tempt, and she was sure her heart would split in two with all the conflict she felt.

She allowed herself this moment so she wrapped her arms around him, squeezing tight. Imprinting him into her memory, to remember the warmth of his body against hers and how well it fit. She may never feel like this for anyone else again, but if she had the memory of it, maybe it would be enough.

But when she felt his hands pulling her closer to him, she knew it would never be enough.

'It's okay, Elena,' he whispered. 'I feel it too.'

She held him, cherished the moment. 'It's

wrong, I know that. But I can't let you go.'

'And I don't want you to. You know how I feel.'

'So take me with you,' she murmured as she laid her cheek against his chest. 'Please.'

He calmly tipped her face up to his. 'You'd give up your whole world for me?' he said, his eyes on hers, glinting in the light. 'Leave everything behind?'

She nodded. 'Yes, everything, if it meant I could be with you.'

A look of satisfaction crept over his face and he leant down, touching her lips with his as she clutched hold of his arms.

'This is not the end,' he murmured. 'But I can't take you with me. Not yet.'

She worked to calm the frustration within her. 'Why not?'

'Because they will always be looking for you, and you'll always be a captive, on the run, with me. You'll be forever looking over your shoulder, wondering if your life still waits for you back home.'

'I don't care about that.'

'No, maybe not right now, tomorrow or next week, but it'll wear you down until you don't know what you want or how you feel.'

'So you want to test me?'

'No, this isn't about a test. It's about clarity.' He paused as he saw the confusion on her face and gently ran his thumb over her cheek.

'You see I know what's going to happen next. You may be clinging to me now. You may be thinking that you can't let me go, but once you're free and within your old life again, logic and outside influences will convince you to do the right thing. And you will try to do it, despite what you really want. I know this. But eventually, it'll be too much, and when that happens, I'll be waiting. That's when I'll know you're sure of what you want.'

'But there's no way I'm going to forget about you and settle back into my old life. No way. And I'm frightened that's all I'll have now.'

'Elena, calm down,' he said. 'I'm simply giving you a choice, that's all. I want all of you, but I want you willingly. And you must be absolutely sure because once you invite me into your life, there will be no going back.'

'But how will I know where you are?' she cried, not ready to let him go.

He smiled again, in control. 'Leave that to me. I will find you, and you will know. You have to trust me.'

'Do you promise? You won't leave me out there, alone? You'll come back for me.'

'You have my word.'

'Then I'll wait,' she said with a sigh. 'And I'll protect you.'

'I know you will,' he said as he trailed his fingers gently down her arms.

Sirens sounded in the distance. Faint at

first, but an unmistakable sound, and they were getting louder.

She wrapped her arms tighter around his waist, feeling his firm torso beneath his clothing. He held her too, and then reached behind himself to pull her arms away. The gesture made new panic flourish inside her. 'I can't leave you.'

'Yes, you can. You'll be fine. The police will take care of you.'

'I don't want their help.'

'You know it has to be this way. It's minutes, only minutes now, and then you'll be out of this room.'

He took hold of her hand and kissed it, his eyes on her as he did. She didn't want him to stop and held on, but he released his grip.

He picked up the gun as he left the room, shutting the door behind him.

She listened as his footsteps faded and a car fired into action, taking him away from her.

She was entirely alone.

*Oh God, oh God. What do I do?*

The sirens were loud, outside now, and her heart skipped a beat at the screech of brakes and doors slamming. Voices shouted her name. The thumps of multiple footfall on the stairs and the presence of many people within the building created too much noise. She didn't like it and held her hands over her ears as her heart rate spiked.

A policeman swung open the door and

called to the others, his voice urgent and hurried. Dread and fatigue made her head swim. She couldn't think. She was going to pass out – something she had fought for so long during her ordeal. Her legs gave way, but the policeman grabbed her, holding firm.

'Don't worry, I've got you Miss Dumont. You're safe now,' he reassured, his voice becoming distant.

Voices were everywhere, and chaos surrounded her, but she was found, rescued, safe. There was nothing more to do. The room closed in, and she didn't fight it. She slumped and let the darkness take over. She had survived and was finally leaving this place, and not in a body bag as she had so feared.

# CHAPTER 11

Elena woke in an ambulance. Tucked under blankets, she rocked with the sway and motion of speed. The policeman who found her sat close by, and a paramedic looked after her medical needs. And she had needs. She was a freed hostage, a little broken, but a survivor.

Within the safety of the hospital's Accident and Emergency Unit, she was housed in a cubicle, the curtains closed, and a police presence outside.

She listened to the sounds of the department – voices of the sick and injured, beeping medical equipment, and phones endlessly ringing. But soon there was a commotion that engulfed all of those sounds. Anguished voices. Voices she recognised. Voices saying her name. Her mother and Charlotte. The curtain was pulled back, and they rushed in.

'Elena, oh, Elena,' her mother cried as she drew close, her face crumpled with emotion at the sight of her daughter. Her jewellery tinkled as she dropped her bag at the end of Elena's bed, and it was a sound that was familiar, and of home. It caused a sensory overload, and the impact of it overwhelmed Elena. She began to cry.

'Mum,' she said, her voice breaking as she

reached for her mother. Any resentment towards her parents was quashed, for now. All she wanted, needed more than anything else, was to be held. To be comforted and soothed as only a mother can. For her to make it better.

'We thought you were dead,' her mother whispered as she held her close, gently stroking her hair. 'I thought I would die with grief. That awful gunshot,' she said as a sob caught in her throat. She pulled Elena closer still. 'But everything changed, and you were alive again.'

She pulled back enough to reach for Charlotte who waited at the side of the bed, huge tears rolling down her cheeks. 'Come here,' Elena said through her own, pulling her close.

'We were so scared,' Charlotte whispered, hoarse with emotion as she hugged her friend as best she could.

'Hey, I'm fine. I'm here.'

They composed themselves from their tearful hugs as the medical team, who had stepped back to allow them their reunion, now made their presence known. One of the doctors stepped forwards.

'While I don't want to break up this happy moment, we really do need to run some tests. See how Elena is doing. Maybe you could come back in a little while?'

Her mother and Charlotte nodded and gathered their things and, after both giving Elena a gentle hug, they left her to the medical team.

The 'little while' became a couple of hours. The nurses took blood and inserted an IV line into her arm to help rehydrate her. Her heart rate was monitored, and questions were asked and repeated by different doctors. She was given a physical examination and notes were made. She was sent for a CT scan, accompanied by the policeman, and returned to her waiting cubicle. The detective leading her case visited, welcoming her back and informed her that he would return when she'd had time to rest. She immediately forgot his name. Everyone who spoke to Elena did so in quiet calm tones, as if soothing a traumatised person. They were only being kind, and at first, she appreciated it, but in time it irritated her. She didn't feel traumatised, but then, she realised she didn't feel anything at all. So she complied, answering their questions, and waiting as they discussed her 'case' as if she was not present. She felt hemmed in, surrounded by the smell of disinfectant, and all she wanted to do was stand in the sun and replenish her body with fresh, clean air. But this was London, and that was not easily done.

Another doctor came in and looked through her notes. 'How are you feeling, Elena?'

'I'm doing okay, I think. Exhausted, but okay, thanks.'

'Well, despite all you've been through, you're in surprisingly good shape,' he said as he flicked through the pages. 'The bruising, although nasty, will fade soon enough and there are no fractures to the bone beneath. You're a little dehydrated, and your leg needs another dressing, but there's no infection and no adverse effects to the drug you were given,' he said as he made his way over to her.

'Your parents have made arrangements for you to be moved to a private room,' he said with a smile as a man in the adjacent cubicle vomited loudly. 'Somewhere a little more peaceful, anyway.'

'Thank you,' she said, eagerly. She was desperate for quiet. Desperate for peace.

As Elena was wheeled along the corridor, she noticed the same policeman positioned outside of her door. She smiled at him, even said hello, although there was no need for him. She wasn't in any danger. It was her decision as to what she did next. But that fact did not fill her with strength, instead only an emptiness at the thought of being alone.

Elena watched the nurse who had accompanied her from the Accident and Emergency Unit settle her into her room. Placing Elena's notes in the folder at the foot of her bed, she filled a jug with water and left it on the bedside locker. She glanced at Elena, eyeing her, and it made Elena uncomfortable. They must deal with a range of scenarios in her department, daily, but it must be rare to have a kidnap survivor to treat. It made her a case study, and she didn't like it. She only relaxed when the nurse informed her that the ward team would be taking over her care and wished her well before leaving.

Elena lay back against her pillows, feeling weak and in a strange limbo – part of life again, and yet apart from it. Disconnected from the world around her.

The door opened, disrupting her thoughts, and a nurse walked in. 'Hello, Elena, how are you feeling?' she asked as she approached, checked her drip, and took her pulse. She was an older lady – probably mid-fifties – and had a kind face. Perfect for this profession. She had an air of efficiency too that came from knowing her job well.

'I'm getting there, thanks.'

There was another knock on the door, and her mother came into the room, alone. 'Hello, darling.'

Elena sat up and ignored the desire to be alone. 'Where's Charlotte?'

'We thought it best if it was just family now. She'll come and visit another day.'

'She's my oldest friend, mother. She's as good as family,' Elena complained.

'You know what I mean,' her mother replied. 'You need rest.'

Elena glanced at her mother who stared at her bruise. Self-conscious now, she touched her face and remembered that awful night Cigarettes had given it to her. Cigarettes, who was now dead. Nausea pulsed through her as the mix of pain and memory jolted her body into action. Empty of anything to reject, her stomach contracted regardless, making her want to retch but she lay still and breathed through it. It was easy now to create a stillness deep within her until the moment had passed.

The nurse noticed though. Even checking Elena's notes at the base of her bed, she picked up the change in her patient. 'Are you feeling unwell?' she asked as she placed the folder back and walked the length of the bed to her.

'I'm fine,' Elena said as the nausea began to subside. 'Maybe a little sickness and pain in my cheek.'

*Let's not mention the irritating mother, the deep ache in my soul, and the threatening insanity. No, let's not do that.*

The nurse checked the monitor again. 'Well, that's no surprise. Completely understandable, I'd say. A terrible ordeal,' she said as she glanced at her mother and went back to the notes. 'We can give you something for the pain. I'll be right back.'

Now that they were alone, her mother fussed over her, fluffing up pillows and straightening her covers, talking about insignificant things. But Elena wasn't listening. It didn't matter. Nothing did. Only him. She remembered his face; his intense eyes. How he had held her face in his hands when he spoke to her. She was empty, and not because of the lack of food. She didn't want to forget him; the feel of him, his scent, and she ached for him. She wanted to keep him etched in a hidden corner of her mind. A secret place, just for her, because perhaps that was all it could be now.

It was over, he was gone, and now that she was free, perhaps that was the right thing to do. Maybe logic was kicking in, just as he said it would.

\*\*\*

Elena held her head to try and contain the pounding there and willed the nurse to come back with her medication. Anxiety gnawed at her, and all she wanted was to be alone instead of listening to her mother wittering on. Dealing with the police loomed ahead like a long shadow and she had no energy for it. But she hadn't changed her mind about what she'd tell them. Of that she was sure.

Aware of her father's absence like a glaring hole in the room, she realised that, actually, all of the men in her life were absent – no father, no brother, and no boyfriend. All too soon, a tiny slither of contempt crept into her consciousness. She waited for it to pass but it didn't, so she decided to raise the issue they had skirted around so far. 'Why isn't Dad here? Why hasn't he come?'

Her mother tensed and moved to the chair by Elena's bed. 'He's at home. We thought it best that just one of us would be here when you arrived. Your release was very sudden and, in the chaos, we decided that it would be me. We didn't want to overwhelm you. Although of course Charlotte refused to be cut out, even though I tried to explain–'

Elena gave a little laugh; her mother was treating her like a fool. Overload her with faces? It was laughable if it wasn't so tragic. Well, now it was time for some honesty.

'Look, let's forget this fiction, shall we?' Elena said as she fixed her eyes on her mother. 'I know what happened. And I want to know why.'

Her mother looked surprised and avoided Elena's eye contact. 'Why what, Elena?'

Elena sighed. 'Why Dad wouldn't pay the ransom?'

Her mother paused, struggling for the words to explain such a decision, and she took too long to answer. Undeterred, Elena leaned forwards and helped the conversation along.

'Why my parents declined to pay a ransom for a daughter they supposedly loved,' she said. 'Putting her in terrible danger.'

Still no reply.

'Do you want to know the danger I'm talking about, mother? Would you like me to describe it?' she asked, her head tilted to one side.

Her mother shook her head, flustered, and

looked down to her lap with slumped shoulders. It was something Elena had never seen in her before. She was always the glamorous, social butterfly, happy and self-assured on her husband's arm. If he was happy, she was happy. But now she was alone.

'Your father can't face you right now,' she said, the bravado breaking down. She focused on her hands, still unable to look her own daughter in the eye. 'He's so ashamed. We both are. I tried to tell him, persuade him otherwise, but you know what he's like when he's made a decision.'

Elena nodded her head as her eyes filled with furious tears. She was well aware of how her father's decisions ruled the family. And now he'd left his wife to mop up his mess, alone. He should be ashamed, but he should be here too, apologising, doing something to put it right. If he cared.

'Ashamed? Let's discuss what you have to be ashamed about.'

'No, Elena... I ...'

But Elena steamed on as anger spilled into a white-hot rage, her only energy source. 'Do you want to know about how a needle was plunged into my arm, drugging me, or how I was beaten when I tried to escape, terrified that I would die in that room? The lack of food or water? I became ill too; shall we talk about my infected leg.'

She reached up and touched her cheek, aware of the twinge of pain it caused, even as a fading bruise. 'Do you want to know the details of how I got this bruise, how the man got drunk and tried to rape me. Shall we discuss that? Would you like to know how long I thought it would take to pay the money, only to discover that you refused? Would you like me to continue?'

'Elena... please.'

Her words were clipped and her voice husky with emotion. 'And do you want to know about the terror when it all went wrong. When my parents did their worst?'

'Enough!' her mother snapped, shaking her head and raising her hand as if to block out the words she was hearing. She closed her eyes.

They sat in silence.

As they calmed, her mother was the first to speak. 'I can only assume you must be in pain to talk to me like this. We will discuss it, yes, but not now. Emotions are running high. It's too soon.'

'It's nowhere near enough. And too soon for whom exactly? Me or you?' Elena's heart raced as she contained the tirade she desperately wanted to let out. Only her own self-preservation stopped it. Weak and in pain, she needed to be calm, to rest.

Looking away from her mother she closed her eyes and rubbed her forehead. 'Where the hell is that fucking nurse?'

'Elena!' her mother exclaimed. 'Please

mind your language.'

'Really,' she shot back. 'You're seriously admonishing me for swearing, here, now, after everything?'

'I... just don't want you to lower yourself like that.'

'Well, maybe it's the company I've been keeping lately, Mother. Ever considered that?'

She expected her mother to show some fragments of remorse, even murmurs of justification for her actions, but not one apology passed over her mother's lips. Not one.

She sighed with irritation. 'You know, I think it would be best if you would just leave.'

'Elena, I'm your mother, and I'm worried about you. I'm not leaving.'

'Of course you're not. Why listen to anything I want?'

'You're upset. When you calm down, we can talk again.'

'Fine.'

They sat in icy silence until the nurse returned, a tray of medication in her hand. Elena watched her take in the vast change in the atmosphere. 'Is everything okay?' she asked as she made her way to Elena.

'Yes, yes, everything's fine. I'm just a little tired,' she said, a little surprised with how much conviction she spoke. But then, she'd spent her life papering over enough cracks in her relationship with her parents to be very convincing at it.

The nurse smiled and said nothing as she handed Elena a tiny paper cup with two tablets in it. She poured her a small glass of water from the jug on her bedside locker.

Elena downed them both, glad to have something to take the pain away and hoped her mother would soon disappear too. The nurse went back to the notes at the end of the bed.

Her mother opened her mouth to speak, but before she could do so there was another knock on the door.

Adam rushed in, his eyes bright with concern. 'Lena, darling,' he said as he hurried to her side.

He was dressed for work. It took a moment to sink in, but soon it wound its way to the front of Elena's mind. *He's been at work. The day of my release and he's been working?* She processed this as he gathered her up clumsily, making her gasp.

'Sorry honey, am I hurting you? Did they hurt you?' he asked as his eyes darted over her face. His gaze lingered on the large bruise, as everyone had done before him. She wanted to scream.

'My God.' He sighed as he brushed his thumb over it. 'What did they do?'

She looked at him as he spoke, took in his handsome features, but he was a stranger to her now. His touch made her skin crawl, making her jittery, irritated by his closeness. She manoeuvred herself out of his hold, creating space between them. If he noticed, he said nothing.

'Adam, have you just left work?'

He blinked in surprise. 'Well, yes, I had to go to the office. They needed me, and I couldn't get out of it.'

She nodded and looked at the nurse. 'Can I ask what time I arrived?'

The nurse checked the notes. 'Ambulance arrival was... ten-forty.'

Elena looked at Adam. 'What time is it now?'

'Elena, please. I've tried my best.'

'What time is it now?' she demanded.

He checked his watch. 'It's two-thirty.'

'Three hours and fifty minutes,' she snapped as she crossed her arms, reeling from the fact that even her release hadn't managed to pull Adam away from his work. 'Well, thank you very much. My place on your list of priorities hasn't improved, I see.'

'I'm sorry,' he said. 'Your release was so sudden. Wonderful, obviously, but sudden. I've been trying to get to you all day. It's been a nightmare, but I'm here now.

She shook her head. 'You know what? I'd really like to be on my own.'

'You don't mean that,' Adam said as her mother began to bristle against her daughter's orders. 'Come on, I've just fought through London to be here. Don't send me away now.'

'I want to be on my own. I'm tired and need to rest. I've been through enough.' She wanted to run, get out of this claustrophobic room, and leave these strangers behind.

'Well, now that's something I want to hear about,' he said as he ran his hand over her hair.

Visibly horrified, her mother interrupted. 'No, Adam. I don't think she should do this now. Elena's had enough trauma for today.'

'I've had trauma longer than that,' she said, glowering at her mother. 'She just doesn't want to hear about it again, Adam. Even the snippets were more than enough for her.'

Adam glanced at her mother and they shared a look, as if questioning who this strange imposter was. Elena wanted to explode with frustration.

She huffed out an impatient sigh. 'You can come back later, I suppose, when I've cleaned up.'

She looked at herself in the hospital gown. Although it was crisp and clean, it did little to suppress her desire to freshen up.

The nurse spoke as if to add weight to Elena's words. 'Elena is right; she needs to rest now.'

'Of course,' Adam said, deciding not to question the nurse's authority. 'But I trust you'll call with an update for me later?'

'Yes, or Elena can do that when she's ready. We all need to give her time, I think.'

Her mother stood, following Adam's lead. 'I have left a bag outside with the nurses. You can change into your own clothes when you've showered.'

Elena watched with indifference, so removed from the people who were her family, who at that moment were nothing more than an irritation that she wanted gone.

'I will call later, darling,' her mother said as she gathered up her bag and coat. She kissed Elena on the forehead, and Adam stepped forwards to do the same. It was something she had never seen; both of them awkward and unsure of how to deal with her. She couldn't deny the sense of satisfaction it provided.

The nurse ushered her mother and Adam out of the door, closing it behind her.

In the quiet of her room, Elena crumpled. It wasn't supposed to be like this. She should be grateful to be free and reunited with her family. She should be floating on air to have her life back, but she only wanted one person – and his absence made her feel worse than ever. Unable to stop the emotion, Elena let sobs rack her body until there was nothing left.

# CHAPTER 12

After finishing a small meal provided by the nurse, which was to be eaten slowly to avoid her body rejecting it, Elena was offered the chance to shower. She did not hesitate. She wanted to wash the memories of that place away, wanted to cleanse herself of it, to remove it from her body, because she was sure she was becoming that room as the scent of must and decay hung from her skin.

The nurse removed her IV line and showed Elena to the ensuite before leaving her in peace. Elena shut the door and turned the dial of the shower, catching herself in the mirror. 'Well, Elena, don't you look the belle of the ball,' she murmured as she stared at her reflection.

She'd lost weight, having little to play with anyway, and her eyes had faint purple shadows circling beneath them. Her lips were pale, and her hair was held together in a braid that hung over her shoulder with errant strands escaping around her face. But these were all insignificant compared to the large, mottled bruise covering her right cheek. It was fading now but was still a rainbow of purple, brown and yellow. But given what she'd been through, it wasn't so bad. The bruise would soon disappear, a hot shower would restore her to herself again, and a good night's sleep in a bed, rather than a wooden floor, would erase the faint shadows under her eyes.

She undressed and grabbed the shower gel and shampoo from her bag. Without warning, something changed. The serenity was replaced by anxiety creeping in, as if an unseen threat was here, with her. She looked up, and in the steam-filled room, the walls appeared to move inwards, closing in on the already tiny space. Her heart rate increased, and she had to inhale huge gulps of air to combat the dizziness and confusion. She fell to her knees, gasping for air and listening to the sound of the water hissing behind her. She was safe and in no danger, but she could not move her body from the crouching position she had put herself in, instinctively, as if to make herself small, to hide, to be unseen, as her mind disappeared into the mist.

When she became aware of her surroundings again, she appeared to have been crouching this way for some time by the way her body ached and the density of the steam that filled the room.

'Jesus,' she whispered as she moved to stand, confusion peppering her mind. 'What the hell was that?'

Desperate for water on her skin, she stepped into the shower, and the feelings of panic soon faded to a rippled aftershock. She lingered under the hot stream of water and let it rush over her, washing away the grime of her ordeal – physically and emotionally. She stayed there, letting the sensation calm her, deciding the soap could wait.

As she lathered shampoo into her hair for the second time, she understood the difference between being clean and feeling clean was a chasm that was vast and wide. She figured she'd need to take a good many showers before she'd feel rid of that place and the events that went on there.

The invigorating scents of honey and lemon mingled with the mist from the shower as she cleansed her body, over and over. Scrubbing, rinsing, and repeating until there was no more gel in the bottle.

She turned off the water and reached for the fluffy towel, wrapping it around herself in a warm cocoon. No more itchy hair or clammy skin, just soft warmth against her body. She dried herself and dressed in an old t-shirt and yoga pants, both of which hung loosely over her frame. Delving further into the toiletries in her bag, she brushed her hair and moisturised her skin, taking care around her bruise. Finally, she slathered her toothbrush with paste and scrubbed her teeth hard. The minty paste burned hot in her mouth and on her tongue, and she relished the clean sensation. But it didn't stop her from adding more paste to the brush and beginning the task again. She finished up, grabbing her lip balm and smearing it over her lips.

\*\*\*

Safe in the care of the hospital, Elena relaxed a little. She had even managed a nap. But her peace was disrupted when the nurse popped her head around the door and advised her that Adam had returned.

'Lena,' he said as he strode towards her. 'Feeling any better now, or am I going to have my head bitten off again?' he said with amusement in his voice. 'I hear you've eaten. I hope that's helped?'

*Just breathe. After all you've been through, you can handle him.* 'Yes, I'm feeling much better now,' she said, keeping her voice steady.

'Great,' he said as he sat on the edge of the bed, close to her. 'Well, you certainly look better, now you're all cleaned up.' He smiled and wrinkled his nose.

Her face flushed with embarrassment. 'Thanks,' she said as she smoothed her hair self-consciously. 'Can always count on you for telling it like it is, even though I wasn't that bad.'

'I was only joking,' he teased.

'Funny.'

'Have the police paid you a visit yet?' he asked, scanning her face.

'No, that'll be tomorrow now. I can't face

any more visitors today.'

'Do you want me to be here when you do? For a hand to hold?' His eyes lowered as they glanced over her body, but she kept hers on his.

'No, I'll be fine, but thanks.' She didn't want him to be anywhere near her when she was going to be Little Miss Deceit. He'd recognise if she was lying easily enough, so she wouldn't risk it.

'So, do you want to talk about it now?' he asked.

'No, I really don't,' she said quickly, feeling that all the things she should be discussing with him required too much energy. The events of the day and her newly found freedom had left her more than a little weary.

He nodded again. 'Okay, Lena, maybe tomorrow,' he said as he ran his hand up her arm. 'You did give us all a fright, you know,' he said with a small laugh as if she had any control over what had happened to her.

'Believe me, it was a lot more frightening on my side of the fence.'

'Of course it was. Are you sure you don't want to talk about it?'

'No, but there is one thing,' she said. 'My phone. Do you know what happened to it?'

He sighed, nodded. 'Ah, yes that. The police found it in a bin just around the corner from your house.'

'Oh,' she whispered as the memory of that

day suddenly filled her mind.

'They kept it I think, but I can speak to them to see if we can have it back?'

She nodded.

'But you know, I could always arrange a new phone for you, if you'd like?'

'Why?'

'Because from the look on your face, I'm guessing you probably don't want that particular one as a reminder?'

'Well, now that you mention it, no, I suppose I don't.' She sighed. 'That would be great, thanks. I'll get the money to you when I can.'

He huffed out a laugh. 'You don't have to do that.'

'I know, but I will. You shouldn't be picking up the tab for this.'

'It's just a phone.'

'Maybe to you, but I feel eternally dependent on everyone right now and I really need some control. I'll be paying.'

'Whatever makes you happy.'

'It will make me happy. That, and the distraction of a phone. It's hard being here and not being able to see what's going on in the world, or speak to anyone; Charlotte, Abigail–'

'Me.'

'Yes, all right,' she said with a roll of her eyes. 'You too.'

'No problem. I'll sort it.'

'Thanks,' she said, catching the way he

looked at her.

'I've missed you,' he said as his hand lingered over hers. Uncomfortable with the sensation, she moved hers away.

'Are you tired now?'

'Maybe.' She was unsure of anything, but his closeness flustered her, making her feel disloyal.

He leaned in closer, his eyes on hers. 'I missed you so much,' he murmured as he brought his lips to hers, quickly moving on to explore and nuzzle her neck.

'Don't, Adam,' she said as she began to struggle. She didn't want him; it wasn't right, so with what little energy she had left, she shoved him hard away from her. 'Adam, I said no. Stop it, just stop it.'

He stopped and pulled away, staring at her, shocked at her reaction. 'Jesus, Elena. It was only a kiss.'

'Only a kiss? What the hell are you thinking?' she spat. 'I've just been released. Why would you think I'd want anything like that? We're in the hospital for heaven's sake.'

Both mute with a mix of exasperation and surprise, the room fell silent for a moment.

After what felt like an eternity, he reached out to her with a remorseful expression. 'Lena, I'm sorry. That was an epic fail on every level. I don't know what I was thinking.' He squeezed her hand, struggling to find the words. 'It's just

... I'm here, you're here, looking so beautiful and alive, and I guess I was confused and I just thought... well, you know.' He exhaled. 'I guess I got a little carried away.'

'But here?' she said. 'Today?'

'Yeah,' he said rubbing the back of his neck. 'As I said, epic fail. I just can't believe you're here. It's amazing. We always hoped–'

'Look, it's no big deal,' she said wearily. 'This is surreal for all of us. We're all dealing with it differently, I suppose.'

'I just want to put it behind us. Get back to normal as soon as possible.'

'Pick up right where we left off as if nothing had happened?' she said, unable to mask the slight mocking tone in her voice.

'Well... yes,' he said, his eyes giving away his surprise that she could think otherwise.

'But so much has changed,' she said. 'I've changed, and I need to pick up the strands of my life again. And I'm not joking when I say I'm really not sure when I'm going to be ready for any kind of intimacy.'

He nodded. 'Of course darling, I understand. It was stupid and clumsy, and I'm racing ahead instead of giving you time. But I do understand the ordeal you've been through; I'm not made of stone.' He sighed. 'Can't we start this evening again?'

'I'm so exhausted, Adam,' she said, feeling more than a little defeated. At what point did getting her life back become so hard?

'Of course you are. Why don't you relax and lay back. I won't try any more of my moves on you tonight,' he said with a grin.

She smiled as he did his best to plump pillows and smooth blankets. Being nurse maid was not a role he was used to playing but she'd wait until he'd gone before she made herself properly comfortable.

'I was so worried, Lena,' he said, serious now, as he sat beside her. 'Every day, I'd wake up and hope the nightmare would be over, but every day it would go on and on. You were just ... *gone.*' He shook his head and stared, focusing on nothing, still there, in that moment. 'There was a large gap in my life where you should've been, and with each day that went past I never knew if that would be the day we'd get the call.'

Her feelings towards him softened and she placed her hand over his. 'I'm sorry Adam, I didn't even consider how hard this would've been for you. I need to remember that.' She smiled and gave a little shrug. 'Maybe we both just need a little time to adjust.'

He smiled too and kissed the back of her hand just as his phone beeped. He pulled it from his pocket.

'It's the New York office. Conference call. I can leave it if you want. Stay with you a little while longer?'

She smiled again. 'No, you take it. I'll be

fine.'

He stood and leant down, kissing her on her good cheek. 'I'll call you tomorrow?'

'Yes, let's talk tomorrow.'

He nodded and chucked her under the chin. 'Get some rest.'

She watched him leave, bringing up the number on his phone, already gone. The only people that would come to her now would be nursing staff, and that was fine with her.

She readjusted the pillows and rested her head; comfortable and warm. Soon, and while listening to the nurses chatting outside at their station, the sleep that she so desperately needed carried her away.

# CHAPTER 13

*She was alone again, in the familiar surroundings of the old, dusty room, but now the door was open. Silence filled the air – it was her chance to escape. She drifted through the door. No one stopped her. Down the stairs. No one stopped her. She tried to ignore the crumpled, broken body at the bottom of the stairs, but the sight of it stopped her. She couldn't get past it. Her exit was clear, but she was stuck, immobilised. She gasped for air as something wrapped itself around her ankle and pulled at her leg – a hand, dragging her down as she began to scream...*

She lurched from her nightmare with a jolt, desperate to snap the fine thread between sleep and the conscious world. Her bedcovers caught in her legs, and her clothes clung to her skin, damp with sweat. She took a moment to register the safety and peace of her room, and when at last she did, she let her head fall back against the pillow and stared at the ceiling. 'It's just a nightmare. I'm fine,' she panted, taking a moment to gain her composure.

The nurse rushed in. 'Elena, are you all right?' she said, checking her over. 'We could hear you from the end of the corridor.'

'Yes, I'm fine, now. Sorry, I didn't mean to startle you,' she said as the nurse checked Elena's steadying pulse. 'I had a bad nightmare, that's all.'

The nurse smiled. 'You poor thing,' she said as she tutted to herself. 'That must have been horrible for you. But I guess it's to be expected, with all you've been through.' She rubbed Elena's arm kindly, and rearranged the blankets. 'Would you like some water?' she asked as she went to the window and opened the curtains.

The morning sun broke through, making Elena squint. 'No thanks.'

'Breakfast then? You must eat; keep your strength up.'

Elena didn't want anything other than to be left alone, but she nodded in agreement. The nurse smiled and checked her charts before leaving again.

After a breakfast of eggs, tea, and toast, she dragged herself out of bed and showered, dressing in jeans and a white t-shirt. She scraped her hair back into a ponytail, and with nothing else to do, she waited – as she had done every day since her abduction.

The nurse entered again with a simple arrangement of flowers. Pink and white roses, wrapped in pink tissue paper and tied with ribbon.

'Now, I know we don't allow these normally,' she said as she bustled over, 'but I am going to make an exception for you, my dear, because of all you've been through.'

Elena sat up as delight filled her. 'They're lovely, thank you,' she said as she glanced over the pretty blooms. Maybe they were from Adam, but these weren't his style. He didn't do simple and pretty. If he had been involved, he'd have ensured the arrangement was of expensive blooms, flowers that made a statement about the sender and his wealth, instead of the sentiment they were meant to convey.

'Yes, they are,' the nurse said as she handed them to Elena. 'They were left on the nurses' station. No one saw who left them, they just appeared, like fantastic flowery magic.' She laughed and waved her hand through the air. 'That'll be your charming boyfriend, no doubt.'

Elena didn't reply but smiled at the nurse, not wanting to burst the happy bubble she was in. She found the small white envelope with her name handwritten across it. She didn't recognise the writing but dismissed it as she laid the flowers in her lap, ripping open the card. The nurse busied herself with Elena's chart, giving her privacy. Elena was glad of it, because when she pulled out the card it was clear they were not from Adam, her circle of friends, or anyone else in her family.

They were from him.

She sat rigid, unable to move as she stared at the sequence of numbers, a mobile telephone number, written across the white card, by hand.

His hand. It was enough to destroy the small amount of calm she had managed to build. He had been here, in the hospital, right outside her door. It was so blatant and bold, and she understood clearly the message that he could, and would, do anything to get to her. The knowledge caused her heart to race and her stomach flip, and it threatened to expel her much-enjoyed breakfast. He was true to his word, and he hadn't wasted any time finding her.

She collected her thoughts as heat flushed her cheeks. She needed to relax, but every part of her was taut with the need to rush out into the corridor, to see him again.

The nurse finished her notes and looked at her with an enquiring expression. 'So, are you going to put me out of my misery? Who are they from?'

'Oh, some people from work,' Elena said, without hesitation. 'They must have seen how busy you all were and decided against visiting.' She wrapped her fingers around the card to obscure it from view.

'Oh,' the nurse said with a little disappointment in her voice. It was obvious that she wanted a more romantic explanation as she admired the flowers once more.

Elena smiled apologetically and shrugged her shoulders. 'Sorry it wasn't more exciting.'

'Don't mind me, dear,' she said in her cheery voice. 'I'm glad you've had something good happen today. Something to put the colour back in your cheeks, as it so clearly has.'

Elena smiled again. *If only you knew.*

'So, all observations are normal. The wound on your leg is looking better, and apart from your nasty bruise, you're recovering well. I wouldn't be surprised if the doctor lets you go home later today. After the police have visited.'

'That's great,' she said with more enthusiasm than she felt. She should want to get back to living her life again, but she didn't want to leave the safety of this room. She sighed. All she had managed to do was to substitute one kind of captivity for another.

'I'll go and find a vase for the flowers,' the nurse said, patting her on the arm, leaving Elena alone with her whirring thoughts.

She turned the card over in her hand and stared at the number again. He had given her no time at all. Her body trembled as she placed the flowers on the bedside locker, unnerved by them, as if their very presence willed her to make contact. She carefully tucked the card into her back pocket. That decision was for another day.

\*\*\*

'The police are outside,' the nurse said. 'Are you happy to see them now?'

Elena had been dreading this moment, but it wasn't going to go away. 'Yes, send them in, let's get it over with,' she said as she sat up in the chair and prepared herself.

Two men entered. The first was a short, bald, overweight man dressed in a well-used suit, his age she couldn't decide. It was clear he did not look after himself, so a late-fifties guess could have been a generous one. Behind him, was a slightly younger man, who was tall, a little better presented, and with a full head of hair. Elena stifled the laugh that threatened. She didn't know if these two contrasting men had been paired together for the 'double-act' humour or if she was losing her mind.

*You're losing your mind, girl. You're losing your sweet mind.*

'Elena Dumont?' the short man asked.

She nodded her reply.

'I'm Detective Sergeant McAllister, we met yesterday, and this is Sergeant Jacobs,' he said as they both held up their ID cards. Sergeant Jacobs smiled but said nothing.

'I'm the investigating officer for your case. We need to get a picture of what happened. Are you up to it?'

'Yes, I think so,' she said, keeping in check the tightening knot in her stomach.

They moved the two tub chairs over to her and sat as the sergeant pulled out a notebook.

The Detective Sergeant smiled.

*Trying to gain my trust.*

He pulled out a small notebook, opening it. 'Let's start at the beginning. Walk me through the events prior to your abduction.'

Elena took a deep breath, her mouth dry. 'In the beginning, everything was normal, except for one particular man. I'd seen him out in the street or passing by, and it was only a couple of times. It shouldn't have unnerved me, he wasn't doing anything wrong, but it did. There was just something about him, you know?'

'And did you not think about reporting it?' Sergeant Jacobs asked. 'If it worried you?'

'Yes, of course I did,' she said with a glare to the Sergeant. 'I'm not stupid.'

'No one's suggesting you are, Elena,' DS McAllister said as he glanced at his colleague. 'We're just trying to understand why you didn't feel the need to contact us, for support.'

She sighed. 'Well, you see, I've done this before,' she said. 'Five years ago, I met a man at a party, had a few drinks with him and didn't think anything more of it. That was until I started seeing him everywhere. Wherever I went, he'd be there too. Glancing at me, giving me an 'oh look, we keep meeting like this' expression. But the more it happened the stranger it became. It was quite creepy actually and I started to question why I'd had a drink with him in the first place. He would be everywhere, always hanging around. He was very odd and together with everything that my parents had instilled into me, I got a little paranoid. When he started showing up near my house, I panicked and reported him to the police. The poor man lived nearby, that's all. He was questioned by the police, hauled out of his home for all the neighbours to see, for no reason at all. If I did happen to see him after that, the glances were always bitter – if he even bothered to look my way. I felt terrible and tried to apologise, but he wasn't having any of it. I vowed not to be so paranoid in future. The man who abducted me was literally there for a moment one day and a moment the next. He wasn't acting suspiciously or anything like that. And I didn't want history repeating itself, so I tried to put it out of my mind. I did try to speak to my parents, get their opinion, but it didn't happen.' She shrugged. 'I didn't want to make a fuss.' She looked into her lap.

'I understand,' McAllister said reassuringly, sensing that his sergeant had knocked her off balance. 'Hindsight is a wonderful thing.'

She managed a smile as he checked his notes.

'Yes. A Mr Richard Casey. Your parents mentioned him too. We've checked him out. He left the country three years ago. Lives in New Zealand now with a wife and family. His passport records show that he has not returned to the UK since, so no chance of retribution there.'

The sound of his name made it all come flooding back. All she went through, and all she put him through.

'Okay, so let's move on,' he said, keeping on track. 'Let's talk about your friend. A Charlotte Lacey?'

Elena blinked back her surprise.

'We spoke to everyone while you were gone. We needed to get a picture of what happened, any leads that would help.' He flipped the pages of his little book. 'You and your friend discussed a man, is that right? That you met in your local coffee shop?'

Her cheeks burned, and she fought to keep her composure. 'That was nothing,' she said. 'I bumped into a man that morning. Knocked my coffee straight into him. It was an embarrassing moment, and I had a laugh about it with Charlotte. Nothing more than that. I couldn't even describe him now,' she said and waved her hand away, dismissing it. 'I'm a little embarrassed that you know about it actually, and I'd rather keep this from Adam if you don't mind. Things have been very stressful since my release.'

He listened and nodded. 'I understand. What we discuss here will remain as private as I can allow. Within the realms of the investigation, of course.' He paused for a beat and continued. 'But to be clear, this wasn't the same man that abducted you?'

'God, no,' she said quickly. If it was as black and white as that, she could be truthful on that score.

He nodded. 'So, Friday was your first day missing...'

'Wait. What's today's date?'

'Seventh of May. Why?'

'And the Friday I went missing was the thirteenth of March?'

'Yes, that's right.'

She inhaled. 'Wow,' she whispered as thoughts swirled in her mind. 'So it was almost two months. I was in that room for all that time.'

He looked uneasy and checked his book. 'Fifty-six days. An unusually long time.'

She absorbed this new knowledge. She'd scratched forty lines into the wall during her captivity. Now, things had changed. These new dates meant that she had unknowingly lost more days of her life to the ordeal, and the knowledge succeeded in intensifying the effects of it. It also highlighted time spent with him, in his care, compared to now, which was just empty, blank space.

DS McAllister leant forwards a little, gaining her attention again. 'Shall we continue?'

She snapped back to the present. 'Yes, of course. Sorry.'

He smiled sympathetically. 'You failed to show up for work, and your employees were concerned when they couldn't make contact with you. They called your parents, who reported you missing after visiting your apartment and finding it empty.'

She nodded. 'I had decided to go for a run. He appeared from nowhere, grabbed me as I tried to get back into my building.'

She paused for much-needed air. 'I elbowed him and ran. But he caught me. A car appeared and he shoved me into it. We ended up in woodland somewhere, I have no idea where. They left me alone in the car so I tried to escape and that's when they injected me with something. After that, I don't remember anything until I was at the house. In that room.'

'It was a terrible ordeal, I can see that,' McAllister said with a kind smile. He paused his questioning for a moment to allow Elena to calm herself before he continued. 'These people then made a call to your father on the Monday.'

She shuffled in her chair, uncomfortable.

'Are you feeling all right?' McAllister asked. 'Would you like to take a break?'

She glanced at him. 'No, I'm fine. I want this over with.'

'I'm sure,' he said as he flicked through more pages. 'Let's focus on the man who abducted you. Could you describe him for us?'

'He was tall, about six foot and lanky, but he was so strong...' She drifted off.

'Take your time,' he said kindly.

'He had black hair that was slicked back, and he wore jeans and a t-shirt. I think he wore a leather jacket too.' She shuddered, remembering the distinct smell of it when he carried her into the shack. 'Is that enough?'

'Yes, Elena, that's just what we need. Were there any distinguishing features? Tattoos or piercings?'

'Yes, he had black tattoos, running down both of his arms.'

The two policemen looked at each other.

'Elena, we have to tell you that a man fitting the description you have given was found dead at the scene,' McAllister said. 'The day you were released.'

'Oh, that's horrible,' she said, needing to keep calm. It was almost over. 'But it does explain those last few hours, I suppose.'

'How?'

'That day, when my father refused to pay the ransom, he came to the room, made another call to my father, pointed the gun and fired it straight into the ceiling. Another one of his sick games to terrify me and my family. The bullet's probably still lodged in the plasterwork – if you haven't seen it already.' She watched him write it down and waited, letting him record all the details. 'I don't think he ever intended to kill me, not that day anyway. But I never knew what was going on in that twisted mind of his, and I'm not sure he really knew either.' She paused for a moment, needing to make this count. 'Anyway, afterwards, I heard raised voices downstairs. Lots of shouting and arguing, and then there was the sound of something crashing to the floor. After that, nothing.' She sighed. 'I don't know, maybe the other person did want me dead and they fell out about it. Badly. I'll never know though as I was still held in the room. When I heard nothing else after that I assumed they'd abandoned the place. A short while later the police arrived. I had no idea he was dead.'

*I'm actually doing this.*

'And you were alone in that room until we arrived?'

'Yes, completely alone, as always.'

'I know this is very hard for you, but we need this information. We're here to help you, so if you remember anything, however small, that may help, now's the time.'

She kept eye contact. 'I know there was another person there, but I never saw him. Or her, I suppose,' she said, shrugging her shoulders.

'Never?'

'Never. I only ever saw the man who abducted me. The man who is now dead.'

He leant forward, his gaze fixed. 'So you're telling me that you never saw anyone else, despite being alone in a house with other people?'

'That's correct.'

'That a man, who never showed you any kindness, who beat you, attacked you and taunted you with a gun, also gave you the dressing for your leg?'

She faltered but fought to regain her composure. 'That's correct. Like I said, who knew what was going through his mind. I didn't overthink it, I just wanted to survive.'

Something in the way he looked at her betrayed his doubt at her recollection of events, but she wouldn't start stuttering and give the game away now, so she matched his stare.

He looked to his notes and spoke quietly with Jacobs as she exhaled slowly and quietly.

'Tell me, is there anyone you know that might hold a grudge? Someone who might see this as payback?'

Elena recoiled. 'What are you suggesting? That this was done by someone I know?'

'I'm not suggesting anything. You come from a wealthy family with a successful father. We need to explore all avenues, that's all.'

'I don't know anyone who'd want to hurt me like this or my father. But he's a barrister. Someone may have a grudge. I really don't know. You'd have to take that up with him.' She rubbed her head. 'Are we done now?'

McAllister nodded. 'Yes, I think we've got everything for now. Thank you for your time. I know that was hard.'

'How long before the case can be closed?' she asked.

McAllister raised an eyebrow. 'We'll need to do a thorough investigation; you'll want whoever was involved to be brought to justice.'

She nodded. 'Of course, but I just want to put it all behind me. Move on.'

'Well, I do have to warn you that we have very little to go on,' he said as he tucked his book into his pocket.

'Have you dealt with an abduction before?'

'Yes, I have. Unfortunately, it's not as uncommon as you might think. I was assisting your parents while you were in captivity.'

Her eyes widened. 'So it was you who advised them not to pay the ransom?'

'No, Elena. It most definitely was not.'

'I see,' she said thoughtfully. 'Do you have children?'

He looked uncomfortable again but answered anyway. 'Yes, I have two.'

'And would you pay a ransom, if the worst happened?'

He considered her question and gave a sympathetic smile. 'It would never happen on my salary, but yes, I would.'

'Of course you would.'

'We all make decisions in the heat of the moment. Don't be too hard on your parents. They did what they thought was right.'

'But right for whom?'

McAllister stood up from his chair, Jacobs following his lead. 'Do you have a place to stay after you're discharged from here?' he asked.

'No. I thought I would just go home. I certainly need the peace.'

'Well, yes, but first we need to make your

building secure – which we've already discussed with your father. He's arranging for all new security to be added to the building. The locks will be changed, including the exterior door, and there will be panic alarms fitted.'

'Wow, it's amazing what a guilty conscience will do,' she murmured.

He smiled. 'It may be best to stay with someone you trust for now, rather than be on your own.'

'Yes, yes, of course, I can arrange that,' she said in a level tone that contradicted the turmoil inside.

He handed her his card. 'If you want to discuss anything, or remember something you think is significant, call me. I can be contacted on the numbers here.'

'Thank you,' she said as she took the card.

'No problem. You rest now. We'll be in touch in a few days,' he said as they replaced the chairs and made their way to the door.

She remained seated as the policemen left. It was done now. Task complete. She'd protected him and wanted no more meddling into the situation. The case needed to be closed, and she would certainly do as little as possible to help any further. He was free, and she was glad. A little damaged but glad. The satisfaction she felt mingled with the knowledge that the old Elena was fading away.

## CHAPTER 14

Elena's desire to be alone was to be denied yet again when a woman dressed in a smart black business suit entered the room after gently knocking on the door.

'Hello, Elena, I'm Dr Jones,' she said as she pulled up a chair and sat down. 'Do you mind if I sit with you?'

'Well, I see that you already have,' Elena said, unable to mask her irritation.

The woman smiled and continued. 'I thought it might be good to have a little chat. You have been through so much and must be very confused about what's happened to you over the last few months.'

'And you are...?'

She smiled again and held up the ID card on her lanyard. 'I'm a counsellor who works alongside the police, helping people who have been through traumatic situations, giving them a chance to work through their feelings. I'm here to offer you a little support, that's all.'

Elena glanced at the woman's ID which neatly confirmed her full name, her profession, and had a photo from ten years ago, at least. 'Well, thank you, but I'm fine. Really.'

'I'm sure you are,' she ventured on gently.

'But DS McAllister was concerned that you might be struggling a little with your emotions at the moment.' She paused and offered another sympathetic smile.

'I see. I didn't realise DS McAllister was fully trained in the complexities of mental health as well as being a detective for the Metropolitan Police force,' Elena replied.

Dr Jones' expression was fixed, her patience outshining Elena's curtness. 'He simply had a few concerns following your interview. Thought a little chat might help,' she said as she opened her black folder and took out a pen.

'But I've told you everything and I'm fine, so there's really no need to waste your time. And I'd really just like to be left alone.'

'I understand that, Elena, but the fact that you want to do just that indicates that you're going through an emotional response that may require attention. You've been through a very traumatic experience.'

Elena rubbed her forehead.

The counsellor continued. 'And these things can creep up on us if we let them.'

'What things?'

'Adjusting back into your life. That alone can bring its own challenges. You may find the transition difficult, which is totally understandable.'

Elena fought the urge to scream. She wanted help from this woman about as much as she wanted to poke herself in the eye.

'Is there anything you wish to discuss with me?'

Elena sat rigid in her chair. 'No. Absolutely not.'

'It's okay, there's nothing to be worried about.'

Elena said nothing, dumbfounded that this woman wouldn't simply disappear.

'Elena, I'm going to be frank with you,' Dr Jones said. 'DS McAllister felt that you might be holding back a little. Hesitant to give us the full picture.' She smiled. 'It's not so much that he understands the complexities of mental health, just that he's been doing his job for many years. Nothing would surprise him, you know.'

'I've told him what happened. Why can't that be enough?'

'It is enough, but there are no rules here. We just want you to understand that you can talk to us. You can trust us and nothing you say will ever reflect badly on you.'

Elena faltered.

'And sadly, it's well known that a range of psychological symptoms can develop in people who have experienced a captive situation such as yours,' Dr Jones continued. 'One of which can be emotional attachments.'

Elena's body tensed, her spine rigid, defensive.

'Do you understand what I'm saying,

Elena? Do you have any unexplained feelings that you might wish to discuss with me?'

'Why would you think that?' Elena blurted out. 'There's nothing like that. Nothing at all.'

'I see,' Dr Jones said with an expression that indicated she understood a lot more than Elena was giving. 'There's no shame in this, really. You were simply trying to survive, and fifty-six days is a significant period of time. Things change. Priorities change, and you won't be the first person to have developed positive feelings for the person that held you. Especially after such a long period of time.'

'But that man was evil, pure evil. Why would I develop an emotional attachment to him? And why would I protect a man who is dead?'

'But perhaps we're not talking about him, are we, Elena.' Dr Jones said gently. 'I'm wondering if there's anything you'd like to share about one of the other captors. You said that there was more than one person there, in the house. Someone who is responsible for what you went through. Someone who is still out there.'

Panic rose within her and she felt smothered by it. 'Really, I can't do this,' she snapped as she sat forwards in her chair. 'You don't know what happened, and you can't possibly know how I feel.'

'Well, that's true, and that's exactly why

I'm here. You do look to be in some turmoil, and I think you'd benefit from exploring your feelings. Stockholm syndrome is a common–'

'No, you're wrong and you're not listening to me,' Elena spluttered as she stood and began to pace the room. 'I don't want to know what you've got to say. Ever. I don't care about a stupid syndrome, and I don't need your help.'

'Elena, please calm down, I'm only here to help you. Why don't you sit down? We can take as much time as you need.'

'Don't tell me to calm down. I don't need to talk or explore my feelings, and I don't want you here. I really think you should leave. Now.'

Dr Jones nodded, took out a small card from her folder, and stood. 'Okay, I can see that you're distressed, and I don't want to add to that in any way. It's clear that this was all a little too much so soon after your release. I'll go now, but here's my card. If you change your mind and wish to discuss this with me, I can be contacted on those numbers. Anytime. The same goes for DS McAllister too, should you wish to discuss anything further with him.'

Elena snatched the card from Dr Jones, just to get rid of her, and watched as she left the room. When she was alone, she ripped the card into tiny pieces and tossed them into the bin.

It took the best part of two hours for Elena to calm herself following her disastrous meeting with the counsellor. She sat in her room, the white card in the back pocket of her jeans, with decisions to make, and she realised that, in addition to everything else, she had also become institutionalised; letting people tell her when to eat, when to shower, and when to sleep. There had been no need to think, and now she was expected to make these decisions for herself – things that used to be so easy but now so daunting. She couldn't even think about how she would tackle her parents.

The door knocked again, and Elena groaned and dropped her head into her hands. 'It's like Piccadilly Circus around here,' she hissed. 'Yes!' she shouted.

She looked up as Charlotte poked her head around the door, and it changed everything.

'Hello, Lena. Now not a good time?'

'Charlotte! Come in,' Elena said and jumped up. 'You've no idea how glad I am to see you.'

She hugged her friend tightly and found that she couldn't let go. This is what she wanted – plain, simple comfort. Something she didn't get from Adam or her own mother, and she began to cry.

'Hey, calm down,' Charlotte soothed as she took Elena's hand and sat with her on the bed.

Elena rambled on through her tears, sharing details about the betrayal of her parents, how she nearly died because of it, and the fact that she had nowhere to go, not able to return to her home.

'Bloody hell, Lena,' Charlotte said, hugging her close. 'I can't begin to imagine how awful it must have been. But listen to me, it's over and you'll stay with me for as long as you want and I guarantee they won't bother you, if you don't want them to.'

'That sounds perfect, thank you.' Elena sniffed as relief calmed her. 'The doctor's visiting today with a view to discharging me, and I can't wait to step outside, but I'm a little terrified too.'

'Well, it's lucky I'm here. Let's get your stuff together right away, so we're ready to go.'

They packed up her things. She called her parents and Adam to let them know what she was doing. Adam was surprised that she hadn't chosen him, but she side-stepped the argument by saying that he was just too busy to have to cope with the added pressure of taking care of her. And he accepted it, for now. Her parents were a different matter. They were not happy at all. Her mother asked when she would visit as they had so much to discuss, but Elena didn't care. They had all but abandoned her, she'd see them when she was ready.

The doctor visited and confirmed that he was happy with her medical progress and agreed that she was well enough to go home. The nurse gave her some painkillers and information leaflets that Elena felt were no more than a generic guide on how to look after your mental health, but she took them anyway. She kept the pretty pink flowers too, tucking them gently under her arm.

'You take care, my dear,' the nurse said as she gathered Elena into a hug.

'Thank you for looking after me,' Elena said, holding on tight for a moment longer.

Hesitantly, she took hold of Charlotte's arm and stepped out into her beloved sunshine.

\*\*\*

Charlotte's garden apartment, a conversion of a large Victorian house, was homely and familiar. Elena relaxed the moment she stepped over the threshold, but despite the familiarity, there was no denying the sense that being here now, everything was different.

Charlotte took Elena's bag from her hand. 'Make yourself at home. Pootle is around here somewhere,' she said as she disappeared down the hall to the spare room.

Elena wandered into the living room, calling out for the cat. She checked the windowsill and the sofa back – favourite places that Pootle liked to inhabit – and soon enough the cat flap clattered and he appeared, a flash of tortoiseshell. His tail high, he mewed and purred, hopeful for food, but she kidded herself it was because he was pleased to see her. She ran her hand down the length of him from head to tail and waited as he turned and let her repeat the process.

'Are you allowed wine?' Charlotte asked as she walked past them, smiling at their little reunion. She continued through to the kitchen, and to the fridge, pulling out a bottle of white.

'Who knows, but if you're opening a bottle, I will have a glass,' Elena said. 'No better way to celebrate my freedom than inappropriate quantities of alcohol, I guess.'

'No better way at all,' Charlotte agreed. 'And I am on it.'

Elena followed her through to the kitchen and sat at the table. Charlotte poured.

'Thanks, Charlotte. You don't know how much all this means to me. It's normality, sanity, and I need that. I really do.'

She took her first sip of crisp, cold wine and let it linger in her mouth before she swallowed.

Charlotte faltered and placed her glass down. 'Elena, I'm sorry, I don't want to spoil your mood, but I can't tell you how awful it was. I can't believe I nearly lost you. I don't know what I'd do without you,' she said, her voice cracking with emotion.

Elena sighed and reached out to give an empathetic squeeze of her arm. Another reminder of how horrifying it must have been for everyone on the outside; helpless and waiting for news.

Charlotte looked into her glass, swirling its contents before continuing. 'I couldn't get any information from anyone. Adam rarely returned my calls, but I guess he had his own circle of hell to deal with. So I only got fragmented snippets from your mum whenever she could take my call.'

'I'm so sorry,' Elena said. 'It seems my parents crumbled under the pressure in every way.'

Charlotte gave Elena a sideways glance, and it was clear she had a question of her own.

'It's okay, Charlotte. Ask me what you like,' she said, helping her along.

Charlotte smiled with a sheepish expression. 'I just wondered how it was, you know, being captive like that?'

'What do you want to know?' Elena said.

'All of it,' Charlotte said immediately but held up her hand. 'Only if you're up to it though. I mean, I don't want to push you.'

'It's fine, of course I'll tell you. But let's grab the bottle first because it's going to take a while.'

Elena began, sharing details from the moment she was abducted, her illness, and the awfulness of Cigarettes to the moment she was released. The only detail she omitted was him, her captor. Charlotte listened keenly, absorbing every detail, her only reaction a lifted eyebrow or widened eyes and the odd murmur of support.

'Oh my God, Elena. You must have been terrified,' she said with a shake of her head once Elena was finished.

Elena nodded. 'I was. All the time. And something like that changes you. I feel nothing at that man's death. Nothing at all. He had it coming and deserved exactly what he got.'

Charlotte nodded, a flicker of discomfort in her eyes.

A wave of sadness moved through Elena's soul. For the first time, they had a gulf between them. An ordeal that was beyond Charlotte's comprehension or understanding. Elena didn't blame her for it and realised that this was something she was going to have to get used to. To be different from the rest, to be altered. But knowing it created an isolation that wrapped itself around her, separating her from everyone she knew.

'As I said, something like that changes you,' she said quietly.

'Have you spoken to your father at all?' Charlotte asked.

'No, not once. You know about his absence at the hospital, and it's been that way since. No contact at all. How fucked up is that?' Elena took another sip of wine. 'I need answers, I really do, but I can't face either of them right now, and they're not beating down my door to see me either, so I'm guessing I'm probably too much for them to handle right now.'

Her bruise twanged, and she put her hand to it without thinking.

'Did he hurt you a lot?' Charlotte asked.

'Yes, he did, but it could have been so much worse,' Elena said as she glanced at her friend's troubled expression. 'And I survived. That's what matters.' She removed her hand and inhaled deeply. 'Anyway, that's enough of ordeals and dysfunctional families,' she said with a smile as she fought the gloom that was creeping into her. 'How's Jake?'

'Oh, he's fine. A chilled-out dude apparently,' Charlotte said, picking up on the change in Elena. 'But skiing in Austria with the boys will do that for you,' she said as she rolled her eyes in mock exasperation. Jake was more likely to walk over hot coals than let a boys' jolly pass him by. Elena smiled, knowing Charlotte didn't mind, despite the eye-rolling. 'Speaking of cool dudes, have you seen Adam?'

Elena spluttered and gulped down her wine before she decorated the kitchen with it.

Charlotte knew him well. He was self-assured, with more than enough money in the bank, but a 'cool dude' he was not and never would be.

'Yes, he came to the hospital,' Elena said with a sigh.

'Hmm. He was so worried about you. He must be thrilled to have you back.'

'Yes, he made a good show of it.'

Charlotte eyed her. 'Oh. Is everything okay on that score?'

'I don't know. I feel so differently now. I can't bear him anywhere near me, you know, intimately.'

'But you've only just come out of the hospital,' Charlotte said, confused. 'Why would you worry about that?'

Elena twisted the stem of her wine glass between her fingers. 'Well, he got a little carried away. Told me how much he missed me, and then wanted to… you know.'

Charlotte held her hands up. 'Whoa there, lady! Back up a little. You mean to tell me that he visited you last night and expected sex, in a hospital bed?'

The fire rose in Charlotte's green eyes, and Elena could have hugged her.

'Yep, and it would have happened too, if I hadn't put a stop to it.'

'I just don't believe it,' Charlotte fumed. 'Bloody hell.'

'It's fine, Charlotte,' she said with a smile. 'He backed off and apologised. He was an idiot, but this is difficult, for all of us. We're all full of pent-up emotions and his just came out like that. No big deal.'

'Hmm, well I think you're being very gracious, and if you need time on that score, you take it. Don't rush anything,' Charlotte said as she poured more wine. 'He'll cope.'

The sense of gloom within Elena had now morphed into a black cloud, hovering over her and seeming to suck all of the air out of the room. She couldn't breathe, took big gulps of air, and fanned her top. 'Is it getting hot in here or is it me? Should we open a window? Maybe we should open a window. Maybe I should have more wine? Or water. Yes, maybe water.'

Charlotte gently placed her hand over Elena's. 'It's okay, honey. Take a minute. You're quite safe here.'

Elena nodded and calmed herself as Charlotte rose from the table to open the large sash window above the kitchen sink. She took a glass from the cupboard and filled it with water, placing it down in front of Elena.

When Elena's heart rate steadied, she took a sip.

'You've been through so much. Do you want to talk some more?' Charlotte said as she brushed some of Elena's hair over her shoulder.

Elena shrugged. 'No, not really. I'm just so tired,' she said, her voice wavering. 'I haven't slept properly in such a long time.' Tears stung her eyes. 'And even now, I can't seem to rest, however much I try, what with the nightmares and my mind buzzing with flashbacks.'

'Come here,' Charlotte soothed as she wrapped her arm around her. 'What you've been through is unimaginable. All these feelings are bound to be expected. You're putting too much pressure on yourself. It's only been a day or so, and you've done so well already. You're out of the hospital, getting on with your life again. It might take a bit of time, but things will improve.'

Elena looked at her. 'But what if it doesn't?'

Charlotte gave a sympathetic smile. 'What do you mean?'

'What if I never feel free?'

'But you are free. You need to focus only on that.'

'No, I'm not,' Elena said.

'Yes, you are,' Charlotte replied. 'No one is stopping you from doing *anything*. You could walk out of that door right now. Do exactly what you want, with whomever you want, and there is no one to stop you.'

'Exactly,' Elena murmured under her breath.

'What?'

'Nothing. Look, I hear what you're saying. I know I can do what I like, but I still *feel* trapped,' she said as she gently tapped her fingers against her heart. 'Do you know what I mean? I survived, but there's no happiness. There's no release of emotion. There's nothing, actually. I feel nothing, only numb.'

'Oh, honey.'

'And I'm suffocating, here in the open air.

Everything is wrong. Everything out there is too loud and too busy. Life, people, crowds. So many people. It's… intimidating.'

Charlotte rubbed Elena's arm.

'It's always there,' Elena continued. 'The experience. The memories. I know it doesn't make sense to you, but I just want to feel safe again. It's all I want… I just want…' She stopped herself.

'What, honey? What do you want?' Charlotte asked.

Elena opened her mouth to speak. Part of her wanted to tell her friend everything, to let all her feelings spill out of her mouth in one incoherent stream, but she stopped herself before any words were spoken. It was too dangerous and too much of a risk to ruin everything by a hurried confession, just to ease her mind.

Charlotte glanced down at Elena's hands, temporarily pausing the conversation. Elena looked down too and saw her hands gripped tight into fists, her skin stretched and knuckles white. It was only then that the sharp pain of nails digging into skin struck her senses. She released them and smiled. *I'm not crazy. I'm not crazy.*

With a kind expression, Charlotte took hold of Elena's hands and turned them carefully to check that no skin was broken.

'I just want to be me again,' Elena whispered.

'But you *are* still you, beautiful,' Charlotte said as she held Elena's hands in her own. 'This doesn't have to define you.'

'Doesn't it?'

'No, you're you, and you have your family, and me, and Adam. When he's not being a prick. We can help you feel better. And it will get better, honey, just give it time.'

Elena smiled, but it didn't help to ease her mind as a tear slipped out and rolled down her cheek.

*There's only one person who can help me, and he's not here.*

'Perhaps you should consider visiting the counsellor? It might help with your emotions, or lack of them, when you've had a bit more time?' Charlotte said.

'No,' she said quickly. 'I don't need their help, and that's not going to change.' She pulled her hands out from Charlotte's hold.

Charlotte smiled, but concern still shone in her eyes. 'Are you sure, Elena? These people can help you heal.'

'Stop the wound healing more like,' Elena muttered. 'Pulling it open to examine every last part of it. I really don't want, or need, people picking through the ashes of my emotions. They want to put me into a neat little box of what they think I should feel, making me at best the victim and, at worst, a new case study. I'm not sure I want that kind of help, not from them. It's too hard.'

'I'm sure it wouldn't be like that.'

'But don't you see, this was my experience, Charlotte. So I have to figure this stuff out for myself.'

'But honey, these people are trained to help you. You don't have to be alone with this.'

Elena nodded and looked away, not wanting Charlotte to see the turmoil in her eyes. 'I just need some time.'

'I get the picture,' Charlotte said, backing off now. 'You have to do things your own way. And there's no pressure or judgement here, so let's park this conversation for now. You've been through enough.' She reached for the wine. 'I suggest that I cook you the dinner of your choice and we drink this. After that, we're going to watch a couple of movies and eat plenty of chocolate and popcorn. We'll wrap ourselves in blankets and crash out on the sofa. These worries can bother us another day. What do you say to that?'

Elena managed a smile, even though her heart hung heavy in her chest. 'I say bring it on.'

# CHAPTER 15

'Lena, wait!' Adam shouted as he hurriedly paid the taxi driver.

Elena rushed to the entrance of Adam's building. 'Leave me alone,' she cried as she pushed open the door.

He caught her up as she pushed the button for the lift and swiped away the tears on her cheeks.

'Why the drama?' he asked, exasperated, as they both stepped inside. 'I thought it would be nice, that's all.'

'What, parading me around your work colleagues and friends like an exhibition piece?' she said as she jabbed at the door button. 'Elena the survivor. I don't think so.'

The lift pinged at his floor, and she strode out towards his apartment.

'Look I'm sorry about the surprise party, and I only did it because I knew you wouldn't agree to the idea of a normal party, but people wanted to see you. To celebrate.'

'Of course I wouldn't have agreed to it,' she cried. 'I couldn't have imagined anything worse. I agreed to you taking me out tonight because you said we'd have dinner and I thought that would be nice. Something normal.'

He thrust his key into the lock and let her in. 'Lena, it's been two weeks, and I'm really glad you agreed to come and stay with me, but you really do need to move on with your life. I just thought this would be a good place to start.'

'Move on? Move on!' she yelled as she tossed her clutch bag on to the sofa. 'Do you know how hard I'm trying to keep it all together right now?'

He moved to her and held her shoulders. 'Of course I do, but at some point things do have to get back to normal.'

Watching his frustration, she began to cry. 'You don't know what it was like. So many people with so many questions. And all your work colleagues too. People I hardly know asking me the most personal of questions.' She didn't mention the only reason she retreated to the toilets was because of an impending panic attack that only subsided once she was within the peace of a cubicle. 'God, it was awful.'

'Yes, I can see how overwhelming that would've been, I suppose,' he said as he pulled her close. 'But please stop crying now.'

She stared at him. 'I am overwhelmed every single day. And why did you not think to invite any of my friends?' Elena said, crossing her arms tightly. 'Life out there is busy and loud, and I'm struggling. Charlotte's support would have helped me so much.'

'Shh,' he soothed impatiently. 'Just calm

down.'

She shook her head. 'I just can't understand why you would think it was a good idea.'

'All right, Lena, I get it. It was a terrible idea,' he snapped.

He stopped, collected himself, and she used the moment to do the same. She wasn't sure she believed him but had little energy to decide if he'd deliberately chosen to push her out of her self-imposed exile, or if he genuinely believed this was a good idea.

'I just thought it would be nice,' he said with a shrug. 'A chance for you to dress up a little and take your mind off everything by meeting new people.'

'Didn't do you any harm either, did it,' she muttered, remnants of anger still bubbling inside.

'Now what do you mean?'

'I saw the nice little chat you were having with your boss. I saw the pat on your back. So, you're the supportive partner *and* the highest achiever at work. Well done. Lots of brownie points there, eh, Adam?'

He rolled his eyes. 'Elena, you really need to get a grip now.'

'Do I?'

'Yes, you do,' he said, frustration furrowing his brow. 'This can't go on.'

'What do you mean?'

'Well, it's clear you're still struggling

psychologically...'

*Nothing to do with having you for a boyfriend, then?*

'So what do you suggest?' she asked. 'Seeing as how you seem to have all the answers.'

'Well, an update from the police might be a start.'

'I'm still waiting to hear. McAllister said he would be in touch.'

'Well, I suggest you chase that up because once the case is closed, it'll mean it's all over and a step closer to getting back to normal. Then this can stop being so... I don't know... so hard.'

'Hard?' she snapped. 'Oh, I'm so sorry this is so hard for you, Adam. I'm sorry what an inconvenience this has been for you.'

'Damn it, Lena!' he yelled. 'That's not what I meant.'

'But you see, I couldn't worry about what you'd be feeling,' she continued, not listening. 'I was too terrified that I wasn't going to survive it. On top of all that, I have to contend with the fact that my own father decided against paying a ransom. So, I'm sorry if all that has been hard on you, but believe me, it's been considerably harder for me. But you wouldn't know because you don't care how I'm feeling.'

'Yes, I do!' he spat.

'No, Adam, you don't. You care about what your friends think, what your boss thinks, but not me. Not the person at the centre of this. You just want to protect your brand, but please enlighten me if I've got that wrong.' She exhaled, attempting to let the anger out with it.

'Oh, please. Stop being so dramatic,' he muttered coldly.

'After what I've been through tonight, I can be whatever the hell I like.'

They both stood in frosty silence, the room electric with the anger that radiated from them both.

She rubbed her temples, trying to ease another headache that threatened as he watched, brooding in the temporary respite of anger.

'I can't do this,' she said with a sigh, stepping out of her heels and striding towards his bedroom.

'So you're going to run away, is that it?'

'I'm going to get changed, that's what I'm doing. And I think it's probably for the best. Get some time out.'

'Fine,' he muttered behind her.

She kept her pace. She hadn't wanted to come and stay with him, but his endless requests had worn her down. He wanted her with him, that's what he'd told her, but he spent most of his time at work, leaving her alone in his apartment with nothing but her thoughts and the choice she had to make.

She lay on the bed and listened to him clattering about in the kitchen and glanced at the door as he came into the room with two glasses of wine. He handed one to her and sat on the edge of the bed.

The distance between them now highlighted the inevitable, she knew that, but she also picked up the feeling that he knew it too. They sat together in silence, drinking the wine that neither of them wanted.

'What do you want, Lena?' he asked eventually.

She sighed. 'I don't know,' she said as she wrapped her hands around her glass. 'I need some time. This set-up isn't working, for either of us.'

He nodded.

'Maybe I should go back to Charlotte's. For now.'

'Yeah, maybe,' he muttered with a stony expression. 'I'm certainly no good for you at the moment.'

'Adam, please don't give me guilt too,' she said. 'I can't take it.'

He stood up and walked to the door. 'Okay, whatever. I'll leave you in peace. I'll be in the spare room if you need me.' He paused and turned in the doorway. 'And you know, maybe we'd feel stronger if we shared a bed again sometime soon. Do what couples do?'

She shrugged. They would never be that again, not now. 'I'm sorry.'

He nodded and reluctantly left the room.

She placed the glass down and flung herself back on the bed with a frustrated groan.

\*\*\*

She woke in an empty bed, and once she'd hauled herself out of it and into the kitchen, an empty apartment. Her phone buzzed in her clutch bag, but she made no effort to get it, not caring who it might be. Only when she had a mug of hot coffee in her hand did she grab it.

Her parents. Wanting answers, and to know when she'd visit. Still unable to face them, she decided her voicemail would take up the slack, for now.

She showered, dressed, and packed up her things. She should finish whatever was left of her relationship with Adam; she wasn't being fair. But to finish it would mean that there was nothing in the way of her other decision, and she wasn't ready for that yet either. So she listened to her conscience, which had become an annoying voice on her shoulder, telling her that she should do the right thing; she should try and make it work. So, for now, some space was what was needed. For them both.

She texted Charlotte and asked if she could go back to hers, to which Charlotte immediately replied with a 'yes'.

Relieved, she busied herself and called the concierge to request a taxi, realising she had become a nomad, living in everyone's space but her own. She didn't care. She needed to be around people – people who could keep her on the right path. Something that was becoming harder by the day. While she waited, she made some calls. The first being her boss at the museum. She said all the right things, how she just needed a little more time and then she would put it all behind her and focus on her work. All the things necessary to garner maximum sympathy and maximum time away from the monotonous distraction of work.

When she was finished, she pulled up her parents' number, paused, and then backed out. She couldn't do it, not yet.

She had just placed her bags by the door when her phone beeped again – a number she didn't recognise. Her body tensed as she gripped the phone tightly.

'Hello?'

'Hello, Elena, how are you?' McAllister asked.

'I'm fine thanks,' she said as she worked to relax her shoulders. 'Do you have news? Have you found something?'

'No, I'm afraid not,' he said and paused. 'And actually, I have to tell you that it's very likely we'll have to close our enquiries on your case.'

'Oh,' she said, surprised. Surprised that it had been so easy.

'I know, I'm as frustrated as you are,' he continued. 'We've had no further leads, and forensics have come up with nothing.'

'I see,' she said. 'Well, thank you for giving me the heads-up.'

She listened to the sounds of paper shuffling and imagined him going through the notes as they spoke.

'These people were professionals,' he continued. 'There is no other theory as to how they got the place so clean.'

She processed the information. The police had nowhere to go. The man they needed was lying in the mortuary, on the road to hell for all she cared, and there was no other evidence. It was over.

'Are you okay, Elena?' McAllister asked after a moment.

She shook her head, bringing herself back to the conversation. 'Yes. Yes, I think so. It's very disappointing, of course, but it was to be expected, I suppose.'

'You're right, it is very disappointing,' he said thoughtfully. 'But we have nothing. Absolutely nothing. That in itself is very odd.'

The tone in his voice hinted to Elena that this was a man who'd probably lived on his wits for a long time, and solved many cases from instinct and gut feeling alone. She was well aware that he didn't believe her version of events, and that there was a glaring missing link, but she wasn't ready to cave in yet. His loss was her gain. She wondered if this conversation had him gripping the phone as much as she was.

'I'm sorry that you haven't had a better outcome.'

'And you haven't given any more thought to seeing Dr Jones?' he asked. 'She really could help you, if you let her.'

His question disarmed her. 'No,' she stumbled. 'I don't think so ...'

The line was silent for a moment. 'I see. And you're sure there's nothing new you want to share with me? Anything at all?'

'No, I'm sorry, I have nothing. As I said before, I was only kept in that small room and saw very little.'

'Of course, yes, that's what you said before,' he said and sighed. 'Well, I'll be in touch again soon to confirm everything, but if you remember anything, you will call me, yes? Immediately?'

'I will. And thank you for all your help. I know this must be difficult for you.'

'Yes, and Elena–'

'Yes?'

'Just remember that people are trying to help you, if you let them. We want justice for you. Nothing else.'

'I realise that,' she whispered. 'And thank you.'

She finished the call and stumbled to the sofa, panic turning her legs to jelly. She sat, took a moment, and waited for the torrent of emotion to subside. And for her legs to carry her weight again.

When she had calmed, she wrote a note for Adam explaining where she was going, and with a strong sense that this chapter of her life was coming to an end, she picked up her bags, scanned the room, and left the apartment.

# CHAPTER 16

Elena couldn't sleep. The nightmares visited most nights and left her drained, soaked in a cold sweat, bedsheets mangled beneath her or in a heap on the floor. She'd even taken to sleeping with a light on in the hope that it would help, but it didn't. Those early hours were the worst because in that quiet time, a sense of emptiness would touch her soul. She missed him, as insane as that was, and his absence from her life demanded her attention until she was a knotted ball of anxiety.

Today was no different. She rose from her bed, pulled on some clothes, and went to the kitchen to make tea. Settling on the sofa with Pootle on her lap, she watched the sunrise, letting her mind flood with memories of him. It always came back to him. She wanted him, and she wanted the safety and protection that he offered. He could take it all away – the chaos, the noise, and the people and their constant questions. It had been just days since she'd left Adam, and although she wanted to do the right thing on that score, she was already gone, out of the relationship and ready to move on.

She pulled the little white card out from her pocket – she always kept it with her, not wanting to risk losing it – and traced her finger over the digits. The numbers jumped out at her and something deep within needed the connection again. It made her reach for her phone.

Opening a new, blank text, she hovered between blind panic and yearning. She paused, her thumb suspended above the screen. What would she say? She remembered his last words to her before he left. *Once you invite me into your life, there will be no going back.*

Faint sounds of movement in the other room brought Elena back. Looking up from her phone to see Charlotte emerge from her night's sleep, she tucked her phone and the card back into her pocket, carefully, so as not to upset the sleeping cat. Whatever she had planned to say would remain unsaid, for today.

Charlotte shuffled into the room, yawning, her flame-coloured hair tumbling down her back – a warrior queen in pink fluffy slippers and dressing gown. Pootle looked up from his sleepy daze, assessing whether he had the energy to ask for more food.

'Morning,' Charlotte sighed as she swiped her hand over Pootle's ears. 'Do you want more tea?' she asked as she grabbed the large mug at Elena's feet and walked to the kitchen. 'Although you shouldn't drink so much of the stuff. You know it won't help you relax. You need chamomile for that.'

Elena said nothing and wrinkled her nose

at the thought. She hated the taste of chamomile tea, and it did nothing for her sleep either. She struggled to see the point of it.

'I know, I know, you hate it,' Charlotte said as she slouched towards the kitchen, her slippers making muted flumps against the floor. 'But you won't sleep any better with all that caffeine rushing through your body.'

'I know, you're right,' Elena said, rubbing her hand over her forehead.

Their conversation was halted when Charlotte's phone rang out. She turned and walked back, picking it up from the table.

'Hello,' she said, putting it on to loudspeaker.

'Morning Charlotte,' Adam said into the quiet room.

Elena's stomach sank.

'Adam,' she said with surprise, 'To what do we owe this pleasure so early in the morning?'

'Thought I'd call in before work. See how you're both doing.'

She looked at Elena and held out the phone for her, but Elena silently shook her head.

'Ah, well if you want Elena, you've just missed her,' Charlotte said as she walked towards the kitchen again. 'She's in the shower.'

Elena listened, the phone still on loudspeaker.

'How is she?' he asked.

'She's someone who's been to hell and

back,' Charlotte said. 'But she's okay. When she manages to sleep.'

'And is that often?'

'Nope.'

'Well, does she have anything for that?'

'I'm not sure. I don't think so. Why?'

Adam sighed. 'I don't know, I just wondered if she'd been prescribed something by the doctors that was making her behaviour a little... strange.'

Elena raised her eyebrows at that. The cheek.

'She's not strange,' Charlotte said defensively. 'She's got a lot to work through, that's all.'

'Hmm.'

'What is it, Adam?'

'I'm not sure,' he replied after a moment. 'I want to help, but she keeps pushing me away. Everything's changed. And so has she.'

'Give her time.'

'I'm not...' he began, stumbling over his words. 'I'm not sure I can.'

'So you want to end it? Now, when she's still really vulnerable, you want to abandon her?'

Elena sat forward, straining to hear.

'I can't give her what she needs.'

'Do you *want* to give her what she needs?'

He answered Charlotte's question with silence.

'Well, you've got to do what you've got to

do,' Charlotte said, her tone clipped. 'But treat her with care, Adam. She's very fragile.'

Elena struggled to hear the muted conversation that followed, and the resounding quiet was overwhelming. So too was the desire to grab her phone and make that call. The conflict between what she wanted most and what was right no longer tugged at her conscience.

Charlotte returned, crossed the room and hugged her.

'I guess you heard most of that?'

She nodded. 'Yeah, most of it.'

'It'll be okay,' she soothed. 'He doesn't know how to handle this. Maybe a little time and space will help him work it through in his mind.'

'What if I don't care how he feels? What then?'

'Well, I think we both know what that means, don't we, honey?'

At that moment, any doubt in her mind cleared like clouds after a storm. She knew what she wanted and what she'd do. She knew exactly what she'd do. And it made him closer than ever.

\*\*\*

Elena's apartment was tidy, and now she was here she realised how much she'd missed it. Her home, mismatched and comfortable. It had the quietness and even on this early summer day, the coolness of a place that hadn't been lived in for a while, as if it had lost the energy and warmth that comes from someone living within its walls.

But that was about to change as Charlotte opened windows, letting warm air breeze in and then selected music to play from her phone. They sang a little and danced a little as they unpacked the supplies they had stopped off to buy on their way, and Elena was impressed with herself and her ability to look happy and normal when all the while the small white card lingered in her pocket.

It was late when Charlotte left, and as she climbed into a taxi, she called out instructions to phone her the moment Elena was scared or regretted her decision to be alone. Elena shut the door to her apartment, locking up with care. Of course she regretted her decision to be alone. It meant that she was free to do as she pleased with no one to stop her. And that was about to prove her downfall.

The room was quiet, except for the slow tick from the large old clock that hung from her wall. She checked her phone. One voice message – from her mother. Elena listened to the frustrated request for her to get in touch and promptly deleted it.

She paced the room. She looked down at her hands clutching the small white card, and her mind raced, surging with new energy. Maybe she had always known that this would be her decision. Maybe what she was about to do was inevitable. But everything was clear now, like the dawn of a new morning, full of clarity and light. It was a clever game he played.

He knew all along what he was doing with her. He hadn't invested so much time and energy in her to simply let her go at the end of it. No, he was never going to do that. But by his own admission, he wasn't a thug to force her either. He had to let her choose. A simple plan, because what's more powerful than free will and the ability to make your own choices in life? Nobody wants to have decisions made for them or thrust upon them. Allowing someone to make their own choice is clever reverse psychology.

Of course he could come back for her – she was certainly no match for him – but what would be the point of that? What he desired was complete and absolute surrender, on his terms, but at her choice, and if he had to wait for it, then so be it.

But now the ticking clock highlighted the movement of time, and it made her anxious. She had given it her best, but it was pointless fighting anymore. She patrolled the room, rearranging photo frames, plumping cushions on the sofa, giving herself one more chance to consider what she wanted most of all – him. And to call that number.

*It's just one call. It's just one simple call.*
...tick

*He'll never let you go. You know he'll never let you go.*

...tick
*I don't care.*
...tick
*I need him.*
...tick
*Move! Now!*

She rushed to the table, urgency filling her as she grabbed her phone and dialled the number. Three attempts. Clumsy fingers. She inhaled deeply but was unable to fill her lungs, dizzy with what she was about to do.

The phone rang three times.

'Hello, Elena,' he said, his voice composed and familiar. 'So, you finally did it. You finally called.'

The sound of his voice sent shockwaves through her.

'I…' She stumbled as the words failed to form in her tense jaw.

'Don't be afraid,' he murmured. 'Where are you now?'

'Home.'

'I see,' he said. 'And you understand what this phone call means? That I'm going to come for you now.'

'Yes,' she whispered, as still as stone.

'Good. Then I'm on my way.'

She hung up the phone and stared at it. No going back now. She wanted to scream as thrill and fear ran through her, but she was mute. So she waited and paced again as shock seeped into her.

Thirty minutes passed like hours, and the door buzzer puncturing the silence marked his arrival. One last chance to stop this, change her mind, but the thought of turning him away now was never a consideration as she dashed across the room and hit the button on the intercom with shaking hands. She released the catch on her door and stepped back from the unmistakable sound of his footfall on the stairs.

The door opened, and her eyes locked onto his immediately. She was surrounded by his power again, and it pulled her tantalisingly towards him. He looked exactly as before – his clothes, his hair, and those eyes – only now he was in her home, at her invitation. If she thought about it too much, she might lose her mind, so she ignored it, instead choosing to relish the sight of him. She'd missed him.

'You came,' she said. A pathetic statement, but she had to start somewhere.

He pushed the door closed and walked into the room, closer, but not enough to touch. 'I keep my promises, Elena.'

She wanted to go to him but hesitated. 'Am I crazy for wanting this?' she said, as the enormity of the situation hit her. 'For wanting you?' She placed her hand on the back of the sofa, steadying her trembling body.

'You're not crazy.'

'I really tried, you know. I really tried living my life, being normal. Fitting in.'

'I know how you fought it,' he said with a sincerity that proved he hadn't kept his distance. 'Just as I knew you would.'

She nodded as the deep ache within her that had been a permanent fixture since she had left him began to lift.

'I didn't like it,' he said, his eyes unfaltering. 'It took everything I had in me not to take you away. But I'm glad you did what you did, because now I know that you're sure.'

She shook her head. 'I don't know that I'll ever be sure,' she whispered. 'I only know that I don't want to feel like this anymore.'

'So don't fight it,' he murmured. 'I can help you. I can take away your pain.'

She hesitated, and although she tried to speak, no more words came.

She watched as he took one step towards her, then another, and another, her heart racing as he moved closer. When he reached out and encircled her hand with his own, she flinched, her breath catching in her throat from the feel of his skin. He smiled at her reaction and pulled her firmly towards him.

And that was it. It was done. The connection was made, never to be broken.

Her legs threatened to give way as she fought to keep control of her own body. He was inches from her now, the warmth exuding from him. Just as before.

'It's okay,' he said softly, his eyes on her mouth and the small gasp that escaped as their bodies touched. 'Don't try to make sense of it yet. You need answers, and I can do that. I'll give you all the answers you need.'

Taking her face in his hands he gently caressed her cheeks with his thumbs. She didn't flinch but let herself be drawn towards him as she slipped into his gaze and his control, happy to give in to it. Everything was so much better when she did. His mouth was enticingly close, and she ached for the feel of his lips against hers again.

He didn't make her wait, and with eyes alive with desire, he pressed his mouth to hers. Instantly, her body sparked into life, craving him too, and she responded to his kiss; exploring, tasting, teasing.

He held her, controlled her, and with his hands on her back now, he pulled her closer, his fingers digging into her skin. Her body reacted like it would any other drug it had been deprived of, becoming quickly intoxicated as her heart raced blood through her veins. Tension filled her. She hungered for more and snaked her arms around his neck, drawing him in as the need between them intensified.

They hurried, their tender kiss transforming into something urgent and demanding. She up and wrapped her legs around his burying her hands in his hair as he held her and strode towards her bedroom. As he did, the sane part of her mind began to compartmentalise.

*I'll put this moment here. I'll deal with this later. I'll make sense of this another time.*

Right now, she could only give in to it, nothing more.

He dropped her down onto her bed, their kisses eager, hungry, as they tugged at clothing, wanting to be free of their constraints. Wanting skin on skin.

His mouth moved to her neck with expert skill, his tongue circling, and teeth nipping at her skin. Her groans of pleasure encouraged him on as he found the soft curve of her breast, the smooth skin of her stomach and lower still to her soft warmth. He lingered; tasting her, teasing her, killing her softly, because she was sure she'd die from the sensation. She arched her back, yearning, offering herself to him and let her eyes close, to become lost in the moment and the soft scent of his cologne. It wasn't love, she knew that, but it was a need, and one that refused to be ignored.

He moved over her, holding his weight as his dark eyes devoured her. She wanted it all and ran her hands up his back, feeling the tense muscles beneath.

Impatient now, she pulled him closer,

wanting him, needing him.

Locked in each other's gaze, her heart hammered in her chest as he plundered her mouth, smothering her gasp with his kiss as he sank himself deep inside her. His groan vibrated against her lips as he took possession, covering her body with his, snaking his arm under her back to hold her close. Finally, he released her mouth and she tipped her head back, needing air, needing respite from the assault of sensations. Her hands reached out, grasped at pillows, a desperate attempt to hold on to something in a world that was falling apart.

She felt the tension build quickly as they moved together, the intensity of their desire and need unhidden. Wrapping her legs around him, she urged him on, seeking the release that hovered so close. 'Don't stop,' she sighed. 'Please don't stop.'

He obliged and pushed deeper, his hands entwined with hers, his mouth close to her ear. 'I'll never stop,' he murmured, moving rhythmically, his words and body claiming her. 'But you know that, don't you.'

She nodded, in no doubt, and cried out as her body shuddered, crashing into an oblivion of pleasure.

Addicted and lost, something was torn up and rewritten in her mind. But she didn't care what it meant to her sanity because, now, she knew she would never be the same again.

## CHAPTER 17

Morning arrived too quickly, the early light breaking Elena's slumber. She stirred, stretched out her sated body and enjoyed the feeling. She kept her eyes closed, not wanting to open them and let the world in just yet. She only wanted to revel in the sensations.

She understood everything now. Why it had to be this way. He'd made her his from the day they first collided, all those moons ago in the coffee shop, but if they had done this during her captivity it would have meant nothing. It would have been marked by the occasion, but this was something separate. Something new and savage, with lightning intensity. But real.

Lazily reaching out, she expected her hand to meet warm skin, but there was nothing, only cold, empty space. Stomach lurching, her eyes shot open. She sat upright, but before panic had time to take hold, her eyes fell on him. Sitting in the armchair in the corner of her room, dressed only in his jeans, and his leg hitched up over his knee, his eyes were locked on her. Her breath caught in her throat at the sight, his presence powerful in her room.

'Good morning,' he said, as casual as he looked.

'Good morning,' she replied. 'How very civil we are in the light of day.' She smiled and ran her hand through her hair to try and tame it, causing new sensations to run through her sensitive fingertips, every part of her alive and electric.

'Indeed.' His eyes never left hers.

'I thought you'd gone.'

'I'm not going anywhere. I told you that last night,' he said as he slowly rubbed his finger over his bottom lip.

She was transfixed. How could such a simple gesture quicken her pulse as it had? She wanted those lips that now knew every part of her body on her again.

'Would you care to share your name with me, then?' she asked. 'Or will you forever be my captor?'

'I think we can move on from that, don't you?' he mused with a dark, half-smile. 'My name is Ethan.'

She studied him. 'Ethan.'

It suited him well, and now she knew it, the connection between them became stronger. Ethan, the man who had altered her so completely. Somehow, he'd made her matter at a time when no one cared. And in a life where so few had ever put her first, she had responded.

'Would you have missed me if I had gone?'

'Yes, I would,' she said. 'You know the effect you have on me.'

'I do.'

He rose from the chair, walked towards her, and sat on the edge of the bed. A little bubble of anticipation danced within her as he leant his arm across her, dominating the space.

'Last night,' she said. 'Me and you. Where do we go from here?'

'Well, we can carry on doing this,' he said, leaning in to kiss her. 'You can let me satisfy your every need.'

She let out an appreciative sigh as he moved down to nuzzle her neck. 'The counsellor would have me in therapy forever if she knew what we're doing. Not to mention my father. He'd have me institutionalised.'

'They've got to find out about us first.'

'Even if they did, I don't care.'

'That's good,' he said as he moved over her, guiding her back against the pillow. 'Because it was time for you to make up your mind. I was getting impatient.'

Her body began to stir. 'I always wanted this,' she murmured, looking up at him. 'But I had to be sure.'

His eyes darkened. 'I know. But now you understand what this means; that I'm not going anywhere.'

With her heart pounding, she nodded.

'Because I've broken a hundred laws to be with you, Elena,' he said. 'And I'd happily break a hundred more to keep you.'

He placed his lips on hers, his kiss soft and warm, and she arched her back, the contact of skin on skin causing every nerve ending to tingle.

He pulled away, his eyes twinkling with satisfaction. 'What do you want?'

'You, Ethan,' she said. 'And then I want answers. You said you could give me that.'

'I can,' he said. 'And will.'

'Good,' she whispered, shifting her body beneath him, ready to invite him in. 'Now, kiss me again.'

\*\*\*

With great effort, Elena dragged herself from her bed and into the kitchen, needing coffee. Anything to give a sense of normality in her new world. She flipped the switch of the kettle and found the croissants she'd bought with Charlotte yesterday, laying them out on a plate.

Ethan joined her and leant against the counter watching as she scooped instant coffee into two mugs and filled them with hot water and a little milk.

'I don't know if you even like coffee,' she said as she handed him a mug.

'I do,' he said. 'And that looks pretty good to me.'

She smiled and grabbed a pastry, toying with it, not quite ready to eat it. She regretted nothing, but the cold light of day brought with it a host of implications from the actions of the night before.

'I can see it, Elena,' he said as he reached for a pastry.

'What?'

'You, thinking. Your mind is racing.'

It felt surreal to discuss this now. She didn't want to break whatever spell they had created last night and was suddenly self-conscious in her own skin.

'Last night,' she said as she swept her hair behind her ear. 'We didn't use any protection.'

He smiled and took a bite of the pastry. 'No, we didn't. So?'

'So, aren't you worried about little things like accidental conception or other... health issues?'

Pregnancy wasn't a worry for her. A contraceptive implant had sorted that after a night out six months into her relationship with Adam. Both reckless with the effects of alcohol, he'd persuaded her to forget the protection, just that once. She'd always wanted children, but in the future, long into the future, and when she was two weeks late, she was consumed with anxiety at the possibility that one wholly forgettable night might have resulted in a baby and a change of direction in her life. The day her period finally did arrive, she'd taken herself to the doctor to have a contraceptive implant fitted immediately, vowing never to get in that position again.

Ethan chuckled. 'Are you blushing?'

'No,' she countered, feeling the heat in her cheeks. 'But for someone who appears to like control in his life, it seems odd that you wouldn't consider the implications of babies in all of this. Unless that's what you want – me, confined and dependent on you, raising our children, the fruits of this strange relationship?'

'You don't need to worry,' he said, still finding amusement in the conversation. 'Even I realise a baby in this scenario would be fucked up. But I also knew it wasn't a risk.'

'How?'

'Because I checked your records.'

'Oh.'

'I needed to know as much as I could about you before you were captured; if you had any life-threatening medical conditions, stuff like that, and that's when I saw you had an implant.' His eyes roamed over the contours of her body. 'And that you're in good health.'

She stared at him, dumbfounded.

'I know, I know, a massive invasion of privacy,' he said. 'And I'll explain more about that later, but right now, I'm sensing that babies are not really the issue here, are they.'

She tried hard to hold on to her indignation but was unable to. 'I guess not.'

'No, so what you really want to know is whether I've just passed on a host of nasty diseases to you. Is that right?'

She kept his gaze. 'So… have you?'

'Of course I haven't,' he assured. 'My body is as clean as a whistle. You have no worries there.' He drank his coffee. 'Not so sure about my soul though.'

She nodded and raised her mug to her lips. 'That we can agree on.'

'Glad we're on the same page.'

'So where do we go from here?' she asked, calmer now.

He put his mug down and went to her, placing his hands on the countertop either side of her waist, any personal space invaded.

'We go to mine.'

She raised her eyes to his. 'Yours?'

'Yes, that's right. What do you think about that?'

'I think it sounds dangerous.'

'Perhaps.'

'Why do we need to leave here?' she asked, butterflies dancing in her stomach.

'Well, apart from wanting you in my space, you have many questions that need to be answered, and that'll be easier to do at mine.'

She considered it, nerves and desire mingling together.

He smiled at her hesitation. 'Question is, are you brave enough to trust me?'

The caffeine swirled around her system, giving her energy and an unfounded sense of confidence. 'Okay, whatever you want.'

'Hmm, you'd better be careful with comments like that,' he murmured under his breath.

'And why's that?'

'Because I might decide to keep you there,' he said, his eyes on hers, like a hawk about to take its prey.

\*\*\*

Ethan waited in his car outside her building, its engine running, watching her shut the heavy front door and make her way down the steps. She had guessed the car would be impressive, quality, and she was right – a black Audi SUV with tinted windows, the driver's side down.

She joined him and buckled up, tucking a bag with a few of her things between her feet. A smile of satisfaction curled his lips as he snaked into the traffic, taking her away from everything that was familiar to her.

He glanced at her. 'Are you nervous?'

'Me, nervous? Of what exactly? Of you taking me somewhere unknown?' She laughed. 'Come on, Ethan, we've been there and done that. I'm not sure nervous is the word I'd use for me right now.' She turned and looked at him. 'Crazy, maybe.'

'I like crazy,' he said.

'I bet you do.'

He placed his hand on her thigh, and she recognised it for the possessive action it was. It didn't bother her and she made herself comfortable in the deep, black leather seat, the car's interior as equally impressive as its exterior.

They headed south, towards the Thames, and soon they were driving through Blackfriars underpass and picking up signs for Royal Docklands. She knew the area reasonably well; she and Adam had found a few restaurants there when he was looking for a place of his own. Working in Canary Wharf meant that Adam had considered all of the surrounding area until he settled on a place in Marsh Wall. Apprehension crept in about the implications of him being so close by. They were over long before she had chosen Ethan and she was content with that, but at the same time she'd behaved a little shabbily, not yet officially ending their relationship. *It's okay. I'll deal with it, like everything else. Baby steps, Elena.*

It wasn't long before Ethan was driving down into a cavernous car park under a large dockside block of apartments. They had arrived, and butterflies began to dance in her stomach again as the realisation of what she'd agreed to suddenly hit her, and the potentially dangerous situation she now found herself. She'd let him take her away from her life, everything that was safe and familiar to her, without anyone's knowledge. She was alone with him, and silently prayed she was right to trust him, that this wasn't some charade to take her away again, captive and part of a new ransom demand.

He switched off the engine and unbuckled his seatbelt. She couldn't move. Something Ethan noticed too as he calmly unbuckled her belt while she struggled to compose herself.

'It's okay, Elena,' he said as he opened his door and got out of the car.

She got out too, functioning in a daze, but soon felt an arm around her waist as Ethan guided her towards the lift bank that would take them to the apartments above.

The doors opened at the fifth floor, the very top of the building, and they walked the length of a white-walled corridor, with wooden beams crisscrossing the ceiling, until they came to a pale wooden door. He unlocked it and gestured for her to step inside.

She glanced around warily, her heart pumping, and took a step back. 'Wait. I just need a minute.'

He saw her hesitation and reached out to touch her arm. 'This is just my place, that's all.'

She nodded, took a breath, and stepped into a large open plan room of white-washed walls, broken up by exposed brickwork running down the length of the room to her left. Industrial-style metal windows punctured the brick and highlighted the river view below, giving a clue to the history of this former warehouse. Wooden A-frame beams ran across the ceiling, exposing the original roof space, making it open and light. A couple of white low-back sofas sat in front of her, and behind them, in the far corner of the room, was a large modern kitchen. To the left of the kitchen was a dining table and glazed double doors leading to a small balcony. The simplistic mix of white and pale wood dominated the space and she was surprised at how welcoming it was.

'This is really nice,' she murmured, cautiously taking it in.

'Take a look around,' he offered as he threw his keys into the small bowl on the side table by the door.

She did just that. Hesitantly at first, she wandered down the corridor to the right of the living room, with matching wooden doors and a soft, cream carpet. She checked out the two bedrooms, the bathroom, and a gym – all with white walls, exposed brickwork, and the same airy pitched ceilings.

The final room at the end of the corridor housed a large desk jammed with computer screens, laptops, tablets, and multiple mobile phones. A nest of leads and wires littered the floor and rectangular black boxes with flashing lights of green and red stood to attention on the carpet. The puzzle was becoming clearer as to how he had obtained her records.

*Better get used to this Elena, because this is part of your life now. You need answers, and he's the one that can give them to you.*

A vintage office swivel chair sat in front of the desk, its wood worn and brown leather faded – a relic of another time – and large canvasses of iconic city skylines hung from the walls. It was a masculine space and it was clear that this was his home. She relaxed her taut shoulders. There was no threat here, no second attempt at abduction that she could see. She had been right to trust him, he'd been true to his word.

She turned and locked eyes with him as he leant against the door frame, his arms folded, relaxed.

'So, this is my office,' he said.

'So I can see,' she said as she glanced over the laptops and tablets. His little enigmas. 'Just how many devices does one man need in order to do whatever it is that you do?'

'It'll all become clear, don't worry.'

'I'm counting on it,' she said as she wandered along the desk trailing her finger over the surface.

'I'm very impressed that you allowed me to bring you here,' he said as he watched her move.

'That's because I continue to trust you.'

'Dangerous.'

'I know,' she said, spinning the chair around to face him.

'So what now, Elena?'

'Well, now I'm here, I think I'd like to know a little of your history,' she said, taking a seat. 'Especially as it's clear you know all of mine.'

'What do you want to know?'

'Everything,' she said, glancing at the screens before turning back to him.

'Okay,' he said. 'Whatever you want.'

# CHAPTER 18

'I gain information. Important, sensitive information,' Ethan said as he grabbed another chair from the corner of the room and joined Elena. 'And I can access and disrupt communication systems around the world as and when I choose.'

She sat back in her chair and rested her elbows against the arms, listening quietly as her heart thundered in her chest.

'Have you heard of a movement called Anonymous?' he asked.

She shook her head.

'They're cyber activists who have the ability to hack into major corporations and government agency sites globally, and they regularly do. They have the power to disrupt, to shut down or compromise sites for the sake of a particular cause, and think nothing of releasing personal information of their targets. They're viewed both as freedom fighters or terrorists, depending on which side of the fence you sit.'

'Are you in this group?' she asked.

'Not really, and nothing I'd ever openly admit to. I've dabbled here and there when I've felt the need, if there's been a cause that was important to me. But it's a dangerous business, they're unpredictable and there have been several arrests from linked activity within the group, so the least amount of involvement I have the better. I'm not ready to spend time at Her Majesty's pleasure just yet.'

'Wise choice,' she said. 'But why are you telling me all of this?' she asked. 'Aren't I a risk?'

'No, because I can trust you. I know you didn't talk to McAllister about me.'

She gasped. 'Oh my God, you're telling me you hacked the Metropolitan Police computer systems.'

He smiled. 'I'm merely demonstrating that like Anonymous, I can gain access pretty much wherever I want, to get whatever information I want.'

'Well, the access to my medical records now makes sense, if still a little shocking,' she mused. 'But why would you do this, Ethan?'

'I provide a service,' he said. 'There's plenty of dodgy celebrities, politicians or high-ranking officials with many, many secrets or bad deeds to hide. But they also have enough money and the right people to help bury their little indiscretions. We all know it goes on but the good people of the world and the media don't like that, so that's where I come in. One of my contacts might pass me data I can work with, or I might find these hidden misdeeds myself. Once I'm sure of what I've got, I let the guilty party know and then it becomes a game of how much that person wants to protect their 'brand', and how much they're prepared to pay for it. It's as simple as that.'

'So, you're on the freedom fighter side of the fence,' she said, clinging to the positives of this conversation.

'I suppose, but that doesn't make me a good person, Elena. I have the power to ruin people's lives with the information I can obtain. Information people go to great lengths to hide from the world. No one wants their reputation tarnished over the internet, but some try and play the game, thinking it'll never happen. Those people soon find out I'm a man of my word. But most of them pay up, and it's made me a lot of money.'

'But what if it's something so bad that it shouldn't be allowed to stay hidden, whatever the price?'

'Then it's non-negotiable and released immediately,' he replied. 'And anything to do with kids ends up in the inboxes of the authorities.'

'So not a completely bad person, then,' she said with a faint smile.

He didn't reply.

Her mind buzzed as she processed this information. 'Ethan, this is huge,' she said after a moment. 'And such a drastic way to make money.'

He shrugged. 'Secrets are a valuable commodity.'

'Even so,' she said. 'Nine-to-five too boring

for you?'

He laughed and ran his hand through his hair. 'I found out very early on that life likes to throw a curveball or two on occasion, and because of that, things changed very quickly for me.'

'What do you mean?' she asked. 'What happened to you?'

'Ah, well, that's a story for another time,' he said, ending that line of enquiry.

'But surely there must have been other options for you?' she asked, tucking the unanswered question into her memory.

'I'm sure there were. I had a good education and found school a breeze, but I was sixteen and damn good on a computer. I learned the basics of system programming and began writing code. Pretty soon I was getting into sites that should have been unavailable to me. It was only a game then, a bit of cat and mouse.'

She opened her mouth to speak and closed it again.

'This is a lot to take in. I get it,' he said with amusement. 'It's not all bad, I did have a legitimate career too.'

'Really?' she said, relived. 'Doing what?'

'Royal Marines. Loyally serving Queen and country.'

'Figures,' she said, her eyes scanning over his strong, muscular frame.

'I paid my dues and learned more tech

along the way.'

'But what made you want to go from legitimate to... well, I don't know what this is.'

He shrugged. 'After a decade of service, I needed something else; freedom to do what I want, when I want, and living like that costs money. So, from there it just kind of spiralled and I've never looked back. Complete independence. Who doesn't want that? And as far as anyone else is concerned, I've got a nice little property business that keeps prying eyes away from what I really do.'

She shook her head and blew out a long breath. 'I don't know what to say.'

He sat back in his chair, unbothered by her reaction. 'We've all got to make a living.'

'But this doesn't explain why you were involved in my abduction?' she said, a dull ache of tension blooming in her chest as they steered towards the root of the conversation. 'You told me that you had to be there, back at the house. Why was that? What happened?'

He scanned her face for what she was not saying, astutely picking up the change in mood.

'Elena, my work is very questionable, I know that, but I am not in the habit of abducting young women from the street. I was pulled in as punishment for hacking someone I shouldn't have; stepping on the toes of a prominent career criminal, here in London. Things got nasty when he discovered he'd been hacked and he didn't take kindly to the information I'd found on him. It was my own fault. These people were "no-go" zones, but I got greedy. I was also well aware of the resources these people would have to intercept me as I was hacking their system, but I thought I was smarter. No, scrub that, I *am* smarter, but I was unlucky. And I paid for it. Some heavies came for me, caught me off guard and roughed me up a bit. Then they gave me a choice – I could meet my maker sooner than expected, or I could do a job for their boss. An offer I couldn't refuse, so to speak,' he said, smiling at the reference.

'So who is this nasty piece of work?'

'You really want to know?'

She nodded.

'Maxim Antonovich.'

'What *the* Maxim Antonovich? Charity advocate and all-round 'good guy'?'

'The very same.'

She looked away. 'Wow. I can't believe it. His daughter, Zina, went to my school. He hosted a couple of major charity fundraisers there.'

'They're the worst, Elena, you know that.'

She nodded. 'I guess, but Zina was really sweet. We were friends for a while until she left for the Royal Ballet. We lost touch after that but I've followed her career over the years,' she said, letting the information sink in. 'But why would he want my father's money?'

'He didn't. He's got plenty of his own, believe me. No, someone had approached him, the one who *did* want your father's money, and because Maxim was controlling the job, he said he had just the person to run it. Me. I just had to lead it, keep things tidy. Keep everyone in check. And keep the transaction safe from prying eyes. Not that there was any transaction to protect in the end.'

'Tell me about it,' Elena scoffed.

'The other men and the venue? Nothing to do with me.'

'And you never met the person who wanted the money?'

'No, I didn't. No names were ever exchanged, with anyone. Only Maxim had all the details. He said it was cleaner that way, but it was just a way of keeping himself in complete control. Do you want me to stop?' he asked, sensing her growing unease.

'No, I'm fine,' she said unconvincingly. 'So you're saying that because my father didn't pay, some random unknown person is still out there. Likely to be very angry that it didn't go to plan, that they didn't get their money.'

He nodded. 'Perhaps.'

The creeping sense of unease changed into a surge of panic. Still, she wasn't safe. Still, she could be taken – at the mercy of another version of Cigarettes. It overwhelmed her, and she craved more air.

'What if they come back for me? And what

if Maxim demands you finish the job you started, or sends someone else to do it?'

'I'm not going to let that happen,' he said as he moved closer to her. 'You're right. He wasn't happy with the outcome but we managed to hash out a mutual agreement, and stuff like that means something to guys like him. I'll keep quiet with the information I have on him, on the condition that he leaves me alone. He won't come for me, and he won't get involved again.'

His assurance calmed her and sent her mind back to something he'd said before.

'Yesterday, you said you'd seen how I was struggling since my release.'

'Yeah.'

'Have you been watching over me? Making sure I was safe?'

He smiled, and reached out to gently cup her cheek, brushing a thumb over her skin. 'As I said, I'm not going to let anything happen to you.'

A warmth rushed through her body at his touch and his words. She should be cautious, still wary to trust, but she finally felt safe, protected, and couldn't fight the feeling that this man was going to wrap himself around her, never to let her go.

'It's been nearly a month since your release,' he continued. 'I'm not saying that puts you in the clear, but if this person wants to come back for you, they're going to have to be very careful. It's a much riskier proposition this time.'

'What do you mean?'

'Well, I'm here now for a start, but they're also not going to know if you'll have some sort of tracking device with you or something that links you to the police. Do you have anything like that?'

She sighed. 'Well, my building is like Fort Knox, panic buttons everywhere, but I don't have anything portable that I can keep with me.'

He nodded. 'We'll have to figure that out then, but in the meantime, we'll just have to be vigilant.'

'Okay,' she said as she processed her chaotic thoughts.

'This was a lot for you to deal with,' he said, watching her. 'We should take a break.'

'No, not yet. There's something I want to ask.'

His eyes narrowed as he watched her, a knowing smile on his lips. 'Let me guess. You want me to find the person who did this to you? You want a window into my world.'

She nodded and leant forwards in the chair. 'Well? Will you help me?'

'Already one step ahead of you,' he answered. 'It was always my intention to find who was responsible, but you want to be part of this too?'

'Yes, I really do.'

He nodded. 'Okay well, we'll be going into this blind and that means no one is off the table as far as suspicion is concerned. We'll be looking into everyone's private lives. Everyone you know too. All of their secrets. Can you handle that?'

'I think so.'

'Even if you discover something you'd rather not know.'

'I'm a grown-up, I'll handle it,' she said. 'I have no choice. I need to know who would want to do this to me, and I need to make sure I never, ever go through anything like that again.'

He sat back in his chair, happy with her answer. 'Well then, looks like I've found my new job,' he said with a satisfied glint in his eye. 'Now, come here.'

She relaxed a little and rose from the chair, taking hold of his outstretched hand. She'd had enough information for the time being, and decided a distraction from her problems was what she needed now.

He pulled her down into his lap. 'That's better. So, how are we going to seal this new deal of ours?'

She wrapped her arms around his neck and felt the sparks ignite within her. 'I'm sure we'll think of something.'

'Already have,' he said as he slid his arm under her legs and stood, carrying her out of the room.

## CHAPTER 19

Elena stepped off the treadmill, reached for her bottle and downed the cool water. She'd slept well, and late, and had managed a few weights and an acceptable run but hadn't pushed herself to the limit, giving her a pleasant post-workout buzz.

She did a couple of body stretches, wrapped a towel around her shoulders, and wandered to Ethan's office, to the sound of him talking on the phone. He glanced around to her as he finished up the call and let his eyes linger.

'Good morning,' he said as he tossed his phone on the desk and reached out to grab another chair. 'Good workout?'

'Perfect,' she replied. 'I should go and shower.'

'That can wait,' he said. 'First, we need to talk. Come here.'

She walked to him and made herself comfortable on the chair. She knew what he'd want to discuss, she had asked for his help, after all. But now that it was happening, she wasn't sure how ready she was for any of this.

'I've been doing some initial digging around, checking out your social media mainly, and your followers, but can you think of anyone who may hold a grudge or might want some sort of revenge? A bitter work colleague? An ex?'

'Well, I mean, I've had run-ins with people in the past, obviously. Who hasn't?' she answered. 'But nothing that would cause this kind of grudge. Nothing so sinister. My parents certainly made sure of that.'

'Your parents?'

'Yes, the Dumont household is full of rules, very strict rules, and high-profile incidents which could damage reputations, namely my father's, are not tolerated. My parents expect only the best behaviour, a rule my brother somehow manages to defy, regularly. And just in case you're wondering, I'm not the kind to go around flaunting my family's wealth like Instagram's richest either.'

'I can see that,' he said with a smile.

'Yeah, well, I leave all that to my brother.'

He nodded. 'I noticed that too. Women, cars and Cristal champagne seem to be the favourites.'

'And private planes,' she said. 'But those images were removed by my father. Too pretentious.'

'It just gets better and better,' Ethan said, sarcasm etched in his tone. 'So, back to this. Was there anything unusual that happened in the weeks leading up to your abduction? Or even longer. A year or so before?'

'No, nothing. Only that awful man lingering outside my building a couple of times, and we all know how that turned out.'

He nodded. 'Yeah, we do.'

'But my life is what it is,' she said with a shrug. 'Maybe it was simply my family's wealth that attracted this person. Who knows? But there were no nasty emails or phone calls or anything suspicious.'

The weight of the task that lay ahead of them rested heavy on her shoulders, like finding that elusive needle in a haystack. She hoped she had the strength for it. 'Okay, what else?' she asked, wanting to power through.

'Well, without any real leads, we'll start with everyone you know and work outwards.'

She looked at him. 'You'll start with my people?' she asked. 'My friends?'

He stopped what he was doing and focused on her. 'Elena, we have nothing to go on, no clues. We have to start somewhere.'

'Jesus,' she whispered. 'But how?'

'Email addresses will be fine to begin with. I'll take it from there.'

'But no one opens dodgy emails these days. We all know the rules.'

'Yes, but my blank email sent to a device through a mail app doesn't even need to be opened to force a crash and reset. Just receiving it is enough. And that little process creates enough of a window for me to get in and access all sorts of data. Simple.'

'But that's terrible.'

'Yeah, but that's the game. I bet you take all the necessary security steps to protect your laptop, don't you?'

She shrugged. 'I suppose.'

'Yeah, of course you do. But people just don't look at their devices in the same way, and the reality is that anything connected to the internet is still a mini processor and just as vulnerable of being hacked: phones, car keys, security cameras, smart speakers, even thermostats. You name it.'

'Well I'm never going to see my phone in the same light again.'

'No, maybe not,' he said. 'Updates help, but they're not bullet proof and hackers just find new weaknesses. It's what we do and it's exactly what you need right now.'

'Wow.'

'This is it, Elena. You asked for my help, and this is what I do. But like I said before, it's a murky world.' He reached out and took her hand in his, a moment of gentleness that surprised her. 'So you need to prepare because my search will trigger a sequence of events that will change everything. I will target everyone you know. I have to. Everyone you've ever interacted with: people close to you – your family, your friends, friends of friends, work colleagues – Joe Bloggs on Facebook who liked a picture you posted two years ago. Everyone, in the hope that there might be something we can find that'll pin down who was responsible. The list is endless, and I will be violating every civil liberty you can think of too. You have to let me do what I need to do. Can you do that?'

She nodded.

'Good. I know this is hard for you, but you have to trust me.'

'Am I right to trust you though?' she asked. 'Or are you about to throw a bomb into my world?'

'You know you can trust me,' he said. 'But I can't guarantee anything else at this stage. The answer is wrapped up somewhere in the threads of your life, and I'm determined to find it.'

'My life,' she said with a sigh. 'Well, maybe now is a good time to discuss some of the other aspects of this life of mine.'

'And what aspects are we talking about, exactly?'

'My parents. The frosty texts from my mother, daily, asking when they are going to see me. Because, suddenly, I'm very important to them.'

He nodded in agreement. 'Standard parental bullshit.'

'Indeed, but unavoidable in my case. They won't shut up, and it's time I dealt with them.'

'Understood. And what else?'

She glanced at him, avoiding for the moment the real reason for this conversation; the elephant in the room that was Adam. 'Well, I should at least call Charlotte. She's been so good to me. I know it's only been a couple of days, but I can't shut her out.'

'Again, understood.'

She cleared her throat. 'There's also Adam …'

'Oh yes, Adam.'

'You know about him?' she exclaimed.

'I know everything about you,' he said, his eyes never leaving hers. 'And yes, I know all about Adam.'

'Oh,' she said, her voice wavering. 'So you understand what I have to do.'

He moved closer to her and rested his arms on her chair, hemming her in, for her full attention. 'Elena, you know I'm not playing around here, and that means not sharing you with anyone – least of all city boy – so the sooner you deal with him, the better.'

She stared at him, her heart pumping in her chest. 'So will you let me deal with it?' she asked. 'Or do you think I would run the moment I'm apart from you?'

His eyes lingered on her for a moment as his lips curved into a dangerous smile. 'Do you want to run, Elena?' he asked, his arms still firm against her chair, not letting her move. Only he would decide when she could do that.

She shook her head. 'No. Not today.'

'Then I'll let you deal with it. I'm no

longer your captor.'

She smirked. 'Oh, really?'

'Yes, really,' he said as he took her chin and pulled her in for a kiss.

\*\*\*

Elena stood at the gate of her parents' house. She hesitated, willing herself to keep going as the first distant rumbles of thunder rolled through the sky. The sound of it raised a question in her mind: did she believe in omens?

She wasn't sure why she was so nervous about climbing the eight steps up to the large black door, but something made her delay. Everything around her was familiar, but it felt a lifetime ago that she had seen her parents here, a time when she was a completely different person. How would they react to this stranger on their doorstep, and what would she say to them? This was the place her mother had uprooted the family to when Elena was six years old, from their four-bedroomed apartment in Chelsea that began as the marital home. Elena understood what pulled her mother to this house, an impressive stucco-fronted villa with columned porch and huge sash windows, its family-sized garden backing on to the beautiful Holland Park – once grounds to the magnificent but now ruined Holland House. Her mother had decided that this would be the place to raise their children, after falling in love with it when visiting a friend nearby. And it had been Elena's home, to come and go as she pleased. Only today she didn't feel comfortable enough to use her key. She didn't want to barge into their space, so she knocked and waited as her heart hammered. She turned to Ethan, and he smiled at her as he waited in his car, making sure she was safe inside before he would drive away, as agreed.

Her mother opened the door, and when they made eye contact, Elena took in the quick succession of expressions; from casual indifference to sudden recognition to final emotional realisation that her daughter was now here.

'Elena, you've come. Finally,' she said. 'Your father said you'd called, but we didn't for a minute imagine you'd come.'

Even now, there was no mistaking the tone of criticism in the statement.

*Finally. Well done, Elena. You've finally managed to see your parents, managed to put other people first before yourself.*

It made her bristle and suddenly reluctant to step over the threshold, but her mother took care of that by reaching out and taking her by the elbow, pulling Elena towards her.

'Oh, Elena,' she said, a little softer this time, perhaps aware of how she may have sounded. 'Come in.'

She couldn't hug her mother, not yet, so they stood awkwardly for a moment, and when it was clear there was to be no happy reunion, her mother smiled formally and spoke. 'Your father's in his study. We can go together. He has been waiting every day for you to call or visit.'

'Well, I'm here now, Mother, let's just leave it at that,' Elena said, wanting to explode.

*Two minutes. I've been here two minutes.*

They walked towards her father's study in a silence only broken by the sound of her mother knocking on the door. 'Charles, Elena is here.'

'Come in,' came the reply. It was the same voice that had been at the end of the phone held to her ear on that fateful day, just to prove she was alive. His voice was high, surprised, as it was then.

Her mother opened the door and walked into the oak-panelled room with Elena following behind, feeling like the schoolgirl sent to the headmaster's office for some minor misbehaviour.

The thunder was louder now, almost overhead, a cacophony of rolling booms that made the windows rattle.

'Elena,' he said as she walked further into the room. He wasted no time in embracing her.

She needed to hug him too, for appearances mainly, but somewhere deep inside there was still the need to be close to him, her father, despite the betrayal. They stood like this for several seconds until she broke away. He gestured for her to sit on the sofa while he sat in the armchair opposite, glancing at her mother. The rain that now fell lashed against the ground outside, drowning out the awkward silence.

'Elena, would you like some tea?' her mother asked, clearly obeying an unspoken order to leave them alone.

Elena knew the score, having been on the receiving end of many of her father's unspoken orders over the years. 'Yes, that would be very nice.'

Her mother nodded and left the room.

'Where's Milo these days?' Elena asked, aware that this needed to begin somewhere. 'I haven't heard from him.'

'He's been away on business for the past two months,' her father replied. 'And you know what he's like. He can't do sentiment and probably doesn't know what to say to you. We all know he's terrible with emotions.'

'Yes, I do know, Dad, but a text would have been nice.'

'Give him time.'

She nodded. More silence. 'I'm sorry I didn't come sooner,' she said and stopped. These were meaningless words, and she immediately regretted speaking them. She wasn't sorry. She didn't want to be passive or to justify her actions, she wanted her father to justify his own.

'I didn't expect it, Elena,' he said. 'Our family has been so fractured by this event that I would not have been surprised if I never saw you again. I was coming to accept it, sadly.'

She looked at him. His words were so concise and said in such a way that it was as if he had spoken them many times in his head, ready for this day. Rehearsed.

More thunder sounded overhead, matching her mood perfectly. Her father stood and went to the mantelpiece, hitting the switch for the wall lights above, flooding the room with a warm glow.

'It was a terrible moment when it backfired as it did, believe me.'

'Backfired?' she snapped, her calm façade ebbing away. 'You make it sound like you had no choice, but paying the ransom was the only option to keep me safe, and you chose otherwise. That's the only reason it backfired.'

His eyes widened in surprise. Had he not expected her to react so passionately so quickly? She couldn't be sure, but one thing she was sure of was that this version of Elena was one he didn't know.

Her mother returned with a tray of tea and biscuits, halting their conversation.

She placed the tray down but remained standing, perhaps sensing the tension in the room. 'I'll leave you two to talk. I'll be in the kitchen if you need me.' She glanced at them both and left the room.

Her father waited for the door to close before he continued. 'I appreciate you're angry, and I understand that.' He sat back in his armchair. 'But when you consider things rationally, especially after the event, things are very black and white. You must realise that we had to take time, be sure that paying the ransom was the best option. For you too.'

'Cut the bullshit, Dad,' she said as heat glowed in her face. 'I'm not one of your clients now. Don't talk as if I couldn't possibly understand the implications. I was there, right at the centre. It was my life you were playing with.' She paused, composed herself. 'There was only one option, just one. You paid the ransom. If you were told that I would be hurt or killed unless you pay, then you pay. There's no negotiating with that.'

'If you need someone to blame, then–'

'You have no idea what I need,' she said defiantly. 'Let's be perfectly clear on that. But yes, maybe I do need someone to blame, and you're certainly not immune from that. You made a choice, and as choices go, it was spectacularly bad.'

He leant forwards. 'Do you think it was easy for me? Do you?' he said with an anger of his own. 'I had everyone giving me advice. The police. Edmond. Your mother was falling apart and was incapable of thinking of anything other than getting you back, and believe me, Elena, there was nothing I wanted more myself, but...' He stopped, paused, and pulled back his composure.

'But what?'

'It… it was something Edmond said.'

A small seed of unease began to take root in her mind. Why would Edmond want to influence her father's decision?

'What happened, Dad?' she demanded, impatient now.

He looked straight at her. 'He asked what would happen if we paid the money and they killed you regardless, if they hadn't already. He suggested that maybe it would be good to delay, perhaps call their bluff. At least make it more difficult than they were expecting.'

'And you listened to him?' she cried. 'You took his advice over the police? You didn't consider the danger that decision would place me in?'

'I'm not perfect, Elena, I wasn't thinking straight.'

He glanced away from her now, perhaps guilt preventing him from looking her in the eye.

'Yes, you were wrong, and it was incredibly reckless,' she said, not finished yet. 'I'm not sure what you hoped to achieve by doing it.'

He nodded.

'I would have died, Dad. You know that, don't you? He attacked me. He'd have killed me. He–' She trailed off, stopping herself from continuing. She should continue, she knew that. She should share more. She should let her father, the man who let her down so badly, know how it was for her – the never-ending fear and terror – but she held it back. She couldn't trust what that would unleash.

'What, Elena?' her father asked, catching her eye. 'What happened to you while you were there?'

'It doesn't matter now,' she said, faltering, her voice cracking. 'I don't want to discuss it. I may never want to discuss it, I don't know.'

After a moment, he spoke. 'If you need to hear that I'm sorry, in order to recover, then–'

'Are you sorry?' she asked.

'Of course I am. I never wanted you to be hurt… or worse.'

She nodded and stared out of the window as she considered it. This is what she came for, what she wanted from him, but somehow it didn't alter how she felt, deep inside. 'It's such a small word, isn't it. Sorry. Five little letters. Can it repair the damage though? Can it do that? I'm not sure. Such a big task for five little letters.' She looked at him again. 'If only it was that simple.'

He sighed. 'If you want to punish me, go ahead. It's no more than I deserve, but you have to ask yourself, will it help?'

'I don't know that either. I feel like I'm swimming against the tide, unable to be sure of anything anymore.' Sadness replaced the fire in her. 'I understand the situation we're in. Your wealth means that we're exposed to a risk that others aren't. I get it. The thought of them getting your money repulsed me, but I needed to survive, and I needed you to help me. But you left me alone in there when I needed you most,' she whispered. 'I was all alone.'

She tried to read his expression. Perhaps he was beginning to understand, perhaps not, but she was growing tired, having been through so much.

'And when I found out you refused their demands, something was ripped out of me, something I can't get back.'

'Elena.'

His reaction halted her and within a second, she realised she didn't want this new burden of guilt. His guilt. It was additional baggage that she did not need. She pulled herself together. 'It's okay, Dad. You don't have to look at me like that. I'm here. I got out alive in the end.'

He nodded, stood and walked to the window, his hands behind his back. 'Well, now, we must move on. For us and the good of the family.'

'Oh yes, for the good of the precious family,' she muttered. 'We mustn't tarnish the gilded cage.'

He turned and stared her down. 'Elena, you may feel it's acceptable to back-chat your parents – your mother shared how you spoke to her at the hospital – but I don't care for this new attitude of yours, so please find a way to curtail it in future. We will find a way, and you will contribute. Am I making myself clear?'

'Yes,' she snapped. 'Perfectly.' She was being told how it was going to be, but for now, she didn't have the energy to fight him any longer. She also realised that, despite everything, there would be no embrace, no affection to heal the wounds. Nothing.

'I appreciate you coming today, but I think we've discussed enough of this for now,' he said, breaking the silence between them. 'But now that you are here, your mother will want to spend some time with you too. We shouldn't deny her that.' He walked to the door and opened it. 'You'll stay for something to eat, yes?'

Reluctance made her stomach sink. 'Well, I–'

'Is it too much to ask that you spend some time with your parents after ignoring them for so long?'

'Excellent,' she muttered through gritted teeth as she rose from her chair.

## CHAPTER 20

After an hour of stilted small talk over a light lunch that Elena barely touched, she was ready to leave. To get out into the air and away from this strange atmosphere.

'Another drink?' her mother asked as they finished up.

'Thanks, but no. I really should get going,' Elena said as she pulled her phone from her bag. One message, from Ethan, telling her that he was outside.

Once at the front door, her mother reached out for Elena and hugged her tight. There was warmth in it, and Elena felt compelled to hug her back.

'That reminds me.' her father said. 'I had a call from Charlotte the other day. She couldn't reach you.'

She recognised his expression. His 'stare-until-you-give-up-the-truth' look. 'Did she? I don't know why.'

'Yes, I thought that was odd,' he said. 'You two are never normally out of touch. What are you doing with your time these days?'

She smiled. 'Just what exactly do you think I'd be doing with my time?'

'I don't know.'

'I've been at home, of course. Where else would I be? I must have missed her call, that's all.'

*Oh yes, daddy dear. You can't reach me now.*

He nodded, with a hint of irritation that this was all he was going to get. He didn't believe her, but she was confident that the last place he'd have guessed she had been was with the man who had held her in captivity for all those days. She was safe enough.

'I'm glad you came, Elena, that you gave your father the opportunity to explain,' her mother said, breaking the moment. She gave Elena another hug.

Elena smiled. 'Yes, well, I'd better get going now.'

'Your mother's right. Thank you for coming to see us,' her father said as he opened the door.

He reached out to hug her too before she had the opportunity to stop him, but it was awkward and clunky; her cheek hitting his shoulder as he clumsily pulled her towards him.

'I'll see you soon,' she said as she walked out of the door and down the steps, listening to the door closing behind her.

The rain had stopped, and the cooled, refreshed air filled her lungs. Everywhere was wet, washed and invigorated by the storm. Little droplets of water fell from rain-soaked leaves, as the emerging sun shone against wet ground.

She'd done it. She'd faced her parents. It hadn't been a great success, but that was to be expected. She'd worry about what happened next another time. For now, she was glad to be free. She looked up at the sky and saw little blue flecks that were starting to emerge from the steel-grey cloud. The thunder had faded into the distance, soon to be gone.

Looking out onto the street she saw Ethan, waiting in his car, a few strides away. There was nothing suspicious about this scene, nothing that exposed who he was and what he did. He was hidden in plain sight. Anyone could walk straight past him and never know the devastating consequences of making his acquaintance. But she knew who he was, and what he was capable of, and at the centre of it all, she was his main concern. She liked that fact a lot.

She pulled open the door. 'Thank God that's over. Please just take me away from here. Mine or yours, I don't care.'

\*\*\*

'And he didn't apologise to you,' Ethan said as he pulled into the underground car park beneath his apartment. 'Nothing at all?'

'Nope,' Elena replied. 'Not a genuine one, anyway. I stupidly expected at least some attempt at remorse, but there was nothing. He seemed more frustrated that he doesn't know exactly how I'm spending my time, rather than how sorry he should be.'

'He's struggling to work you out,' Ethan said as he parked the car. 'I think you were probably an open book before the abduction, and now he doesn't know you. He's losing control, and that's making him panic.' He switched off the engine and glanced at Elena. 'But if you want more answers, you know what we need to do.'

Elena opened the door. 'Really, Ethan?' she said, exasperated. 'You want to include my parents? Already?'

He shrugged. 'You know I do.'

She couldn't find the words to answer as they made their way to Ethan's apartment, and once inside, she headed straight for the balcony and pushed open the doors, needing the air. The afternoon sun was still high, the sky an unbroken blue. Any trace of the earlier storm had evaporated into the air.

She listened to the sound of water lapping at the small shingle bank below, its rhythmic sounds soothing her as she watched boats chug down the river, their destinations unknown. Leaning against the railings, she tipped her face up towards the sun and allowed herself to calm. Ethan had disappeared to his office, and that was fine with her too. Right now, she didn't want to know what the next phase of his game would be, especially if it involved her parents. That might be too much to bear and it made her play the conversation between herself and her father

...n her mind, unpicking every ...hidden meanings.

...sound of feet padding through ...nterrupted her thoughts.

...ppreciated how the sound of the river against the urban landscape could be so soothing,' she said as she shielded her eyes from the sun to watch Ethan join her.

'I suppose it is,' he said, standing by her side, leaning against the railings too.

'It definitely is,' she said with a sigh. 'Peace in all the chaos.'

She caught him watching. 'What?'

'Everything okay? You looked deep in thought there.'

'I don't know,' she said looking out over the river. 'Meeting my parents today has brought everything to the surface. All the bad stuff. My parents, my brother, my entire dysfunctional family.'

'You call it dysfunctional, I call it borderline psychopathic.'

She smirked and nudged him. 'Well, if we're going to get brutal about it, okay, but I have mentioned this to you before. You have been warned.'

'Can't argue with that.'

'My father dominates the family. He makes the rules that we all have to abide by and God forbid anyone who breaks them. And now, my brother seems to be following in his footsteps. I'm sure he hates me and I really don't know why. He always has. I could bore you with stories from our childhood, stories that from the outside appear to be trivial sibling rivalry, but to me they were so much more sinister than that. And now, weeks after my release, I've had nothing from him. Nothing at all. Maybe it's because we're so different, who knows. Maybe he thinks I'm weak.'

Ethan brushed his hand over hers. 'You're far from weak.'

'Then there's my mother,' she continued. 'The mouse who is too frightened to rock the boat, and finally there's me, on the outside of all of it. I'd accepted that a long time ago, and don't get me wrong, it's no big deal. You can't choose your family, and my life is full of wonderful people who I adore.'

His eyes found hers and he smiled. 'Adore?'

She smiled back. 'Yes, so I'm not in need of any pity. But it's just this... my father's refusal to pay the ransom, it makes me feel so... abandoned. And their hurry to brush everything under the carpet now that it's over, to move on under a veneer of normality – whatever *that* is – is just so strange. So cold. Could that be motive?' She sighed. 'You already know this, I'm sure, that I work at the British Museum?' His face gave away that yes, he was well aware.

'It's all I've ever wanted to do. I spent as much time as possible at the museum as a child, fascinated by different civilisations and how they lived, how they loved their families and friends. The social order of things. I studied if it was so greatly different from ours. Anyway, the ancients: the Greeks and the Romans, do you know what they used to do to unwanted children?'

He shook his head. It didn't matter what he knew, just that she needed to express herself.

'They used to "expose" them,' she explained. 'They literally left them outside, exposed and at the mercy of the elements if they were going to be a burden on the family. Left outside to die, bundled up, in the street. Especially girls. Girls were always unwanted, boys the expected heirs. And girls came with the expense of a dowry, you see, so it was downhill all the way for us females. Sometimes there was salvation though. Sometimes the parents would try to sell them or perhaps a childless couple would take them.' She shrugged. 'It was an awful, terrible thing to do, but it was their culture. It was what they did. Another mouth to feed was a serious consideration.' She was momentarily lost in her knowledge and the safety and grounding it provided. 'They did what they did for a reason. But I can't seem to get past the fact that my parents exposed me and left me for dead, and all for what? This wasn't about culture, the prejudice of gender or the worry of another mouth to feed. It was just about money, protecting their wealth.'

'And how does that make you feel?' he asked.

She looked at him, understanding where he was going with this. 'Like I owe them nothing. Particularly my loyalty.'

He nodded. 'So let me widen the search to include your parents.'

She considered it and something flipped in her mind. A switch, replacing the sadness with a strange force that began to take over and spread: a new synapse firing in her brain, sending waves through her body and bloodstream like a virus, infecting her. She liked the feeling, found strength from it, and discovered a sense of control in her own life again that had been lacking for so long.

'Yes, okay,' she said, her voice low but unwavering, as was her eye contact. 'Include my parents and brother in your search now. However unpalatable, I need to know everything.'

He faced her, satisfied with her answer, a telling smile on his lips. 'You're sure?'

'Completely.'

Elena decided on something there and then: that from now on, people would be punished for mistreating her. No more was she the passive bystander in her own life. She was taking charge, stronger now and had the talents of a man who did things differently – a merchant of secrets – and that meant so did she. Knowledge would be her new power, and Ethan would get it for her. He'd bring her the world if she asked for it. And she would, regardless of how long it would take. She would put her faith in the man opposite her, watching her intently now.

'Welcome to my world, Elena,' he said. 'Let me show you more.'

He took her by the hand and led her indoors.

Ethan led Elena back into the living room and she followed, empowered with a strength to face whatever lay ahead. She walked with him towards his office, her hand in his, until they were standing in front of the many computers.

'You're fully on board now,' he said, pulling up a chair. 'I can see it.'

'So?'

'So I suggest we take things up a notch. Up the stakes a little bit.'

'Tell me,' she said, taking a seat.

Ethan shuffled wires and boxes about on his cluttered office desk, before settling on a small chrome stick, the size of his thumb. 'Ah, here it is. The very familiar flashdrive.'

'Yep, I've seen one of those before.'

'I'm sure you have,' he said. 'And at first glance my flashdrive looks pretty much like yours or any other, but it's not.'

She smiled. 'Of course it isn't,' she said, taking the small metal bar from his grasp to inspect it.

'No, because with this little gem, while it's plugged into a device, it's making a helpful little backup of all the laptop's documents, passwords, internet history and cookies. Without anyone ever knowing. It'll give me everything I need to see all the recent activity. Very simple, and very effective.'

She glanced up at him. 'I thought you ate cookies.'

He raised an eyebrow, finding the humour.

She continued to twist the small metal object between her fingers, watching him as he watched her hands move. 'I assumed you'd check everyone out from all your computers here,' she said. 'And via that email.'

'Yes, everyone will obviously be covered in my global search, but we need some immediate results and this will get them for us.'

'So you want me to sneak around.'

He shrugged. 'Your parents will expect another visit soon and you're going to be tying up some loose ends with Adam and Charlotte, yes? So this will be a good opportunity to look at their home systems to see what they may be hiding, if anything. Maybe we can kill three birds with one stone. Do you think you could do that?'

She stared at him, understanding that this could plunge her into a darkness she may never resurface from. She placed the flashdrive on the desk. 'I'm not including Charlotte.'

'We can't exclude anyone at this point.'

'No. Charlotte doesn't come into this. She doesn't deserve this.'

He faced her, his eyes demanding. 'How do you know?'

'She's my friend, Ethan, that's why,' she replied, ignoring his reaction. She wouldn't back down on this. 'Look, I'm on board to search my family, that's fine. They have it coming. And the same with Adam, that's fine too. But none of my friends deserve this kind of invasion. There's no way they'd be involved.'

'Well, I'll pick it up then,' he said. 'From here. I won't be excluding anyone.'

She blew out a sigh. 'Fine, I can't stop you, but I can't be part of it.'

'Fine. I get it,' he said, his expression softening. 'Maybe I was asking too much too soon.'

She didn't reply.

'So, let's get back to this,' he continued. 'If you can get creative enough to gain access to any laptops lying around, this will be perfect. Plug it in and let it do its thing.'

'I'm sure I'll find a way,' she said. 'But what if there are problems? What if I don't get a chance to do it, or I'm not left alone for long enough?'

'Ultimately, it won't matter, but I'm sure you can think of something. Be creative.'

She sat back. 'Leave it with me.'

'Hmm, you're learning well. I like it,' he said.

'I've had a good teacher.'

'Indeed you have,' he said checking the screens. 'Is there anyone else that we should look at within your immediate family?'

Her mind went back to her conversation with her father and she thought of one person in particular. 'My Uncle Edmond, my father's brother.'

He nodded. 'I'm aware of him.'

'He's one creepy guy. Always has been. He mainly keeps himself to himself on the family farm in Somerset, so I rarely see him and that's fine by me. But there's something my father said, about his reaction during my abduction.'

'What's that?'

'He wanted my father to delay, to consider refusing to pay the ransom.'

'Did he now?'

'Yes, he thought they'd be playing into the captors' hands. Giving them too much control, especially as I might be killed anyway.'

'I see. Another facet of your strange and intriguing family.'

'I know. I've never been a fan of him with his beady little eyes, watching everyone, but he's always seemed harmless enough. He likes to come to London every now and then. Always gets fed well at my parents' house. He scoots between theirs and a couple of old-style gentlemen's clubs in town.'

'Leave that with me,' he said. 'He'll go to

the top of the list for now. And I think I'd like to meet this bunch of people you call your family. And soon.'

'Well, that's a hard no,' she said assertively, as the thought of Ethan and her family in the same room together left her with a horrible sense of dread. 'Investigating them is one thing, but meeting them? No way. Too dangerous.'

'Hmm, maybe,' he said with a telling glint in his eye. 'But fun.'

'For me or you?'

'Me, obviously,' he said, giving her a wink.

She couldn't mask the sound of laughter that spilled from her lips. She liked the playful Ethan. 'You're a bad man.'

'I've never pretended otherwise, Elena,' he said with a mix of humour and deadly seriousness. 'So, who do you want to visit first?'

She sighed as she considered it. Neither option of her family or Adam was an appealing one. 'Adam, I think. Let's get that over with. It's not going to be an easy conversation to have.'

Ethan nodded. 'Interesting. I see you're up for this more than I thought, tackling the most awkward situation first. Fair play.'

'I'm glad I surprise you,' she said with a hint of sarcasm.

'Baby, you surprised me the day I first met you.'

She smiled and nudged his leg with her foot.

He soon became lost in the information on the computer screen but glanced at her and smiled when she continued to watch him. 'Okay. Can hear you thinking again. What is it?'

'It's a nice place you have here.'

'Thanks,' he said vaguely as he worked.

She rose from her chair, went to the pictures on the wall and studied them. The light falling against the canvas almost brought them to life. She turned to him. 'Hmm. I just wondered if, you know...' she cleared her throat, '... you had anyone else in your life, or...'

'There are no other women, Elena,' he said, keeping his eyes on his screens. 'Only you.'

'Well, it's not a problem or anything,' she said, attempting a blasé attitude, despite her face flushing as his words spoke to her body as well as her mind. 'I mean, you and me, we're not... this doesn't have to be... well, anyway... I just wondered.'

'Okay,' he said, chuckling. 'Whatever you say.'

She paced the room, a lightness within her from the instant relief of knowing she was the only one. Like Ethan, she too didn't want to share.

He continued working and she remained silent for as long as possible, until she could bear it no longer. 'But now we're here,' she ventured, going back to her chair, leaning towards him a little, 'maybe you could share a bit more about your life?'

'Well, I have a brother,' he began. 'Oliver. He lives in France. He's an artist and couldn't be more stereotypical. You know the type, living a torturous existence, always searching for his muse. But I make sure he's okay financially, so he's also an irritatingly happy son of a bitch.'

Elena saw that while he may have wanted to express casual indifference, the affection he felt towards his sibling shone through anyway. 'How often do you see him?'

'When I can. I go over there, spend a couple of months with him until we can't bear the sight of each other.'

'And your parents?'

'My parents? Well, they died 20 years ago,' he said, stopping what he was doing to face her. 'Car accident.'

The curveball. She reached out and placed a hand on his arm. 'I'm so sorry.'

'It's fine. It was a long time ago.'

'Do you want to tell me about it?'

'No. There's no need. They're gone and it was very sad, but that's all there is to it.'

She nodded and decided not to pursue it. She'd find out what happened on that score another time. Smiling, she changed tack. 'Friends?'

The humour in his eyes assured her that he was happy to continue. 'Yes, of course. My line of business may make me look like an outcast of society, but I'm not. Nor am I a hermit or anything. I see my friends often enough.'

'But this job of yours, has it been worth it?'

He sighed. 'No, not always, but I've been living this way for so many years, I let myself become locked into it.' He adjusted in his seat and leant towards her. 'But now I have something else to occupy my time. Something much more rewarding.'

'A nice little arrangement,' she said as she tilted towards him too.

'A mutual agreement,' he replied.

# CHAPTER 21

Ethan and Elena sat in silence for most of the short journey to Adam's. The morning had been tied up with Ethan showing her some basic self-defence. The condition on which he would allow her to leave his side.

The instructions were clear – stay aware of everyone. Don't get caught wondering who's behind you. Look around. She remembered the feel of his arms wrapped around her as he explained what to do if someone jumped her from behind. How important it was to turn fear into a rage; a power. He had calmed her fears of not being able to fend off an attacker by explaining that it wasn't about studying for a black-belt in Taekwondo, but targeting vulnerable areas on an attacker's body – a punch to the face, or a knee to the groin. Anything to disable the attacker for long enough to get away.

Ethan pulled up at a safe distance from Adam's building and switched off the engine. The paved pedestrian area in front of the building, dotted with ornamental trees, was almost deserted, only a handful of people going about their weekend business. She couldn't decide if that was a good thing or bad, but she tried to put it out of her mind and focus on what she needed to do. But she was jittery and worked hard to control the nerves that raced.

'You okay?' he asked.

She nodded. She wouldn't share that she wanted to back out of this idea, to be taken home again where she was safe.

'There's some admin you need to know,' he said as he faced her, serious now. 'I've set a tracking app on your phone, so I know exactly where you are at all times. But I also want you to wear this,' he said as he handed her a small silicone square. 'It's a GPS tracking device. Clip it to your clothing but keep it hidden.'

She nodded, understanding. 'Of course,' she said tucking it into her dress, fastening it to her bra. 'I'll make sure it stays secure.'

'Good. I'll wait for you here. I've got a good sight of the entrance. I'm not too far away, and if he tries anything funny, you get yourself out of there immediately. If you can't do that then get somewhere safe, the bathroom for example, where you can lock the door. Then, you call me.'

'Oh, I will, no doubt about that.'

He handed her the flashdrive. 'Ready?'

'As I'll ever be.'

She leant forward in her seat, kissed him and got out of the car.

Walking across the paving towards the glass-fronted building, she glanced over her shoulder to check that Ethan was still there, watching. The air was humid, a sign of the heat that would fill the day ahead, and she was glad of her cool linen dress.

Once inside the lobby, she walked through the reception area and past the long oblong desk, a continuous curve of cream marble.

'Good morning, Elena,' the concierge said brightly, recognising her.

'Good morning,' she replied with a smile, masking her anxiety. She had no idea what she was walking into and felt alone in the truest sense. Her mind raced. Would Adam be hostile? Was what she'd come to say expected? And most importantly, would she be safe in his company?

She made her way to the bank of lifts and pressed the button, playing Ethan's self-defence tips over in her mind. *Stay aware. Target vulnerable areas on the body. Punch, fight and get away.*

'I can do this,' she whispered to herself, an attempt to calm her nerves. 'It's Adam. It's only Adam.'

The ascent to the eighteenth floor was rapid and pinged her arrival, the doors opening out into a corridor filled with natural light, flanked by windows at each end. As she made her way to Adam's apartment, a sense of foreboding scratched at her consciousness. She rang the buzzer, keen to get this over with.

He opened the door. 'Elena,' he said in a stilted tone.

Saying no more, he stepped back, allowing Elena to enter. He walked down the hallway and she followed behind, leaving the door ajar.

His living room was as bright as usual, the floor to ceiling glass letting in all the sunshine and offering a grand view of Canary Wharf. It was a familiar view, one that she had witnessed in each passing season. She had often sat here waiting for Adam when he had 'just one more email to send.' Night time was her favourite; the twinkling lights from other buildings, street lights and the mood lighting from the bars and restaurants below, all reflected in the rippling water of the river.

The apartment, as always, was tidy, which was easy to achieve with its minimal decoration. Only when Elena stayed did it seem to clutter up. The kitchen to her left, its black gloss units immaculate and smear free, was empty of activity. There would be no offer of refreshment from Adam today, but she was far from thirsty anyway.

She stared at the large abstract artwork, which looked like a cow dancing, above the small square LED fireplace to her right, unsure of where to begin.

'I guess you're not here to talk about the weather,' he said as he glanced out of the window. He was dressed in a black short-sleeved shirt, a couple of buttons left open at the neck, and linen trousers, his feet bare. It was a long time since Elena had seen him look so informal. Dressed like that, she remembered the early days and what had attracted her in the first place, even though it no longer affected her. But she was suddenly sad that things had deteriorated so badly, that it was unlikely that they could even be friends now.

She glanced at his open laptop on the glass table in the kitchen that quietly beeped its notifications, as if aware of the tense conditions it found itself working in.

'I've come to talk about us.'

'Us?' He snorted a small bitter laugh. 'Surely there is no 'us' anymore? People need to speak to one another to be an 'us'.' He didn't shout, but the venom was clear.

She flinched, not expecting the conversation to start with such bitterness.

He sighed. 'Come and sit down. I don't bite,' he said as he moved to the large L-shaped taupe leather sofa in the middle of the room, next to a glass-topped coffee table. He sat and hooked a leg under the other, resting his right arm across the back of the sofa. She crossed the room and joined him, sitting far enough away from the potential embrace of his arm, tucking her hair behind her ear.

'Two years, eh?' he said. 'And what did we get out of it? Apparently, nothing.'

'Adam, it's not like that. It wasn't all bad, I realise that, but there's no denying how distant we had become.' She shrugged. 'And I think we have to face the facts that sometimes, it just doesn't work out.'

'It could have.'

'Do you truly believe that?' she asked.

'Yes, I do. We were happy.'

She bristled at his version of events. 'Were we though, Adam? I mean really?'

'Things were fine,' he snapped.

'Well, you carry on creating a history that isn't true, but I don't agree,' she said, in no mood to be manipulated.

'We were perfectly fine before your "ordeal".' He made little quotation marks, trivialising all that it meant. 'But you're a little mouse, aren't you, and instead of confronting it head-on, you're using it as an excuse to end our relationship.'

Anger rose in her like heat and soon replaced any concern for his feelings. If he wanted a fight, he was going to get one. 'I'm not using anything as an excuse. It suits you to play the victim here, but don't think I don't know how you were considering ending things between us. I know about your conversation with Charlotte.'

He rolled his eyes. 'I should have known that would've got back to you.'

'Whatever, but I'm certainly seeing things clearer now, so thank you for that,' she snapped. 'Thank you also for enlightening me on what you really think I've been through. It just proves my point that you don't know or understand me at all. And if we're going to throw character assassinations into the mix, here's mine. If you weren't so busy with work, you would have taken the time to understand what I have been through, and would have taken the time to talk it through with me. But no, workaholic Adam is too busy for that.'

'Ah, so the true colours are coming out now, eh?' he said, his anger rising to match hers. 'I tried to talk it through, but you pushed me away.'

'Seriously?' she asked. 'That was a token effort, and you know it. You never really took the time to discuss how I felt, or what I'd been through. You just wanted me to snap back to the old Elena; pick up where we left off, while you continued to work 17 hours a day.'

'So I work hard for a living. Shoot me.'

'Oh, but that only happens to me, remember, Adam? But, oh no, wait,' she said as she held her hand over her mouth in mock realisation. 'Maybe not, because you still have no idea of the "ordeal" I suffered,' she said, making sure to use her own air quotation marks.

'It's always been this way, and I've never heard you complain about the benefits before,' he snapped.

'No, maybe not, and that's my mistake, but there's one thing I know and it's that this life is not enough.'

'Oh, I *see*. It's not enough,' he said as if it was all becoming clear. 'Well, what the fuck do you want, Elena? The fucking moon?' He threw up his hand and let it slap down against his side, his eyes bright, cold, and full of anger. 'Well, fine, if that's what you want, go. Leave me.' He waved his hand. 'Have a nice life. There. Is that what you want, for me to make this easy for you?'

'No, of course not,' she said, trying to calm the conversation. 'You're obviously hurt and angry, and I'm sorry.'

'Don't flatter yourself,' he snapped. 'I'm the one who's sorry. Sorry that I wasted so much time and effort on you. Someone with the world at their feet but with too many daddy issues to appreciate it.'

She was done. 'That's enough, Adam; enough of you talking to me like that. Who do you think you are? I didn't have to come here today, I was trying to be civilised about this, but it's clear you're not interested in ending things amicably, you just want to score points. That's what you care about. Well, fine. Have it your way.'

He smiled sarcastically. 'Well, well, well. Seems like this mouse has found her teeth.'

'Shut up, Adam,' she snapped, her voice hoarse from shouting.

Cold, snide laughter fell from his mouth.

'Oh, forget it. You're just not worth it.' She stood and hooked the strap of her bag over her shoulder. 'You know what, there's no love lost here, if there ever was. This is about the fact that

I ended it before you did, and you don't like it, do you? You can't bear me having one up on you.'

'I don't care what you do, Elena.'

'No, and that's abundantly clear, again. As it has always been.'

She could feel his anger. A visceral force of hurt pride. She knew the line between love and hate was thin, but she realised if he ever did love her, he flipped over that line remarkably quickly.

He huffed a response, looking uninterested, as he always did on a subject he didn't agree with.

A lump formed in her throat and she needed a moment to control her breathing. She'd be damned if she would let him see her cry.

The temporary respite from their exchange of words perhaps gave him time to consider things too. He stood, his face calmer, the anger now replaced with a reluctant acceptance. 'Look, I'm sorry. We shouldn't fight.' He shrugged. 'Maybe you're right. Maybe we weren't the right fit. But we tried. I guess we should be thankful for that.'

'We should,' she said, calmer now too. 'And I don't want us to part as enemies.'

'You're right, we should part on good terms, at least.' He smiled and brushed his thumb over her cheek. 'Are you sure about this, Elena? Is this really what you want?' he asked, in a moment of sincerity.

She nodded. 'Yes, it is. I'm sorry.'

He nodded too and gazed at her for a moment. 'What we could have been, eh?' he mused. 'I hope you find someone to meet your lofty expectations. I know I couldn't do it.'

She firmly removed his hand. She had no time for his games. 'I suppose this is it then, Adam.'

'I suppose it is.'

She exhaled. 'Well, I guess I should collect my stuff. Maybe you could grab the gold bracelet I left here?'

'Really?' he said, checking his watch, all signs of patience disappearing. 'You want me to get it now?'

'Well, yes. It makes sense while I'm here. Surely you can grab it for me?'

'Can't I just get Jill in the office to courier it to you?' he asked, irritated now.

'It was a gift from my father, so I'd rather take it back with me now, thanks. You know what he's like about gifts.'

'Well, do you know where it is?' he asked.

'In your bedroom perhaps, or maybe the bathroom. I can't remember.'

'For Christ's sake,' he muttered as he walked towards his bedroom.

As he did, she reached to pull the flashdrive out from her pocket and moved quickly to the laptop. She pushed it into the port and after a few clicks of the mouse, let it do its thing. With her heart thundering, she stood in front of it, blocking it from view.

'Where exactly do you think you put it?' he shouted from the other room, still clearly put out at this inconvenience.

'I'm not sure. Maybe by your bed or on your chest of drawers,' she called out, knowing he would have no idea that she didn't even own such an item. He took no more notice of her and what she wore than he did the stars in the night sky.

She listened to him fumble about, pulling open drawers and moving ornaments, cursing under his breath. Glancing at the stick, she watched the erratic flicker of its little red light, the only indication that it was busy infecting the hard drive.

'Come on, come on,' she whispered and waited a moment more, her eyes darting between the laptop and the doorway to his bedroom. He said something undecipherable as she stared at the stick, willing it to hurry, sweat beading on her forehead at the prospect of being caught. Feeling that time had temporarily suspended itself, the last tab on the screen finally closed. Search complete. She yanked the stick free and plunged it back into her pocket.

'Look, don't worry,' she said as he strode back into the room. 'I guess I must have taken it home after all.' She smiled and shrugged. 'Nothing more final than collecting those last items from each other's homes.'

'I guess not,' he said as he made his way back to her.

'So, this is goodbye then,' she said, desperate to leave.

'Yes, it is.'

Close now, he looked down at her, a dullness in his eyes. It was the final moment of their chapter, and it was coming to an end. He reached out and they hugged awkwardly.

'Goodbye, Adam,' she said, pulling away first.

'Goodbye, Elena.'

She turned to go, and glanced over her shoulder to see him standing in the middle of the room, watching her leave. She shut the door to his apartment and leant against it for a moment, breathing a long sigh of relief.

It was over. It was done.

Her hands trembled as she pushed the button for the lift, adrenaline surging at what had happened. She wanted to be with Ethan again, and the thought of him waiting for her made her hurry.

Leaving the building, she checked over her shoulder and scanned her surroundings as she made her way to Ethan's car.

'So?' he asked as she climbed in. 'How did it go?'

'It was not pleasant,' she said as she closed the door. 'He was angry.'

'He'll get over it,' Ethan said, dispassionately.

She nodded, knowing a sympathetic viewpoint on this subject would be something Ethan couldn't provide. She looked back at the block of apartments that were already disappearing from view as Ethan drove away.

'Did you manage to get what you needed on the stick?'

'I did, but there's no threat there, Ethan. I really believe that.'

'Let's wait for the data to prove it.'

She sat back in the chair. 'I suppose, but Adam is Adam and yes, he was angry, but only because I ended the relationship before he had. He doesn't like to be outwitted, that's all. But I'm sure he'll soon find a pretty little thing to hang on his arm and enjoy the lifestyle he has to offer, no questions asked. After his wounded pride heals, he'll soon be back in the game.'

'And did you enjoy the thrill of our little game?' he asked.

She smiled. 'I'm not sure my heart can take that kind of adrenaline again soon.'

'Of course it can. You're stronger than you think.'

She stared out of the window and considered his statement. Strong was not an emotion she was familiar with right now. It was something else. Something she couldn't define.

# CHAPTER 22

The radio played softly through Elena's kitchen as she popped the tops off two bottles of beer. Screams of delight erupted from a caller who had just won a coveted prize, but she missed what it was.

'Must be the cash prize,' she murmured to herself after a mouthful of cold beer. 'No one screams like that for a household appliance, that's for sure.'

The entry door buzzer sounded so she carried the beers through to her living room, placed them on her table, and answered the phone. 'Hello.'

'Your pizza delivery, madam.'

'Great, come on up,' she said as she hit the button and moved out onto the landing.

Ethan climbed the stairs holding two boxes of pizza and winked at her as he strode into her apartment and placed the boxes on her table, next to the beers.

She followed and opened up the boxes, taking in the cheesy, doughy aroma. 'Hmm, delicious.'

'So, how did it go with Charlotte?' he asked as he grabbed a beer.

She had been hungry and ready to devour

the pizza, but his question made her abandon the slice in her hand, plonking it back in the box, no more able to eat it than down a box of nails.

'It was fine,' she said, taking a seat, opting for her beer instead.

She thought back to their catch-up. The afternoon they'd spent together was almost like old times; familiar and relaxed. They'd connected with Abigail and Louise on a group call, and managed to easily lose a couple of hours chatting and laughing together. It was good, just what she needed, and probably long overdue. Nothing was more soothing to her than getting lost in the detail of other people's lives. She was glad to have the distraction and managed to close her mind off from the suspicion, searches, and flashdrives, and just enjoy the company of her friends. It was only when it was time to leave that Elena snapped back to the present and the tasks that lay ahead of her.

He took a bite of the slice of pizza in his hand as he grabbed the chair beside her and sat. 'You know, when all of this is over and we find the person responsible, things can get back to normal.'

'Normal?' She raised a brow. 'Things will never be normal again, but I know what you mean.'

'And did you change your mind about the flashdrive?'

'Nope. I still feel the same way,' she said,

picking at the label of her beer with a fingernail. 'I won't do it.'

He looked at her. 'I see.'

She'd had all the opportunity to use the flashdrive during her visit, but none of the desire. There had been a moment when Charlotte was on a call to Jake, but it meant nothing. She was adamant that she would not betray her close friend, so the stick remained buried in her pocket, where Ethan had tucked it, for the duration of the visit.

He wiped his fingers on the serviette and pointed to the remaining slices. 'You need to eat those.'

She nodded, and reached for a slice, forcing down the doughy pizza with occasional mouthfuls of beer.

'That's better,' he said as he picked up his own beer and drank.

'Did you find anything from Adam's laptop?' she asked as she packed up the empty boxes.

'He runs a pretty tight ship there. I couldn't find anything of significance. It was very sterile.'

Elena smirked. 'Sterile is a good word. That's exactly how he likes to live.'

'Was he always so meticulous with his housekeeping?'

'Yes, with everything. His home, his work. There is no place for disorder anywhere in his world. He's on a ladder to the top, and nothing will get in the way of that.'

'He sounds like a right bundle of laughs.'

'Hmm, yes, some may call him anally retentive.'

Ethan laughed and drank some more. She liked the sound of it and the effect the beer was having on her mind – a haze, blurring the edges of her life.

She continued. 'And I didn't realise just how different we really are until, well, you know.'

He nodded. 'Yes, I do, and I'm glad to hear it,' he said as he went to the kitchen and popped the cap off another beer. 'He has folders for everything. Very thorough. Everything initialled and bookmarked,' he said as he came back into the room and handed her another beer. 'He even had you in there.'

'Makes sense, I suppose,' she said. 'We were together for two years, and I don't need to see the inner workings of his laptop to know he'd keep a list of expenditures on me. He'd want to keep a record of everything he bought for me – birthdays, Christmas, holidays. Made sure he'd claim for it I bet, where he could.'

Ethan took another swig of beer, thoughtful. 'Well, the deeper search on him will give us more, I just thought the flashdrive might give us a clue.'

Elena stared at him. 'No, you just wanted

to play.'

He said nothing but his smile confirmed it.

She continued scraping at the label on her bottle and tossed the fragments onto the empty pizza box. 'What about any other searches. Have you found anything?'

Ethan placed his bottle on the table. 'No, not really.'

His hesitation spiked something in her, grabbing her attention. She caught his eye. 'Ethan?'

'Okay, look,' he began, holding his hand out. 'I didn't want to discuss this yet, not until I'm sure of the facts, but I had started a little digging on your uncle.'

'Go on.'

'Well, he seems to have very little tech on board to give him an online presence I could check out. I was also struggling to find any important information via my usual methods, so I tasked someone I know to take a little trip to Somerset. Have a look around.'

'What?'

'It's fine, Elena,' he assured quickly. 'You don't have to worry. He didn't know a thing about it. No harm done.'

'No harm done? A little thing like breaking and entering?'

'He was away. No damage was done to the property, and nothing was taken. It was for information only.'

She looked at the ceiling and groaned. 'Whatever. We're already in deep, what's a little housebreaking between friends,' she said as she glanced at him. 'But I'm guessing by the look on your face that's not the worst part.'

He grimaced. 'Yes, you'd guess right.'

'So hit me with it then,' she said, bracing herself.

'First, you have to understand that the information I have is not the full picture yet, okay. Try not to panic.'

'Ethan, will you just tell me.'

'It seems that your dear old uncle is pretty rubbish with his money. In fact, he goes through it like water on a hot day. He's squandered most of his inheritance on a few bad property deals and has allowed massive mismanagement on the farm. He also has memberships to a few expensive members' only clubs in London. You get the gist.'

'I do.'

'Your uncle was obviously in need of a bailout, because in amongst the mess of paperwork scattered about his office was a letter from your father, replying to your uncle's request for some money. A loan.'

'A loan? For how much?'

'For an amount pretty close to your ransom demand. He must have been desperate because there were also several decline letters for the same amount from pretty much every bank in the country too.' He watched for her reaction as he continued. 'But the problem is that your father refused, said hell would freeze over before he paid a penny towards the farm. That it was not his responsibility, only Edmund's.'

'Oh God,' she whispered. 'That's motive, surely?'

'Well, it might be innocent enough,' Ethan said. 'It's possible that he found the funds he needed elsewhere; managed to sweet-talk somebody else into giving him the money, or even resorted to a loan shark, but we'd be wrong to ignore it at this point.'

Her breath caught in her throat which seemed to be tightening with every inhale. She gulped down the beer, hoping it would help to ease the constriction. 'Yes, you're absolutely right. We should take this to the police.'

'Not so fast,' he said, carefully, as he scrutinised her reaction. 'We need to think about this, figure out what our plan needs to be first.' He placed his hand over hers. 'Yes, we could go to the police and hand over the information but, essentially, he hasn't done anything wrong. Not in the eyes of the law. Even a barrister like your father would agree, this is only circumstantial.'

'But that's for the police to decide.'

'Yes, of course, but if they go down there asking lots of questions, he'll know he's under suspicion, and then we have the added danger of how he might react. Do we want to push someone into a corner where attack becomes the only form of defence?'

'No,' she said with a long sigh. 'I don't know.'

'Think about it,' he continued. 'He's down there in Somerset, blissfully unaware of what we're doing and what we know. That gives us a little time to continue the search on him, find out more.'

'I know what you're saying, but it doesn't stop me from feeling so trapped.'

'Listen, we're far from that. We'll do some more digging, then we'll go to the police. We just need to hold our nerve for a bit longer. Wait it out. Can you do that?'

She thought it through. 'Yes, I think so,' she said finally, calming herself. 'It's not like I have a choice.'

The buzzer for the front door sounded loudly into the room, puncturing their conversation.

She looked towards the door.

'Expecting anyone?' Ethan asked as he glanced at her.

'No one.'

The door buzzed again, jolting Elena in her chair.

'All right, look, we're going to answer it,' Ethan said as he stood and moved across the room. 'If it's Charlotte or your parents, fine, just get rid of them, but if it's someone you don't know, I'll handle it.'

The buzzer sounded for a third time and she tensed, unable to move her body into action.

'Elena, just answer it, or I'll do it,' he ordered.

She stood and crossed the room, grabbing the phone. 'Yes?' she said, keeping her eyes on Ethan.

'Er, hello,' a woman's voice said at the other end. 'Is this Elena Dumont?'

'Who wants to know?'

'I have a delivery for her.'

'Well, I don't want–'

Ethan snatched the phone out of Elena's hand.

'I'll be right down,' he said, his tone calm as he pressed the entry button.

'What are you doing?' Elena cried, as he hung up and went to the door.

'We don't know what this is about, but it's better that we understand it than ignore it. Keeping one step ahead, remember?'

'But I don't like it. I'm not expecting anything.'

'It doesn't matter, because I'm going down instead of you. Anything strange and I'll soon sort it out.'

She grabbed his arm. 'No, I don't want you going down there. What if it's dangerous? I don't want you getting hurt.'

He looked down at her hand clutching his

arm. 'Elena, I can look after myself. Nothing's going to happen to me, so you can let go.'

She paused, nodded, and released her hand.

He hurried down the stairs to the front door, and she hugged her arms around herself as she watched him disappear. She was unable to hear what he was saying, but the muted conversation was calm, and nothing that gave away any kind of danger. Breathing easier now, she waited for him to return.

In his hand was a large posy of white lilies, edged with gypsophila and evergreen leaves, arranged in a little green pot. In the centre of the arrangement was an envelope, clipped onto a long plastic stalk.

'What are those?' she asked as she moved back to let him into her apartment.

He shut the door, and she noticed immediately his rigid posture and clenched jaw.

'I think you need to open the envelope.'

Nervously, she took the arrangement from him and pulled out a hand-written note.

*R.I.P Miss Dumont. Loved, and sadly missed.*

She stared at the words, her eyes wide with horror, as the hairs on the back of her neck prickled her skin. 'What the hell is this?'

He took the posy from her and tossed it onto the table. 'It does change things a little.'

'A little?' she said as she felt the pulse of her heart beating in her throat. 'The person who did this to me is back, and they've just let me know they want me dead. This is as real as it gets.'

'Elena, relax, no one can get to you while I'm here,' he said as he reached for her.

His words pricked her senses into overdrive, making her take a step back from him, as she questioned every decision she'd made since her release.

He watched, his eyes narrowing as he studied her. 'What are you doing?'

'Yes, that's right,' she whispered. 'You're here. How convenient.'

'What, you think this is me?' he exclaimed, his eyes bright with indignation.

'Well, you're the only one who knows I'm here right now.'

'This is your home. Everyone who knows you has this address.'

She shook her head. 'Yes, I know but ...'

'But nothing,' he said, moving closer to her. 'You need to think this through.'

'I'm trying,' she stammered, taking another step back. 'But you're talking too quickly. You're trying to confuse me.'

'I'm not trying to confuse you,' he said, his composure firmly in place as he continued towards her.

'Is this a game to you?' she asked. 'Are you playing with me?'

'No.'

'You, so keen to help. But is it all a lie?'

'You know it's not.'

'Do I? I mean, you and me, it's totally out there,' she said. 'I trusted you so quickly. Maybe too quickly.'

'Elena, this needs to stop right now,' he ordered.

'Why? Why should I stop? What if I said I want you to leave?'

He shook his head. 'You know that's not going to happen.'

Momentarily overwhelmed, she glanced at the door. His eyes followed hers.

'Ah, I see,' he said, the corner of his mouth curving to a smile. 'So now you're deciding whether to run. Is that correct, Elena? To escape.'

She shook her head, tried to deny it, but she couldn't shape the words in her mouth.

'Yes, you are. You're doubting me, aren't you? You think this is my doing. The person who wants to help you.'

'I have plenty of people who want to help me,' she managed, immediately angered by her feeble statement.

He moved closer.

*Don't touch me. If you touch me, I'll never be able to leave.*

'But do they know you like I do?' he questioned. 'Do they care for you like I do? Want to keep you safe?'

He reached for her, but she pushed his hand away. 'Don't.'

He raised an eyebrow, a silent reprimand, and reached out again. She faltered and let him take her hand. He pulled her closer as confusion blurred what was real and what was feared, causing a noise in her mind that was deafening.

He held her close in a tight embrace, but there was no threat, no sense of impending danger. He gently kissed her hair, but said nothing, perhaps understanding that all she needed was time for the storm to pass. Feeling her body slump, she leant against him, the will to resist drowned out by the unused adrenaline saturating every muscle and fibre within her.

She lost herself for a moment, encased within his arms, and steadied, wishing that touch alone could infuse his courage directly into her. Resting her head on his chest she focused her breaths, wondering if this was what madness felt like.

'Am I ever going to be free?' she breathed.

'I'll make sure of it,' he answered. 'I'm going to find the person responsible, I promise you that.'

She looked up at him, stared deep into his eyes, desperate to believe him. And by the way he held her, it felt right to rely on her instincts again. 'I'm sorry for doubting you, Ethan. This is messing with my head.'

'You don't have to apologise. I understand.'

She nodded. 'I'm just so terrified.'

'I know you are, and that was the aim of this little message.'

'Well, whoever sent it should pat themselves on the back, because it succeeded.'

'I hope they enjoy it because it'll be the last time,' he said firmly. 'Now, go and pack a bag because we're going back to mine. It's too risky for you to be here now.'

She hurried to her bedroom, in no mood to argue. Working quickly, she rifled through her wardrobe and drawers, pulling out clothes to throw into a bag, adding a few essentials – toiletries, make-up, shoes. She finished up and went back to Ethan, numb at the thought that she was about to abandon her home, a place she loved; her haven. But it was time to be pragmatic, this was necessary to her survival. Still, she couldn't help but wish for an ounce of confidence that this nightmare would ever be over.

## CHAPTER 23

Five days had passed since the sinister floral arrangement had been received, and there was no denying how much safer she felt by being here with Ethan; how good it felt to be hidden away from prying eyes. She worked hard not to let the knowledge that someone was out there, waiting for their chance, to overwhelm her.

Ethan was watchful, attentive, perhaps aware that whatever trust they had built had taken a hit by the events at her apartment. They continued with their plan and followed up leads, but most would frustratingly fall apart upon closer scrutiny. A small glimmer of hope came when Ethan successfully managed to eliminate her friends, their partners and any of her work colleagues. And although he wouldn't fully eliminate Adam, he could find nothing of any consequence there, either.

Now, it was time for a date she could delay no longer; to revisit her parents and use the flashdrive. Something she had fought to do alone, despite dreading it, and despite Ethan's initial refusal. She'd called her parents, suggested a visit, persuading them she wanted to start again.

Once showered, and with a towel

wrapped around herself, Elena leant against the sink to apply her make-up, swiping her hand across the mirror to de-mist it first. Her mind played out every kind of awkward conversation with her parents, and the logistics of how and when she'd use the flashdrive.

Ethan strolled into the bathroom and slid his arm around her waist, tearing her away from her thoughts, as the warm, spicy scent of his cologne filled the air.

Smiling at his reflection in the mirror, she twisted the mascara wand back into its tube. 'What a good impression of domestic bliss we're creating here. Anyone would think we're a nice, normal couple.'

'Don't ever let us be that,' he murmured as he nuzzled her neck and trailed his hands down the length of her sides, lingering against the curve of her breast under the towel. 'Such a shame you have to go. I could think of far more interesting things to be doing.'

He didn't need to elaborate, she understood, remembering the delights of the night before. Delights of his skillful mouth, causing pain which, when she cried out, was quickly replaced with soft kisses that left her senses confused but craving more. Of hands that had held her tightly as he teased and caressed her body, ignoring her pleas to stop and then not stop, deliberately tempting and depriving it of the pleasure it yearned until she thrashed in a frenzy of need.

Only then did he hit her with an onslaught of sensations that had her screaming out incoherently, unable to breathe. No, he had no need to elaborate.

'Well, if you will keep sending me out on these missions,' she goaded, as she turned to face him, gently pushing her body against his. 'You'll be demanding that I call you 'Sir' next.'

'Now, that's a tempting concept,' he breathed, a smile on his lips. 'And one for later.'

She bit her lip and looked up at him, her gaze lingering on his lips. 'Really?'

'Yes, really, and I suggest you go and get dressed now, before I change my mind.' He moved back reluctantly and gestured for her to walk by.

'Have you always been this officious?' she asked, as the glint in his eye made her tingle.

'Always,' he replied, smacking her behind as she moved past him.

She went to his bedroom, a little peeved that he'd seen through her delaying tactic, and pulled out some underwear and a navy dress from her bag. 'This will have to do,' she sighed, remembering how hurriedly she'd packed, resulting in a dress that was slightly creased. She slipped it over her shoulders, the cool fabric hugging her body, the skirt draping in delicate folds at her knees.

'It looks to be doing very well,' he remarked, leaning against the door frame, his eyes roaming over her. 'You look beautiful.'

'Thank you,' she said with a smile when she caught his gaze linger at the V-shaped neckline.

She grabbed her clutch bag on the chair and stepped into the heels she'd dropped beside it, quickly checking herself in the mirror, smoothing out the fabric of the dress. It was already looking better, and she knew that by the time she arrived at her parents, the creases would be gone.

'Ready to go?' he asked.

'Yes, I think so,' she said, his words suddenly causing nerves to dance in her stomach at the daunting task ahead of her. She felt the beaded pattern of the clutch begin to imprint itself into her hand and loosened her grip.

'Elena, don't panic,' he soothed. 'It's going to be fine.'

\*\*\*

Ethan pulled up outside Elena's parents' house, switched off the engine and walked around the car to open her door. As she got out of the car, he opened the back door and pulled out a smart jacket.

'Ethan, what are you doing?'

'I've changed my mind,' he said as he swung the jacket on.

Panic filled her. 'I thought we'd agreed, I'd do this alone.'

'Yes, but I'd like to see their faces when we walk in together,' he said as he looked at her parents' imposing home. 'I feel like playing the game tonight.'

'No, Ethan, please,' she hissed. 'This is too dangerous. You must go. Before they see you. I'm serious.'

'So am I,' he replied. 'Unless, of course, you don't want to play along?'

He fixed her with a gaze that suitably expressed that the idea was non-negotiable.

'Damn it, Ethan,' she said with frustration, understanding that this was an argument she wasn't going to win.

He looked back to the house. 'Anyway, it's irrelevant now.'

'What do you mean,' she said as she followed his gaze and saw her father standing in the open doorway.

'Elena?' her father said, watching their altercation on the pavement below.

'Jesus,' she groaned under her breath and hurried up the steps to her father.

'Dad, hi,' she said as Ethan followed behind. 'I'm sorry, there's been a slight change of plan. This is my friend, Ethan. It's late notice, I know, but I'd like him to join us this evening?'

'Of course,' her father said as he looked him over, sizing him up, considering what the connection was between this man and his daughter. But he kept his charm and his manners, not giving anything away just yet.

'Ethan, this is my father, Charles,' she continued. She could have laughed at the absurdity of the situation, but there was far too much to lose, so instead, she settled on blind panic.

'Hello, Mr Dumont,' Ethan said, cool and composed as he shook his hand while she worked hard to control her heart rate. 'What a beautiful home you have here.'

'Thank you,' he said with a guarded smile. He tentatively placed a small kiss on Elena's cheek and looked Ethan in the eye. 'Please, come in,' he said as he stood back from the door. There was none of his usual exuberance, only a cautiously friendly greeting in the circumstances, and Elena was glad of it. He had a lot to make up for still and, if he was trying, he was taking it seriously. But maybe because of that, and somewhere deep within her, was the feeling of guilt at the underhand nature of their visit.

'Shall we go through to the others?' he said as they made their way through the lobby and down the corridor towards the study.

Her father opened the door and there, standing before her, was her family: her mother and brother – more a stranger than a sibling, the only link their same coloured hair, which he wore short and very well-groomed. But the sight that caught her off guard, making her suddenly rooted to the spot, was her uncle, standing with his back to the fireplace, drink in hand, staring at both herself and Ethan as they walked into the room. The work she had done to bring her heart rate down slipped away as it began its fast pace again. The four of them watching her and Ethan in the awkward atmosphere was intimidating, and it took all of Elena's strength to calm and compose herself while considering if they had done it this way deliberately, knowing it would fluster her?

'Elena,' her mother said. She jumped up from the sofa and walked over to her as her brother and uncle eyed them both suspiciously.

Elena greeted everyone with as genuine a smile as she could manage. She hugged her mother, picking up the hostility that filled the room.

'Hello,' her uncle piped up, his eyes on Ethan. 'So, who is this cuckoo in the nest, eh, Elena?'

'Who indeed?' her brother muttered as he drank his champagne.

She looked at them hard. 'That's enough. He's a friend, his name is Ethan, and you should know right now that if you can't be pleasant, we will be leaving.'

'No, Elena, there's no need for that,' her mother said hurriedly. 'Charles, get them both a drink.'

'Of course,' he said as he moved to the cabinet behind the desk and poured two glasses of champagne. He walked over and handed one to

and turned to face the interroga-
right; it's her business and nobody

'Ethan, it's very nice to meet you, and you are welcome here,' her mother said warmly.

'Thank you, Mrs Dumont. It's very nice to meet you too,' Ethan said, giving Elena's mother a smile that caused her cheeks to flush.

'Please, call me Sophia, and this is Edmond, my brother-in-law, and my son, Milo,' she said as she flashed them both a stern look. 'They may sometimes need reminding of their manners, but they'll get there in the end.'

They both mumbled a half-hearted greeting and Elena noted their discomfort. She also saw the strain in her mother's expression as she too struggled to understand who this new man was in her daughter's life. But despite the awkwardness it didn't stop the warm satisfaction of subtle triumph as Ethan turned his attention to her brother and uncle, smiling again as he raised his glass to them, not in any way intimidated by the moment. Taking it one step further, he then placed his other hand against the small of Elena's back, an action that was picked up by everyone in the room, like bees to honey. Another maddening piece of the puzzle that she would decline to share. She should have known that Ethan would do something like this. It was too much to ask someone who felt the way he did not to stake his claim in some way, but she enjoyed the way her family reacted and made no attempt to move or conceal it.

Milo scowled at Elena as she drank, knowing he was forbidden from any further questioning, but there would be more comments made before tonight was over, she knew. He'd soon revert to type. She was ready though, and would face it in a way she had never done before, because that was just it; how she dealt with her family was all *before.* Before the abduction, before the betrayal by her father, and before Ethan had come into her life. These were new traits in Elena that they didn't yet know, but by the end of the evening, they would understand.

Elena watched as her flustered mother hurriedly thought of something to say. 'Let's go to the dining room, shall we?' she said. 'I'll speak to the caterers to add an extra setting to the table.'

'That sounds like a very good idea,' Charles said, happy to move them on as he made his way to the door. The others followed, and Elena hoped the move to another room would help to melt the ice that was beginning to form. Her father led the way, and Elena held back so that they would be the last to follow.

Ethan's arm snaked around her waist as he moved close enough beside her to speak quietly into her ear. 'You underestimate how well you cope,' he whispered, 'but let's not forget the other reason why we're here.' He squeezed the metallic object into her hand which she took and wrapped her fingers protectively around.

She nodded and kept her eyes front as her uncle turned his head, eyeing them, checking them out.

Elena and Ethan entered the dining room. Every effort had been made – a beautiful arrangement of fresh flowers sat in the middle of the table, and the best crystal was out. In any other family, this would be a show of love, an effort to bring a family together, perhaps. But not in Elena's. Instead, this was a show of power and a lesson in who was in charge. They waited to take their seats as the caterers laid an extra place at the table. She knew that the evening would consist of only the best food and wine, but it didn't help her. She had no appetite whatsoever. Her mother gave out her seating instructions, and Elena was relieved to be placed next to Ethan. Her brother sat opposite, next to her uncle and her mother was by her side at the head of the table, her father the opposite end, in his usual spot.

Elena subtly dropped the flashdrive into her clutch bag just as the waiting staff entered the room to serve the wine. Her uncle spent much time deliberating, asking if there would be a fish course and what the meat would be. She inwardly cringed at how pretentious he sounded, guffawing like a buffoon, a harmless fool. But his steely eyes emphasised that the joviality never reached that far, hinting that there was much more to this man than his inoffensive exterior. She watched him, trying to find a glimmer of something that might expose him, and was only distracted when she too was asked for her choice of wine. She opted for a glass of white, ignoring her brother's watchful stare, perhaps waiting for a slip-up that he could jump on and attack.

# CHAPTER 24

Plates of seared scallops were placed in front of them all, and her father quietly thanked the waiting staff before they moved to the back of the room. It would have been impossible to ignore the atmosphere, and Elena imagined the staff having a good laugh about it later, over a cigarette outside.

'Have you had any more thoughts about when you are going back to work, Elena?' her father asked as they began to eat.

Milo snorted noisily, placed his cutlery on the plate, and took a large slug of wine.

'Milo,' Charles said. 'I would like us to have a pleasant dinner.'

Elena drank her wine too. Her father was trying hard, causing another twinge of guilt at what she was about to do, but now was the time to begin the plan. 'Actually, I have some documents I have to print out for work, I don't know if Mum mentioned them to you?'

'Ah, yes she did. Of course you can print them here.'

'Great, thanks.' She pushed the food around her plate and took a few bites, but she was unable to eat the rest. So she twisted the stem of her wine glass between her fingers and glanced at Ethan who was enjoying the food before him. He noticed and gave a sideways look and smiled; a show of support.

Milo caught the exchange and glared at them. He opened his mouth to speak, but Edmond spoke before all of them.

'Are you local, Ethan?' he asked as his eyes narrowed. 'I'm in Somerset. Charles dragged me into town. Can't stand the place, except for my brother's hospitality and maybe White's in St James's Street.' He gave a strange laugh as the drink in his glass threatened to spill out onto his napkin. 'Always get a good meal here, though,' he said as he tapped his belly.

'I live on the other side of town,' Ethan said as he finished his food, keeping an eye on Milo.

Milo made his move. 'What part of town, exactly?'

'Docklands, near the Wharf.'

'Ah,' Milo said, giving a good show, making a steeple of his fingers, deep in thought. 'But, isn't that where Adam lives, Elena?' He waved his finger between the two of them. 'Does he know about this little arrangement?'

*And so it begins.*

'No, he doesn't,' she replied curtly. 'Not that it's any of your business, but I've ended my relationship with Adam.'

'My, my, Elena,' he said with a tight-lipped smile. 'What have you been up to?'

'Back off, Milo,' she warned.

'Milo,' Sophia said, but it was soft and he ignored it.

'Maybe it's the influence of her new friend,' Edmond said with a glint in his eye, enjoying this exchange.

'That's enough,' Charles warned.

'Well now, Edmond, that's a very good point,' Milo said, ignoring his father. 'What's the deal between you two, eh? Did the two of you meet over a pile of bones at the museum?' he asked with a chuckle.

'How funny you are,' she replied sarcastically, through gritted teeth.

'Yes, that's right, I'm hilarious,' Milo replied, his tone empty of humour. 'So come on Elena, tell us all where you met. I'm sure we all want to know.'

Elena sensed the tension in Ethan, feeling the heat of anger radiate from him.

'Why do you suddenly care about me and what goes on in my life,' she asked. 'You certainly never cared in the past.'

Milo glanced round at Edmond. 'Well, could it be that Elena has something to hide?' he said. 'She certainly seems reluctant to share.'

'Oh, come on, Milo, we all know that's got nothing to do with it,' she replied. 'For someone who cares so little for me, you do seem very keen to know about every intricate detail of my life. Does it frustrate you that I won't share?'

'No,' he huffed like a cocky adolescent. 'Couldn't care less.'

'Oh, really,' she said, rolling her eyes. 'Well, whatever, Milo, but this conversation is over now.'

He locked eyes with her, his lip curled in anger. 'Oh, is it?'

'Yes, it is, and you're going to stop with the glaring, the remarks, and the belittling now. Am I making myself clear?'

'That sounds awfully like a threat, Elena. Who's going to make me?'

'I am,' she replied, not willing to back down.

'You?' He laughed. 'You? And who's army?' he goaded.

'How about mine,' Ethan interrupted, leaning in with an arm resting on the table as he glared at Milo.

The mocking smile was knocked from Milo's lips as if Ethan had swiped it away with his fist. Glancing at Elena, he did a double-take when he saw her small triumphant smirk.

Sophia laughed nervously. 'Milo. Behave,' she lightly reprimanded as she glanced at Ethan.

'What?' Milo spat, his hand outstretched towards Elena. 'Can't you see what she's doing?'

'You can apologise to Ethan and your sister too, I think,' she said with a gentle point of her finger, in an attempt to keep things from deteriorating any further. 'She has been through enough recently.'

Milo was indignant. 'Why would I want to do that?'

Ethan kept his eyes fixed on Milo, his demeanour betraying the amount of physical damage he could do to her brother. And somewhere in her mind, Elena considered how much she'd like to witness it.

'Milo, that is enough!' Charles thundered, throwing his napkin down onto the table, startling Elena and her mother. 'You will apologise to your sister immediately, and I suggest you cut back on the wine and remain quiet until you can be civil. You are embarrassing yourself in front of our guest.' He glanced at his brother. 'You are not helping either, Edmond.'

Edmond sank back into his seat, opened his mouth to speak, but then thought better of it.

Her father was the epitome of etiquette, and despite whatever he may be feeling about this situation, he would not let his family behave so shabbily in front of others – especially one they knew so little about.

'You have my apology,' Milo replied tersely, without remorse.

Calmer now, Charles gave Ethan a small smile. 'I apologise for my son, Ethan. He's headstrong, but it has made him a very successful career as a barrister like myself, and sometimes his assertiveness spills over into his personal life.'

Ethan returned the smile, his composure

restored, but his eyes gave away the anger that lay just beneath the surface.

'Can I get you more wine?' he asked, pointing to Ethan's empty glass.

'Thank you, but no. I'm driving later.'

'Some water, then,' he said as he gestured to one of the waiters who approached the table and filled Ethan's water glass. 'You would benefit from the same, Milo.'

'I am *not* drinking water,' Milo huffed.

Her father sighed, returned to his food, and bought up an innocuous subject that could safely move them on from the confrontation. Everyone acted with quiet civility, eating their food, and joining in the conversation. All except Milo, who continued to brood like the spoilt child he was.

'I think we'll have coffee in the drawing-room,' her father said to the head of the waiting staff as they finished up. The man nodded as the other waiters moved forwards ready to clear the table.

Now was the time to get to work. Elena got up and smoothed her dress, her hands clammy and her heart racing. 'I'd like to use your computer now please, for these documents?' she said under Ethan's watchful gaze.

'Of course,' her father said as he moved to the door. 'Use the laptop in the study.' He held his hand out, gesturing everyone to leave.

She glanced at Ethan. 'I'll just be a minute,'

she said as steadily as she could.

***

Elena's heart thundered as she hurried to the study. Was it because of the guilt? It should have been the guilt, but that was not the reason. It was because she was excited, thrilled even, living this way. On the edge, with Ethan. She turned the little chrome stick over in her hand – so small, and yet ready to unleash so much damage.

As she turned the door handle, she inwardly thanked her legs for getting her there and began to tremble as she fired up the laptop. She just needed to let the flashdrive work and then close it down. Simple as that, and he wouldn't know a thing about it. She watched the screen as it kicked into action and listened to the faint voices coming from the drawing-room. She hoped Milo would be behaving, but even if he wasn't, and if earlier was anything to go by, Ethan would be fine.

The system was open and ready, so she plugged the stick into the computer and watched as its little red light at the tip flashed repeatedly. It was working, sending out its code, invading every corner of the system. Stealing all of the information the computer held, with nothing to stop it. Her hands were shaking as she waited. Ethan was right, no one would have any idea of what the device was doing behind the scenes. No clue at all. A bit like her.

The handle on the door turned, making her jump. Her father walked in, catching her eye. 'Are you all right, Elena?' he asked. 'You look like you've seen a ghost.'

She smiled. 'You startled me, that's all. I didn't hear you coming,' she said as she grabbed some paper from the printer and folded it in two, her fake documents. The light on the stick went out, its work done. She hurriedly released it and closed the lid of the laptop as he walked across the room towards her.

'I'm glad we are alone,' he said. 'It's nice to be able to talk, away from the bravado of your brother. Even though you seemed to enjoy challenging him a little tonight.'

'More defending than challenging, I'd say, and it's nothing more than he deserved. I apologise if I was rude, but I'm not sure either of us will get a genuine apology from him for his behaviour.'

'I think, in the circumstances, you handled yourself very well. We all know what Milo can be like. He needs to be brought down a peg or two sometimes. It won't do him any harm, and you're right, there will be no apology from him.'

She nodded, happy to have her father's attention, but something about this moment made her uneasy. Something didn't feel quite right.

He walked to the cabinet in the corner of the room behind his desk and poured himself a glass of whisky. 'How are you?'

'I'm fine, Dad. Well, I'm getting there,' she said, listening to the others.

'So, you and Adam, that's over now, is it?' he asked.

'Yes, it is. I know you liked him, but it wasn't right, even before... you know...' she said, unable to say the words.

'The abduction.'

'Yes, the abduction,' she said, faltering. 'And I couldn't go on the way it was after. We were not getting on.'

She heard muffled laughter, mainly from her mother, and she wanted to get back, but her father seemed happy to keep her talking here.

'And Ethan, who's he?'

'Dad, please,' she said, running her hand across her forehead. 'He's a friend. A good friend,' she said, despondent that this was the real reason he wanted to speak to her.

'A friend?' he said as he folded his arms, his eyebrows raised, disbelieving. 'You have plenty of other friends to help you. Friends I have met. Why him?'

She was indignant. 'Why not, Dad? Anyway, I'm not a child, you're in no position to judge or interrogate me.'

'You're right, of course,' he said. 'It's just, so much has changed, and you seem so different.' He sighed. 'I hope you're being careful.'

'Well, that's because I *am* different Dad.

How do you expect me to stay the same with everything I've been through?'

'We have all been through an awful lot, Elena.'

'Oh, I see. Well, I don't recall seeing you in that dank room with me,' she said curtly.

'I don't appreciate your attitude, young lady. You know I wasn't, but I had a loaded gun at my head with the decision I had to make.'

She felt her blood boil. She was travelling down a path from which there was no coming back.

'Oh yes, more like the decision that you didn't make, that left me with an actual loaded gun situation. Yes, that fantastic decision.' She folded her arms, not giving a second thought to the fake document.

Her father drank down his whisky and poured himself another. 'Is this how it's going to be now?' he asked. 'Bitterness and recriminations?'

'You'd like me to forget all about what happened, wouldn't you? Brush it under the carpet, like all the other things in my life. Well, I'm sorry, Dad, but I'm not going to do that. Not anymore. I'm going to live my life how I want and with whom I want, and I'm not going to apologise for it.'

He placed the glass down with a firm thud. 'No Elena, this stops now. I'm not going to stand by and let a daughter of mine go off the rails and hang around with God knows who all because of an event in her life that's now over.'

'It's not over. Not for me,' she spat. 'But that's all you actually care about. Isn't it? That your daughter might ruin your reputation?' Anger made her tremble. 'Have you seen your son? Have you seen the people he associates with? Do you have the same conversations with him?'

'No, of course I don't.'

'So you won't stop me either.'

'I'm your father, and you'll do as I say!' he thundered.

'Really? You're actually using those words?' she cried. 'You can't tell me what to do.'

'Can I not?' he challenged.

'No, I'm not a child, Dad. It doesn't count anymore. You didn't care about me enough to part with your precious money, so you don't get to bark orders at me now. We all know that's your real offspring, isn't it? Money. Well, I hope it buys you the love I'm incapable of feeling for you now.'

He blinked back his surprise. She had said it, had spoken the words that had been buried within her for such a long time, and they both paused as they absorbed what it meant.

'Elena...'

'Oh right, so now you're the injured party. Yes, of course you are. That's just great and just what I need.'

They were no longer matched evenly in this fight. He was faltering, but she was still soaring on the wind of anger as it spilled from her, unable to stay contained.

'I loved you, Dad, in spite of it all. I placed you sky-high on a pedestal and loved you even through the disappointment you couldn't hide from me. All my life I've tried to live up to your expectations. All my life. And it's left me exhausted. I can't do it anymore.'

He said nothing, perhaps knowing how much she needed this moment, perhaps shocked that she had finally spoken out. She didn't know or care as she hurried on, her voice husky from the lump that had formed in her throat.

'Why was I such a disappointment, Dad? Why? Why was I not enough to consider paying the money?'

Unable to control her emotions, anger gave way to hurt, and she began to cry. He walked towards her, but she side-stepped it, not wanting his false concern.

'It wasn't like that, Elena,' he said. 'It wasn't about whether or not I paid the money. I didn't want them to get what they asked for and to take you from us too. They would have taken everything. I couldn't let that happen.'

'I know, you said that before, but I still don't understand. Why would you listen to your brother and not the police, the bloody experts in their field?'

Huge, hot tears now rolled down her cheeks. She swiped them away. She didn't want him to see her weak, because she wasn't that person anymore, so they had to go. She was stronger, hardened, and all too aware of the way her family had treated her.

He sighed, weary, and moved closer despite her reticence. 'Elena, please believe me, I wasn't thinking. I made the wrong decisions, in so many ways, and I'll live with those for the rest of my life. It had nothing to do with the love I have for you.' He sighed again. 'You are worth more than you know. And I see that you have no idea the love I have for you. It's not your fault. I realise I have made a mess of showing you over the years. I'm not, and never have been, disappointed in you, but the damage has been done, I realise that too. I'm sorry I lost my temper. Of course you can live your life how you choose, with whomever you choose and I'll support you however I can.' He reached out, wanting to hug her, but he held back, unsure. 'I'll also understand if you can never forgive me. But I will keep trying, in the hope that you do.'

She had never heard him speak with so much love. Resistance slowly changed to surrender, and she let herself lean against him, resting her head against his shoulder as he wrapped his arms around her.

'Do you think you can forgive me?'

She nodded and found herself hugging him

back, having no control of it, but it was what she needed, and the anger was quick to subside. Whatever rage had been residing in her had erupted and was already dissipating to nothing.

They stood together, letting the moment pass, and deep within herself she began to heal. Perhaps she was forgiving him, and she might let that happen. Perhaps they would achieve a father and daughter relationship that was based on honesty and respect. Perhaps he would respect her as her own person with her own choices. Perhaps.

He took hold of her shoulders and gently pulled away. He smiled and smoothed her hair over her shoulders, like he did when she was a child. It felt good.

'Thank you for letting me in,' he said. 'Feel better now?'

'Yes, I think so.'

He took her hand and kissed it. 'Good.' He looked towards the door. 'We'd better get back. Are you ready to face them?'

She wiped her face with her hands and nodded. She did feel better.

As he shut the door behind them, she was relieved that he hadn't bothered to check the laptop. She looked down, checking the flashdrive and the pink imprint it had made in the palm of her hand.

She found the others talking and laughing, easy in each other's company and surrounded by a vastly different atmosphere from the one she left. Whatever charm offensive Ethan had initiated, it was working. Only Milo refrained from participating, more content to sit and brood. She joined them and sat down on the sofa opposite Ethan, but what she really needed now was to be alone with him, to let him soothe the chaos in her mind.

'All done, Elena?' he said, smiling.

'Yes, all done.'

An expression of satisfaction crept over his face as he finished his drink. She glanced around the room and shoved the crumpled paperwork into her bag together with the stick.

'Elena, we must do this again soon,' her mother said cheerily, slightly flushed in the face, clearly enjoying the effects of the wine and the male attention.

Elena smiled and checked her watch, deciding to give them one more hour of her time before making her excuses to go.

'We never did find out how you two met, did we?' her uncle said to Ethan as they all stood in the lobby of the hallway, saying their goodbyes.

'No, I suppose you didn't,' Ethan replied, with no more of an explanation before moving on to her father.

'Thank you for your hospitality tonight, Charles. It was a wonderful dinner and a pleasure to meet you,' he said, shaking her father's hand.

She watched as her father smiled, still trying to read him.

'The pleasure was mine. Please make sure my daughter gets home safely.'

'Of course,' Ethan replied. 'You have no cause to worry.'

'I do hope not.'

Ethan and Elena made their way to the car as the others stepped into awaiting taxis.

'Well, that was interesting,' she said with a sigh as her parents disappeared back into the house.

'Your family are definitely... eccentric,' he said as he pulled open her door. 'Your carriage awaits.'

She stood close to him. 'Why thank you, Ethan,' she teased as she brushed past him, climbing into the car.

'Just getting you home safely as promised,' he said as he shut the door and walked around to his door.

'Little does he know, I'm in the lion's den... *Oh*.'

He reached over and took her face in his hands, smothering her words with his mouth and a kiss that cleared all thought. Reluctantly, he pulled back. 'Jesus, I have been waiting to do that all night.'

'Yes,' she whispered, struggling to compose herself.

He smiled and kissed her again.

'Ethan,' she murmured with a glance through the window when he pulled back. 'What if they see us?'

'They never believed us anyway, and you're with me now, Elena. I don't care who knows it. We're not hiding from anyone.'

He sat back, happy to have silenced her with that statement, and started the car, pulling away, taking her to where she wanted to be.

'Did you manage to load the flashdrive?'

'Yes. It's all done.'

He nodded. 'Good. And how did it go with your father? I noticed you looked a little emotional when you returned.'

'It was fine. We spoke. Well, we argued actually, and maybe I said a few things I shouldn't have, I don't know. But he apologised for everything, genuinely this time, and I really needed to hear that,' she said as she felt her shoulders relax a little. 'We've never argued like that before, I've never really spoken my mind, and perhaps it's changed things between us. Perhaps we've found something we can work on. I can hope, I suppose.'

'Good,' he said. 'He certainly seemed to be trying. But your uncle and Milo? They're on another level of fucked up.'

'That's the understatement of the century, right there,' she replied. 'And I thought I did well to spend the evening with someone potentially involved in my abduction, and not to scream into his face to admit it. And my brother, well, now you've seen it for yourself.'

'I did. What the hell sparked that kind of attitude?'

'I really don't know. He's always been that way. Competitive. Ruthlessly so. I think over the years he's become entrenched in some sort of power struggle with our father. He wants to be top dog of the family, but he can't quite do it yet. My father won't allow it.'

'Well, his attitude made me want to knock him out.'

'That was obvious,' she said as she got comfy in her seat, muzzy-headed from the wine. 'Maybe one day, I'd like to see that.'

'You would?' he said as he glanced at her, a glint of dark amusement in his eye.

She shrugged. 'I'm adapting every day.'

'And at a fast pace.'

'I have a good teacher showing me the way.'

'The best, obviously,' he said as he took her hand and kissed it.

She smiled as he did but for all her bravado, and after this evening, it was clear that her feelings for Ethan were intensifying much more rapidly and profoundly than she had ever expected. And whatever it was that she was feeling, it surged through her system, burning like a beam of light, and it would soon sear into her soul.

## CHAPTER 25

Elena woke late and in an empty bed, but the sound of Ethan's feet pounding against the treadmill in his gym assured her that she wasn't alone.

She'd slept well. Joining Ethan in the gym was the sensible way to start the day, but instead, she decided that coffee and breakfast were necessary first, having eaten so little at her parents' house last night.

Cool morning air danced over her skin as she threw back the covers and slung her legs out of the bed, causing a quick shiver to pucker it with goose bumps. Dressed only in her underwear, the hazy memory of the night before flitted into her mind; how she'd left Ethan to his computers while she relaxed in his living room, and how sleep had quickly claimed her. She remembered the feel of Ethan scooping her up from the sofa and carrying her to bed, his hands gently undressing her before pulling her into a warm embrace and whispering goodnight.

She threw on Ethan's shirt, fastening a couple of the buttons as she padded barefoot to the kitchen. Pulling open the fridge, she grabbed a bowl of fresh strawberries and pre-made pancakes. Her phone buzzed against the countertop where she'd left it last night.

'Hi, Charlotte,' she said, picking out the largest strawberry in the bowl.

'So you'll never believe who called me this morning,' Charlotte said excitedly, launching into the conversation.

Before Elena could reply, Charlotte continued. 'Your mother. She shared all the details about the man they met last night who's suddenly burst into your life.'

'Oh.'

'Yes, exactly. Ethan, isn't it? So, come on, share. Who is this gorgeous new guy, and why did I have to hear about him via your mother, of all people?'

'He's just a friend,' Elena replied, caught out and unprepared, rolling her eyes at her pathetic response.

'Yes, your mother said the same thing. She didn't believe it either.'

Elena laughed, hoping to mask her nerves, but it caught in her throat in an awkward squeak instead. 'I don't know why it's so hard to believe.'

'Don't you?' Charlotte said, the humour beginning to fade, being replaced by the tiniest glimmer of suspicion. 'Your mother said that she could almost see the sparks bouncing off the pair of you.'

'Really,' Elena huffed. 'That's just ridiculous.'

'Okay,' Charlotte said. 'You're being weird now. Spill, Elena.'

'There's nothing to spill. Yes, he's a little more than a friend, I'll admit to that, but I just wanted him for myself for a while, that's all.'

'But you show up at your parents with him?'

*Damn it, damn it.* 'Well, yes, but I couldn't help that.'

'And more importantly,' Charlotte continued, 'we've not discussed him at all.'

'There hasn't been time,' Elena said quickly.

'Really?' Charlotte exclaimed. 'You're actually going to use that as an excuse? What about the other day?'

'I don't know. I just wanted to spend the time with you, that's all.'

'Right, that's it,' Charlotte said assertively. 'This is totally weird. I'm coming over.'

'No, wait,' Elena blurted. 'You can't.'

'Why?'

'Because I'm not at home,' she said, feeling that bailing out of a burning plane would be less stressful than this conversation.

'So, where are you then?'

'Well, I'm…'

'*Oh*,' Charlotte said, the pieces falling into place. 'I get it. You're with him, aren't you?'

'Maybe.'

'So give me his address and we can meet

up.'

'No, I'm sorry,' Elena said, rubbing a finger hard against her brow. 'I can't do that.'

Silence followed and Elena began to pace.

'What's going on?' Charlotte questioned. 'I thought I'd rib you about your secretive new man, but now you're acting really strangely. You're with a man you hardly know, somewhere unknown, and I'm guessing you're alone with him?'

'Yes, but–'

'And you won't share who he is or where you are?'

'I can't.' She desperately wanted to share everything with her friend; Ethan, the searches, the death threat, but she couldn't. She couldn't risk Charlotte going to the police and opening up the investigation until she and Ethan were ready.

'Are you mad? With everything you've been through? Think of the danger, Elena.'

'I'm not mad, thank you very much, and I'm not in any danger, Charlotte,' Elena said, trying to mask the irritation. 'Honestly.'

'How can you be so sure, you have known him for what, five minutes? This is not you, Elena. You don't do stuff like this.' Charlotte's tone changed in a heartbeat. 'Please tell me where you are. I'm worried about you.'

'I'm sorry, I can't. So much is going on, but really, it's better – safer – if you're not involved.'

'Come and stay at mine,' Charlotte pleaded. 'That's the safest option. Just for a while. We can talk this through, make sure you're all right.'

'No,' she said, exasperation spreading through every part of her. 'Charlotte, please. I'm staying here.'

'Are you in trouble?' Charlotte persisted. 'Have you got yourself involved in something you can't discuss right now? Is he with you, monitoring what you can say?'

'Of course he's not,' Elena said as calmly as she could, despite her insides knotting tight, panicking that everything she'd worked so hard to protect was beginning to collapse around her. 'Nothing like that at all. This isn't some cheap TV drama.'

'Then what's going on?'

Elena continued to pace as she fought for the words, her hand gripped around her phone and pressed hard against her ear.

Charlotte sighed. 'We used to share everything, Elena. Every tiny detail about our lives. But you can't tell me, can you? You can't tell me who he is.'

Pain sliced through Elena's heart. She was deceiving her friend. Something she'd never done before. She should give Charlotte what she wanted to hear, she should be able to trust her friend, but she was mute, her mind racing, wanting to repair the damage this conversation may cause.

'Do the police know?' Charlotte asked.

'No, and it's going to stay that way,' Elena warned, her jaw tense, her voice low. 'He has no need to be included within the police investigation, do you understand?'

'But if he has nothing to hide, why would you worry.'

'I'm not worried, because you won't be going to the police about this. And don't underestimate the damage it will do to our friendship if you go against me. I'd never forgive you if you go behind my back like that.'

'But this is insane,' Charlotte said with frustration. 'You should be around family. You need time to heal.'

'Ha, you're joking aren't you?' Elena cried. 'You have met them after all.'

'All right, I take your point, but there's always me. I want to help you. Jake wants to help you. So do Abi and Louise.'

Elena paused for a moment, listening to the concern in her friend's voice. 'Charlotte, I don't want to fight you over this,' she said, her heart heavy.

Charlotte paused, thinking. 'I feel I should do something,' she said. 'I should discuss it with someone. I couldn't live with myself if anything happened to you and I did nothing.'

'And tell them what? That your friend, an adult, is spending time with a man that you don't happen to know. Yes, big problem there. The police would be round here like a shot, dusting the place for prints, I'm sure.'

'I'd appreciate it if you lost the sarcasm.'

'And I'd appreciate it if you took a moment to consider how you're treating me,' Elena replied. 'You haven't been through what I've been through. It's my battle to fight, and I get to choose how, and with whom.'

'Elena, can you hear yourself?' Charlotte asked. 'What could he have possibly done to convince you to abandon everything in your life and go to him, just like that?'

'It's complicated, Charlotte. I'm not going to deny that, but I'm fine. I'm not vulnerable or at risk. I'm with someone who understands, that's all.'

Another silence, Charlotte's mind evidently racing as much as Elena's. 'Elena, this isn't about drugs, is it? He hasn't got you hooked on something?'

Elena looked to the ceiling, feeling the need to stifle her laughter, understanding how much easier that explanation would be. 'No,' she said calmly. 'It's nothing to do with drugs. I'm as sober as a judge.'

Charlotte muttered something inaudible.

Elena continued, not about to give in. 'Don't test me, Charlotte. It'll destroy us. I want you in my life. I don't know what I'd do without you, but all I know is that I need to be with him right now. I'm in no danger, I promise, and you have to trust me on this. I have a lot of stuff to work through and he's helping me with that. I'm sorry if that's hard to take, but I'm not going to change my mind.'

'Okay, okay,' Charlotte sighed, defeated. 'I'll let you be. You're clearly determined to do this your way, but while you are still my friend, I'm going to be the sanity in all of this craziness.'

Elena released her breath.

'I want to hear from you regularly, to check that you're all right,' Charlotte ordered, in full parent mode. 'The minute I feel something is wrong or you're acting strangely, more strangely than you are right now, I will intervene.'

Elena could have screamed, but if it made Charlotte feel in control and away from outside interference, she'd agree. 'All right, yes. Fine,' she said, finally. 'I realise this is hard for you ...'

'No, it's fucked up and crazy, but, like you say, I haven't been through what you've been through, and if you're going to stay with him anyway, at least this way I can still be in your life, a stable force.'

'If you feel you must,' Elena said, wondering what it was in her personality that made others want to control her.

'And I'd like to meet him,' Charlotte continued. 'See what the fuss is about.'

'Yes, if you'd like,' Elena said, already mentally preparing her excuses to delay that from happening.

'I'm always here for you, Elena,' Charlotte said, her voice softer now, perhaps as exhausted as Elena had become from this conversation. 'Anytime. Okay?'

'Yes, I know,' Elena said as tears welled in her eyes. 'And thank you, but I'm fine. Really.'

She hung up the phone and resisted the urge to go back to the bedroom, curl under the covers and disappear from her life for a while.

Feeling more than a little flustered, she tossed the phone on the counter and reached into the cupboard for a mug. She needed coffee now more than ever. Ethan appeared, and she flicked a glance over her shoulder, registering his naked torso and the sweatpants that covered the lower half of his body. He was beautiful, even like this, a bright sun that scorched your eyes if you stared directly into its light. But his expression was dark, serious, and it didn't take a genius to figure out why.

'I suppose you heard that,' she said.

'I'm happy to hear that I have your loyalty,' he replied as he strode across the room to join her in the kitchen. 'But who spoke to you like that?' He crossed his arms and leant against the counter opposite her.

'Charlotte,' she said bluntly, reaching up to grab another mug and the jar of coffee. She loaded the machine, hit the switch and watched as it began to hiss into action. 'She's spoken to Mum, about our dinner last night,' she said. 'Clearly, everyone knows we're far from friends and that has made everyone suspicious of who you are. Especially Charlotte – hence the heated conversation. I'm vulnerable, apparently, at risk.'

He didn't say anything and she turned to face him, watching as he stared out of the window, thoughtful. The quiet moment intensified the electricity that filled the room, a magnetic pull between her frustration and his anger. 'Do you trust her?' he asked, still and unmoving.

'Yes, for now. I wouldn't tell her where I was, so she thinks I'm under some sort of spell with you. She's stipulated that I have to get in contact with her regularly to prove I'm still alive.'

'Do you now?' he murmured, disliking being dictated to, as much as she did.

'I know, it's not perfect, but what else can I do? She wants to meet you too at some point. I don't want her to go to the police, and she threatened to do that.'

'Would you like me to search a little deeper into her life, find something that could be used? For leverage?'

Elena stared, shocked at how easily the words spilled out of him. 'No. Absolutely not. She's my friend and although a little heavy-handed, she's just looking out for me. I'm not going to blackmail her with a past misdemeanour.'

'If you're sure.'

She was pumped up from Charlotte's conversation, overwhelmed.

'I'm not sure of anything,' she snapped as she turned back to the coffee, clattering about, busying herself with the task in hand, but making a simple cup of coffee was an impossible task with tears clouding her vision.

She felt his stare sear into her back. 'Elena, calm down.'

She threw her head back and closed her eyes in frustration, 'Jesus, Ethan, I'm trying. This is all so fucked up. And now I feel like everything is falling apart.'

She turned to face him as he walked to her. 'No, it isn't,' he said. 'We can handle Charlotte. Give her what she wants.'

'And you're happy with that?' she asked. 'She's going to be looking for something, anything, that's going to allow her to go to the police.'

'So let her, I'm not going to do anything to you that will give her that opportunity. At least not anything that she'll be able to see,' he murmured as he tilted her face up to his.

'I thought you would protect me from harm?' she said, the air between them alive with heat and tension.

'Yes, I will,' he said with a dangerous smile, 'but how I protect you from myself is, in itself, a little trickier.'

He placed his arms either side of her, locking them straight, and they stared at one another; fired up. His phone rang out in his pocket, and she waited, expecting him to answer, but he didn't break his gaze; his focus entirely on her. She shifted slightly under the weight of his body pressed against hers.

He smiled again, entwining both hands in her hair now, tugging at it to tilt her face up to his. 'Are you under my spell?' he asked as his eyes clouded. 'Is Charlotte right?'

The game was beginning, and she felt as if she'd stepped into the eye of the storm.

She held his gaze, refusing to be the one to break first. 'Does it matter?'

The slight nod of his head acknowledged her question. 'No,' he said as his hand trailed from her hair, his fingers softly clasping her jaw, his palm against her throat. 'I don't believe in spells and magic.'

'Neither do I,' she said, her eyes hungry for him. 'I know what I'm doing. I want it all, everything you can give me. Everything I know you'll give me, and I don't give a damn what anyone else thinks.'

'Perfect,' he breathed as his mouth found hers, firm, and demanding a response. She let out a moan as his lips travelled to her neck, and his teeth grazed over her skin. 'I like this,' he said, pulling away only an inch to speak, his fingers trailing down the back of the shirt.

'Well, it is yours.'

He brought his eyes up to hers. 'Don't be smart with me,' he warned. 'I meant what's under it.'

'I know exactly what you meant, and again, it's yours.'

That was it, whatever it was that was holding him back snapped, right there, and he picked her up and carried her to the bedroom, throwing her down on the bed, making her gasp as he took hold of her hips and hauled her underneath him in one quick move. His eyes burned with desire, almost unseeing as he relied only on the sense of touch, losing the control he always immaculately maintained. She revelled in the knowledge that it was all because of her. He gripped both edges of the shirt and ripped it open, exposing her body to him as the sound of buttons clattered to the floor. He treated her underwear with the same respect and let his hands roam over her skin, caressing her with firm purpose.

'Jesus, Elena, you drive me crazy,' he said as his eyes drank in her naked body. He cupped a breast with his hand before seeking it with his mouth. She squirmed at the pleasure of it, lost in the euphoria of being the object of his obsession. He plundered, until her ability to think at all began to fade.

It had never been like this before, and the

pace became frantic, his mouth ravaging skin, causing her to buck underneath him and cry out. With one hand he held her face firm, his fingers digging into her skin, and with the other he pinned her wrists above her head, keeping her exactly where he wanted as he kissed her furiously. She moaned, not wanting him to stop.

But just at that moment, he did stop, suddenly, as if he had just awakened from a dream or a nightmare. He looked down at Elena, really looked at her, clamped tight in his grasp.

'Ethan?' she said, looking up at him.

He released his grip and moved from the bed and her. He pulled on the sweatpants that had, only a moment ago, been hastily discarded. 'I'm sorry.'

'What?' she said and sat up, shocked. 'What's wrong?' She watched him dress. 'Ethan. What went wrong?'

'Did you not feel it?' he asked.

'Feel what? I don't understand.'

'We were close to the edge there, Elena. Really close,' he said as he walked out of the room.

She hurried off the bed, discarded the torn shirt, and quickly slung a summer dress over herself. 'Ethan, wait.'

He stood in the living room and turned to face her. 'I had to stop myself from losing it in there, and I could have. So, so easily. I could have hurt you. I was capable of anything.'

'But you didn't hurt me,' she said as she took a few steps towards him. 'I let you do all those things you just did. I'm not a nervous virgin bride on her wedding night, I'm capable of telling you if I had wanted to stop, but I didn't.'

'And why didn't you? I was too rough with you. You should have told me to stop,' he said, shaking his head. 'You should have *wanted* me to stop.'

She could only stare at him, confused at what was happening.

'Can't you see what I've done to you?' he continued. 'I wanted you, so I set out to do everything to get you, and now you'll do anything I want. Whatever the cost.'

'No, it's not like that,' she said, her heart fluttering with a new panic. 'I know what I'm doing.'

She thought of her visit from Dr Jones at the hospital and the apparent syndrome that she could be suffering from. She had dismissed it then and although it rolled through her mind now, it was of little consequence, because whatever she may have, it was set deep within her, and there was no cutting it out.

'Do you?' he said. 'I thought we could do this, but maybe you should have walked away when you were released. Had a normal life.'

She let out a small gasp, the horror of what he was suggesting shaking her fragile world. 'But I don't want normal and neither do you.'

She moved towards him again, close enough to touch, but he backed away. An action that made tears prick her eyes. 'Ethan …'

'But having a relationship with your captor is something else entirely,' he said with resignation.

He walked to the kitchen, grabbed a glass, moved to the fridge for water, and poured. He turned to face her and she wanted to go to him, wrap his arms around her again, but something stopped her.

He swirled the water but didn't drink. 'I can't lose control like that. I don't want to hurt you.'

Her heart pounded. His conscience had finally emerged, but she was too caught up in him to leave now. She stared, frozen, not able to move, not able to think.

He softened when he saw the desperation in her, put the glass down, and held out a hand. 'Come here.'

She rushed to him and hugged tight, needing to be close again, to have the contact. 'Please stop this, Ethan. We can do this, we can work it out. You wouldn't have hurt me, it would never have gone that far, I know it. I know you.'

He held her face. 'Can't you see? I've only been thinking about my own needs. I want to own you, to possess you.' His eyes were deep pools as he looked down at her, pools that she could drown in. 'I like making you scream,' he said as she watched his mouth move. 'I like taking you to the edge and bringing you back.' His hands squeezed her hair tight, but there was restraint in him too. 'But what happens if that moves on to harming you, Elena. What then?'

Everything slowed, her world full of fear and panic. What they had was nothing like that, nothing at all. She felt that deeply.

She gently placed her hands over his. 'You won't, I know you won't.'

He released his hold and laid his hands on the counter, lost in his own torment, somewhere she couldn't reach him.

'My desire for you makes me dangerous,' he murmured, his body rigid and still. He exhaled deeply. 'I know what I said before, about needing you to be mine and I still feel that, like a fire in my fucking chest, but I need to do what's right too.' He paused and shook his head. 'Fuck, I can't believe I'm doing this.'

'No, no, no,' she cried. 'Don't say it.'

'But I'm giving you the opportunity to get out of our little arrangement.'

The grenade was thrown. Her life blown apart. 'No! You can't do that! You can't end it,' she cried as she shoved him hard. '*Now* you have a conscience? *Now* you want to let me go? After all you've said and done?' She thumped at his chest, sobbing. 'You can't do that to me.' She couldn't breathe, couldn't live in a world where he no longer wanted her and she began to cry.

He took her hands in his and looked at her, both anger and frustration burning in his eyes. 'Elena, I'm doing it *because* of you. I don't want to let you go, I would rather tear my eyes out, but I am trying to do the right thing for once in my life.'

'Well I don't want you to,' she said, her face wet with tears. 'What about before? You said you'd never leave. What happened to that?'

'Elena...'

'No. Please.' She clutched his face in her hands, frantic. 'Ethan, please. Don't do this. We can work it out. Stay with me.'

He held her close, buried his face in her hair and she clung to him, desperate to hold on to the most precious thing in her life. Too soon, he pulled himself away and grabbed his phone and strode towards the bedroom, listening to the voice message from the rejected call earlier. She followed.

'Well, you'll have to throw me out,' she threatened, swiping the tears from her face, 'because I'm not leaving. I refuse to make this easy for you.' She was paralysed by the moment, watching him change into a t-shirt and jeans while she fell apart. He strode back to the living room and she followed close behind. He collected his keys and hesitated, a tortured expression giving away that he wanted this no more than she did.

'Where are you going?' she sobbed. She

had dealt with so much abandonment since her release, but this one hurt the most – deep into her soul.

'I need to go out, and I think it's best that I do,' he said with a sigh.

'You can't go now.'

'I won't be gone long. When I come back, we'll work out what to do. I can continue with the search here and I'm sure I can find somewhere safe for you to stay while I do.'

'No, you're not listening. I'm not going anywhere,' she spat as anger burst inside her, a firework erupting. 'You can send me away but I'll just come back. Do you hear me? I'll just come back.'

'Elena.'

'I'll walk through the streets of London to get to you. I'll be alone too. All alone.'

'No, you won't,' he growled with frustration.

'Oh, I will, and you'll have to keep a close eye on me then because I'll put myself into every conceivable situation of danger until you come for me. Do you get it? Do you want to test me?' She rushed to the door and opened it. 'You want me out here, wandering the streets, where it's most dangerous? Fine. I'll go. Maybe then you'll listen.'

'Elena, come back here. Now.'

She walked out into the hallway, her heart so raw it hurt to breathe. She had no idea where she'd go, but it didn't stop her. She had to make him understand, to see sense. The sound of footsteps thudded behind as he rushed to her. She continued on to the lifts and hit the button.

He grabbed her arm. 'Okay, you've made your point.'

She flung it away and turned to face him. 'I haven't begun to make my point,' she cried. 'You gave me a choice, and I made it. I turned my world upside down to be with you. My choice, Ethan. Mine. And you're not going to take that away from me.'

'Do you think I want this?' he said as he grabbed her hands. 'I want nothing more than to keep you here with me, forever, but I'm not going to be responsible for destroying the one good thing that's come into my life.'

'But you're not destroying me. I'm happy. For once in my life, I'm happy. Fucked up as that may be. But if you carry on with this, you'll be destroying us, and I won't let you do that.'

They stared at one another, locked in battle, as the lift pinged and the doors parted. The man inside, ready to leave, blinked back his surprise at the sight of them and their heated silence. They composed themselves and stepped aside, allowing him to go on his way. The awkwardness of the moment calmed them.

'What do you want?' she asked as the doors closed and the lift began its descent. 'What more do you want me to do to prove how much I need to be with you. Do you want me to drop to my knees? To beg?'

'No, of course I don't.'

'Well, stop it, just stop it.'

He looked her over and gently smoothed away the hair that clung to her face, wet with tears. 'Come back with me,' he said, frustration still simmering in his eyes. 'We don't need to have this drama out here.'

He wrapped his arm around her and walked her back towards his apartment.

# CHAPTER 26

Ethan closed the door and dropped the keys onto the table. The storm had passed, leaving them spent, and with nothing left to do but assess the damage. Elena went to the sofa and sat down.

'Ethan, please talk to me,' she said. 'We need to work this out, because I am not going anywhere. I mean it.'

He sighed, looked to the ceiling, and joined her on the sofa. Sitting forwards in the seat, resting his arms on his legs, he began. 'I'm fighting demons every day with you,' he said. 'I want you, I've never hidden that, but it's all consuming, as I knew it would be. So I had to be in control of it, and I was doing okay, but you're like my blue touch paper. Seeing the fire in your eyes earlier just tipped me over the edge.'

'But you can't control everything,' she said, reaching out to place her hand on his back. 'Especially your emotions. Or mine.'

He nodded and stared into the distance. 'My parents died when I was fifteen. You know this. My brother was two years younger and fell apart. A complete breakdown. It was truly the worst thing. I was expected to hold it all together. Everyone said I had to be strong, and I was happy to do it – for him. I wanted to help him, look after him, and in some way, it helped me too. Gave me a purpose.'

She was desperate to hold him, take away his pain, as she imagined how hard it would have been for him. The grief he must have gone through, all alone, only a teenage boy, just starting out in life. The sudden expectation of having to be the adult, to cope. But she resisted and let him continue.

His lip curled into the faintest smile as he remembered. 'I managed it, Elena. I took care of everything and looked after my brother. Obviously, we were too young to be left alone, so we lived with an aunt and uncle. We were in their care, but I created the routine for him. I kept us in school, kept things stable – for him and for me. I kept all the balls in the air and took over, but it took control and that gave me what I needed. I began to live my life by it – control in all things. I made the decisions.' He ran his fingers through his hair. 'I lived my life and it was fine, it was easy. Don't get me wrong, I was no monk, but I didn't let anyone get too close to me and that was fine too, because then I didn't have to feel.'

He sat back and reached his arm around Elena, pulling her towards him. She let him do it and tucked herself under his arm, gripping tightly, cleaving herself to him. He had given her too much rope. He would have to prize her body off him before she'd let him go now, but he seemed happy to let her do so as he continued.

'But then you came along, and I knew that was it. Something inside me fired into life again at that house.' He smiled. 'I wanted to keep you safe, but it was more than that. I wanted *you*. I was well aware of what I was doing. I charmed you, made you feel safe enough to want me too, enough to be confident that you'd call the number eventually. I kidded myself that it was as simple as wanting you, so I had to have you. And maybe it was, at the beginning. But now, it's so much more than that. I need you, Elena, there's no doubt about it. You make my life worthwhile. You give me something pure, something decent. You make me want to be a better person. Better than I was before. But sometimes the demons come out to play, and when that happens, how can I be sure that it won't tip into something more damaging?' He looked in her eyes. 'Look at you, so, so beautiful, looking at me like that. What if it's already happened?'

'I don't care,' she said without hesitation. 'There's nothing wrong about you and me. It's complicated and a little... strange... but it's not wrong.'

'And that answer just proves what I've done, Elena,' he said.

She smiled. 'No, it doesn't. I don't care what you say. You're a man with a conscience, that's all.' She moved to kneel beside him, taking his face in her hands. She kissed him.

'So many demons,' he whispered.

'I know, Ethan,' she said as she held him. 'But I want all of you, including your demons. It's what makes you who you are.' She offered another kiss. 'Let me make you happy. I can do that.'

His breath caught, and he moaned.

She traced her finger over his jaw, watching his resistance give a little, breaking down the barriers. 'I belong with you,' she murmured, her fingertips warm and enticing against his skin. 'You won't hurt me. I know it. Only if you make me leave.'

'Elena.' His eyes scanned hers, heavy with the knowledge that he was losing the will to fight the conflict in his mind. 'I'd tear down the stars for you.'

Taking his hands in hers, she placed them on her body. 'If I'm not with you, I'll have nothing. Is that what you want?'

He shook his head. She kissed him, gently, languidly, pouring all the feelings she had for him in it. All the want, the need. The addiction.

She leant in closer. 'Come back to me,' she whispered as she drew him close. 'I want you as you are, the Ethan I know.'

He pulled her close and kissed her, taking control. She allowed it, encouraged it as his touch set off an explosion of desire within her.

He was careful at first but gained his equilibrium as he held her and pressed his hands firmly against her. She went willingly and savoured the feeling that this little drama was passing them by. She raised her hands and buried them in his hair as the hot sensation of longing radiated through her body, picking up again, where it had been abruptly cut short earlier.

A new feeling raged through her with fierce ambition. She was never going to leave him and, more than that, she was never going to let his conscience get in the way of their relationship again.

\*\*\*

Music from the radio filled the room as Elena worked the coffee machine. The morning had been perfect. They had woken, tangled together in Ethan's bed, bathed in morning light, letting the world and all of its chaos pass them by. Hands had trailed over warm skin, finding a newness in everything they touched. Eyes had searched, connecting on a deeper level, and their bodies had moved together, giving and receiving pleasure.

Now, thrust back into the reality of their situation, she carried the two mugs of coffee to the office, and Ethan, and pushed aside a cluster of wires to place the mugs down.

She sat and watched as he concentrated, lost in his world as he flicked between screens.

She glanced at the screens too, watching

lines of code scroll up in one continuous roll. 'How do you do it?'

'Do what?'

'Get into people's systems.'

'A bit of java script goes a long way,' he said with a smile. 'You write some code, manipulate the order of things; confuse the system. It creates a weakness I can work on until I'm in.'

The computer beeped, interrupting their conversation.

'What's that?' she asked as she cupped her mug in her hands.

'It's just the system's attempt to get into another file,' he said. 'It's encrypted and won't break. It's so heavily protected, whoever owns it has chucked everything at it. That's what you're hearing, all of my coded attempts to confuse. It'll break, but it might take a while, that's all.'

'And what's that,' she asked, pointing to another screen. 'Whose details are you looking at there?'

'Those are Maxim's files.'

'You're hacking him again?' she said, suddenly afraid. 'But I thought you two agreed to leave each other alone?'

'Don't panic, we did. I've just gone through the information I already had on him.' He grabbed his mug of coffee. 'A set of dates in his diary, around the time of your abduction. I didn't pay it much attention before, but something about this is off somehow.'

'But he organised the abduction. It makes sense that he would have dates.'

'Yes, and that's exactly why I skimmed over it. But looking at them again I noticed these two specific dates he's kept in his diary,' he said, highlighting them on the screen. 'One of them is not consistent with when you were taken. It's too far in advance.'

'Maybe he was micro managing the situation at the beginning?'

'Yeah, but that's not how he works. He keeps his involvement as minimal as possible and gets others to do his work for him. He puts out the word, fixes up the basics and then takes his payment. The less he's involved, the less the police can tie him to the event and that's just how he likes it. But this is different. He's taken a risk for you here, and that's out of character.'

'And what's the other date?' she asked, wanting desperately to believe they were edging closer to the truth.

'Three days into your abduction.'

She stared at him. 'But what does that mean?'

'I don't know, but if we find the person he met, we find the person responsible.'

'Speaking of which, do you have any more on my uncle?' she asked.

'Nothing, his lack of technology makes him frustratingly invisible. I can see that he's used his passport though. He's out of the country right now.'

'Really, he gets to holiday?' she said and tutted. 'Not sure if that makes me unbelievably happy that he's not around, or furious that he gets to take off with no worries, while I'm here, fighting for survival.'

'I think we'll go with happy,' he replied. 'At least he's not around to cause any trouble.'

The screen beeped again.

'Now what is it?' she said.

'Another document,' he said, sitting up in his chair. 'Well, this is interesting.'

Ethan stared at the screen for a moment and then enlarged the details which showed an online bank statement. 'Your brother. It would appear he's been very busy too.'

She leant in to get a closer look at the long list of transactions as her mind began to race. What she saw were innocent enough indications of where he was during the month and what he was doing. Nothing wrong there. But at the end of each month, a sum of money would show up, always five thousand pounds, and always titled 'Rental'.

'Rental?' she murmured. 'What does that mean? My brother lives alone, and although he owns two properties, neither are rented out.' She looked at Ethan. 'What has he been doing?'

'I'm not sure. I'll need to check it out, but I think he's been syphoning money from his employer for himself.' He pointed to an account. 'You see this,' he said as he highlighted the digits. 'This is the account where his salary originates.' He moved to the other. 'There are a few differences between this account and his salary account, but the source is the same. I think he's managed to open another company account without their knowledge and has been transferring money over each month.'

'I can't believe it,' she murmured. 'I know he's capable of many things, but this? He's paid a fortune; he doesn't need to do this.'

'Considering the small amount and the fact that it's such a large company, it's likely to go unnoticed. For a while anyway. But look, it's disappearing. Each month it's being transferred.' He clicked to run another scan. 'I need to investigate this, find out where it's going.'

She sat back. 'He obviously needs the money for something. Maybe he's being blackmailed? Maybe he's got a secret to protect.'

Ethan nodded. 'Well, perhaps, but this could be drug use, or some other form of unhealthy pastime, but you're right, it could be blackmail. I understand very well the lengths people go to ensure dirty secrets never come out into the open. Perhaps he's no different.' He glanced at her. 'But I'm not the one doing it.'

'I know,' she said with a faint smile just as a realisation hit her, suddenly and without warning. 'Oh,' she whispered. 'What if that's true? What if he is being blackmailed? And what if the blackmailers wanted more? A higher amount. Considerably higher.' She stared at him, wide-eyed. 'Like an amount that could be obtained from a ransom demand?'

He nodded. 'Exactly like that.'

'I've got to do something,' she said. 'I should go to my parents, let them know.' She placed her mug down and stood. 'No, I can't do that. Not right now,' she said, pacing now. 'Things are too strained. What should we do, Ethan? Where do we go from here?'

'Elena, slow down,' he said as he moved to her.

She nodded, but couldn't shake the feeling that the four walls of the room were closing in on her. 'Could it really be my own brother?' she asked, needing to take large gulps of air. 'I mean, what if it is? The bastard.'

He took her by the hand, his brow furrowed with concern. 'Take it easy. Take a couple of breaths,' he said, rubbing her cold hands, giving her a moment to calm.

Saying nothing, she nodded and focused on her breathing, trying to calm her heart rate.

'That's better,' he said and smiled. 'As with your uncle, we don't want to panic your brother. We don't want to give him time to destroy files or evidence either. But I think now is the time to bring in DS McAllister.'

'Yes, absolutely,' she agreed. 'We need to go to the police. We can't wait any longer. And we need to hand over the information on my uncle too. They need to see it all.'

Ethan nodded his agreement. 'I'll get my keys.'

'What?'

'I'll drive us there.'

'No way,' she said firmly, at the very limit of her patience. 'There is absolutely no way I'm strolling into a police station with you. That is *not* happening.'

'Well, there's no way I'm letting you do this alone,' he shot back. 'They'll have no idea who I am. You know I've made sure there's no links between me and your abduction.'

'I don't care, I'm not risking it,' she snapped. 'I haven't gone through all this, uprooted my life, to lose you if you're arrested now. Your presence will be difficult enough to explain and it might make them dig a little deeper.'

'You need to think about this, take more care.'

'Oh, for God's sake, what can possibly happen to me?' she said, bucking against logic like a frustrated child.

'What, like the day you were snatched off the street, in broad daylight?'

His words halted her. They injured her too, a harsh reminder of their history. 'I can take a cab. Where's the danger in that?'

'Where do you want me to start?' he

snapped back, angry now. Angry that she refused to see it. 'You are not travelling alone. It's simply not happening. I can drop the information into DS McAllister's inbox, or something.'

'How will that help when it's likely to bring him round to mine to ask if I know anything about it, only to find I'm not there? He could go sniffing to my parents and they'll waste no time informing him about you, then where will we be?' she argued, refusing to back down. 'Where's the danger? Edmund is out of the country, and I'll make sure Milo is accounted for at his office before I leave.' She sighed, feeling suffocated by the weight of her situation. 'I'm not some stupid damsel in distress that needs saving. I need you here, you have that file to break into. It might be important.'

'I don't know, Elena.'

'I need to do this, Ethan. I won't change my mind.' She edged closer and reached out to touch him. 'Please, I can't risk you going to the police with me. I can't lose you.'

His eyes softened. 'And I can't lose you either. Going out there without me is too dangerous. Can't you see that?'

'Let me do this my way,' she pleaded. 'Don't make me feel weaker than I already do.'

He leaned in and placed a soft kiss at her temple. 'Look, I'm not trying to make you feel weak or helpless, but we need to keep you safe.'

She was silent, resolute, and he caught her

unwavering expression. 'You're determined to go without me?'

She nodded. 'Yes, I am. This is my life we're talking about. My uncle, my brother. I need to sort it out, and I won't have the police sniffing around here.'

He sighed and took a moment, thought it through. 'Okay, look, there is someone I trust. A friend of mine. Someone that can take care of himself as well as you. He can take you. Are you happy with that?'

'Sounds great,' she said. 'And thank you for understanding.'

'I'll give him a call,' he said as he grabbed his phone. 'And you need to call Milo's PA.'

'I'm on it,' she said, hurrying into action.

Elena managed to reach her brother's PA, only to be informed that he was tied up in meetings all day with the Board of Directors. Elena thanked the PA and ended the call, satisfied that whatever he was up to, right now, he was busy with other things.

In the quiet of Ethan's office, she heard the faint sounds of voices in the living room. Two to be precise. The familiar sounds of Ethan, and another. She left the office and made her way towards the living room.

'You just need to take her where she needs to go, wait for her, and then bring her back to me,' Ethan said.

'Seems a little over the top, but if that's

what you want, I can do it.'

'Good, because that *is* what I want.'

'Can I ask you something?' the unfamiliar voice asked.

'Yeah.'

'This is all a little intense, isn't it? I don't know what you've got yourself into here, buddy, even for you.'

He sighed. 'I know, it's complicated, but it's real, and I need to protect her. And walking into a police station with me seems to be her hard limit. She doesn't want me involved. I guess she's had enough anxiety to deal with, so I've got to respect that. But it doesn't alter the need to keep her safe. So, right now, it means someone staying with her, and if it can't be me, I'd rather it be you. I still don't know who's out there, so I'm not taking any risks.'

The other man laughed. 'Mate, we all know you're one big risk.'

'Yeah, whatever,' Ethan said and laughed, comfortable in this person's company, one of his friends.

'But if this helps, I'm happy to assist.'

She walked into the room, and the conversation stopped as they both turned to her. It was unnerving. Conversations never stopped on account of her entering a room, and she didn't know how to respond. The doors that overlooked the Thames were open, letting humid air drift in.

'Hello.'

Ethan walked to her. 'Elena, this is Jack,' he said as he slid his arm around her waist. 'He's going to stay with you, make sure you're safe.'

'Hello, Jack,' she said with a smile and held out her hand to shake his.

'Hi, Elena.' He shook her hand firmly and smiled back. He was tall, with short brown hair and a neatly trimmed beard; almost in the same league as Ethan as far as looks were concerned. Almost.

'You know what you're doing?' Ethan said as he handed Jack a set of car keys.

'Yes, absolutely. The police station. DS McAllister and straight back.'

'I have one file to unscramble. It's tied up with a fucking ribbon, but I'll get it. It'll be done by the time you get back.'

Ethan looked at Jack. 'Better get going. Just keep a lookout; you know what it's like.'

'I do, and I will. She'll be fine.'

Ethan went to Elena as she grabbed her bag. He wrapped his arms around her. 'You have your tracker on you?'

'Yes, right here.'

'Good,' he said and kissed her. 'Get this done and get back here as soon as possible.'

'I will.'

Elena followed Jack across the room and looked around at Ethan one last time before leaving his apartment, shutting the door behind her.

# CHAPTER 27

'Thanks for doing this,' Elena said as they jumped into Jack's car. 'You must have more interesting things to do than ferry a stranger around.'

'It's no problem,' Jack said. 'And no, at the moment I don't have anything more interesting to be doing, so it's all good. Given myself a little break from the world of graphics and design – that's what I do by the way – legitimate career, no off-grid stuff here. But when Ethan asked me to help you guys out, I have to admit to being a little intrigued.'

'So, you know what happened, between me and Ethan?'

'Yes, I do.'

'Oh.'

Whatever self-esteem she was beginning to claw back was floored again at the fact that he was well aware of what she'd been through, yet still chose to be with Ethan. She'd fooled herself into thinking that she could remain in a private bubble, not having to explain her actions, but it was clear their secret was blown.

'You probably think I'm a lunatic, doing this, being with him,' she said as she looked out of the window, not wishing to see his expression. 'And I guess I probably am.'

There was a pause and both were silent. This was not going to plan. She glanced at him and took in his contemplative expression and then settled on the cars ahead of them, sure this conversation was over.

'No, actually I don't think that at all,' he said. 'Yes, this is all a little strange,' he looked at her and smiled. 'Actually, it's one of the strangest situations I've ever known, but I've never seen Ethan like this either; kind of free and content. It's good.'

She smiled. 'Have you known him for a long time?'

He nodded. 'Since we were kids,' he said as he worked his way easily through the light traffic. 'There's a group of us, and we've always been around for each other. Grown up together. Been there and done it all – some of it a blast, and some of it we'd probably rather forget,' he said with a wink. 'Most of the time we're all in touch, but there are times when he disappears, no contact at all, and then he's suddenly available again. It was to be expected when he was in the Marines, but with what he's doing now, well, I've learned not to ask too many questions. I guess you might want to do the same.'

'Maybe,' she said. 'But right now, I need to know who would have wanted to do this to me, and he's helping me with that.'

'Did you know his parents well too?' she

asked, tentatively steering the conversation to where she wanted it to be.

'Yes, I did. They were good, straight-down-the-line kind of people who worked hard and paid their dues, and I think Ethan would have been a very different person had they not died.'

'He said it was a car accident but didn't elaborate. Do you know what happened?'

He sighed at the memory. 'It was all the clichés; bad storm, heavy rain. They were driving home from somewhere, I can't remember where, and didn't see the drunk driver swerving towards them. Suddenly, *bam*, their lives were lost and Ethan and Oliver's changed forever. Happens all the time, I guess, but the devastation it causes…'

She looked out of the window. Tears pricked her eyes. She wanted to go back to him. Tell him she'd never leave, but she had a job to do first.

'Are you okay, Elena?'

'Yes, I'm fine. It's just so sad. But it's helping me to understand him more, and I need that if I'm going to make sense of what we've done. And his need for control.'

'Hmm, that,' he said and smiled. It was enough for her to see that his friends were probably very familiar with that aspect of Ethan's personality.

He glanced at her. 'Can I ask you something now?'

'Yes, if you'd like.'

'How was it, you know, when you were captive? What was *he* like?'

She sighed. No words would effectively convey the full horror of what she went through, but she told her story anyway, enjoying how cathartic it was to be able to talk freely, sharing her and Ethan's bond that developed during her captivity, and how he protected her from the other violent man.

Jack looked quietly horrified, shocked that a close friend had been involved in something so appalling. 'Jesus Christ, what was he thinking?' he muttered, as much a spoken thought as responding to what she had said.

'You know why he was there, don't you? Why he had to do it?'

'Yes, although the details he shared with me were very sketchy. He didn't want to discuss it. Hurt pride, I guess. He'd pissed someone off big time, yes? Had to settle the debt? That's all I know. Like I said, I've learned not to ask too many questions.'

'Yes, that's right. He was in charge of it, and I thank my few lucky stars that he was there. It would have been very different otherwise.'

He rubbed his hand over the back of his neck. 'I don't know what to say. I'm sorry you had to go through all that.'

She shrugged. 'It was life-changing, for

both of us, I think. And I guess people bond in those moments, don't they?'

He nodded. 'Yes, I guess they do.'

'It's hard to explain why I chose to be with him, and I suppose it's harder still for anyone to understand the connection we share.'

'Well, you don't have to explain anything to me,' he said sincerely. 'I can't imagine what you went through.'

She nodded. 'He always tells me that he's–'

'A bad person?' Jack said, surprising her by finishing the sentence. 'Yeah, I know. It's not just a line though, I think he believes it.'

'Do *you* believe it?' she asked, silently hoping on his answer.

'No, I don't, and in all the years I've known him, he's never left anyone behind, so to speak. He makes sure anyone he cares about is suitably looked after, and that's all I can tell you. That actions speak louder than words.'

She felt love swirl inside her, as if it was a physical presence in her body, for the man who was at the centre of her world. And who wanted nothing but her.

She smiled, relieved. 'Thank you, Jack.'

He smiled back at her. 'Not a problem.'

She was grateful for their discussion and understood why Ethan trusted Jack as he did. It gave her new strength. Her self-esteem even managed an elevation from rock bottom.

\*\*\*

Elena and Jack spent over an hour at the police station, handing over a flash drive containing details of Milo's transactions and her uncle's loan request, carefully avoiding the exact specifics of how she obtained the information. It wasn't much to go on, DS McAllister admitted that, but he assured her he'd look into it and get back to her.

As they made the journey back to Ethan's, Elena remembered that there were some things she needed from her apartment. A few more of her toiletries and some clothes. She suggested it to Jack, who was happy to oblige, and he called Ethan, who was not so happy, but agreed when she said she'd check in with Milo's PA and return immediately afterwards. Jack drove to the end of her road, turned the car around, and found a space just a few strides from her building.

'Right,' he said with playful determination. 'I have my orders,' he said as he switched off the engine and unbuckled his seatbelt.

He smiled at her confused expression. 'I will come up with you. I'm not to leave your side, remember?'

She smiled. 'Of course. His control knows no bounds, clearly.'

'With you? No. But I'm happy to assist.' He grinned. 'Today, I am Jack the Protector.'

She smiled. 'Do you have a superhero outfit to reveal under there?'

'No, but if I did, it would have a JP on the

front in big red letters in the middle of a yellow circle, edged in blue. What do you think? Sound good?'

'Okay, that was a lot of detail, Jack,' she said. 'And *a lot* of thought. Is that the graphic designer in you, or would you really like to be a superhero?'

He considered it. 'Both, I think.'

'Well, I now know you a little better than before,' she said. 'Now, let's get this done. We both have our orders.'

They got out of the car, and Jack followed her into her building and closed the door firmly behind him. She grabbed the pile of post on the table in the lobby and they made their way to her apartment. Once inside, she sorted through her post, mainly junk mail, and grabbed some clothes and toiletries, packing them into a bag. As they made their way down to the main entrance, she remembered her phone.

'Damn it,' she muttered and paused on the stairs.

'What's up?' he asked a little ahead of her.

'I've left my phone up there.' She mocked hitting the side of her head with the heel of her hand. 'If I had a brain. You go to the car, I'll only be a second,' she said, already running back up the stairs.

She opened her apartment door as the thud of the front door closing sounded in the hallway, and grabbed the phone from the table.

She locked up but as she made her way back down the stairs, the hairs on the back of her neck stood on end. She was alone, for the first time.

Caution made her pause as she opened the main front door.

She glanced at Jack's car only a few steps away, a few steps to safety. But she couldn't do it. Fear meant she couldn't move. She couldn't see him either, but that was because the driver's side was just beyond her field of vision. 'Just stop,' she said to herself. 'You can do this. There's nothing to fear.'

She peered out to her left and her right as she walked down the steps to the pavement. The street was clear, and she made her move, belting across the road to the car. Any sense of relief at being with Jack again was quickly replaced by ice-cold horror at the sight of him lying across the two front seats, his phone on the floor, playing music to deaf ears. He was out cold with a large welt covering the side of his face; sprung upon without warning while looking at his phone, waiting, and only moments ago joking around with her.

'Oh no, Jack!' she cried out as she pulled hard on the door handle and reached in, leaning over him. 'Jack, Jack, can you hear me?' she shouted, part in fear and part to be heard. Carefully, she put her shaking fingers against his neck, and, after a few adjustments, she felt the steady beat of his pulse. He was out for the count but alive.

*Thank God.*

'Hang on, Jack. I'm going to get help,' she said and turned and pushed the door shut. She checked up and down the street and ran across the road, up the steps to her front door. She needed to get to the safety of her building and call for an ambulance. And the police. This wasn't a random attack, her instincts told her that. Someone had come for her, and they were terrifyingly close. She rammed her hand into her bag and frantically searched for the cold sharp metal of her keys. Finding them deep at the bottom, she grabbed them, and hurriedly jabbed the key in the lock. But her shaking fingers made it an impossible task. 'Come on. Come on. Damn it,' she muttered as she worked.

'Hello, Elena,' a voice said from behind.

## CHAPTER 28

She shrieked and turned, fear ready to take over. It took a moment to recall the familiar face looking up at her from the pavement.

'Adam,' she cried as she ran back down to him, peculiarly happy to see him; a familiar face. 'You've got to help. It's Jack. He's been attacked. He's over there in that car. He's unconscious.'

'Really? That sounds terrible,' Adam said with concern as he looked at the car and then to Elena. 'Who is he?'

'He's a friend,' she said quickly, trying to focus her mind. 'I'm scared, Adam. They're coming back for me. I'm not safe. I need to call an ambulance… I need to call…' The insidious feeling of panic crept up on her. 'Oh God, oh God. Please don't lose it now,' she muttered through forced gasps. Now was not the time for a panic attack. She calmed her breathing and held on to the railings that ran alongside the steps to her building.

'Hey, hey, it's not a problem, I'll help. Calm down,' he said with a smile as he rubbed her back. 'You go up and get a blanket for your friend, and I'll call for an ambulance.'

'Great, thank you,' she said, relieved, and after turning the key in the lock on the first attempt, she dashed back up to her apartment.

Once there, she reached into her bag and grabbed her phone, ready to make a call as she swiped the throw from the back of the sofa. There was only one person she wanted here with her now and, as if fate was stepping in, Ethan's number appeared on the screen.

'Elena. Thank God,' he said when she answered, his voice raised and urgent. 'I'm coming to get you,' he said over the sound of movement and keys rustling. 'Right now.'

'Ethan,' she cried. 'Ethan, come quickly. Jack's been attacked. I think they're coming for me.'

'Jesus,' he snapped. 'Are you in your apartment? Are you safe?'

'Yes,' she said as she rushed to the living room window.

'Elena, listen to me,' he ordered. 'I know who was behind your abduction. I got into the encrypted file.'

She closed her eyes and held her hand against her forehead. 'Oh God. Who was it? It was my brother, wasn't it?' She looked down at the car. It was just as she had left it, with Jack still slumped in the chair. But there was no Adam.

'No. It wasn't your brother.'

'What? Then who?' she cried, desperate.

Ethan sighed. 'It was Adam,' he said as he revved his car into action. 'Adam organised your kidnapping. He wanted your father's money. He was the one behind it.'

'Adam?' she whispered. 'No, that's not possible.' Her body tensed. Cold tendrils of fear wrapped themselves around her legs, like ivy to a tree, rooting her to the spot.

'It's him, Elena. I guarantee it. Look, I'm on my way, I never should have left you alone. Lock yourself in. Don't let anyone in. Do you hear me?'

She was paralysed, terrified, as she listened to the sound of footsteps behind her. He was here. She stopped listening to the rest of Ethan's words as they faded into silence, carried away.

She couldn't breathe.

'Hang up the phone Elena, there's a good girl,' Adam said behind her.

Ethan heard it too. 'Elena, who is that? Who's there?'

'He's right here,' she whispered as Adam's hand covered hers, prising the phone from her grasp.

'What? No! Elena… *Elena!*' Ethan bellowed down the phone as the call was disconnected.

She turned as the puzzle fell into place. He wanted her dead, and now he had come to finish what he had started. And she had made it so easy.

He looked down at her, a strange smile across his lips. 'Don't you know that you should always be sure to close your front door, sweetheart?' he said as he tucked her phone into his pocket. 'It's the first rule of home security. You never know who's out there, waiting.'

His eyes were disturbingly empty, and the fear of what that meant sent Elena's body into action.

She pushed him hard and rushed for her door, and was halfway across the room when he grabbed at her arm and gripped it, shoving her back.

'Not so fast,' he said as he turned her to face him. 'I think we need to have a little chat, my darling. Now, I know there are no rules as to how long one waits before throwing themselves at another, but, really, you've wasted no time with your little friend down there.' He wrinkled his nose. 'A bit disgusting really, don't you think?'

She stood still in his grasp, trying to get her mind to work. She needed to keep him calm.

He smiled, taking her silence as an admission of guilt. 'My, my, you have been a busy little girl, haven't you?'

'Adam, it's not like that. He is just a friend, that's all.'

'You expect me to believe that?'

'Yes, I do. It's the truth.'

'And just who were you on the phone to, eh? Another one, like him downstairs?'

'No one.'

He paused, considering what she'd said. 'Really, then where have you been all this time.'

She didn't reply.

'Maybe I should have installed a tracker

on your phone when I replaced your old one,' he mused. 'Maybe I would have been able to find you sooner, but I really didn't think it necessary. You are the most predictable person I know, after all. Well, so I thought, but now I'm not so sure.' He was momentarily lost in thought and then shook his head. 'But it doesn't matter now. I really don't care, and I don't care if you sleep with the entire male population of London.'

He released his grip enough for her to back away and glance at the door. 'Adam, why are you here?'

He said nothing, but his eyes remained on hers. He looked like the Adam she knew: his build, the contours of his face, but behind his eyes he was different – a stranger. A stranger who wanted her dead. And it frightened her.

'Look, I don't know what you're planning, or why you're here, but the police are on their way. I called them when I came up,' she lied. 'They'll be here any minute.' She truly wished she had.

He stared, assessing her, and shook his head. 'No, I don't believe that at all.'

He stepped forwards a little, noticing the space she had managed to create between them. 'Do you really want to know why I'm here, Lena?'

She nodded, keeping the door in her sights.

'Well, fine, I'll share,' he said. 'This year has been particularly stressful for me. I've made a couple of big deals, but they were risky and one went wrong. Badly wrong. Lost a couple of mil. A shoddy deal, I know that. I rushed it you see? Didn't think it through.' He shrugged, pragmatic. 'Bound to happen in my line of business, but I didn't need anyone to know about it. So, I made plans. Plans that included you. I decided you were going to help me out with that, one way or another.' He laughed. 'And I chose the other.'

'With the help of Maxim, your new friend?'

He stared. 'How the fuck do you know about him?'

'I know a lot of things,' she said, taking the smallest step away from him. 'Made it my business to know.' She didn't know where she was going with this, she just knew she had to keep him talking.

'Doesn't matter, I suppose,' he said with a small shrug. 'In fact, it feels good to be able to talk about it. Get it off my chest. So thank you for that.' He moved closer still. 'You can't imagine what a mess everything became when the whole abduction thing went wrong. Those people still wanted their share, and they didn't take no for an answer. I spent a lot of time and effort to get that money, and lost a lot in the process. Your fault. Again.' He sighed. 'Why didn't you just die?' he murmured in a low tone, suddenly filled with hatred.

'What?' she gasped.

'It would have been so much easier if you had. Now I have to do it all myself, and that was *not* part of the plan.' He tutted and rolled his eyes. 'So, you're going to be a good girl and make this easy. For both of us.'

Suddenly, in an action that she didn't even register, he snapped out his hand around her throat, like a lizard catching a fly.

She let out a strangled cry and scratched at his hands. 'Don't you touch me!'

'What are you going to do, Elena?' he goaded.

She answered that question by ramming her knee firmly into his groin. He cried out and bucked backwards. 'You stupid little bitch!' he yelled as he shoved her hard, making her stumble backwards over the arm of the sofa and onto the floor.

She turned, scooted away and saw him pull out a long plastic box from his jacket pocket, revealing a syringe that was identical to the one used to sedate her before.

'This is a little stronger than the others,' he said with a cold stare. 'Just so you know. You won't wake up after this one, I'm afraid.'

She cried out and grappled to her feet, rushing for the door. She nearly made it too, but as she reached for the handle to drag it back, his hand reached out from behind and firmly pushed it shut. He wrapped his arms around her forcefully, so that her own were trapped by her sides, leaving her unable to move. He dragged her back, away from the door and freedom.

'Adam, stop it! Stop it!'

'Now, it's time for a little nap, and I'm going to help you with that,' he said as they shuffled across the room in a strange dance until he managed to turn her to face him and push her against the wall, ramming his arm across her chest.

'Get your hands off me!' she screeched as she thrashed and fought to free herself, staring at the dangerous chemicals in his hand.

'Fuck, just... stop... struggling,' he panted as he pushed his body against hers and put the cap of the syringe between his teeth, pulling it free.

She stared straight into his eyes, absent of any humanity; absent of any emotion at all. He breathed heavily as he clamped his hand around her chin and forced her head to one side, exposing her neck.

'No!'

'Keep fucking still!' he yelled as he tried to steady his hand, but in the fight and without any proper control of the syringe, he stabbed the needle into her shoulder, making her shriek out with pain and fear. Still unable to get a good hold, he attempted to plunge the liquid into her, to invade her with the poison.

*He's going to do it! He's going to kill me!*

In that moment, a primal force grew

within her. The need to survive. She wasn't going to let this happen again. Memories of everything Ethan had taught her rushed into her mind and, within a second, she hugged her arms close to her body and pushed her hands against him with such force that she managed to propel him away from her. He grunted as he staggered backwards, plucking the syringe from her skin. With no time to think twice, she charged forwards and struck him hard under his chin with the heel of her hand, letting out a loud, shrill cry that merged with his. His head jerked back, and the motion sent him tumbling backwards, cracking his head against the corner of the table before he fell to the floor.

Silence.

He was out cold.

She coughed, gasping for air as she stumbled against the sofa and bent over, resting her hands on her knees. She took a moment to check the damage, holding her hand over the stinging wound. 'I'm okay,' she panted. 'I'm okay.'

She shook her head and snapped into action. She had little time. Reaching down, she fumbled into his pockets and grabbed her phone. The syringe lay by his side, its needle embedded in the carpet, bent and out of shape. She stared. It was half-empty.

She kicked it out of reach even though it was useless now, and dialled the emergency services.

*Hurry.*

She pressed the panic button and hit the buzzer to release the main front door. She hauled open her own and launched herself out into the corridor, hurrying to her neighbour's apartment. Hammering on their door, she yelled for help as the first sensations of wooziness started to take hold.

No reply.

She banged repeatedly, glancing back at her apartment and began to cry. 'Please. Answer the door.'

Still no reply. With no other option, and having to use the wall for support, she stumbled to the top of the stairs. *Got to get down. Got to get outside. Ethan.*

The stairs swayed and danced before her eyes as her legs trembled with the effort of keeping her upright. 'Come on,' she cried. 'Get out of here.'

A faint voice. She looked down at the phone in her hand. *Emergency services.*

'Hello.'

Her legs gave up the fight, and she collapsed to her knees. 'Somebody please, help me,' she said as she held on to the bannister. She wasn't going anywhere.

Events began to blur; hazy, snippets of actions that didn't splice together. Another quiet voice, but when she looked down at her hand, her phone was gone.

'Hello,' she said again as the sound of plastic and glass splintering against the floor below rushed through the silence. That, and the sound of him behind her.

'What's the matter, Leens?' he asked. 'You look a little unsteady on your feet there.'

She turned to face him, slowly, giddy from the drug.

Very much awake now, he stood by her apartment door, a small trickle of blood running down his face. He watched with amusement as her body processed the drug.

'You murdering bastard,' she hissed as she gripped the bannister.

Closer now, he crouched behind her. 'Let's go back inside, shall we? Get you more comfortable.'

She wrestled uselessly and was easily overpowered. 'You won't get away with this,' she cried.

'Oh, Elena. You're such a cliché,' he said. 'And I don't see anyone here to stop me. Do you?'

She looked to the stairs. 'He's coming. He's coming...'

*Stay awake. Don't let him win.*

'Who's coming, Elena? Who is this imaginary person?' Adam said with a chuckle as he tucked his arms under hers and pulled her back to the privacy of her apartment.

'No, Adam, no,' she sobbed, weakly bucking against his hold.

The hinge of the heavy front door downstairs squealed as it was thrown open, a distinctive sound, and it brought Elena back to the present. Ethan's voice echoed through the hallway as he frantically called her name, a sound that mingled with footsteps climbing the stairs.

She began to fight. 'Ethan.'

*'ELENA!'* he bellowed as he reached the top of the stairs and rushed towards them.

Adam hurried along the corridor, but Ethan was quicker and grabbed hold of him, dragging him away from her.

'What the hell have you done?' Ethan growled, his voice laced with fury.

'This little whore is getting what she deserves.'

Through a haze, she steadied herself and watched as Ethan knocked Adam down with one blow. He straddled him, holding him by his collar to deliver three hard blows to his face until his head lolled backwards, unconscious.

Releasing him, Ethan rushed to Elena as she attempted to stand.

'Elena, I'm here,' he said as his panicked eyes scanned over her. 'Jesus, what did he do?'

The room spun. 'He's injected me with something. I don't know what it is. I'm frightened, Ethan. I don't want to die.'

'You're not going anywhere,' he said holding her close as she slumped against him. He pulled out his phone and began to dial. 'Where's the syringe?'

She waved her hand in the direction of her apartment as her legs buckled beneath her again, the pull of unconsciousness starting to win.

'No, no, no,' he ordered gently as he wrapped his arm tighter around her. 'Stay with me.'

He shifted his arm to gently cradle her as he kneeled down. 'I need an ambulance,' he demanded. 'My girlfriend, she's been attacked. She's been injected with something.' His voice echoed in the hallway. 'She's losing consciousness.'

His words rolled through her blurred mind. *Girlfriend.*

'Well, where is it? We need it right now.' He stopped and listened, taking instruction. 'Yes, okay, okay. I'm keeping her still. She's still awake, yes, but only just. Jesus, just hurry,' he said. 'She doesn't look good at all.'

Sirens in the distance.

'Hold on, Elena, hold on,' he whispered in her ear as he pulled her close. 'Stay with me; they're coming. Just stay with me.' His hands brushed over her face, smoothing away her hair, and she was aware of how warm they were. How warm they always were. But they were trembling too and it confirmed her worst fears.

It was no good; Adam had won. She mourned the bad timing of it all. She had so nearly found happiness, found a meaningful connection with someone, but just as she'd grasped at it, it had slipped through her fingers, like sand. If she had the energy, she would've sobbed at the loss of it. Instead, all her body managed to do was to allow a few tears to slip from her eyes as they fluttered and closed.

'Elena, open your eyes. Look at me,' Ethan demanded softly.

She wanted to look at him, she wanted his face to be the last thing she would see, but the weight of her eyelids were too heavy.

More footsteps thundered up the stairs, just like before when she was a survivor, and not as the ghost she was becoming – one foot in this world and one in another – lying in the arms of the man she loved, in the corridor of her apartment building.

Other voices mingled with Ethan's hoarse demands, and someone said her name, talking to her, trying to bring her back to the world she was clinging to by a fine silvery thread.

Something sharp stung her arm, but it was meaningless as the blackness surrounded her like a warm blanket.

# CHAPTER 29

The rhythmic beep of a machine swirled in Elena's mind. Distant at first, it became louder, clearer as she came to. Opening her eyes, her vision cleared to the sun shining, gloriously. It never let her down. It stood by her, bringing her round, waking her up; it was her symbolism of hope and the living world.

Her body was heavy but comfortable, laid out under warm sheets and blankets. The only part of her that suffered from any discomfort was her shoulder, which ached when she attempted to move. The action set off a flash of memory. Someone standing above her. A doctor, talking to her with a sense of urgency, asking her to open her eyes, encouraging her to wake.

It didn't matter now. She was alive and seemingly in command of her senses too, with no apparent disablement from the drug in the syringe. She couldn't help giving thanks to an unknown being for allowing her to survive her ordeal.

She glanced around. Another hospital room. For a moment, she worried that she was back at the hospital just after her release and all that had happened since had been a dream. But as she registered the sensation of her hand encircled by another, a warm hand, it proved that was not the case at all.

A monitor was by her side, and a drip fed into her arm. But all of that was secondary, irrelevant, as the sight she focused on completely was the man sleeping close by. At the side of her bed, with one hand wrapped around hers and his head resting in the crook of his other arm, was Ethan. The dark circles that underlined his eyes and the full stubble indicated that he hadn't left her side. She reached out and caressed his hair, delighting in the softness of it under her touch, her senses bright and sharp. Alive.

He jumped and blinked his eyes into wakefulness and looked straight at her.

She smiled. 'Hello, Ethan.'

'Elena,' he gasped as he kicked back the chair and hurried closer. He cradled her face with both hands. 'You came back to me,' he breathed. 'You came back.'

With reverence, he repeated her name and kissed her eyelids, her cheeks, her forehead and nose, before placing a soft, gentle kiss on her lips.

He strode to the door and called for the nurse before returning to her side. Sitting on the edge of the bed, he rested his forehead against hers. 'I thought I'd lost you, Elena,' he murmured, his voice deep and raw. 'It was the worst moment of my life, and there was nothing I could do about it.'

He disappeared into the memory.

She held him close and ran her fingers through his hair. 'It's okay, I'm here,' she said. Her eyes brimmed with tears, but she fought them. They had no place here because this was a new beginning that would never be taken for granted. They were together, and that was all that mattered.

Their quiet reunion was broken by a nurse entering the room. 'Hello, Elena,' she said as she strode quickly over to her. 'We're very glad to see you're awake. How are you feeling?' she asked with a kind smile as she took Elena's pulse.

'I feel good. Very woozy, but good,' Elena said as she kept her eyes on Ethan.

'Any pain or discomfort?'

'No, not really. My shoulder is a little sore, but that's it.'

'We'll get the doctor to check you over, but you certainly have the colour back in your cheeks, and your pulse is strong. That's very good news considering your condition when you arrived.'

'And what was that?' Elena asked.

'Very poorly indeed. Thankfully, the paramedics brought the syringe with them, so the doctors tested for the drug and gave you something they hoped would counteract it, but it was touch and go. We could only watch and wait and hope it was enough.'

'Well, I'm so grateful to all of them,' she said before pointing to the drip in her arm.

'What's this for?'

'That's to hydrate you,' the nurse said. 'It'll help to clear your system of toxins. Now, take your time to properly come round, and if you need it there's a bowl here if you get a little queasy. I'll give you a minute and go and notify the doctor.' She updated the notes and looked to Elena again. 'Would you like me to notify your parents?'

'Yes, I suppose,' Elena said. 'But please keep them away for a while. I need some space to be with Ethan.'

'No problem,' she said and directed her gaze to Ethan too. As she did, the warmth in her face receded. It was only for a moment, but Elena caught it. The nurse said nothing more and left, leaving them alone again.

'Ethan,' Elena asked. 'What did you do, because if looks could kill ...'

He looked at her sheepishly as he ran his hand through his hair. 'Fine, I admit, I *may* have been a little overbearing with the medical team when they brought you in.' He brushed his thumb over her hand. 'I may have been... a little overprotective.'

Saying nothing, she let her weak smile tease the answer out of him.

'Okay, so I went into full military mode,' he said as he took her hand and kissed it. 'I backed off instantly when I realised, but the damage was done, hence the evil stare.'

She reached out to take his hand, but the motion made nausea swell in the pit of her stomach. 'Oh,' she sighed and pressed her hand over her abdomen, waiting for the queasiness to pass.

Alarmed, he moved to stand. 'What's going on? Shall I get the nurse?'

'It's fine,' she said as she tugged him back. 'It's just a bit of nausea, that's all. I'm alive; I can easily cope with a bit of sickness.' She stroked his arm. 'I'm okay, thanks to you. You saved me. Again.'

He shook his head. 'I got there in the end, but it was you who did the rest. They told me that an ambulance and the police were already on their way when I made my call. You'd managed to activate the panic button and dial for the emergency services. The doctors told me that those few extra minutes probably saved your life.'

'Yes, I remember making the call, but after that things are hazy.' She pulled herself back from the memories. 'How long was I out for?'

He checked his watch. '14 hours, 45 minutes and 37 seconds.'

'That's very specific,' she said as a smile crept across her lips.

He shrugged. 'I can't guarantee the seconds, I'm not going to lie, but it was hell on earth waiting, and I never want to go through that again.'

'You don't have to,' she said warmly.

'Where's Adam, now?'

'He was treated at the scene and then arrested. He deserves to be six feet under, but I guess prison is the next best thing.'

'I guess the police will want to see me too.'

'They will, but I told them they can wait until you're stronger.'

She nodded, relieved that there would be no more questions to answer, just yet. 'Ethan, what happened at yours? When I called you, you already knew it was Adam. How?'

He frowned. 'I finally accessed the encrypted document. It had everything on it, Elena. Details of the abduction – dates, times, the venue. Information he'd put together. Photos of you plastered all over it. Times of when you went out, times you came home. When you were alone, and when you were with him or friends. There were details of an off-shore bank account. It was empty, and from what I could make out, never had any deposit. The bank account was set up one month before your abduction and closed the day after your release. The most terrifying document was an invoice for a sedative – two vials of the stuff.'

'And nothing of you in there? Nothing to incriminate you?'

'No, nothing. Adam was in the dark about me, but that also meant I was in the dark about him. When I finally found out, it was clearly too late. He was already there, with you.'

She held his hand tightly. 'Adam would have found his moment, and if it wasn't for you, there would have been no one to stop him.'

With a long exhale, he continued. 'There has never been a man so ready to destroy another human being as I was when I knew he was there with you. And when I got there and saw what he was doing, I didn't need any more motivation to knock him out. I could have done so much more. I really could. It was only you that stopped me.'

'I'm glad you hurt him,' she said, an obscure and black satisfaction blooming inside her. 'I hope he rots in hell.'

'I know,' Ethan said. 'But prison will have to do.'

She wished it was enough.

'How will the police know about it, if it's encrypted?'

'Already thought of that,' he said. 'All the information has been passed to McAllister, anonymously. He'll deal with it. Adam may be able to afford a firecracker of a defence lawyer for his involvement in your abduction, but there's no denying that he went to your apartment and injected you with a powerful sedative, enough to finish you off. That's attempted murder, and holds a significant term at Her Majesty's pleasure.'

'I'm so glad about that.' She sighed. 'How did I not see it? His contempt for me, enough to want to hurt me? The signs must have been there?'

He laid his hand over hers. 'You can't blame yourself. He fooled everyone. He'd lost everything. He was penniless, the bailiffs were coming for his apartment. He wanted revenge and had nothing more to lose. The doctors told me that this particular drug doesn't leave a trace once it's been metabolised by your system, so apart from the puncture wound on your neck, there would have been no other evidence. If things had gone his way, he'd have had plenty of time to cover his tracks and make sure nothing would place him at the scene. Who knows what was going through his mind, but he'd certainly thought it through.'

'That's just horrible,' she whispered, her voice hoarse as tears threatened.

'I know, but it's over now. You're safe.'

'And Maxim? He's not going to snitch?'

'No. Like I said, I've got enough dirt to bury him. He'll leave me alone, and he's got so many people in his pocket, including the police, no one will go after him.'

She tensed again, remembering someone very important. 'Oh God. Jack?' she cried. 'I forgot about Jack. Is he okay?' she said as she gripped Ethan's hand. 'Tell me he's okay.'

Ethan hushed her gently. 'He's fine, Elena. Absolutely fine,' he said with a smile. 'He's been checked out and is back at home. Apart from a black eye and feeling terrible at having been caught out like that, he's good.'

'You didn't blame him?' she asked nervously, well aware that in his anger he'd have been capable of it. 'It was moments, just moments that we were apart. It wasn't his fault.'

He smiled. 'Don't worry. You'll see him later, when we get out of here. But I'll call him, he'll be glad to know you're awake.'

She nodded and smiled, relaxed a little. 'Adam assumed Jack was my new man,' she said. 'He had no idea about you though.'

'Well, he found out about me soon enough,' Ethan said with a dark smile.

'He did indeed.' She squeezed his hand. 'And Milo and my uncle? What are we going to do about them?'

He shrugged. 'Well, I can't find anything more on your uncle and his need for a loan, but that's his problem. And your brother, well, he's a grown-up, and not a very nice one at that. He's made his bed. It's up to the police what they do next, but we don't need to be involved anymore. I'm guessing his employers, at the very least, will want to know where the money has gone though, so I'm sure he'll get what's coming to him.' He glanced at her. 'Your relationship is probably well and truly fucked though.'

'I'll cope.'

He smoothed the frown from her forehead. 'You need to rest. You look tired.'

'I don't want to rest yet,' she said. 'I want to know what happens next.' She took a deep breath. 'Between us.'

He leant forwards and brushed loose strands of hair over her shoulder. 'Elena, I'm not going anywhere. And neither are you. My feelings haven't changed, and they never will. And by the way you're looking at me, I think you feel the same.'

'I do. You fought for me in a way that no one has ever done, and it means everything.' She brought his face close to hers and kissed him gently. 'But I don't know how to step back into my old life again. I'm a different person now. I want different things. Is that crazy?'

'No, that's not crazy. You were caught up in a game, and you came out fighting. It has changed you, but you're strong and you're a survivor.' He moved closer. 'But I can take you away from it all, if you'd like? We can start again somewhere new, without our history dragging along. Can you do that?'

'Yes, I think I can. I'm sure there are other museums in the world that need people like me. And wherever we go Charlotte and the others can visit as much as they want. Everything else is irrelevant.'

He raised her hand to his lips and kissed it, his eyes firmly on hers. 'You're sure?'

'Completely. I never want this crazy passion I feel for you to end.'

'Well, that's good to hear,' he said, amused. 'I'll take crazy passion any day of the week.'

He pulled her close as his lips met hers, soft and warm, igniting the fire again.

They eventually pulled apart but remained close, unable to break the contact.

'I do have one request though,' she said after a moment.

'What's that?'

'Take me to France,' she said. 'Take me to meet your brother. I'd like that a lot.'

He smiled and kissed her again. 'That, sweetheart, is a deal.'

There was a knock on the door that broke their quiet moment and it startled her. Old habits. She laughed. 'Come in.'

Charlotte walked in, and her eyes widened as they fell on Ethan.

Poor Charlotte. Elena understood how it was to meet Ethan for the first time, and she pitied her friend who was so unprepared for it.

Charlotte turned her focus to Elena and walked straight to her, perching on the side of the bed, carefully managing to hug her.

'Thank goodness you're all right,' she whispered, tears spilling down her cheeks. 'I was so scared. I don't know what I'd do if I lost you. I'm just so thankful you're okay.'

'I am,' Elena said as she hugged Charlotte back. 'Because of him.'

Charlotte looked straight at Ethan, the

mistrust in her eyes. 'I suppose I should thank you.'

He smiled, unfazed. 'I appreciate that, but I'd prefer it if you could find a way to deal with this situation and not let it destroy your friendship, because whether you like it or not, I'm not going away.'

Charlotte looked at Elena.

'He's staying in my life,' she said, confirming it. 'I want to be with him too.'

Charlotte tutted and crossed her arms.

'I know you don't like it, but this is my choice, Charlotte.' She reached out and took her hand. 'But I need you too. I don't want to lose you or fight with you.'

Charlotte weakened, and smiled. 'I'm not going anywhere either.'

'I'm glad,' Elena replied. 'But I need you to be able to deal with it. Can you?'

She looked at Ethan and seemed to be summing him up. 'I suppose I will always be grateful that you got to her when you did. It shows you won't harm her.'

He nodded. 'That's the last thing I want to do.'

'And maybe one day you can share the truth about how you two met?' Charlotte said, turning her attention back to Elena.

'There's plenty of time for that,' Elena said, knowing that a heavily edited version of events would need to be hashed together before she would do that. But that was something for another day. She reached out to take a hand of both of them. 'And who knows, one day you might get along?'

'Don't count on it,' Charlotte said before Ethan had his chance to charm her, but there was humour in her voice and a glint in her eye that gave Elena hope.

It wasn't long before Elena was ready to be alone with Ethan again. She only had to rub her forehead a few times before Charlotte got the hint and made her excuses to leave.

'Is this really the end of it,' she asked once they were alone.

'It is,' he said. 'It's over. I've found all I can relating to your abduction.'

'Even those unexplained dates?'

'Yes, I dug a little deeper and found a reference to your initials – E.C.D. I think he kept those dates because of the fact that he remembered you being friends with his daughter. It probably piqued his interest, that's all.'

Elena's stomach lurched, and this time she fought the urge to vomit. 'E.C.D. You're sure that's what you saw? Those specific initials.'

'Yes, your initials, right?' he asked. 'Although I didn't think you had a middle name. Maybe you'd care to share?'

She said nothing, lost in her thoughts as she gripped the blanket, hidden from view.

'Elena?' he said gently. 'They are your initials, right?'

'Sorry, what?' she said vaguely and then smiled, snapping her focus back to Ethan. 'I don't know what he was thinking. That was sloppy. Letting that information slip for people like you to find.'

Ethan looked at her, perhaps trying to read her, and Elena moved her gaze towards the window. She needed time to process this new information. About her, her abduction, and the impact it had made. She calmed her breathing and let this new jigsaw piece fall into place.

He gently brushed his finger over her cheek. 'Hey, relax,' he said. 'I can see your mind racing but believe me, it is over.'

'I wish it was,' she whispered.

He squeezed her hand.

'I'm fine, honestly,' she said reassuringly. 'It's a cliché, but I think I just need closure. I need to put this all behind me.'

'You will. Give it time.'

She nodded, thoughtful. 'Will you help me with that?'

'I will do whatever you want me to. I am at your command.'

She smiled. 'That's very good to know. Maybe you could start with a double espresso, if I'm allowed? Kick start the removal of the sedative from my system.'

He laughed. 'I'm on it.'

With Ethan gone and in the silence of the

room, her mind raced. Adam's part was done. He would now pay for his crime. The other, the lynchpin of her pain, was for her to deal with.

She needed to heal, and she would do whatever it took to make that happen.

# CHAPTER 30

'You know you don't have to do this,' Ethan said as he pulled up outside the building that stood amongst scrubby wasteland. 'It's only been a month since you were released from hospital.' He switched off the engine and faced her. 'Is this really necessary?'

Elena glanced out of the window and then to Ethan. 'Yes, it is. It's something I have to do. I need to see this place again, now that I'm free.' Her face twitched into a nervous smile. 'It was the place of my abduction, and I can't have it lingering in my nightmares anymore. A place of horror and fear.'

He nodded. 'Well, let me come with you at least. We can do it together.'

'No, Ethan,' she said quickly. 'Thanks, I really appreciate your support, but I need to do this by myself. I need to say goodbye to this part of my life, and I've got my phone right here if I need you.'

He studied her for a moment. 'I get it,' he said and leant forward to kiss her. 'But I'm right outside. I'm right here.'

She reached to touch his face. 'I know you are.'

She shut the car door and walked determinedly to the building, taking in her surroundings. An area of abandoned buildings on the outskirts of London, derelict and only reasonably free of the crimes that were committed here because it was still daylight.

Stepping over the collapsed streetlamp, she pushed at the broken front door as memories of the fateful night she tried to escape quickly flooded her mind. A time when she had resisted what was happening to her, not as she was now; surrendered to it, accepting of it, and creating a new life for herself within it. She walked across the hallway. As her shoes thumped against the wood, echoing through the musty air, she tried to block out the image in her mind of Cigarettes' body crumpled at the foot of the stairs, broken, dead.

Shaking her head, she cleared her thoughts as she slowly climbed the stairs, careful to avoid broken wood, keep a sure footing.

There was a quietness that implied an empty building, but she knew otherwise. She began to hum a childhood song, quietly, almost under her breath, but loud enough to be heard in the quiet air around her. She heard the shuffle, the sound of movement above as someone else registered her arrival, listening and reacting to the footfall on the stairs – just as she had, all those days ago.

Turning at the top of the stairs, she made her way to the familiar room, her heart beating fast as she turned the key of the lock and opened the door. She strode towards the man slumped before her, hands and feet bound, his mouth covered with tape.

Crouching to his level, she smoothed his straggled hair and gently ran her fingers over a bloodied cut, just above his brow.

He struggled hard, his hands straining against the ties.

'Hey, hey. Careful. You'll cut your skin,' she soothed. 'The best thing I found was to relax my hands. Don't fight it. That's what I did, in here, when I was all alone, depending on my family to save me.'

She caught hold of the corner of the tape covering his mouth. 'This might hurt a little,' she said as she whipped it away in one swift action.

'Elena,' her father snapped through furious breaths. 'What the hell have you done? Untie me, immediately.'

'Ah, I'm sorry, I can't do that.'

She rose and wandered around the room. 'So here we are. The place of my abduction. What do you think?'

'What the hell are you talking about,' he demanded, his eyes cold and impatient. 'You will untie me. Right now.'

'Can't do that,' she said as she moved about the room, finding a spot and marking it by tapping the floorboard with the tip of her shoe.

'Right about here is where the thug tried to rape me,' she said. 'Thank God for Lycra sports clothing, that's all I'll say about that little incident. Won't rip easily, you see. Slowed him down.' She caught his expression. 'Oh, does it disgust you, Dad? To know that someone tried to rape me? Does that contaminate me in some way?'

He looked away.

'Ah, I see. It does,' she said. 'Well, never mind.'

She continued. 'And up there, in the ceiling, is the gunshot. Do you remember? You should, he was on the phone to you at the time.' She pointed to it. 'Look carefully. See it? Can you see the little black death star?'

He didn't look up, but kept his stare on her. 'I don't know what you hope to achieve here, but you are playing a dangerous game.'

'Oh, but that's not a problem because I like dangerous games now, Dad. Didn't you know that?'

'I see a woman who is having some sort of breakdown and my patience is wearing very thin.'

'I'm having no such thing, and my sanity is not your biggest problem right now. It's your corrupt soul and the mess it's got you into that you should be worrying about.'

She saw the confusion on his face and stepped a little closer. 'Would you like me to continue? To fill in the blanks? How about starting with your little friendship with the head of one of the most powerful Russian syndicates in London?' She folded her arms. 'How is Maxim Antonovich these days?'

He curled his lip in anger and lurched towards her.

She raised her foot and pushed it against his shoulder, shoving him down to the floor. 'Now, now. Calm yourself down.'

She took a step back, smiling. 'I thought that might get your attention.'

'You know nothing!' he spat.

'No, no. I know *everything*,' she threw back. 'My new friend has been very busy for me, doing a lot of work. He told me all about Maxim.' She laughed. 'He even discovered your brother's pathetic attempt to extract money from you. What a ridiculous exercise that was for him. Doesn't he know you at all?'

Now she saw something else in his eyes, something that looked like fear.

'And when my friend found a seemingly irrelevant document with a couple of dates and just three little initials in it, I saw everything for what it was. Simple as that. Isn't that right, Ètienne Charles Dumont?'

His eyes shot to hers.

'Of course, it's common knowledge within the family how much you hate your birth name, Ètienne, don't you? How you always resisted the French name given to you by your mother. So you buried every trace of it; some legal, some not so legal, choosing to be the English gentleman instead. You would never even respond to the name, even when dear old Mamie refused to call you anything else. But my friend somehow didn't manage to join the dots on this one.' She leant towards him, her voice almost a whisper, sharing a secret. 'But, then again, only someone close would have known that. Someone in the family. Like me.'

'Doesn't mean a thing,' he blustered.

'Well, yes I suppose, but let me present my case for the prosecution.'

He smiled cynically. 'I wouldn't want it any other way. The burden of proof is now yours, Elena. Do continue.'

She nodded. 'Good. Well, let's start at the beginning. The part where I carried around the hurt at your refusal to pay your daughter's ransom until it ate me up inside. And, stupidly, I believed the bullshit that you were sorry, that you loved me. But then I learnt of those three little initials, and it all became clear. A kind of revelation. Lots of memories came flooding into my mind. Like the time you met Maxim at my school. How you hit it off immediately. Organised a charity event that would bolster both your egos.'

'Again, doesn't mean a thing.'

'No?' she said as she slowly paced in front of him. 'Well, let me paint a little picture here.

See if I've got this right.' She paused for breath. 'Adam needed money to cover a failed business venture. He found Maxim and a deal was arranged. But Maxim recognised your name – and maybe mine, being Zina's friend – so he came to you with details. Some sort of code of honour amongst men like you. I don't know how he discovered your real name, maybe you let it slip in some whisky filled evening with him, while you plotted my downfall. I don't really care.'

'Wait,' her father interrupted. 'Adam was the one behind this?'

'Yes, that's right. Adam.' She sighed. 'You really do need to do your homework. Please try and keep up.'

Her father's face fell. 'Maxim always refused to share that information. I thought Adam had just lost it because you ended the relationship.'

'Of course Maxim kept you in the dark. It kept him in control.' She crossed her arms. 'Do you really think Adam decided to go to my apartment, inject me with enough sedative to floor a rhino just because I had the audacity to end our relationship? I mean, yes, crimes of passion do happen, but he never really cared enough for me to be that affronted.' She smiled. 'No, he was playing for much higher stakes.' Her smiled changed to a chuckle at the absurdity of it all. 'I bet he doesn't seem like such great son-in-law material now, does he? Someone only after your precious money?'

Her father stared, absorbing this new information.

She leant against the wall, eyes on him.

'Anyway, we need to keep on track. I thought you might be in Maxim's pocket somehow. But I thought, if you were, why would he feel the need to involve you? So, instead, I considered that maybe it's not that you're in his pocket. Maybe he's in yours.'

Her father was still, listening.

'You're important. Obviously you are. I get it. A high-profile barrister such as yourself gets to take on the best cases. Especially the controversial ones. In your line of work you meet all the people – the high, and the low. The people with enough money to pay for your services. And, with you, it doesn't matter where that money comes from, does it, just as long as it's paid.'

She paused, waited for an answer. Nothing came.

'What did you do for him, Dad? Did you represent him, get him off a charge and out of prison? So much so that it meant his gratitude bought you a few favours?'

'You're a fool if you think we don't have any dealings with these kinds of people in my world' he said. 'Of course we do. I've crossed paths with that man many times. Yes, I overturned a couple of cases, got a couple of his people off charges. And, yes, it did earn me a few favours. He saw your name, put two and two together, and figured he'd speak to me about it.'

'So, you sanctioned it?' she said, her composure slipping. 'You let what happened to me, happen. And you met up with Maxim just before the abduction and again just afterwards.' She clenched her fists. 'When I was living through that hell, you and he had a meeting to decide my fate. Nothing but a business arrangement?'

He sighed. 'Elena, you were never meant to get hurt. Really you weren't. The agreement was simple. Yes, you'd be taken, but no money would exchange hands, and you'd be released. We had to go through with the charade, it was the only way to panic the perpetrator into backing off. We figured a botched kidnap would ensure they would avoid targeting the family again. Nobody makes the same mistake twice.'

Burning fury ran through her at his emotionally detached explanation of why she had to go through her nightmare, as if it was the only reasonable option. It wounded her, but she refused to let it show.

'So you decided to use me as a bartering tool *and* a deterrent?' she said. 'But how could you have such a casual disregard for what I would go through, even for appearances sake? Did you know the men who were involved?'

'No, of course I didn't. Again, Maxim wouldn't share.'

'So how could you have possibly ensured my safety?' She paused, needing to gather her thoughts. 'Now I realise what your speech meant the other night when you said how much you wanted to make amends. It was guilt, wasn't it?'

'No, I meant those words.'

'You're not capable of meaning those words!' she spat. 'You even tried to imply that Edmond had suggested not paying the ransom when that was never part of your plan,' she said, exasperated. 'Is there any low you won't sink to?'

'I was just trying to protect my family.'

'Well that's been a pointless exercise because there's nothing left of it now,' she said. 'And none of what you've said changes the fact that, while you and your criminal friend were making all the rules of your game, you failed to share these details to the man who abducted me from the street. The man who would have happily killed me – after he had abused me in whatever way he chose. And you didn't account for Adam either, losing his mind and wanting revenge. Coming back for me when it all went wrong. Those people didn't get the memo and that's shoddy.'

'I'll admit, that was a mistake.'

'The whole thing was a mistake. Even now you don't know the damage you have caused with your toxic egos. And it's left me more than a little bruised, both physically and psychologically.'

Her father worked to free his hands. 'This needs to stop now,' he said, irritated that the cable ties refused to snap. 'If you release me now, I'll let this go.'

'But I can't let what you've done go, so it's no wonder I feel the need for... oh, what's the word now? Oh yes, that's it, a little retribution.'

'Elena, I mean it–'

She ignored him and moved to the window. Gently tracing her fingers over the loose piece of wood, she remembered how she had pleaded for it to remain that way, just so that she could enjoy a glimmer of the sunlight above.

'Ours has been a strange relationship, hasn't it?' she said thoughtfully. 'To the outside world and all your glitzy friends, you were the loving father, while I played the good daughter. What a fiction we created. What a smokescreen.' She took a breath. 'The truth is that you delight in playing with people's lives, whatever the cost. Destroying them if you wish.' She gestured around her. 'And so here we are.'

'None of this was about you.'

'Oh, that's where you're wrong. It was all about me. I was the pawn in your game, and somewhere along the line, you forgot who you were dealing with, not just that this was your own daughter, but another human being. So this time, I get to decide when this is over. Not you.'

He snorted. 'You? I don't think so.'

She continued with a smile, letting his jibe bounce off her. 'We'll see.'

He glared. 'Elena, I'm warning you...'

'No, you're not doing anything. You've got enough problems right now.'

'And you think you can do this. Leave me here and say nothing.'

'Yes, I can. I'm getting very good at secrets. Especially with the help of my new friend.'

'Ah, yes. The elusive Ethan. Did he help you with all of this?'

She tutted. 'You underestimate how resourceful I've become.'

'And just where did you find him, Elena? This man who is suddenly your main focus in life? I don't remember you talking of him before your abduction.'

'No, that's because I didn't know him before the abduction,' she replied, allowing herself to enjoy the moment. 'But fate ensured our paths crossed in the most dramatic way.'

She watched him figure it out, and laughed a little when his wide-eyed gaze turned to her.

'He was involved?'

She nodded her agreement and watched as a look of contempt spread across his face.

'That's abnormal. Abhorrent,' he said. 'Where the hell did you go, Elena?'

'I survived,' she said. 'I had to, because, as it turns out, I couldn't rely on my family to help, could I?'

Another shot fired that left her father mute.

'He was the good cop,' she continued. 'But I'm being flippant, because he's so much more than that. He's special. He understands me. He helped me and I've developed a very deep *affection* for him because of it. And before you say anything, he likes me too, thank you very much. Can't get enough of me actually. Those who don't understand it might call it an obsession, but it's powerful. Powerful enough to turn my poor, little love-starved mind, according to the dippy shrink at the hospital anyway.'

Her father tutted. 'You've finally gone mad, girl.'

'Nope, wrong again. I've never felt more clarity. And unlike you, I'm loyal to the ones who care for me. I protect them and I keep my promises, so don't underestimate what I wouldn't do for him.'

'So where is this man you feel so strongly about?'

'He's downstairs, waiting in the car for me. He thinks I'm up here getting some sort of closure, and in a way, I suppose I am.'

'This is a sick game, Elena.'

'Maybe. Just as my abduction was a game to you,' she replied.

'You won't win.'

'I already have. And at least I understand you now,' she murmured. 'At least I see the real you.'

'Oh, and who's that?'

She moved towards him and crouched to his level. 'I see your poison, seeping deep into the layers. Penetrating and warping everything you touch until it's exactly as you want it. And so now you need a lesson in what I'm capable of too. Because you need to learn that you can't abuse people. You can't play with people's lives, especially for the sake of money. Because they can snap and break.'

'Just like you?'

'Yes,' she whispered. 'Just like me.'

They stared at each other until she moved to stand, stretching her legs. 'Anyway, you should be proud of me. This little gem is all my own work. I just had to do a little research. Find someone desperate enough to do whatever I demanded. No questions asked. It got you here, trapped, and no one will ever know I was anywhere near. You see, still playing the good and ever so slightly traumatised daughter.'

'So your plan was to knock me about a bit. Give me a taste of my own medicine?'

'Oh no, it's much more than that, and something that I have no need to be involved with any longer,' she said as she glanced at her watch.

'How do you think this is going to end, Elena? You must realise I will find you and once I do, I'll expose you. You and Ethan. Everything.

I'll ruin you.'

'You see, that's where you're wrong again,' she said with a sigh. 'Because I have enough on Maxim and you to bring both your houses down. All the nasty dealings you've made will be released, everywhere. Would you like that? A nice little scandal, perhaps? Let the world see the kind of man you really are. Life as you know it would be over. How do you think Mum would react to that, eh?' She drew close, to make herself perfectly clear. 'And we all know how people like Maxim would react to being outed in such a way, so don't go mistaking the havoc I can wreak in your life.'

His eyes narrowed. 'You wouldn't dare, girl.'

She stared him down. 'Question is, do you want to try me? Surely someone like you is aware of what they do to corrupt lawyers in prison?'

She watched him, waited for his response, but no sharp reply came.

'I have this situation locked down. This conversation didn't happen and you'll find nothing on Ethan and nothing on me.'

He broke her gaze, and she knew she'd won.

'But, right now, this is what you need to focus on,' she said as she glanced around the room. 'I thought it might be nice to let you experience this place, see how well you do. How good is your agility, old man?'

She watched with amusement as he struggled against his ties.

'I'm not completely without heart though. Here, have this,' she said as she pulled out a small mobile phone from her pocket and laid it down on the floor, just out of his reach. 'Better be quick though, I forgot to charge it up. Not much juice left.'

She checked her watch again and moved to the door. 'So, Dad, I guess this is it. I won't be seeing you again. I need to get as far away from my toxic heritage as possible. Give my love to Mum though, not that she ever wanted it.'

'Elena, get back here! Do you hear me! *NOW!*'

'Now, now, you need to focus. You've got enough on your plate with figuring out how to get out of here. You've already wasted enough time. Think of that fading battery.'

She opened the door and glanced back, watching her father furiously grapple with his ties.

'Goodbye, Dad.'

She closed the door and walked purposefully out of the house, calming her body as he pounded his feet violently against the dry floorboards, still bellowing her name. She enjoyed the thought of how she'd got here; how she'd done it. A miracle really. A nugget of good fortune when she was last in hospital. Never expecting it, she failed to hide her surprise when, during a graveyard shift one night, she came face to face with the doctor from her captivity.

Having left her room when sleep evaded her, and without Ethan by her side, she had seen him sitting at the nurses' station. The surprise on his face was evident, his pen frozen in his hand. His presence at the hospital was proof of his attempt to go legitimate, and someone trying to do that had a lot to lose. She learned quickly that people in those situations were open to persuasion. Hers was a simple request – bring her father here, secure him, and leave. Not the end of the world. Quite reasonable really, given his past experience. And in payment, she'd keep her silence. She wouldn't send the letter exposing him and his dubious past to his employers at the hospital. She'd let him have his new start. After all, everyone deserves a new beginning.

She knew her father would escape, but that was okay. She didn't need him to die. She didn't need that kind of retribution. He would figure how to get out of the room, shuffle down the stairs, and get himself out. It was easy enough. He'd be humiliated, yes, having to ask for help, get himself back to his gilded life, but if that's all he suffered, it would be enough. Enough to know what she'd gone through, enough to know that she knew who he really was, and that he held no power over her anymore. It was over, on her terms.

She exited the building and moved in time to the beat of her tainted heart and climbed into the car, glancing at Ethan who watched intently.

'Feel better?' he asked as he started the car. 'Laid your ghosts to rest?'

She smiled and nodded. 'Much better, thanks. Laid all my ghosts to rest now.'

He looked at her, and when she noticed the intensity of his gaze, she knew she was in trouble. 'Good, and later you'll tell me exactly why you decided to go it alone to punish your father.'

Speechless, her heart threatened to jump from her throat.

'You realise I knew what you were doing,' he continued, his arm outstretched, his hand resting on the steering wheel.

Rushing from shock to disbelief, she finally settled on acceptance. 'I suppose at some level I would have known that you'd be aware, yes. It's what you do, after all. Why would there be different rules for me.'

'Elena, I threw the rule book out of the window when it comes to you,' he said warmly and free of anger. 'I just noticed your reaction at the hospital when I mentioned those initials and I knew something was wrong, so I did a little more digging. I found out that I'd made an incorrect assumption about your name, that you actually have four middle names, none of which begin with 'C' and that E.C.D were your father's initials. And, by that point I saw that you'd already begun.'

She turned to face him. 'I was always going to share what I had done with you, I just needed to do this. By myself.'

He gave an understanding nod. 'I get that, and it's why I backed off, watched from a distance.'

She let the tension in her body go. 'I enjoyed it actually. It was quite the thrill.'

'You're a quick learner.'

'I'm always learning. You know that.'

'Maybe I'll show you everything one day,' he said.

She sat back in the chair. 'Maybe. Or maybe that's not necessary. Maybe I already know more than you think.'

He chuckled. 'Let's not get ahead of ourselves.'

'I pay attention, Ethan,' she said, feeling herself pout.

'Yes, I see that,' he said.

'And I adapt.'

He kept her gaze. 'I see that too.'

'So why are you looking at me like that?'

'Because I think you're going to keep me on my toes, Elena Dumont.'

She laughed. 'You wouldn't want it any other way.'

'You've got that right,' he said as he looked

towards the derelict house. 'And you're sure about this?'

'I'm sure,' she said without hesitation. 'He'll be fine. This is over. I'm ready to go.'

'Happy to hear it,' he said as he pulled away from the desolate surroundings. 'You look beautiful by the way.'

'Thank you,' she replied, feeling strangely empowered. 'I'm adjusting to living in my new skin. Do you like it?'

His lips curved into an assured smile. 'I like it a lot.'

'Good, because I don't care what it all means anymore. You, me. Our history. I'm in love with you. And if that makes me crazy, I'll live with it. Happily.'

He stopped the car, shifted it into neutral and faced her. 'What did you say?'

'If that makes me–'

He shook his head. 'No, the bit before.'

'What, that I love you?'

'Yes, that part.'

She shrugged. 'Well, I do. Does it bother you?'

'No sweetheart, not at all,' he said as he took her face in his hands. 'Because I'm crazy about you too, Elena. Like nothing else I've ever known.'

He pulled her towards him and smothered her smile with a kiss. It was warm and filled with love, proving that he was hers as much as she was his. She lifted her hands to his hair, keeping him close, prolonging the kiss. She would never tire of him. She would always want him.

Pulling away now, she gently traced her finger over his lips. 'Let's get away from here.'

'I'll take you anywhere you want to go,' he said.

She smiled. 'So take me home.'

'And where is that?' he asked.

'Wherever you are.'

# ACKNOWLEDGEMENTS

So many people to thank who have supported me through my writing journey. I'm lucky enough to have great people in my life who have continually spurred me on, even when I was ready to throw in the towel.

To Richard Bradburn at Editorial.ie for his manuscript critique, copy-edit, and honesty. To Lorena Martin for providing such a fantastic book cover for me, and for her endless answers to all my queries. To Paul Martin at Dominion Editorial for his proofread after a significant rewrite.

To my friends and family for all their unending support and genuine interest in my writing journey; to my mum and sister who have utter faith in me and give their total love and support every single day. And for my dad who sadly never got to read the finished copy but who supported me to the end. To Caroline and Sarah, who provide endless support and love, despite the miles between us.

To my readers, thank you, I hope you enjoyed the book and if you ever want to get in touch I can be found at @GemsLawrence on Twitter, @GLawrenceWriter on Facebook and www.gmlawrencewrites.co.uk. Come and say hi!

Finally, a massive thank you goes to Paul and Emily for putting up with me; for their endless patience and for letting me have the space I needed to disappear into the story with the laptop for a couple of hours, or giving me that much needed hug when things were hard. You two are the best and I couldn't have done this without you.

Printed in Great Britain
by Amazon